BLOOD TRACKS

BLOOD TRACKS

PAULA RAWSTHORNE

USBORNE

For David, Stan, Archie and Sadie.
The loves of my life.

First published in the UK in 2013 by Usborne Publishing Ltd., Usborne House,
83-85 Saffron Hill, London EC1N 8RT, England. www.usborne.com

Copyright © Paula Rawsthorne, 2013

The right of Paula Rawsthorne to be identified as the author of this work has been
asserted by her in accordance with the Copyright, Designs and Patents Act, 1988.

Cover photography: raindrops on glass © istockphoto/Thinkstock; girl © Hemera/
Thinkstock.

The name Usborne and the devices ♀ ⊕ are Trade Marks of
Usborne Publishing Ltd.

A CIP catalogue record for this book is available from the British Library.

ISBN 9781409532156 JFM MJJASOND/13 00892/2

Printed in Reading, Berkshire, UK.

1 THE LIFT

Gina waved goodbye to her friends as she dashed from the shelter of the sports centre into the torrential rain. Nearing her dad's car, she could see that he was engrossed in a conversation on his mobile.

She reached the door of the Fiesta and lifted the handle, but it didn't open. She tried the back door but all the snips were down, denying her access.

Gina rapped on the window. "Dad! Let me in, will you? I'm getting soaked out here!"

Without even looking at her, Martin Wilson raised a hand, signalling to Gina to wait. As he continued his call, Gina peered in at him, outraged. She watched the muscles in her father's face tense; his expression was stony and then suddenly agitated as his lips formed rapid words that she couldn't hear, his eyes flashed once towards her and then he was back in his conversation.

Gina banged on the window, glaring at him. She squirmed as the rain began to trickle down the back of her tracksuit top; her trainers were soaking up the puddles like a sponge. Her thick black hair was plastered to her cheeks by the lashing rain. She watched her dad switch off his phone and look across at her, apologetically. He snapped the door open.

"Thanks a lot!" Gina said sarcastically as she plonked herself down in the passenger seat. "Who were you on the phone to? Couldn't you have just let me in? I nearly drowned out there."

"Sorry, love. It was business; I needed to concentrate."

"Well," Gina said, "it doesn't seem fair, you being all dry and warm, and me soaking." She started to shake herself like a dog coming out of a lake, her long curls spraying her dad with water.

Gina waited for his mock outrage, but instead her dad just gave a weak smile, put the headlights on and started up the engine.

"You're a right laugh tonight," Gina said disappointedly. "Are you okay?"

"It's nothing. I'm just tired."

"Well, aren't you going to ask me how I got on at training?"

He shook his head, as if trying to clear it of some obstruction. "Yeah, of course. How did you get on?"

"Well, I'm glad you asked because I've only gone and

smashed my personal best!" Gina grinned with pride and looked at him expectantly.

"Good," her dad replied, without taking his glazed eyes off the illuminated road.

"Good?" she said indignantly. "It's a bit better than good. You should have been there to see me. You would have loved it. I ran the fifteen hundred in four minutes fifty. That's seven seconds off my PB. Coach said he's going to let me run for the county. He said, if I put in the work, I could easily make it into the under-sixteen squad."

When there was no answer, she shoved his arm. "Are you even listening to me?"

"That's great, Gina. Really great." Her dad's voice was monotone.

"Yeah, but we'll have to up our training, Dad," she continued excitedly. "What do you reckon? Can you come out with me *three* times a week? I know things are busy at the warehouse and it's getting dark about four, but maybe if you ask Uncle Tom, he'll let you off early? He owes you loads of time – all those extra hours he has you doing."

"Umm," her dad replied.

"I thought you'd be chuffed," Gina said. She felt deflated, but then her eye was caught by the large, rectangular box on the back seat of the car. She twisted round to investigate.

"Wow!" Gina said, impressed. "Is this for Danny's birthday? He's been going on about wanting a tropical fish tank for ever. At least he'll shut up now. Hey, Dad, the box is open, did you know? Have you checked everything's in it?"

There was no reply but Gina carried on regardless.

"Well, I hope Danny doesn't get bored of it after a few weeks. You know what he was like with the goldfish. He never fed it, then he'd panic and put a ton of fish flakes in. Ugh, remember that poor fish floating on the top of the bowl? It looked like someone had used a bike pump on it."

She stared at her dad's blank face.

"Why aren't you listening?" she shouted in frustration. "You know Danny will probably kill any fish you put in there!"

"Yeah," he said, staring straight ahead. Gina wasn't convinced that he was even focusing on the road. He seemed to be on autopilot, though it did cross her mind that right now her dad might agree to anything.

"By the way, Dad," Gina chirped sweetly, "you don't mind if I go into town on Saturday with Becky and a few mates? We were thinking of going ice skating and then for a pizza. Is that all right? Maybe you could you drop me Zoff, *and* pick me up later? And maybe I could have a couple of weeks' pocket money early – or better still, you could just give me the money. Go on, Dad, please?" She gave him a dazzling, toothy smile, but he still seemed a world away from her.

Gina narrowed her eyes in concern. She leaned across

and felt his forehead with the palm of her hand. "Well, you don't feel too hot or anything, but you *must* be coming down with something. This is like sitting in a car with a zombie."

She fell silent, her eyes focused on her dad, willing him to smile or speak, but the only sound was of the squeaking windscreen wipers and the hot air blasting around the car, fighting back the steam that was misting up the windows.

Her dad indicated right at a sign for a no-through road. "Why are we going down here?"

He didn't answer.

None of the street lamps, dotted along the cracked pavements, were working. They bumped slowly along the cobbles, past rows of derelict, boarded-up houses. Beyond, unseen in the darkness, was an old bridge over the railway line and a little way after that the street petered out.

"Planet Earth, calling Dad." She was trying to sound playful but tension riddled her voice. "You've gone the wrong way."

He pulled over onto the pavement, turning off the headlights but keeping the engine running.

"What's up? Is there something wrong with the car?" Gina asked.

"No," he said, looking into the blackness. "I just need to answer a call of nature."

"What! You're going out in this, to have a wee? Can't you just hold on till we get home?"

"No…I can't. You stay in the car, put the radio on, don't go anywhere."

"Put the radio on? How long are you going to be?"

But he didn't answer. Instead he suddenly turned to her and clasped her hands between his callused palms.

"I love you, Gina, you know that, don't you?" he said earnestly, his eyes locked on hers.

As she searched her father's pensive face, she saw herself reflected in him more sharply than ever. She was looking at the same dark, feline eyes, the same thick, black eyebrows. Her skin was caramel, whereas his was a deep brown, but she'd inherited his bow-shaped mouth, his wide cheekbones and strong jawline. All the features that left people divided over whether Gina Wilson was unusually attractive or just the wrong side of handsome for a girl.

Gina let out a nervous laugh. "Oh my God, Dad! What is wrong with you tonight? You're freaking me out!"

He gave Gina a weak smile. "I'm sorry. How about we go for a run tomorrow?"

"Okay then," she beamed. Wriggling her hands free, she noticed his palms were encrusted with dirt. She tutted. "Your hands are filthy and your overalls are even worse! Honestly, Dad, what are you like? Get going, will you? I want to get home."

He picked up his phone, put it in the pocket of his work overalls and opened the door to the driving rain.

Gina watched as he was quickly consumed by the darkness. She pressed various buttons on the radio, hoping that music would shake off her unease. She found a song she liked and, slouching down in the seat, put her feet up on the dashboard and proceeded to untie her trainers and peel off her soggy socks. She wriggled her damp, puckered toes, letting the hot air dry them. Her hands beat out the rhythm of the song on her legs as the windscreen wipers swished back and forth like a frenetic metronome.

She groaned, remembering that she had a science project due in the next day. She always waited until the last minute to get her homework done. Usually she'd panic and end up throwing herself on her dad's mercy. He'd always give her a hand to look answers up and find all the worksheets she'd lost, but there was no way she could ask her dad to bail her out tonight, not when he was acting so weird. And there was no point asking her mum. Mum's thoughts on the matter were very clear.

"You're too soft on her, Martin," Clare would lecture. "Gina's fifteen, not five. It's her own fault if she leaves everything until the last minute. Just let her get into trouble. It's the only way she'll learn."

Another song started on the radio.

"What's he doing? He's been ages."

Gina contemplated going to find him but now that she'd just got dry, she didn't fancy venturing outside in the dark and the wet. Instead she leaned over to the steering wheel and pressed down on the horn, emitting two long blasts of protest. "Come on, Dad!" she pleaded.

She slumped back in her seat, and heard her phone beep from inside her tracksuit pocket.

That'll be Mum wondering where we are.

But it was *Dad* that flashed up on the screen. She clicked on the text and her stomach muscles clenched as she stared at the message.

Forgive me. Dad

She hit the button to silence the radio. "Dad?"

Her eyes scanned the blackness outside as panic rose in her. She strained her ears but all she could hear was the squeak of the windscreen wipers and the rain pummelling the car. But then, seconds later, came the ear-piercing sound of train wheels, sparking and squealing along a track in a desperate attempt to stop.

Gina sat on the sofa in the living room, her freezing body wrapped up in a duvet. She stared blankly at the uniformed officer sitting opposite her. He'd introduced himself as Constable Jason Rogers from the British Transport Police. Danny was hunched up in her dad's armchair, pressing a cushion to his mouth to stifle his sobs. Her mum walked into the room carrying a tea tray. The cups and sugar bowl rattled as her shaking hands placed it down on the table.

"Thank you, Mrs. Wilson," the constable said, taking a mug.

Gina's mum sat next to her on the sofa. "This won't take long, Gina." Her voice trembled. "Constable Rogers just wants to ask you some questions."

Gina listened, unblinking, as the constable explained that he was helping to investigate her father's death and that he needed to take a statement from her about what had happened earlier that evening.

Gina recounted the details without a flicker of emotion, as if she was a journalist reporting the news. The constable scribbled furiously in his notepad. When she stopped talking, he thanked her and said that he'd leave them to rest but that he'd keep them informed.

"It will take a few weeks, but there'll be an inquest. There has to be in cases like this," he said.

"Good, good," Gina muttered, as if talking to herself.

Her mum stood up unsteadily and showed him to the front door. Gina could hear the constable in the hallway, saying, "Your daughter is obviously still in shock. People involved in traumatic events often seem detached and matter of fact. This must be a terrible time for you all. I'm so sorry."

Danny slopped over to Gina, and snuggled under the duvet with her. He looked at her with mournful eyes as they sat in silence. Mum returned to the living room. She gave a pained smile on seeing them together. "Do you think you can manage something to eat, Gina?" she asked.

"No," Gina said, exhausted. "I just want to go to bed. Promise that you'll tell me if anything happens."

"Of course I will, but you heard what Constable Rogers said – it's going to take a while. It's best not to think about it yet," her mum replied, biting her lip.

* * *

Gina spent the next few weeks drifting around the house like a ghost; she didn't want to go out, and was losing all sense of time, spending hour upon hour on her bed, falling in and out of sleep. Even when she was awake, she felt like she was sleepwalking – nothing seemed real. She had vague images of her mum flitting in and out of her room, trying to coax her to eat something. She knew that she should have been ravenously hungry but she had no appetite. The aching emptiness inside her couldn't be filled by food.

For long periods she wouldn't utter a single word but then, suddenly, her silence would be shattered by bouts of uncontrollable crying. The outpourings came upon her without warning, like a wall of water breaking through a dam. Her whole body would start to tremble and choking sobs would mount up in her throat, until they erupted in a howl that sounded like it came from a wounded animal. Each time it happened her mum would run to her, throwing her arms around her, rocking her and kissing her head until the crying ebbed away and Gina fell asleep, exhausted.

Every knock on the front door made Gina tense. She listened to the sound of visitors, recognized the hushed voices of friends, teachers, neighbours and relatives, but she just wanted all of them to go away. One day, however, Mum came into her room to say that a friend had called. Mum told her it would do her good to chat and, before Gina could object, Becky was ushered into the bedroom.

Gina sensed Becky's awkwardness as her friend perched on the end of her bed. She could see in Becky's widened eyes that she was taken aback by her appearance.

"I'm so sorry about your dad. He was such a lovely man," Becky said, looking down at the duvet.

"Thanks," Gina whispered.

"Your mum thought you might want to talk about it. Do you?"

Gina shook her head.

"Well, when you do, I'm here for you. You know that, don't you?"

Gina managed a weak smile. There was silence between them as Becky chewed her lip, thinking what to say next. "Want to know what's been going on at school?" she said at last.

"Okay," Gina answered politely. But as Becky began recounting all the latest gossip, Gina slumped back on the pillow, her eyes glazing over, as her friend's words became a drone in her ears. Becky had stopped talking long before Gina realized.

"I'd better go. You're tired," Becky said quietly.

"I'm sorry, Becky."

"It's okay. I understand. I just wanted to see you. When are you coming back to school?"

"I don't know. We're waiting for the inquest and the funeral. I can't do anything until I find out what happened to Dad."

"Do you mean why he did it?" Becky said gravely.

"What are you talking about?" Gina looked baffled.

"You know, why he…killed himself."

"My dad didn't kill himself," Gina said firmly.

Becky blushed. "Oh…okay, well, er, I'd better go. I'll see you soon." She squeezed Gina's hand and hurried out of the room.

At first her mum would gently suggest that Gina might feel better if she went out and got some fresh air. Gina hadn't been for a run in weeks. Normally there was no stopping her. So the more she refused to go out, the more worried her mum became. Then, one afternoon, Gina felt a determined tap on her shoulder. As her eyes flickered open she saw her mum standing next to her bed in the darkened room. Gina licked her dry lips and croaked, "Is it about the inquest?"

"No. It's doing you no good sleeping all the time. You need to get up, get washed and get dressed," her mum said firmly.

Mum pulled back the duvet, swung Gina's leaden legs out of the bed and wrapped her in a dressing gown that hung from her shrunken body. Gina shuffled to the bathroom, where her mum turned on the shower and waited outside, calling through the door, "If you don't shower, Gina, I'll come in there and wash you myself."

Then Mum escorted her back to the bedroom and sat her at the dressing table. Gina could feel the brush tugging at her knotted curls as she stared down at the table.

"There, that looks better," her mum said sweetly, lifting up Gina's face to the mirror. The image that stared back at her was gaunt, with shadows under the eyes. The skin was dull and the eyes lifeless, but Gina didn't care; she stood up and headed back to bed.

"Oh no you don't! You can't stay cooped up in here for ever," her mum said, getting some clothes out of the wardrobe.

Before she knew it, Gina found herself in the breezy park being led along the paths. Her mum's voice was full of forced cheerfulness, talking about how good it was to be in the fresh air and how this would make Gina feel "that bit better", but Gina could only think about how she and Dad used to run around this same park. She could picture them jogging side by side. Gina suddenly stopped walking. She felt like she was going to throw up as the realization hit her. She bent over, retching.

"Gina, love, what's wrong?" her mum asked in alarm.

"I'll never see Dad again," Gina spluttered. "He's gone for ever."

Danny was already back at school and each day, on his return home, he'd go and crouch at the end of Gina's bed, his big brown eyes full of concern.

"Shall I make you a cup of tea?" he'd say. Or, "Do you want to come downstairs to play on the Xbox?"

Gina continually said no, but Danny didn't give up. One afternoon, when their mum was out shopping for food, he struggled into Gina's room, carrying a stack of old family albums.

"I thought we could look at some photos of Dad," he said, plonking the pile on the bed and opening the curtains.

Gina sat up groggily, her eyes stinging as the light flooded her room.

As Danny started to flick through the albums, Gina's blank face lit up.

"Okay, let's take out photos of Dad and stick them on my wall."

Danny smiled, delighted that at last he'd found something to cheer Gina up. However, two hours later the smile had been wiped off his face.

Gina had seemed gripped by the idea and she'd jumped out of bed, going from inertia to mania within minutes. She kept frantically flicking back and forth through the albums, peeling out photo after photo. She barked orders at Danny, telling him to get Blu-tack from downstairs, telling him to bring more albums upstairs. She spent ages deliberating where each photo should go but then she'd change her mind, rearranging the images, discarding others. She ignored Danny's huffing and pleas for a break. Only when she was completely satisfied did she stand back and survey the fifty or so photos she'd stuck on her wall. Every one of them featured her dad: from fading black-and-white baby pictures to the last photo ever taken of him, surrounded by his family at the kitchen table for his birthday meal.

"It looks great." Danny gave a tired smile. "Can I go now?"

"Yes, thanks, Danny," Gina said. She waited until Danny had left the room and then she addressed the wall of photos. "You're not to worry, Dad. This inquest will find out what happened to you. Then you can rest in peace."

Finally, the morning Gina had been waiting for arrived. Mum called her into the kitchen. Gina sat opposite her at the table, noticing for the first time the pasty whiteness of her mum's face and the ageing bags that had formed under her eyes over the past weeks.

"Gina, we've got a letter from the coroner's office… There's a date for the inquest hearing."

Gina gave a great sigh of relief. "We'll find out what happened!"

"Yes."

"We'll find out that Dad didn't kill himself," Gina said.

Her mum hesitated before saying gently, "Gina, it's

time that you knew something. Your dad wasn't well before he died."

"What do you mean? What was wrong with him?"

"He was very down, depressed."

"What? No he wasn't. He was fine. It was only that night he didn't seem right," Gina protested.

"No. I've been trying to find the right time to tell you. I've only known since he died, but it seems as if your dad had been depressed for a while. He hid it from us." Her mother's eyes filled with tears.

Gina shook her head violently. "You can't believe Dad killed himself! No way! Just you wait. The inquest will prove that he didn't."

3 THE VERDICT

Gina was surprised that such an ordinary-looking room was used to dissect such terrible matters. It didn't look like a courtroom at all – no jury, no people in wigs, no witness stand; just a table from which to give evidence, its only distinguishing feature the box of tissues placed, expectantly, in the corner.

A clerk led them to their places. Gina sat next to her mum in the first row of chairs. Her mum patted her knee, asking nervously, "Are you okay, love?"

Gina nodded, though her head throbbed. She'd spent the six weeks since her father's death waiting for this inquest, and now she was about to find out what had happened that night; she really wanted to be alert and focused.

The witnesses filed into the seats behind her. Gina looked towards the desk set aside for the press. Two local journalists sat chatting, notebooks at the ready. She resented their presence – they had no business being there, making a story out of someone else's misery; making the details of her dad's death public property.

An old man entered the room and the clerk instructed everyone to stand. The man took up his position at the raised bench in front of them and bowed slightly, indicating that everyone should sit down. Gina realized that this was the coroner. He had the air of a kindly but firm headmaster as he explained that his job was to establish the facts and find out when, where and how her father had died. He told the courtroom that relevant statements and reports had been gathered and that witnesses would be called. He informed them that, after he had finished questioning a witness, family members and interested parties could also ask questions, if they felt the need.

He shuffled through his bundle of papers and announced that they should begin with a summary of the post-mortem report. Gina screwed up her eyes, as she visualized her father's mutilated body lying on the mortuary slab. She chased the distressing image away, determined to remain focused on everything that was said in this room. She couldn't understand all the information that the coroner read out, but she registered the explanation that her dad had died from multiple trauma injuries which were consistent with being struck by a train.

The coroner explained that, "The deceased suffered a

fracture to the skull which, in the pathologist's opinion, was probably sustained as his head struck the railway line after he had fallen from a significant height. This blow would almost certainly have rendered the deceased unconscious before the train made impact."

A flicker of relief crossed Gina's face. Her mother squeezed her hand, whispering, "Did you hear that, love? Your dad wouldn't have felt any pain."

Gina continued to listen intently as the coroner read out that the toxicology report had revealed no traces of alcohol or drugs in her father's body; the pathologist found no underlying medical problems at the time of death, and her dad's GP confirmed that, to the best of his knowledge, Martin Wilson had been fit and well at the time of his death – his last appointment had been over two years earlier for a chest infection.

The driver of the intercity train was the first witness called. Gina gave an involuntary shudder as the man walked across the room and stood at the witness table, his head bowed. She'd seen him on the night of her father's death, the look on his face emblazoned in her mind.

The driver's voice was frail as he swore the oath. His eyes were downcast as he delivered disjointed answers to the coroner's questions about what had happened that night. He appeared to be a broken man, wracked by an irrational guilt; still off work with stress.

"I couldn't stop in time…I just couldn't," he kept repeating, glancing over at Gina with eyes that begged forgiveness.

Constable Rogers nodded to Gina and her mum as he took his place at the witness table. The police investigation had concluded that the train driver had, indeed, done everything in his power to try to stop the train from the moment he saw the body on the track. However, the time available, coupled with the speed of the train, had made it impossible for the driver to prevent the impact.

This was not the first time he had investigated a "jumper". It was an inevitable part of the job, but not one that he'd ever get used to. As he read from his statement, he turned pale at the memory of the scene that had greeted him that night. His voice cracked a little as he began describing the impact on Martin Wilson's body by the seventy-ton train travelling at ninety miles per hour. Seeing the look of horror on the faces of Gina and her mother, the coroner hurriedly interrupted.

"I don't think we require quite so much detail, thank you, Constable. I have it in your written statement."

"Sorry, sir." Constable Rogers cleared his throat and continued in a chastened tone. "The only item recovered at the scene was Martin Wilson's mobile phone; the phone that was used to text his daughter. It was found strewn around the track, smashed to pieces. He was most likely holding it when he jumped from the bridge."

The constable finished his statement and was dismissed by the coroner. The coroner then addressed Gina. "I believe that Martin Wilson's daughter wishes to make a witness statement," he said. He beckoned her forward. "Please, Gina, come to the witness stand."

Gina rose, shakily, from her chair. She leaned over to her anxious mother and kissed her tenderly on the cheek. Her mum hadn't wanted her to attend the inquest, worried that it would prove too distressing for her. But Gina had insisted on coming. She needed to be there, to hear every word spoken about that night, about her dad. She wanted to stand up and give her own evidence. She needed to have her say.

Even so, she found herself trembling as she stood at the witness table. The coroner gently asked her to tell him, in her own time, what had happened that night. For a moment, she felt as if she'd been struck dumb, unable to utter a word. She looked over at her mum, who nodded at her and mouthed, "Go on, Gina." Then she swallowed hard, took a deep breath and the words started to come. Gradually her speech gathered momentum until the words were tumbling out of her. She hardly dared pause for breath – afraid of being stopped before she got it all out.

"Dad came in the car to pick me up from my running club like he always did, but there was definitely something wrong. He had a phone call, a work thing, he said. He wouldn't let me in the car until he'd finished. Whatever was being said seemed to be winding him up, and after he opened the door for me, he hardly spoke. He was miles away, not paying attention. He said he was tired but I thought maybe he was ill. Usually he'd have been mucking around, having a laugh. He loved to hear about my running. He used to be a bit of a runner himself, so he trained with me, came to every meeting to cheer me on. But that night, he didn't ask me anything. And then he went down that dead-end street and got out of the car saying he needed a wee, but then he told me he loved me. I thought it was a bit weird to say out of the blue like that, so I just laughed at him and didn't even say 'I love you' back. He must have wanted to hear me say it, and I didn't, and now it's too late. Then he seemed to have been gone for ages. I was getting a bit worried, so I beeped the horn. Then that text came." Gina fell silent; her ragged breathing filled the room. She couldn't bring herself to repeat the message.

The coroner took control of the situation.

"Thank you, Gina. I realize how difficult this is for you. You can go back to your place now. We have a record of the text," he continued. "For the purposes of the hearing, let it be known that it read, *Forgive me. Dad.*"

But Gina didn't move. She hadn't finished. She fought back the sobs that were gathering in her throat and continued. "And then I heard the train screeching, trying to stop and it was my dad on the tracks and I know what you're thinking, but you see –" she looked imploringly at the coroner – "it doesn't make any sense. My dad wouldn't kill himself and anyway, just before he got out of the car, he said that he'd go for a run with me the next day. Why would he say that if he knew he was going to kill himself? He wouldn't, would he?" She looked desperately around the room, waiting for someone to agree with her, but all she saw were downcast faces etched with pity.

"You've got to believe me!" she cried out. "My dad would never do that to us. He loved us! If you'd met him, you'd know he wouldn't leave us like this." Her shoulders shook as her sobs finally erupted. Her mother rushed across the courtroom and Gina felt arms around her, cradling her quivering body.

The coroner spoke up. "I think we should stop there for the day. We'll resume the hearing tomorrow."

Gina begged, "No! Please, don't stop. If I leave this room now, I won't have the guts to come back tomorrow and I need to be here. Please! I'll pull myself together."

"But it's *your* welfare I'm thinking of," the coroner assured her.

"Then please, just carry on and let me stay."

The coroner paused. "Mrs. Wilson, if you believe that it's in the best interests of your daughter to remain here, then I'll abide by your judgement," the coroner said.

Gina looked pleadingly at her mother.

Her mum gave a sorrowful sigh. "Yes, I think she should stay. Gina needs to hear *everything*."

"Then, if you go back to your seat, Gina, we'll continue," the coroner announced. "Would Mr. Thomas Cotter please come to the witness table."

Gina dried her eyes as she tried to compose herself. She wanted to take in every word that he had to say. She scrutinized Uncle Tom as he stepped up to the table. She knew how he liked to keep himself well groomed and fit. She knew that her dad's boss was never short of female admirers, but today his handsome face looked grey and drawn. Gina realized that her dad's death had hit Uncle Tom hard.

She heard Uncle Tom's voice thicken with emotion as he answered the coroner's questions.

"Yes, sir. I knew Martin very well. I first met him sixteen years ago when I opened my warehouse on the docks and I employed him as my foreman. We had a great working relationship which became a friendship. Marty and Clare always made me feel welcome in their home. The kids even call me uncle," he said, giving Gina a weak smile.

"And how would you describe Martin Wilson's character?" the coroner asked.

"Well, he was a great bloke – warm, kind, a real family man. The other lads at the warehouse really respected him. But I'd been worried about him in the weeks before his death. He was putting up a front for the others at work but I noticed he seemed down, withdrawn, not his usual self at all."

"And did you ever ask him about this?" the coroner said.

"Of course. I asked Marty outright. I was really concerned and I thought it might help if he confided in someone. He did tell me about this feeling he had; this dark cloud. That's how he described it, 'a dark cloud' that hung over him. I asked him why…what was worrying him? I thought maybe I could help him, but he couldn't even explain what had brought it on."

"And was he seeking help for his feelings of depression?"

"No." Tom shook his head despondently. "I did my best to try to persuade him to tell Clare. He needed her support, but he wouldn't tell her. He kept saying that he didn't want to burden her or the kids. At home he was carrying on as if everything was normal.

"I said I'd go to the doctor's with him, see if he could get some antidepressants, but Martin wasn't having any of it. He insisted that he'd snap out of it, be back to his old self soon. I was feeling completely out of my depth. I really needed to tell someone, to get him some help, but he made me promise to keep his condition to myself. So I didn't tell Clare, but I kept an eye on him, took him out for drinks, sat and listened, but I still didn't get to the bottom of what was bothering him."

"And can you tell us what you know about what happened on the day of Martin Wilson's death?" the coroner asked.

"Yes, okay." Tom braced himself and began. "On the day…the day it happened, I was up in Glasgow on business. I'd only been there a couple of hours. I'd already had a business meeting and I was en route to check in to my hotel when Marty phoned me – it must have been about one o'clock. He wanted to let me know that one of the shipments of cocoa beans from the Ivory Coast had docked early – it wasn't due for another couple of days and the GPS system hadn't been tracking it, so it caught us by surprise.

"Anyway, Marty had gone ahead and got the lads to unload it into the warehouse – I could always rely on him to deal with things when I wasn't there; he was a fantastic foreman. I thanked him and was about to put the phone down but he seemed to hesitate, so I asked him if there was anything else he needed to tell me and then, out of the blue, he started this…this *outpouring*, telling me what a great mate I'd been to him and how much he loved Clare and the kids, and then he started to cry… It was terrible. I could hear him down the phone, weeping like a child. I didn't know what to do, what to say, so I just ended up saying something useless, like, 'Everything's going to be all right, Marty.' I told him he had to ring Clare, let her know how he was feeling. I told him that I'd be back from Glasgow the next day and we could have a good talk. I said to send the lads home and shut up the warehouse early. We didn't have any deliveries going out and he sounded in no state to work and, to be honest, I never trusted anyone else to run the place.

"Then he seemed to pull himself together. I could hear he'd stopped crying. He just said, 'Don't worry about me – I'll be fine. Thanks for everything, Tom,' and hung up. That's the last time I ever spoke to him." Tom's voice trailed off. He looked over at Gina, who was shaking her head vigorously, her lips pursed in protest.

"I'm so sorry, Gina," Tom said gently.

Gina had been listening to his evidence with mounting anger. She couldn't believe what he was saying. Without thinking, she was suddenly out of her seat, shouting at him. "No way! My dad wasn't depressed. I would have known if he'd been depressed."

"Gina, if you wish, you will have a chance to question the witness after I've finished," the coroner said. He started leafing through the papers in front of him.

"Gina, listen to me," her mother whispered. "It's true. Tom's told me all about it. Your dad kept it hidden from us. He didn't want to worry us. Isn't that typical of him? Doesn't that sound just like your dad, to put us before himself?"

"How can you believe that?" Gina hissed. "He couldn't have kept it from us. He was my dad – *your* husband!"

"I know it's hard, Gina, but it makes sense. Why else would he have done this? People *can* hide their true feelings. Please don't go making things more painful than they already are. Come on, love, sit back down."

Gina looked at her mother's distressed face and reluctantly took her seat, glaring at Tom as she mumbled to the coroner, "No. I don't want to question him."

The coroner gave her an acknowledging nod and, having found what he was looking for within his bundle of papers, he began his questions.

"Now, Mr. Cotter, you've just said that the last time you spoke to Martin Wilson was around one p.m. when he was at the warehouse. Are you sure about that?" he asked.

"Yes," Tom Cotter replied without hesitation.

"As Martin Wilson's mobile was destroyed by the train, the police liaised with his network provider to gain a record of calls he made and received on the day of his death." The coroner held up the sheet of paper. "Their records show that he made a call to you at around one p.m., as you've said. They also confirm that he sent a text to his daughter just before his death and that, earlier that day, he'd received a text from his wife, which I know from Mrs. Wilson's written statement was to remind him to pick up a fish tank for their son's birthday. However, this document also shows that he received a call from you, which would have coincided with the time he was picking up his daughter from the running club."

Gina's eyes widened. She sat forward in her chair, staring at Tom. He appeared momentarily flustered but then he tutted as if annoyed with himself. "Yes, of course.

Sorry. I did phone Marty around that time. I'd completely forgotten. It's been such a stressful time."

Gina grimaced in disbelief.

"I phoned to check he was okay," Tom continued. "I'd been worried about him all day."

"So this would have been the phone call that he received when he wouldn't let his daughter into the car?" the coroner quizzed.

"Yes." Tom shrugged. "I suppose it must have been. Marty wouldn't have wanted Gina to know that anything was wrong with him. He wouldn't have wanted her to hear our conversation."

The coroner nodded in agreement. "Yes, I can see that. Thank you for shedding light on that call, Mr. Cotter. You can stand down now."

Gina didn't take her eyes off Tom as he returned to his seat.

The coroner looked over to her mum. "Mrs. Wilson, I know that you have submitted a written statement to the inquest rather than give verbal evidence here today."

"Yes, sir," her mum replied meekly.

"I've studied your statement and I see from it, as Mr. Cotter says, that you were not aware of your husband's depression."

Gina's mum flushed with shame. "No, sir, I hadn't realized. Martin didn't tell me how he was feeling."

"And it would seem that you have checked your

husband's emails and bank statements in an effort to find an explanation for his depression."

"Yes, sir," her mum said quietly. "I checked on the family laptop to see if he'd used it the day he died, but he hadn't. There were no unusual emails over the weeks before he died and the websites that came up on the history were running sites, West Indies' cricket scores, gardener's forums – it was the stuff he always looked at. There was nothing out of the ordinary."

"And your husband's finances?"

"Well, we'll never be rich but we've never been in any serious debt and I haven't found any credit card statements that would imply Martin was in trouble."

"And in the years you've known your husband was he ever prone to depression?"

"No, not that I ever saw, but maybe he was hiding it. We've been together since we were sixteen but I've been thinking about it a lot since that night, and I've started to wonder if the death of his mum and dad affected him more than he let on. You see, they both died a couple of years ago, within months of each other, and his brother Joseph, well, he was only twenty-one when he was killed in a car accident. Martin often talked about him. So, of course, he was the only one left on his side of the family. All that loss could have really got to him, couldn't it?"

The coroner didn't offer an answer. Instead he said, "Thank you for your input, Mrs. Wilson. We will break for an hour and when we resume I will be ready to sum up and deliver my verdict."

Gina spoke out, surprised. "But there must be more evidence to look at; more people to question?"

The coroner turned to her, and said gently, "Gina, I'm satisfied that there has been a thorough investigation which has provided me with the evidence I need to conclude this inquest. I will see you back here in an hour."

Gina refused to sit with her mum and Tom in the court's cafe. Instead she paced around, chewing at her nails, throwing icy stares at Tom. "How could you have forgotten you made that call?" she asked in a raised voice.

"I'm sorry but, like I said, I forgot because I've been stressed out of my mind about your dad's death, wondering if I could have done more to help him. Thinking that maybe I should have just told your mum about his depression, even though he didn't want me to. Maybe then this wouldn't have happened."

"But he wasn't depressed," Gina retorted.

Her mum shook her head sadly. "Please, Gina, it's been a shock for us all. I know it's hard to take in, but it's not Tom's fault. He tried to help your dad."

"Well that phone call definitely didn't help! Dad looked wound up," she snapped.

Her mum looked at her disapprovingly, but Tom gave

a gentle smile. "It's okay, Gina. I know you're angry about losing your dad. I don't mind if you take it out on me."

Gina scowled at him and walked to the other side of the room.

On returning to the courtroom the coroner launched into his summing-up. He spoke with authority and a clarity that was unclouded by emotion.

"Due to the lack of witnesses to how Martin Wilson came to be lying on the train tracks that night, I am obliged to draw my conclusion from the evidence presented here today and contained within the statements and reports at my disposal. Given the pathologist's findings, it seems reasonable to believe that Martin Wilson jumped from the bridge that night. After considering the information I have about the height of the sides of the bridge it would seem improbable that he could have, accidentally, fallen from it.

"As we have heard, Martin Wilson was not under the influence of alcohol or drugs. This fact, coupled with the text sent to his daughter and the evidence given by Tom Cotter regarding Martin Wilson's state of mind at the time, seem to rule out any suggestion that this was an accidental death. On the basis of these facts it appears beyond reasonable doubt that Martin Wilson must have climbed up on the side of the bridge that night and jumped onto the railway track with the intention of killing himself."

Gina was stunned, but her mother's head dropped in resignation.

The coroner continued. "From what I have heard here today, I am in no doubt that Martin Wilson was a good man and a devoted father, but in my duty to document the truth, I must return a verdict of suicide. I offer my deepest condolences to the Wilson family."

Everyone in the courtroom stood as the coroner went to leave the room but Gina ran up to him, blocking his exit.

"No! Please wait! That's not what happened. Didn't you listen to what I said – I knew my dad. He wouldn't kill himself. He wouldn't. I wanted this inquest to find out what happened that night. I wanted you to find out the truth! Why haven't you found out the truth?" she cried.

The coroner turned his intelligent eyes on her. "Gina, I know that this verdict is hard to accept but an inquest can't make judgements based on your feelings and instincts. I examined the facts very carefully before reaching this conclusion. I hope that one day you will understand that it is better to know the truth, no matter how painful." He smiled sympathetically and walked past her, but Gina shouted after him.

"Your verdict is wrong and if this inquest won't find out the truth then I will. I *will!*" She clenched her fists tight, her body trembling with fury.

4 THE CONDOLENCES

The funeral took place a week after the inquest. Throughout the day Gina felt like she was suffocating: first in the funeral car that took them to the windswept crematorium, then during the service in the freezing chapel, where Gina listened to the vicar trying to console the inconsolable. The vicar's sermon spoke of her dad "finding peace and being in a place where the burdens of the world were lifted from his shoulders". His words were obviously chosen to bring comfort to the family of a suicide victim but they made Gina's blood boil. She had to fight the impulse to stand up in the pew and shout "Don't talk about my dad as if he killed himself".

And when Tom Cotter stood at the lectern to deliver his eulogy, she couldn't focus on his stories of how wonderful her dad was, all she could feel was bitterness and anger towards Tom for telling everyone that her dad had been depressed.

Gina remained stony-faced as she watched her father's coffin glide backwards through the green velvet curtains, on its way to be consumed by flames. Her mum gripped her hand so tightly that it went numb. The sound of stifled sobbing filled the chapel, but Gina refused to let herself cry. *This isn't a proper goodbye for you, Dad,* she thought. *All these people believing that you killed yourself. It's not right, it's not fair!*

After the service, the gathering in the Social Club seemed to go on for ever.

Are these people ever going to go home? Gina thought to herself. She looked over to Danny in concern. All day, her brother's face had remained blank; he hadn't uttered a word; people were speaking to him as if he was a toddler, not a ten-year-old boy.

She noticed her dad's workmates being shepherded towards the family by Kylie, Tom's secretary. Gina liked them all, but Kylie was her favourite. Whenever Gina had visited her dad at work, Kylie always made her feel welcome. She'd often sit in the office in the corner of the warehouse, eating biscuits and listening, wide-eyed, to tales of Kylie's love life, and all the while Kylie's decorated nails would carry on tapping the keyboard at the speed of light. Tom would often pop his head round the office door – always dressed smartly, every inch the businessman amongst his workers in their overalls. He'd wink at Gina and slip a ten-pound note into her hand, whispering, "Don't tell your dad."

Growing up, Gina used to find any excuse to visit the warehouse, although her mum would warn her that it wasn't a playground. But Gina loved it in that vast space. She felt like Alice in Wonderland as she entered the warehouse through the tiny door cut into the immense sliding shutters. She loved to stand and fill her lungs with the sweet-smelling clouds of chocolate dust that rose, like magic, from the thousands of sacks of cocoa beans. She loved it when her dad plonked a yellow safety helmet on her head and swamped her in a high-viz jacket. Then, if she was really good, he'd let her sit next to him on the forklift truck, and help pull the levers that raised the bulging jute sacks onto the miles of towering shelves.

Whenever she had wandered down the wide aisles with him, as he checked a shipment, she'd hear one or other of the men singing along to the radio. Often the cavernous space echoed with laughter as rude jokes went flying between the aisles. "Gina, cover your ears," her dad would say urgently. She couldn't see how anyone would dislike working there, especially when they went home covered in a layer of chocolate dust every evening. But today there was no singing, no laughter. Her dad's workmates were barely recognizable with their sombre suits and solemn faces. Even Kylie was dressed demurely.

In turn, each of the seven men kissed her mum's cheek and told her what a great bloke Martin was, and how much they'd miss him. Then they reached over to ruffle Danny's hair and kiss the top of Gina's head. Kylie tottered forward, and despite her best intentions to remain composed, she burst into tears as she hugged the life out of Gina's mum.

"I still can't believe it, Clare," Kylie wailed. "I keep expecting him to come in. Every morning I'm sitting in that office thinking, 'Martin's going to come in now', but he doesn't!"

Her mum buried her head in Kylie's leather jacket.

"He was one in a million, Clare. We all loved him. He used to keep the lads in line; make them apologize if they said any of that sexist stuff to me. And he never let them swear around me – which was lovely of him, although, the truth is, I know more swear words than the lot of them – but it's the thought that counts, isn't it? And your Martin was *so* thoughtful."

The queue of mourners was now growing behind Kylie, as people waited to offer their condolences. Kylie gave Gina's mum a last squeeze and hugged Danny too, before stepping sideways to Gina. She opened her mouth to launch into another memory, but Gina got in first.

"Kylie, what happened that morning at work? What was Dad like?"

Kylie rocked back and forth on her stilettos.

"Are you sure you want to talk about this *now*, Gina?" she asked, looking uncomfortable.

"Yes," Gina said emphatically. "I need to know."

"Well," Kylie sighed. "He seemed fine when he first came in, but I didn't get to talk to any of them most of the morning – they were all too busy unloading a shipment – it had arrived earlier than we'd expected. Next time I saw your dad was when he came into the office, after he'd spoken to Tom; Tom was on business in Glasgow overnight, staying in this swish hotel. Anyway Martin said that Tom had told him we could all go home early. He asked me to pass the good news on to the others. Well, you can imagine, the lads were ecstatic. They were out of the place in five minutes flat. Your dad told me to go home, said he'd shut the warehouse, so I got off into town. There was a pair of lovely leather trousers on sale that I was desperate to get my hands on."

"And how did he seem?"

"To be honest, he seemed a bit stressed, not his usual chatty self. I asked him why we were closing the warehouse early but he didn't answer, he just told me to go and have a good time."

"Had Dad seemed depressed to you?"

"Oh God, Gina. You know me; I'm too busy talking *at* people to pick up on stuff like that. Anyway, your dad wasn't letting on that he was in a bad way, was he? It's easy to plaster a smile on your face and pretend like everything's

43

all right. I did it for six months once! There was this fella, he bored me to tears, but he was loaded. He ended up proposing! I tell you, I was tempted. I would have had the life of Riley – but even I have my standards." She nodded, proud of herself.

Gina searched Kylie's face. "Kylie, do *you* think he killed himself?"

"Oh, babe," she answered, her eyes refilling with tears. "We know he did. The facts are the facts, Gina. Don't go driving yourself crazy trying to change them." She pulled Gina to her and planted a kiss on her forehead, leaving an imprint of blood-red lipstick, before tottering off towards the door.

Gina suddenly felt overwhelmed by the noise and heat generated by over a hundred mourners. So, when yet another person came to hold her mother's hand, she took her chance.

"Where are you going?" her mum asked anxiously.

"Just outside. I'll be back in a minute."

Gina wove through the heaving room, head down, avoiding eye contact with people. Many she hardly knew, but some of them stopped her, hugged her, planted unwanted kisses; by this stage, it wasn't just the tea and sandwiches that had been polished off. The bar was doing a brisk trade as people raised their glasses to her dad. And, as more alcohol was consumed, people were becoming less careful with their talk.

One huddle of people didn't notice Gina was passing.

"The poor kid," Gina heard someone say. "Did you hear about her outburst at the inquest? She won't believe that Martin killed himself. What was Clare thinking of? She should never have let Gina get up and give evidence. A coroner's court is no place for a child."

Gina stopped in her tracks and listened.

"How's she ever going to get over this? She's always been such a daddy's girl and Martin loved the bones of *her*."

"It's bad enough that he killed himself but how could he do that to his own daughter? Leaving her in the car like that, while he went and jumped in front of a train."

"Well, I don't like to speak ill of the dead, but killing yourself like that is such a selfish way to do it. He could have caused a terrible accident."

"Why do you think he did it?"

"Don't know. Probably money troubles – it often is."

"He must have had a guilty conscience about something. People don't go killing themselves for no reason."

"Maybe he was just out of his mind. They say he was depressed, not that you would have known it."

"Well, you never can tell what's going on in someone's head. Depression is a terrible thing, you know. My cousin Alan had it. He killed himself too, and none of us saw it coming."

Gina wanted to scream; she screwed up her face with anger and started pushing past the guests, fighting her way to the exit. She flung the door open and rushed outside into a corner of the car park, where she remained, huddled up, shielding herself against their voices and the biting wind.

Minutes later Tom appeared, scanning the car park until he spotted her.

"Gina," he said, crouching down to her. "Your mum's been asking for you. You'll freeze out here. Come back inside."

"No! I'm not going back in there with those people, talking about why my dad would have killed himself," she spat.

"They should keep their opinions to themselves," Tom said, annoyed, "but I suppose it's only human nature to look for an explanation, to try and make some sense of it. You were so brave at the inquest, Gina, telling everyone what happened that night, but I've been wondering whether you've remembered anything else? It may be something that didn't seem important at the time; something he did, something he said. Anything to help explain the way he was feeling."

"Why are you asking me? *You* seem to know far more than I do; telling everyone that my dad was depressed." She scowled at him.

Tom shook his head sadly. "But he *was* depressed. He hadn't been well for weeks."

"What exactly did you say to him on the phone that night? He was so wound up."

"Well, maybe he didn't appreciate me checking up on

46

him, because that's all I was doing. I told him that we'd go out for a drink when I got back. I told him everything was going to be all right."

Gina eyed him with suspicion.

"Don't look at me like that," he said imploringly. "Come on, people are starting to leave at last. Your mum and Danny are waiting."

Gina followed him without resistance. She longed to be back in her room where she could hide away from people who were full of pity and gossip. She squeezed into the back of Tom's sports car. Her mum insisted on sitting in between her and Danny, clutching their hands. They all sat in exhausted silence.

"The Social Club put on a nice spread, didn't they?" Tom said to break the quiet. "And it was a magnificent turnout, Clare. A real testament to Martin."

Her mum nodded silently, biting her lip.

"And the vicar did a nice service, didn't he?" Tom continued.

"Oh God…the vicar! With everything going on, I forgot to pay him. And I didn't even ask where I get Martin's ashes from," Gina's mum flapped, tears welling in her eyes. "Where will they be? Do they keep them in the crematorium or at the funeral director's?"

"Don't worry about anything," Tom said calmly. "I'll drop you off and go back to sort everything out. You all just need to get home and rest."

Her mum dabbed panda eyes, as the tears mingled with mascara. "I don't know what we'd do without you, Tom."

"Listen, I'm always here for you. Anytime, day or night," he replied.

"And thanks so much for volunteering to do the eulogy. It was lovely, really lovely. Wasn't it, kids?"

"Yeah," Danny muttered.

Gina remained silent. She felt a prompting squeeze of her hand, but still she didn't reply.

"Everything you said about him…it really summed him up," her mum continued.

"Well, I only told the truth. Martin was a lovely man, who thought the world of you and the kids. I doubt I'll ever meet such a good man again."

"Could I have a copy of what you said, Tom? It was hard to take it all in. To be honest I feel like I've been sleepwalking through today."

"Of course, Clare. Look, we're here now," Tom said, slowing down. "Let's get inside and I'll put the kettle on." He manoeuvred into a space amongst the vans and ageing cars parked along the street.

The family peeled themselves off the back seat and Mum opened the glossy green door of their immaculate terraced house.

Gina noticed her mum stop abruptly as she stepped over the threshold.

"What is it?" Gina asked, following her in. Immediately she saw that the drawers of the sideboard in the hallway were open and their contents strewn on the tiled floor.

Gina rushed past her and into the living room.

"No!" she cried as she saw the mess. The sofas had been turned upside down, their linings slashed, all the trinkets and trophies from the shelves had been dashed to the floor. The family laptop, which normally lived in the far corner of the room, was nowhere to be seen. Their DVDs and CDs had been cleared out and there was a gaping space where their TV should have been.

Gina picked up one of her dad's running trophies that she'd put on display. She then fell to her hands and knees and started frantically to gather up fragments of broken glass and pottery. Tears streamed down her face as she tried to piece together a garish mug emblazoned with the words *World's Greatest Dad!*

She heard Tom call out: "I'm going to check the rest of the house. Don't touch anything. They might have left fingerprints."

"I'm coming with you," she sniffed, picking herself up from the ground and walking past her mum, who stood surveying the room in shocked silence, and Danny, who was sitting on top of the upturned sofa, staring into space.

In the kitchen all the cupboard doors were open and drawers had been pulled out. The window hung off its hinges and the back door was ajar.

"They obviously got in through the window. It looks like it's been jemmied open. Then they've just unlocked the back door and taken the stuff out through the yard," Tom growled. "I'll see how things are upstairs. You're best to stay down here with your mum." Gina ignored him and followed. She peered into the bathroom at the top of the stairs. They'd even rifled through the cabinet. Soaps, scissors and ointments lay discarded in the sink.

Gina gasped as she saw her bedroom. It looked like a hurricane had hit it. Her dressing table had been upended, leaving her mirror shattered and perfume from cracked bottles seeping into the carpet. Her clothes had been pulled out of the wardrobe and the contents of her underwear drawer had been emptied onto the bed. She shivered with disgust. She looked at her wall of photos. At least they hadn't been touched.

Gina walked into her mum and dad's room but quickly retreated. The sight of her dad's clothes thrown around the floor made her stomach lurch. She found Tom in Danny's ransacked room.

"Who would do this?" she whispered.

"I've heard of this happening before," Tom spat. "The bastards read the obituaries in the local paper. They know the house will be empty the day of the funeral and the neighbours will probably be there too, so they plan to rob it when there's no one around."

"Really? That's just sick."

"I'll call the police." As Tom reached for the phone in his pocket it beeped. Gina watched his face turn ashen as he opened the text. He went straight to the window and, lifting the net curtain just a fraction, he peered out. Immediately he let the curtain drop and seemed to shrink back into the room.

"What's wrong?"

Tom cleared his throat. "Nothing," he replied sternly.

Gina lifted the net curtain and spotted a bulky, bald black man leaning against a silver Mercedes on the opposite side of the street. His arms were folded across his shiny, smart jacket and he was looking straight at her house. Gina noticed that he had rings on several fingers and a stud sparkled in one ear.

"Who's he?" She turned to Tom.

Tom shrugged his stiff shoulders. "How should I know? Just some man by his car, I guess."

"What was your text about? Is everything all right?"

"Of course it is," Tom said. "Come on, Gina. Let's go and see your mum and Danny. I'll phone the police from downstairs."

Gina frowned as she saw the slight tremor of his hand as he put the phone back in his pocket and walked briskly out of the room. She returned to the window and looked out. The man and his car were gone.

5 THE ALLOTMENT

A police officer called round early the next morning. Gina recognized him from the previous evening. Gina, Danny and her mum sat, exhausted and bleary-eyed, at the kitchen table.

"Just letting you know that you can start tidying up now. The forensic team finished late last night and we've interviewed your neighbours," the officer said.

"And did anyone see anything? Did you find any fingerprints?" her mum asked anxiously.

"No. It seems that most of your neighbours were at work or at your husband's funeral and the initial findings by the forensic team aren't looking like they'll turn up any prints."

"Someone told me that burglars read the obituaries and then rob people's houses when they know they'll be at the funeral; is that true?" Gina asked.

"Yeah, unfortunately it is. I've seen it happen a few times before. All we can do now is go and have a chat with some of our usual suspects and keep our eyes open at car boot sales and in the pubs we know deal in stolen goods. If you're lucky, we may be able to retrieve some things but I'll give you a crime number and you can look into claiming on the house insurance."

Within minutes of the police officer leaving, the doorbell rang and Gina opened it to reveal a gaggle of neighbours.

"We've come to help," Bob from next door said, waving a dustpan and brush. "Don't let the scumbags grind you down."

"Thanks." Gina gave a grateful smile as they filed past her and set to work.

Bob turned back to her. "By the way, Gina, you know you've been asking people if they saw your dad the afternoon he passed away?"

"Yeah," she said. Since the inquest she'd knocked on every door in the street asking the neighbours the same question and getting nowhere. "I'm just trying to find out what he did."

"I know, love," he said sympathetically. "And, well, the neighbours may not have seen him, but I've just met someone who did."

Gina gasped. "Really? Who?"

"Well, I was over at the allotments at the crack of dawn

today and I bumped into Stefan Poliakoff. I don't think you know him. He's an old Polish man, his plot is on the row up from your dad's. Anyway, I was telling him you'd been broken into on top of all your other troubles and we got chatting, then he comes out and says that he saw your dad the afternoon that he passed away."

"And what was he doing?"

"Stefan said he was working on his plot. But you're best to talk to him. If you hurry, he may still be there."

"Which plot has he got?"

"Number twenty-eight, third row."

"Thanks, Bob," Gina said, her heartbeat quickening.

She went into the kitchen and searched through a drawer until she found two small bronze keys with *Allotment* written on the fob. She headed out of the front door and looked down the slope of the street to the unmistakable skyline of the docks; she could pick out her dad's workplace from the complex of warehouses within the port walls. Gina walked briskly down the hill and onto the dock road before crossing over to the canal. The patchwork of allotments was on the other side of the water. The large green space sat incongruously between the streets of crammed terraces. Gina walked over the footbridge and up the grassy path that led to the allotment entrance. She used one of the bronze keys to open the main gate and trudged along the rows until she came to plot twenty-eight. She was relieved to see an elderly, ruddy-faced man sitting in a deckchair, admiring his neat rows of weeded earth.

"Mr. Poliakoff?" she asked, approaching him a little nervously.

"Yes?" he answered.

"I'm Gina, Martin Wilson's daughter. Bob just told me that you saw my dad on the day he died."

Mr. Poliakoff tutted, shaking his head. "Oh, it is terrible for you. I am so sorry for your loss."

"Thanks," she said hurriedly, anxious for information. "So what was my dad doing? What time did you see him?"

The old man narrowed his eyes in concentration. "It must have been around three o'clock. I was on my way home. I'd been here since first thing and I could see the dark clouds gathering. I walked past your father's plot and I saw him digging, digging, digging…like a man possessed. I called to him, 'Don't work so hard, you'll give yourself a heart attack.' He turned round to me; sweat was pouring down his face. He did not smile. He did not seem himself. Your father and I have often spoken in the past. He was always such a cheerful man. He said to me that afternoon that digging helped him to think. 'And what is it that you think about?' I asked him. 'I'm thinking about what I should do,' he answered.

"He looked like he had the weight of the world on his shoulders so I said to him, 'Listen, I have a flask of vodka here. Why don't we sit down, have a drink and you can tell me all about it?' But he wouldn't. He thanked me and told me that he wanted to keep digging. I warned him that the heavens were going to open and I went on my way."

"And that was it?" Gina asked.

"Yes, and then I heard what happened. I'm so very sorry. I only wish he had confided in me that day; maybe I could have stopped him." Mr. Poliakoff sighed.

Gina walked over to her dad's plot and stood, deep in thought. *So that's why his hands and overalls were so dirty when he picked me up. He'd been here, digging.*

She surveyed the random holes that had been dug and the mounds of earth piled next to them. It looked like an army of giant moles had been at work. She felt a physical ache in her chest, thinking about him on that day, wondering what had been going on inside his head. There was so much of her dad in this allotment: all the years he'd spent trying to grow his vegetables. How ecstatic he'd been at the sight of some deformed carrot that had survived the life-sucking soil. All the mud fights he started when he could see that she and Danny were getting bored with helping, and the hours they'd spent playing cards for pennies in the rickety shed that he'd transformed into their den.

How many times had she caught her dad, standing amongst his failing crops, eyes closed, filling his lungs with the fuel-filled air from the docks and city roads.

"Are you in Trinidad again, Dad?" she'd ask him, amused.

"Oh, yes," he'd sigh. "Lush, rolling hills cascading down to golden beaches, turquoise waters lapping at our toes. Paradise!" And she'd look out at the looming docks and the grey waters beyond and give him a shove.

"We'll keep saving. We'll go and visit one day and then you can bore us to death, showing us all the places from when you were a kid."

She unlocked the padlock on her dad's shed and opened the double doors. Light flooded into the cramped interior. She stepped inside and inhaled the comforting smell of creosoted wood. Their picnic table and folding chairs sat in the middle, surrounded by gardening equipment. Layers of music posters adorned the walls. Some were Danny's choice and others were hers, dating back years to singers she was now embarrassed to admit she'd ever liked. Gina picked her way around the shed. Everything seemed just as it should be.

Three little stacks of playing cards were dotted around the table, with a glass jar of pennies in the centre. For a second she had an overwhelming feeling that her dad would stroll in at any moment and sit down to resume their last game, filling the shed with his laughter and groans as he won and lost. Tears filled Gina's eyes but she dug her nails into her hand until the pain distracted her. She sniffed and wiped the tears away defiantly.

Crying isn't going to help. I've got to stay strong. I've got to be organized. I should be looking everywhere, writing everything down.

She took off her muddy shoes as she entered the hallway and slipped upstairs, avoiding the busy neighbours. She popped her head round Danny's bedroom door and saw him and her mum silently picking through the mass of clothes, books and broken bits of games that had been dumped in the middle of his room.

"Where have you been?" her mum asked.

"I've been talking to an old man at the allotments. Dad was there that afternoon."

Her mother's face tensed. "And what did he say?"

Gina told her mum, who listened intently.

"What was troubling him?" her mum whispered, staring into the distance.

"Didn't he tell you he was feeling sad that day, Mum?" Danny asked.

Her mum's face crumpled. "No, love, I wish he had, but he didn't. I didn't even talk to him that day. I just texted to remind him to pick up a fish tank for you."

At these words Gina jolted. "The fish tank! Of course! That's another place he must have been that afternoon, before he picked me up from running club. Where did he buy it from?"

"I don't know," her mum answered.

"Well where's the receipt?" Gina asked impatiently.

"I'll find it. I haven't even looked at the tank yet. It didn't feel right without Dad," Danny said, as he scrambled under his bed and pulled out the box with the fish tank still inside it from under a mound of dirty clothes.

"Danny!" his mum tutted. "What have I told you about putting your dirty clothes in the wash?"

"All right, but at least they hid this from the robbers. They might have smashed it up if they'd seen it."

Gina examined the contents of the box. She lifted the hood of the tank and pulled out a pump and filter, plants, several bags of bluish bedding stones and another one of fine gravel.

"There's no receipt in here," she said, disappointed. "I need to know where he got it from."

"Maybe it's somewhere in the house," Danny said.

"But I don't think Dad came back to the house; no one saw him."

"Then maybe it's in the car," her mum suggested.

"Have you got the keys?" Gina said, eagerly holding out her hand.

Her mum handed over the car keys and Gina rushed to the Fiesta, which was parked in front of the house. She rooted through the glove compartment and found what she was looking for. The receipt was from Neptune's Aquarium. She gripped it like it was a golden ticket, and searched frantically for the sales assistant's name and the time of purchase.

She was desperate to go to the shop straight away but her mum wouldn't allow it.

"But I have to talk to them, Mum. They saw Dad that day. They might know something important."

"No, Gina. It can wait until tomorrow. Let's tidy up the house and then I want us all to have an early night. You've got to look after yourself, love. And you need to try and relax."

But Gina couldn't relax. That night she sat up in bed until well past midnight, scribbling page after page of notes into a book.

Eventually she put her pen down, exhausted. But still she couldn't sleep, with her mind whirring and her body a jangle of nerves. She got out of bed and stood in front of the collage of photos on her wall. One picture showed her dad holding a newborn baby; it was her. The look on his face was of pure joy.

"Everything I know is in here, Dad, but there's more, isn't there?" she said, waving her notebook at the picture. "If I can piece together your last day, I'll start to get answers." She kissed his smiling face. "You know I will, don't you?"

6 ENQUIRIES

Gina stood amongst the rows of tanks that housed fish of every imaginable colour. The soft glow of light and the warmth from the tanks made it feel like twilight inside Neptune's Aquarium even though they'd just opened up for the day.

Gina approached a long-haired man wearing an Iron Maiden T-shirt.

"Hi, can I help you?" he said drowsily.

Gina peered at his name badge. "Yeah. You're Jamie, aren't you? You're the person I want." She put the receipt on the counter. "You served my dad on this day." She pointed to the date. "He bought a fish tank here in the afternoon at seventeen fifty-five. You see, it says so on the receipt."

"Yeah, sure," the man said.

"Do you remember him?" she asked, showing him a photo. "He was buying the tank for my brother. He was probably wearing his overalls from work. He works... worked at the port."

Jamie looked at the photo. "Yeah, I do actually. Your dad told me it was a birthday present for your brother."

"And how did he seem?" She stared at him, her brow furrowed.

Jamie pulled a confused face. "Ahh...fine?"

"I mean, did he seem upset, depressed?" she interrogated.

"I don't know what to tell you," he answered, surprised. "I'd never met him before, had I? But he just seemed normal to me... Well actually..." Jamie pondered. "Maybe he was a bit stressed. He certainly wanted to get everything just right. I spent so much time going through things with him that I was late closing up. Not that I'm complaining," he added quickly. "You can't rush these things. You know, choosing the best tank size, all the equipment, getting tips on maintenance."

"So he was stressed, not depressed," she asked earnestly.

Jamie shrugged. "Yeah...well. I'm not sure. All I know is that once he chose the right Starter Kit, he spent ages choosing all the accessories. He looked at the different plants, coral, gravel, bedding stones – I mean, we have *forty* different types of bedding stones, all colours, shapes and sizes and your dad looked at every single packet until he found the ones he liked best. But, by the time he left we'd put together a kit any kid would be chuffed with."

"So did he say where he was going?" she asked with bated breath.

"No, I'm sorry. He didn't." Gina saw his look of concern as he asked, "Has your dad gone missing or something?"

"No." She couldn't look at him. "He's dead...he died."

Jamie's mouth sagged open. "Oh God...I'm really sorry. That's terrible. Listen, don't take any notice of me. What do I know? Stressed? Depressed? I haven't got a clue."

"It's fine, it's been useful," she reassured him.

"Well, it's nice that he was able to buy your brother the tank; it's something special to remember him by, isn't it?"

Yes it is. He's right. Danny needs to see that fish tank teeming with life, not sitting in a box under his bed.

"Thanks for your help," Gina said. "I'll bring my little brother with me next time. We need to choose some fish."

Gina sat on the top deck of the bus heading home, her face rigid with concentration.

So, if it was nearly six o'clock when he paid for the tank and seven o'clock when he picked me up from the running club, that just leaves an hour where I don't know what he did or where he went. I suppose he could have just gone to a cafe, sat and had a cup of tea – but which cafe? Dad didn't have a favourite cafe and I don't think he went to a pub – there wasn't any trace of alcohol in the coroner's report. It's worth asking though, isn't it? Maybe he met up with someone?

She got out her notebook and wrote: *Go to local pubs and cafes – ask if they saw Dad – take the photo.* She kept clicking the top of the pen, mumbling to herself, "Come on, Gina, get organized!"

She was getting strange looks from the passengers around her, but she ignored them. She turned to a new page and started to draw a timeline of the day her dad died, from when he had left the house for work, to the minute she'd heard the squeal of the train wheels, braking on the track. She studied it carefully and suddenly she knew where she had to go next. Her dad had spent from seven-thirty a.m. to, at least, one-thirty p.m. at the warehouse. So far she'd only questioned Kylie about that morning, though she'd already heard at the inquest what Tom had to say, but what about her dad's workmates? They'd been with him that morning. Maybe one of them would remember something important. They were all under one roof, right now.

Gina got off the bus on the dock road and walked to the main entrance to the port. She knew the security guard in his uniform and peaked cap, sitting inside the hut at the barriers.

"Hi, Dave," she called to him. "Can you let me through?"

"Oh, hi, Gina, love." He poked his head out of the

sliding window, surprised to see her. "I'm so sorry about your dad."

"Yeah, thanks. Can I go through to Tom's warehouse?"

Dave looked uncomfortable. "I know it's ridiculous, Gina – I've known you since you were little – but I'm not allowed to let unauthorized people through without checking first. You've always been with your dad before and you know how it is with port security. They think everyone is here to steal cargo or to pick up a container full of illegal immigrants." He rolled his eyes. "You name it, they're paranoid about it."

"But you don't need to check with Tom. He knows I'm coming." She smiled sweetly.

"Okay, hang on then." Dave's head disappeared back into the hut and he produced a sheet and visitor's badge. "Sign in and put this badge on. Just remember to give it back on your way out." He smiled.

Gina made her way through the port. CCTV cameras loomed at her from every wall. As she reached the quayside a huge shadow fell over her like there'd been an eclipse. She looked up to see a vast red container hovering high above her. It had been lifted from the deck of a ship by the towering gantry cranes. She watched with a mixture of awe and fear as the crane swung round slowly and lowered the container down, stacking it on top of a row of matching boxes like they were giant Lego blocks. She walked along the dockside, past the immense cargo ships, their gigantic chains tumbling into the waters as they dropped anchor. Everything about the docks was on such an enormous scale. She felt tiny and vulnerable amongst the tons of metal and machinery.

She looked out at the grey murky sea, perpetually churning with the constant traffic of ships sailing in and out of port, their horns blasting, their bodies creaking. Squawking seagulls suddenly skimmed overhead as they swooped in to steal fruit from a damaged crate.

For Gina, the docks were a part of her life. They never slept, producing a cacophony of noise, day and night, as ships from all over the world were loaded and unloaded. The sound of the docks floated on the wind into the surrounding neighbourhood. Visitors to Gina's house would ask, "How the hell do you live with that constant noise?" But, just like all the other residents, she had become immune to it.

She walked on and made her way through the cluster of giant buildings until she came to the cocoa warehouse. Entering through the Alice-in-Wonderland door, Gina was taken aback by the sight that greeted her. She saw half a dozen dogs, each in a different aisle, methodically making their way over the piles of bulging jute sacks, stored on the miles of shelving. With wagging tails and heads in constant motion, they moved from one pile to the next, sniffing at the sacks of cocoa beans.

Tom strode out of the office, Kylie tottering behind

him. "What are you doing here?" His voice was less than welcoming.

Kylie gave Gina a hug. "Hiya, babe. Lovely to see you."

"What's going on?" Gina asked.

"It's just the port police doing a spot check," Kylie said, waving at one of the police officers who stood at the end of the aisle.

"It's routine. They do them all the time," Tom added.

"Well, it's not that routine, is it?" Kylie disagreed. "We haven't had one for at least a year."

"Whatever," Tom said impatiently. "I just wish they'd hurry up. I'm trying to run a business here." He gave Gina a half smile. "So what can I do for you?"

"I just wanted to speak to Dad's workmates."

"What about?"

"About that morning…before he died."

Tom looked puzzled. "They've already said everything they know."

"But *I* haven't spoken to them properly. They might have remembered something new."

"As you can see, it's not a good time," Tom replied gruffly. "I'll let you know when's best to come in."

Gina stuck out her chin defiantly. She wasn't going to obey the man who'd told everyone that her dad had been depressed. "Don't worry, I won't be long," she said, walking past him and approaching a forklift truck driver who was stacking sacks.

Half an hour later, after Gina had spoken to all seven men, Tom came to find her.

"Are you done now?" he asked, irritated. "Because we need to get on and I've only just got rid of the bloody port police."

"Yes."

"So what did the fellas have to say? Did you learn anything useful?"

"No." Gina looked despondent. None of the men had told her anything new. They'd all agreed that her dad had looked as if he was okay, though they hadn't really had a chance to talk to him that morning because of the big delivery. It seemed her dad had done some random checks on the sacks and the only unusual thing that they could remember happening was that they got to leave work early.

Tom looked concerned. "Can you see now that there's no point to all this questioning? People've already said what they know."

"I'm just trying to find out the truth about what happened to my dad. Somebody's got to." She glared at Tom.

Tom sighed, sadly. "I think you'd better go home now."

As Gina walked away from the warehouse, Tom called her mother. The sound of a busy supermarket filtered down the phone.

"Hi, Tom," she said.

"Clare, have you got a minute?"

"Yeah, I've just finished on the checkout. I'm on my break. What is it?"

"I think we need to talk about Gina…"

"So what kind of fish do you think we should get?" Danny asked Gina excitedly. They sat on the slashed sofas that their mum had covered with brightly-coloured throws.

"We'll go to the aquarium and choose," Gina answered distractedly, as she looked through more old photo albums that she'd found.

"Do you think the coppers will find our TV and my Xbox? It's dead boring without them."

"I don't know. They said that they'd keep us informed."

They heard the key in the door and their mum's voice: "I'm home."

Clare's pale face appeared around the living-room door. "Hi, Danny. Did you have a good day at school?"

"Yeah, it was okay. Everyone had heard about our house being robbed. Michael Morris reckons they were druggies. He said they always are."

"Maybe he's right. Only people off their heads would tear a house apart the way they did, unless…" Gina's brow creased.

"Unless what?" Danny asked.

She shook her head. "Nothing, it doesn't matter."

"Anyway," Danny continued, "everyone's being dead nice to me. Miss didn't even give me any homework."

"Well that's good," Clare said. "I just need a word with Gina in the kitchen, if you don't mind, love?"

Gina sensed the anxiety in her mum's voice and followed her immediately.

"What is it? What's wrong?" Gina asked.

Her mum looked uncomfortable. "You went to the aquarium today? Did you find out anything?"

"Not much, but it was helpful. The guy there didn't think Dad seemed depressed and now I know how long he spent in the shop I've started a timeline of where he went that day."

"*And* you went to the warehouse and questioned your dad's workmates."

"How do you know?" Gina frowned.

"Uncle Tom phoned me. He's concerned about you. He thinks that you're just upsetting yourself, questioning everyone."

"He just didn't like me interrupting his business," Gina snapped.

"That's not the reason. He can see that you're struggling with all this and he thinks that you should get back to school; focus on other things."

"Oh, does he now?" Gina said indignantly. "Who does he think he is, telling me what to do?"

"He cares about you, Gina, and he's right. You need

routine, you need company. We have to try and get back to something like normality."

"Why are you siding with him? We can't trust him. Why didn't he mention that it was him who'd phoned Dad that night? Why have you just believed him about Dad being depressed?"

"Gina, ask yourself, why on earth would Tom lie?"

Gina's eyes darted around. "I don't know, but it can't be true."

Her mum cupped her hands around Gina's angry face, saying softly, "When you're older, you'll understand things better. You'll understand about depression. You'll understand what stress can do to people and you'll realize that the only person I'm 'siding' with is you. Until then, you've just got to trust me to do what's right for you – and that means sending you back to school."

7 THE DEPARTURE

The family had been surprised when, a week later, Tom stood in their kitchen and announced that he'd decided to go travelling for a few months and that he'd hired a manager to run the warehouse until his return. Gina saw the look of disappointment on her mum's face but she felt only a mixture of relief and suspicion at the news. Gina wanted him gone; she didn't want him spreading any more lies about her dad, and she didn't trust him.

"Why are you running away?" Gina asked.

Tom laughed. "I'm not running away. Please don't be angry with me. I know it seems selfish to leave now, but Marty's death has made me realize that I shouldn't delay things. I've worked hard all my life and I've always wanted to see the world. I've got to seize the day. You do understand, don't you?" He looked towards Clare.

"Of course I do. I know how hard losing Martin has

been for you, too. You've been such a help to me, but you *should* go – we'll still be here when you get back," her mum replied with a forced smile.

Tom seemed relieved to have her mum's blessing. He held his arms wide open, saying, "Come on, I need a hug."

Mum and Danny stood up and embraced him but Gina held back.

"Aren't you going to give your Uncle Tom a goodbye hug?" Tom asked.

"No. You're not my real uncle, are you?" Gina replied icily.

"Well, no, but…" Tom stumbled.

"Gina! Don't be so rude." Her mother looked mortified. "Say goodbye to your Uncle Tom."

"Goodbye, TOM," Gina said, walking out of the room.

Even after Tom had gone and she was back at school, nothing could stop Gina's constant thoughts about what had happened to her dad. She spent her days in a state of agitation that bordered on mania. She'd only been back in school a few weeks when she approached Becky and some other friends on the playing field and overheard their loud whispers.

"Look, Gina's coming. It's time we said something."

"What are you going to say?" Gina asked them.

There was silence as her friends exchanged embarrassed looks.

"Nothing," Tanya replied.

"We're her friends. She needs to be told," Becky said firmly.

"What is it?" Gina asked in a whisper.

"Listen, Gina," Becky said gently, "you know that we've been trying to get you through this. We understand how terrible it is but we're finding it really difficult to help. We've tried to take your mind off it all, but you won't go anywhere or do anything. All you talk about is how your dad wasn't depressed and didn't kill himself. I'm so sorry, Gina, but we don't know what to do. We've been thinking that maybe you need to talk to someone who knows about these things. Someone who can help sort your head out."

Gina was stunned. All these weeks they'd been listening to her and then talking behind her back; saying what? That she was crazy? Cracking up? Well, if they weren't going to believe her then she'd find out the truth without them. Gina turned around and rushed away before her friends saw her crying.

The school was trying to be supportive, keeping a close eye on Gina, and teachers had noticed how isolated she was making herself. The headteacher eventually phoned Clare to share his concerns.

"It's not her academic work we are worried about – Gina seems to be plodding on with that. To speak frankly,

Mrs. Wilson, we're more concerned about Gina's mental health. We appreciate that she's been through a dreadful trauma and it's only been a few months since her father's death, but she seems to be having real difficulty coping with it all, and it's driving her friends away, frightening them even. We'll do our best to support Gina through this, but perhaps she needs some professional help – bereavement counselling, maybe?"

Clare thanked the head and said she'd think about it, but then she put the phone down and wept.

Gina knew that her mum was desperate for her to focus on other things; to go back to her running club, go out with her friends, spend time with the family, but Gina couldn't; she had more important things to do. On her way home from school she'd go into pubs and cafes in the area, showing the staff a photo of her dad and asking whether they'd seen him on the day he died. Her enquiries were met with a range of responses, some sympathetic, some disinterested, but all negative.

Once she got home each evening, she'd often head straight up to her bedroom. Her mum would knock on the door, trying to coax her downstairs and Gina would call out that she was busy doing her homework, but when her mum retreated, she'd open her notebook again and pore over her words, trying to recall how her dad had behaved in the weeks before his death. Some days Gina felt like her head was going to explode as she tried to conjure up every word her dad had said, every gesture he'd made.

One evening she was talking to her gallery of photos, asking, "What were you like before you went to work that day? I didn't actually see you, did I? I was in the bathroom, I hadn't even made it downstairs before you left. Mum was shouting for Danny to get out of bed. But you shouted up to me, didn't you? You said, 'I'll pick you up from running tonight. If I get a chance I'll get there early; watch you train, pick up a few pointers.' I opened the bathroom door and called down to you, 'Well you need them, old man!' and you laughed – I heard you laugh and you weren't faking – you seemed normal…happy. So why were you like a different person when you picked me up from the running club? What were you thinking about at the allotment? What did Tom Cotter say—"

She stopped abruptly as her door flew open and Danny entered.

"Who are you talking to?" he asked, looking around the room.

"To Dad," she said matter-of-factly, pointing to the photographs.

"Oh, all right." Danny shrugged. "Anyway, Mum sent me up to get you. There's that copper downstairs who came about the house getting robbed. Mum phoned them ages ago to find out if they had any news, and he's here now."

Gina rushed downstairs and into the living room. She automatically walked over to the display shelf on the opposite side of the room and cupped the grey urn that contained her dad's ashes. Holding it between her hands made her feel more connected to him. After a few seconds she released it and said to the puzzled police officer, "So what's the news?"

"Well, nothing positive, I'm afraid. We haven't been able to retrieve any of your stolen goods but I'm glad to see that you've replaced them," he said, nodding towards the new TV.

"Yes," her mum said, "the insurance paid out."

"Good. That's new, isn't it?" The officer pointed to the tropical fish tank in the corner of the room in an effort to lighten the atmosphere.

"It's mine," Danny said proudly. "It's off my dad. It's looking good but it's going to look even better. I'm going to keep adding more fish and stuff."

"Haven't you got anyone for the burglary?" Gina wanted to stick to business.

"No, I'm afraid not. It's been very frustrating. We thought we'd made a breakthrough a few weeks ago but it came to nothing."

"Why? What happened?" her mum asked.

"Well, we heard on the grapevine that a couple of young men had been boasting down the pub about how they'd been paid to break into a house."

"What! Our house?" Gina asked.

"We don't know for sure. We've had a few burglaries in the area but the timings would fit with yours."

"Oh my God! So what happened to them? What else did they say?"

"Well, that was the problem. They wouldn't say anything. They had previous convictions so we hauled them in, fingerprinted them, interviewed them, but it was just 'no comment' all the way. We held them while we searched their flats but we found nothing we could use against them. If they were guilty, they'd covered their tracks well. We couldn't charge them. Their solicitor argued that it was all hearsay and she was right. We had no evidence, so we had to let them go. I'm sorry."

"But you've got to ask them more questions," Gina said.

"Look, unless we have very strong suspicions we can't get them in again. The whole thing *may* have just been hearsay."

"You can't leave it like that."

"We have to. The depressing statistics are that most burglaries are never solved."

"But why would someone have paid them to break into our house?" Gina asked.

"It happens. Some people don't want to do the dirty work themselves. They pay some local yobs and split the profits. But we still don't know that happened in your case."

Gina started chewing at her nails, speaking rapidly. "What if it had something to do with what happened to Dad? What if it was someone with a grudge? Someone who did it for revenge?"

"Nobody has a grudge against your father," her mum insisted.

"And if it was a grudge, then they would have done all sorts to the house; written abuse on the walls and much worse," the officer said.

"Then they were looking for something! Somebody paid them to search our house," Gina announced.

"But we were robbed, Gina," her mum said.

"Yeah, but they could have just taken the TV and other stuff to make it look like an ordinary break-in. That would be the clever thing to do, wouldn't it?" she said to the officer.

"Possibly, but what would they have been after?" he replied.

"Nothing! It's a ridiculous idea. There's nothing in this house of real value." Her mum sounded irate.

"But look what they did," Gina persisted. "Danny's mate thought it was druggies, but couldn't it have been people looking for something? Why else would they turn the place upside down?"

"The fact that the house was turned upside down doesn't mean that they were after anything specific," the officer said. "Burglars search for hiding places, in case people have stashed a load of cash or valuables."

Gina's eyes suddenly looked wild, her mind was racing. "Listen, when we got back to the house and saw we'd been burgled I was upstairs, in Danny's room, with Tom. He got this text and he went and looked out of the front window and then he shot back; he looked shaken, so I looked out too and there was this big man standing by his car on the opposite side of the street."

"And what was he doing?" the officer asked.

"Well, nothing. He was just standing there."

"And who was he?"

"I don't know. Tom said he didn't know him."

"Well, what was the text about?"

"I don't know, but—"

"What's the relevance of all this?" her mum butted in.

"Well, it felt odd at the time but now we know someone paid them to break into our house, maybe it was that man and Tom Cotter knows him," Gina garbled.

Danny jumped up from the sofa. "So is that big man after us?"

"No he isn't." Her mum threw Gina an annoyed glance. "Gina's being silly. There is no 'big man', just some man who happened to be on our street."

"Young lady, you can't jump to conclusions," said the officer. "As I've said, we don't even know if the men we questioned were guilty, we don't know if they were paid and, if they were, we can't even be one hundred per cent certain that it was your house. As for this tale about the man in the street, well, it's hardly likely to be anything connected with the burglary. You wouldn't be waiting outside the house that you'd just had robbed, would you?"

"But shouldn't you write this down so that you can look into it?" Gina demanded.

"Well, I'll make a note," the officer said half-heartedly, "but I don't imagine it'll come to anything."

"Tom was up to something," Gina insisted.

"Love, you must stop fixating on Tom Cotter," her mum said, exasperated. "You're determined to blame him for everything. Your imagination is out of control."

"But—" Gina began.

"Be quiet, Gina." Her mum sighed. "Officer, maybe it would be best if you left now. As you can see, all this has just put unhelpful ideas into my daughter's head. It's not good for her."

Gina scowled as her mum walked him out of the room.

You're not the only policeman, she thought. *I'm going to talk to one who might actually listen to me.*

The next day, after school, Gina sat in the office of Constable Jason Rogers of the British Transport Police. He'd been surprised to see her.

"Does your mum know you're here?" he asked.

"Yeah, of course she does," she lied.

"How can I help you, Gina?"

"I've got new information. It might be connected with what happened to my dad."

"Okay." He sounded sceptical. "Let's hear it."

She told him about men being paid to break into their house when they were at her dad's funeral. She told him about Tom Cotter, the text and the man in the street. She told him that they might have been looking for something.

"I don't see how the burglary connects to his death. It happened weeks after your dad died," Constable Rogers said.

"Yeah, but it was the best time to get inside the house. Everyone was at the funeral. Please, you need to question those two men to find out who paid them and why. And can't you find out who that man in the street was and how he knows Tom Cotter?"

"There's already an officer in charge of investigating the burglary. He will have looked into all this."

"But he doesn't understand; you really need to take over."

"I certainly can't take over another officer's investigation, but if it will put your mind at rest, I'll give him a call. What's his name?"

Gina gave the officer's name and watched Constable Rogers disappear to make the call.

Gina sat chewing her nails in the hot, stuffy room. Beads of sweat started to form on her forehead as she waited.

Constable Rogers returned, his face a mixture of annoyance and concern. "It seems that you haven't been straight with me. The officer gave me a very different perspective on your *facts*. He explained the situation and said he won't be pursuing any further enquiries, and neither will I. Listen, Gina, you know that I was part of the investigation into your dad's death. But the inquest gave you a verdict, and in my view, it was the correct one."

"No it wasn't!" Gina cried. "There's other things that don't add up and they all involve Tom Cotter."

"Go on," the constable said impatiently.

"Well, only Tom Cotter says that my dad was depressed. No one else noticed!"

"People can hide depression," he answered firmly.

"But then Tom lied about the last time he spoke to my dad."

"But he didn't lie, did he? He forgot."

"That's what he *said* when the coroner found him out. Tom said he was checking up on my dad, but he couldn't have been, because he was winding Dad up so much. He wasn't helping him at all."

"Gina, this is just your word against Mr. Cotter's."

"Then there's the burglary and Tom and that man," she continued, undeterred.

The constable puffed out his cheeks. "Haven't we just established that is all unsubstantiated? It seems to me that you're twisting things to fit in with your belief that your dad didn't kill himself. So what are you saying, Gina? Do you think your father's death was suspicious?"

Gina was taken aback for a moment. Her mouth went dry. "Yes…yes, I suppose I am," she whispered. She'd had the thought at the back of her mind all this time, but somehow saying it out loud made it seem real – and terrifying.

"Okay, so in that case, do you believe that your dad was attacked on the bridge that night?" He sounded like he was interrogating her.

Gina stumbled around in her head looking for coherent thoughts.

"Maybe…I'm not sure."

"You either believe he was or he wasn't," he said. "And who would want to attack your dad?"

"Nobody would want to attack him. Everybody loved him."

"So do you think Tom Cotter attacked him?"

"No! Of course not," she protested. "But I think he knows something about what happened."

"Well, at least you don't think the man is a killer." The constable sounded sarcastic. "Especially as he was in Glasgow when your father died. So who was it, Gina? Who was this *attacker*?"

Gina gnawed at her nails, stress tensing her whole body. "I don't know, maybe it was a mugging that went wrong."

"But nothing was stolen from him and the bridge road is a dead end and you didn't see anyone else there. So I think we can rule out an attack, don't you?"

"But he *didn't* kill himself. He *wouldn't* do that!"

There was a heavy silence before the constable said gently, "There are no grounds for your suspicions and, on top of all that, how do you explain the text he sent, asking you to forgive him?"

"I don't know," Gina replied in a whisper.

"Gina, listen to me, you are still upset. You're clutching at straws. The inquest found that your dad was depressed. It's tragic, but sometimes people kill themselves when they're depressed. The investigation and the inquest have given you the answer. I'm sorry."

He opened the door and Gina slowly walked out, feeling like she'd been punched in the stomach.

8 THE COLD CALLER

As time passed Gina continued to contact Constable Rogers, insisting that he kept investigating her dad's death. Eventually, he stopped answering her calls. She didn't see her friends, and even a visit from her running coach had failed to persuade Gina to return to the club. Her mum's frequent bribes of outings and tickets to gigs were rejected and, as her sixteenth birthday approached, Gina became increasingly anxious. Her mum tried desperately to persuade her to invite all her friends over but Gina refused, mumbling, "I don't want to do anything. Becky and the girls wouldn't want to come anyway. We don't hang around together any more."

"But that's because you don't go out, Gina. I'm sure that they'd love to celebrate with you," her mum replied brightly.

"No, Mum. Please stop going on about my birthday," she pleaded. "I've got nothing to celebrate."

*　*　*

When the day arrived, Gina was woken up by her mum and Danny singing "Happy Birthday". Danny dive-bombed her bed and handed her a large rectangular present, wrapped in newspaper.

"Come on." He shook her. "Open it up. It's a massive bar of chocolate. It cost me all my pocket money, so you might want to share it with me."

"Happy birthday, love," her mum said, kissing her cheek. She handed Gina a small box. Gina sat up and faked a smile for them. She opened the box and stared at the watch. "It's a special one for runners," her mum explained. "It's got a stopwatch and all these other things that I don't understand, but they'll tell you how you're doing when you run."

Gina didn't respond.

Her mum smiled tensely. "I thought it would be good for when you start running again."

Gina's face crumpled. She covered her eyes with her hands as tears started to trickle down her cheeks. "I'm sorry. I'm so sorry. I can't do this without Dad."

Her mum rubbed her back. "It's okay, it's okay."

"But it's not. I want Dad here too, baking me one of his rock-hard birthday cakes, leaving work early to pick me up from school and taking us all out for pizza. I want him to embarrass me like he always did by getting the whole restaurant to sing 'Happy Birthday'. I want to go and choose a movie with him and let him talk me into renting an old film that he knows I'll love. I want us all to sit on the sofa and eat popcorn until we feel sick. I want him to make his speech about the day I was born as me and Danny throw popcorn at him and tell him to sit down and, at the end of today, I want to be able to hug him and kiss him goodnight and thank him for another great birthday."

The bedroom was filled with the sound of frantic gasping. Gina looked up and saw Danny, shaking with crying.

"Come here, Danny," Gina said, feeling guilty for upsetting him. She stretched an arm towards him, but her brother just turned and ran out of the room.

A few days later Gina was the only one in. She sat cross-legged on her bed and looked over at the collage of photographs which dominated the wall. The fifty photos had become nearly eighty, as she'd hunted out more and more images of her father to add to it.

"Every day that I don't find out what happened to you, I feel like I'm letting you down, Dad," she said bitterly.

She felt under her mattress and pulled out her notebook. Its cover had become tatty and frayed. She flicked through page after page of information, thoughts, interviews and timelines. The further on she flicked, the more scrawled and chaotic the writing on the page appeared – words became illegible, ink smudges obscured information and deep pen lines scoured through pages as her frustration and distress grew.

Gina gently rocked back and forth, her eyes closed, her fingertips massaging her aching temples. "Think, Gina, think. Who can help you find answers?"

The doorbell rang, interrupting her thoughts. She ignored it. She didn't want to see anyone, but then it rang again.

Ding dong! Ding dong!

Whoever was at the door wasn't going to give up.

Gina stomped down the stairs.

She opened the door to a young, greasy-haired man holding a clipboard. She noticed that his baggy suit hung off him, so he looked like he was merely dressing up as an adult. He greeted her with a rictus smile. "Good morning. I'm Olly and I've come to see you today to make you an offer you can't refuse," he said, as if reading an autocue.

Gina crossed her arms, scowling. "Oh yeah and what would that be?"

"Well, Madam…erm…Miss… I've noticed that your guttering may need updating and, luckily for you, our company, Gutted!, is in the area for one day only and can offer you an exclusive half-price deal on replacement guttering, with a lifetime guarantee."

"No thanks," she said, closing the door.

"Please," the young man pleaded, "could I speak to the householder – see if they're interested?" He looked down at his list. "A Mr. Martin Wilson. Is he in? Maybe if I could convince him of what an unmissable offer this is…"

A wave of nausea washed over her; she'd never get used to people asking for him.

"Maybe I should call back later. Catch him then," he said uneasily.

"He won't be back later. He won't ever be back. He's dead. He died seven months and five days ago."

"Oh…I'm sorry…" Olly squirmed.

"But the thing is," Gina continued earnestly, "they said it was suicide."

The young man started to look twitchy.

"It wasn't, you see, but nobody believes me, nobody will help me. You'd know if your own dad was depressed, wouldn't you?" she asked, nodding manically at him.

The young man backed away nervously. "I'm sorry. I haven't got a clue. I'm only trying to sell guttering. I'll make sure we cross him off our list." He lowered his head in embarrassment and started to walk away.

She shouted furiously after him: "Doesn't anybody care about what really happened to my dad!? Well you can piss off! You can *all* piss off!" She slammed the front door and ran up the stairs to her bedroom.

Her whole body shook as she stood there. She walked

over to the photographs and slowly ran her trembling hand over each one, studying them, until her eyes fell on one particular picture. She peeled it off the wall. Her churning insides were immediately calmed as she was drawn into the scene.

Her dad's face was creased with laughter as he kneeled by a mound on Scarborough beach. Only her head and neck stuck out of the sand that he'd buried her under. She was grinning, showing off a gap-toothed smile. That was the last summer her hair had ever been short. It looked like a halo of glossy curls on her little head. Even though she was only six, she could vividly remember a woman passing by, remarking to her dad, "Isn't he sweet? He looks the image of you."

After that Gina had insisted on growing her hair as long as possible so that no stupid stranger would ever mistake her for a boy again.

Gina walked over to her dressing table, opening several drawers before finding the long-bladed scissors. She sat down, placing the photo in front of her. Her fingertips stroked her father's smiling face and she smiled back at him. She looked at her gaunt reflection in the new mirror, as she gathered a bunch of the curls that cascaded halfway down her back. She narrowed her eyes with satisfaction as she listened to the sound of the blades slicing through the mass of hair. She held the first decapitated clump aloft like an American Indian warrior triumphantly displaying a scalp. She threw it onto the floor and gathered together another bunch. She cut through the hair with such reckless disregard that the scissors nicked her earlobe; she winced, but didn't stop, even when droplets of blood fell on the dressing table. The blades of the scissors were struggling to cut through her thick mane, but undeterred, Gina continued hacking, pulling at half-cut strands until they came away. Then she placed the cold steel blades against her forehead and began to chop into her fringe, blowing away the clumps that floated into her eyes, obscuring her sight.

The front door opened. "Gina, we're home! Are you still in your bedroom, love?" Mum called, making her way up the stairs. "Danny's got a pirate ship for the fish tank. I've bought some new clothes, but I could do with your opinion. I don't know whether they make me look like I'm wearing a tent. Oh, and I've got a couple of tops for you. I hope you like them. I know you think I've got no idea about fashion but…"

Her mum stood in Gina's doorway, her jaw dropped open.

"Gina!" she cried. "What have you done?!"

Danny shot up the stairs to see what was wrong. He saw his sister, scissors in hand, surrounded by a carpet of hair; her butchered tresses rollercoastered around her head. She sat staring, as if she could see right through them.

His moment of shocked silence swiftly erupted into laughter, as he howled at her, "Oh my God, Gina! You're proper *mental*!"

9 THE APPOINTMENT

Gina slouched on the straight-backed chair, her arms crossed, scowling at Dr. Havers.

"My waiting list is ridiculously long. I'm so sorry you've had to wait for this appointment," Dr. Havers said.

"I'm not sorry. I didn't want to come in the first place," Gina huffed. She patted her head self-consciously. She had been reluctant to let anyone touch her hacked hair but, eventually, Mum had persuaded her to let a hairdresser sort it out. The hairdresser had performed a minor miracle, turning Gina's butchered curls into a cropped style which brought out the gamine quality of her face.

"I realize that you don't want to be here, so I appreciate you coming," the doctor said warmly. "People have all kinds of strange ideas about psychiatrists, but you might be surprised to know how many people come to us for help. Now, Gina, are you sure you want your mother to sit in on our session?"

Gina grabbed her mum's arm. "Yes, my mum stays. I've got nothing to say to you anyway."

"Well, it would be much better if you'd talk to me, but if you'd rather listen this session then that's fine." The doctor came out from behind her desk and positioned her chair so that the three of them were sitting in an intimate circle. "I've studied the referral from your GP and your mother and I have spoken on the phone."

Gina flashed her mum an angry look.

"I'm worried about you, Gina," her mum said sadly. "The doctor needs to know what's been going on."

"Your mum has done the right thing by bringing you to see me. I can help you to deal with your father's suicide."

"My dad didn't kill himself," Gina growled at Dr. Havers.

"Would you like to tell me why?"

"I've got nothing to say to you. You'll only twist it and make out that I'm mental or something," Gina fumed.

"No," Dr. Havers said gently. "I don't think that at all, Gina, but you *are* traumatized."

"You don't know what you're on about," Gina mumbled, sinking down into her chair.

The psychiatrist's kind face creased in thought. "I'm not going to patronize you, Gina. You're obviously a bright girl and I'm going to talk to you as such. I believe the best way to help you is to be direct, to share my explanation for your behaviour, even if it makes you angry at first."

Gina rolled her eyes but her mum squeezed her hand supportively. "Please listen to Dr. Havers."

"Go on then," Gina said challengingly.

"From what I've heard from your mum, you were very close to your father. The shock of him leaving you in the car and killing himself with no warning has clearly left you traumatized and unable to accept what has happened. I believe that, even if it's at a subconscious level, you are experiencing deep feelings of guilt that you were unable to prevent his death and maybe even that you were in some way responsible for his death."

"Come off it!" Gina protested.

"Really, Gina, this is a very common feeling in teenagers. They are naturally egocentric. They tend to think that everything revolves around them so you may believe that your dad's actions were because of you. I think that you're also struggling to deal with powerful feelings of rejection. You find it hard to believe that your dad would do this to you."

"This is such crap," Gina interrupted.

Dr. Havers held her hands up. "Just hear me out. The reality of what happened is too overwhelming for you and therefore your mind has been searching for an alternative explanation, no matter how irrational it is. This is why you are convincing yourself that your dad didn't kill himself and, in turn, treating your 'obsession' more like an 'investigation'. From what your mum has told me, you seem to be focusing much of your suspicions on a family friend who tried to support your dad. This is perfectly understandable – you're angry with him. Your dad confided in this man, Tom, but he wasn't able to stop your dad killing himself. You feel he let your father down and you want to punish him."

Gina jumped up with such force that her chair fell backwards. "You don't know what you're talking about. I'm not punishing Tom Cotter. He's a liar. He must know stuff about how my dad died. I'm not kidding myself – Dad would *not* kill himself. He loved me. He said that he'd go for a run with me the next day. People don't say things like that if they're about to kill themselves!"

"But they do," Dr. Havers said calmly.

"He wasn't depressed! I would have realized."

"Listen, Gina, I've worked with many depressed and suicidal patients, and let me tell you, they can be experts at hiding their feelings. Suicide often comes as a complete shock to the people closest to them."

Gina saw her mum's shoulders slump and tears start to roll down her cheeks.

"Are you okay, Mum?" she asked gently.

"Yes, it's just such a relief to hear a doctor say that. I've been feeling so guilty that I hadn't picked up on how your dad had been feeling."

"There's nothing for any of you to feel guilty about,

and you have to understand, Gina, that your dad's suicide wasn't *your* fault and it *wasn't* a rejection of you. He was depressed and not in his right mind. It doesn't mean that he didn't love you or that he wanted to leave you."

"Look, I know that you've probably got a ton of degrees and that you're really clever, but you're still wrong about my dad and you're wrong about me. Thank you, but I really don't need to be here." Gina gestured to her mum. "Are you coming, Mum?"

"Give me a minute with the doctor, will you, Gina? Why don't you go and wait in the car?" Her mum gave Gina the car keys and waited until she left the room.

"Do you think you can help Gina?" Clare asked Dr. Havers.

"She's a very distressed, confused and angry young woman, but if she keeps seeing me, I'm confident that I can help her through this to some kind of acceptance of what's happened."

"But what if I can't persuade her to come again?"

"Please do, Mrs. Wilson, otherwise your daughter's long-term mental health may suffer."

"What do you mean by that?"

"Well, if Gina can't move out of this stage of denial, then she's in danger of losing her grip on reality and developing psychotic behaviour which would require more drastic intervention."

Clare looked shaken.

"The truth is, Mrs. Wilson, Gina desperately needs someone who can reach her and she needs them now."

10 DECLAN

Declan groaned as he stepped out through the doors to be greeted by the evening gloom and the heaving rush-hour traffic. He booted a discarded can along the pavement, deep in thought. *You're such a balls-up, Declan Doyle! Mum and Dad have only been gone two months.*

It was his parents' fault that he hadn't wanted to move to Ireland with them, even though he loved the place. How could he not love it? It was in his blood; he'd spent every holiday of his life there. Okay, so it rained most of the time, but in his head his uncle's farm was always bathed in sunshine, with lush fields as far as the eye could see; him and his cousins running wild, drinking cider in the hayloft and joyriding on the tractors.

In England his mum would have had him tagged given half a chance: always wanting to know where he was going, who he was with, giving him embarrassing curfews that his mates laughed at. But at the farm in Ireland, normal rules never seemed to apply. His parents seemed happy to let him and his cousins camp out all night in the middle of nowhere, or roll in after midnight, without having to explain himself – yeah, the *craic* was great, the place was beautiful, but still, it was this heaving, grimy city across the grey water that felt more like home.

After all, this city was where he'd been raised, amongst the sea of crammed-in houses. The cobbled back alleys were where he'd honed his football skills and accidentally smashed a few windows. All his mates were here, his football team was here, sometimes the whole of humanity seemed to be here. He was happy that his parents had fulfilled their dream and returned home to help Uncle Shaun with the farm, but he wasn't ready to give up the buzz of his city for the joys of the Irish countryside.

His parents had taken some persuading, but his dad had eventually convinced his mum to let him stay in England. "I know he's only seventeen but it'll be the making of him," his dad had proclaimed. "You're going to get a job, aren't you, Declan? Make me and your mammy proud."

His mother's attitude had been somewhat different. "You get one chance, Declan Doyle," she'd said, "and if you mess this up I'll have you over in Ireland quicker than you can say 'Guinness'!"

Declan checked his watch. *Six-thirty! God, I'm late for tea. Mrs. Mac will have a search party out for me.*

He started to sprint down the road, cutting down the side streets and through the back alleys until he reached the unique forecourt that marked Mrs. McManus's house. The tiny space in front of the terrace was overflowing with window boxes containing luridly coloured silk flowers, their stems sunk into concrete. As all the local cats had taken to using her floral display as a litter tray, a distinctly unflowery aroma rose from it, though Mrs. McManus still maintained that it "brightened up the street".

Declan's heart sank. He could see his landlady's wizened face peering through the thick lace curtains.

He greeted her with a winning smile as she ushered him in, tutting.

"Evening, Mrs. Mac," he said cheerily. "You're looking particularly lovely today. Have you done something with your hair? It takes years off you."

"Where have you been, Declan? I've been worried," Mrs. McManus scolded. "Your dinner was going cold. I had to put it back on the stove. Get in that kitchen and wash your hands."

Declan did as he was told and then waited at the kitchen table for a further telling-off.

Mrs. McManus stood at the stove, stirring the contents of a pan with some difficulty. "I hope you don't mind, but I went ahead with mine because I'm away to bingo in an hour and you know I like to be ready in good time."

After living with Mrs. Mac for the last two months,

Declan did indeed know that she liked to be early for everything. If she was going out at eight p.m. she'd be ready in her hat and coat by seven thirty. Declan couldn't imagine that Mrs. Mac had ever done anything spontaneous in her whole life.

"Bridie is picking me up," she continued. "Do you fancy coming along? I know you love the bingo."

It was true that Declan had accompanied Mrs. Mac and her best friend, Bridie, to a few of the bingo nights, but this was solely to make the old ladies happy. There was no way he could face it this evening. Anyway, going out with Bridie was too traumatic. She drove her mini at twenty miles per hour on the ring road, shouting "Feck off" to the queue of beeping cars behind her and, even worse, once she'd had a couple of brandies at the bingo hall bar, she started to get a bit flirty towards him.

"No thanks, Mrs. Mac," he answered quickly. "I'm a bit tired. I think I need an early night."

"Ah, God love yeh. Have you been walking the feet off yourself all day, looking for a job?"

"Kind of," Declan replied uneasily.

"Well, don't you worry. Your mammy and daddy have left you in my care and you know I take that responsibility very seriously. I've seen you struggling to find work these last weeks so I thought I'd give you a helping hand."

Declan looked worried.

"I know how upset your mammy was when you failed

all those exams, especially when the school said you were more than capable if you'd bothered applying yourself."

Declan cringed. Mrs. Mac may have been a family friend for years but did his mum have to tell her *everything*?

"So, I've had a word with Mr. O'Rourke. He knows you come from a good, church-going family – though I didn't mention that I hadn't seen you at Mass once since you've been here." She let out a theatrical sigh of disappointment. "Anyway, he's willing to give you a try. Be at the parlour on Monday morning, eight a.m. sharp. He even provides your work clothes, although he said the only suit available may be a bit big. The last fella who used it was on the large side. Mr. O'Rourke was very upset with him when he went off on the sick after only a few weeks and tried to claim compensation for injury at work. He said carrying the coffins had given him a slipped disc. I assured Mr. O'Rourke that you wouldn't be having any slipped discs; you're a strapping young lad who would brighten up any funeral."

Declan looked at her in horror. "I'm not sure working in a funeral parlour is really for me, Mrs. Mac."

"Nonsense! It's a solid trade. Recession-proof, Mr. O'Rourke calls it; always got a good supply of customers. The only thing certain in life is that we're all going to die," she proclaimed cheerfully.

"I don't think I'll be very good around dead bodies," he protested.

"You'll soon get used to them. And, if you play your cards right, you might end up in the mortuary section, helping to get them looking all nice and peaceful for the families. Mr. O'Rourke's a real miracle worker; once *he's* finished with them, some of those corpses look better than they did when they were alive."

Declan's face was now tinged with green as Mrs. McManus ladled steaming heaps of stodge onto his plate. He picked at his food in brooding silence.

"Get it down you, Declan. You're going to need plenty of fuel to carry all that dead weight." She smiled wisely.

He disguised a grimace as he spooned in a mouthful of charred food.

"It's delicious, Mrs. Mac, but I'm not very hungry," he said, getting up from the table. "I hope you won't be offended, but I've given Mr. O'Rourke's job offer some thought and decided it probably isn't for me. But thanks anyway." He bent down and kissed the old lady's cheek.

Mrs. McManus rolled her cloudy eyes. "Think on, Declan. You shouldn't look a gift horse in the mouth."

Declan went up to his bedroom and lay on the plump eiderdown. He looked up at the wallpaper that covered every inch of the room. The old lady's taste in décor didn't complement his own. Her penchant for floral wallpaper and matching curtains left him feeling claustrophobic. Her obsession with putting lavender-scented liners in all his drawers left him smelling less than manly. But he'd managed to introduce a hint of testosterone into the flowery flurry, cluttering the top of the chest of drawers with his male grooming products and stockpiling football magazines on the bookcase next to Mrs. Mac's Mills & Boons.

Life as Mrs. Mac's lodger wasn't what he'd had in mind when he'd asked to stay in England, but it was the compromise he'd had to make. Mrs. Mac wasn't the most liberal of landladies. She wouldn't let him have a TV in his room; she would never be sure what he was watching! So, if he wanted to watch television, he had to go in the sitting room, where she'd often join him, especially for the gruesome cop shows that absolutely thrilled her. The problem was she could never follow the plot and so asked Declan a constant stream of questions, making him miss all the important bits. And, when she was in the room, she never relinquished control of the remote. At the first glimpse of naked flesh, she could change channels faster than Billy the Kid could draw his gun. She'd suck in her teeth, protesting, "Now, there's no need for that kind of thing, is there?" Declan found it hard to agree.

As he lay on the bed he thought about the events of the day and his stomach churned. He didn't have long to make up his mind; the offer was only open until midnight and then his fate would be sealed. He chewed his lip, weighing it up. If he didn't, then this man could ruin his life, his parents would be devastated and the truth was, he was scared, really scared. What option did he have? He'd be a fool not to make that call. He didn't want to, but if he didn't, the alternative was much worse, wasn't it?

Declan took the card out of the back pocket of his jeans and flipped it back and forth between his fingers before phoning the number. When the voice answered he didn't bother with any pleasantries.

"This is Declan Doyle," he said coldly. "I'll do it."

11 THE WANDERER RETURNS

Gina sat in stony silence as they drove home.

"You should give Dr. Havers another chance," her mum said. "She seems really nice. I think she could help us."

"No way!"

"But what she said made a lot of sense. She has years of experience in these things."

"I'm not seeing her again," Gina said, staring ahead. "And you shouldn't have made me go there in the first place. I'm not mad, you know."

"No one thinks you're mad, Gina. You just need a bit of help to get through this."

"I'm fine. There's nothing wrong with me," Gina said, tugging at her cropped hair like she was attempting to make it longer.

"Do you think that your dad would want you to be like this? Cutting yourself off from people, all those silly thoughts whirling round your head. No! Your dad would want you to get on with your life, get out running again, go out with your friends. That's what he would want. Don't let him down, Gina." Her mum's voice trembled.

Gina didn't answer. She turned her sorrowful eyes away from her mother. She felt so alone.

When they reached the house, Danny was waiting excitedly at the front door. He ushered them in.

"We've got a visitor!" He smiled. "You'll never guess who it is."

Before they had time to answer, Tom jumped out from behind the living-room door. "Tada!" he said, his arms open wide.

"Tom!" her mum shrieked. She rushed towards him and Tom wrapped his arms around her, lifting her off the floor. Gina shrank into the background. Her heart was pounding.

"God, Clare, you don't know how wonderful it is to see you." He held her at arm's length, inspecting her. "You're looking great!"

"Give over." She blushed. "I'm twice the size since you saw me last."

"You always needed more meat on your bones." He grinned, his teeth dazzling white against his deeply tanned skin.

Gina's mum rolled her eyes, tutting. "So the wanderer returns and not one postcard in six months."

"Sorry." He looked remorseful. "Were you worried about me?"

"No," she replied dismissively. "I knew you'd be having too much of a good time to even give us a thought."

"I just really needed to get away from it all. Have a complete break from normal life. I mean, the places I got to see were mind-blowing: Vietnam, Cambodia… I even spent some time with Tibetan monks in India – it was amazing."

"Gina, come and see Tom," her mum ordered.

Gina stepped forward, glaring at him. "So, did you 'find yourself' then?" she asked sarcastically.

"Gina!" His eyes widened. "That's a radical haircut."

"Yeah, she had a fight with a pair of scissors and lost," Danny chuckled.

Gina walked past Tom and over to the shelf which displayed their trinkets and trophies. In the middle of the shelf sat the shiny grey urn. She cupped her hands around it and stood for a moment in silence.

Tom shot her mum an unnerved look. Her mum shook her head to warn him not to comment on it.

This ritual had been going on ever since her dad's ashes had been collected from the undertaker's. As soon as her mum had brought them into the house, Gina had taken the urn from her, marched into the living room and placed it prominently on the shelf. Her decision had gone unchallenged; her mum didn't want to upset her, so there they'd remained, the presence of this small vessel overwhelming the room. Now, every time Gina entered the room she'd make a beeline to touch the urn, even when she thought no one was around. Her mum was concerned, but decided to ignore Gina's behaviour, hoping that it might be comforting to her in some way.

"Are those presents for us?" Danny said. He pointed to a pile of packages on the sofa.

"Danny, don't be so rude," Mum laughed.

Tom wrestled Danny into a headlock and ruffled his hair. "Yeah, Danny, you won't be getting anything until I've heard you've been looking after your mum and sister while I've been away," he teased.

Danny laughed, wriggling out of the hold, grabbing Tom's wrist to give it a Chinese burn, but then he let Tom's hand drop in shock.

"What happened to your fingers?" Danny asked.

"Oh, these things," Tom replied blithely, wiggling the two stumpy fingers on his left hand. "They're a souvenir from my travels. It's not too bad. I only lost them down to the first knuckle. I wish I could tell you it happened doing something heroic, but I'm afraid it was just a jet-ski accident in Australia. I was lucky it was just the two. If I'd fallen any closer to the propeller it would have cut through my whole hand."

"Oh you poor thing," Gina's mum said, wincing. "You're safer staying at home."

"Well, that's where I'm going to be from now on," Tom announced.

"Not this home," Gina hissed under her breath.

"Great! Are you back for good?" Danny beamed.

"Yep! I've well and truly got my wanderlust out of my system. You won't believe it, but you can get bored of paradise. I started longing for grey skies and a decent cup of tea and, of course, the people I'd left behind."

Gina bristled as she noted how Tom's sky-blue eyes fell on her mum.

12 THE RUNNER

*S*he was trapped in the car, panicking and helpless as she kept trying to silence the white noise that hissed out from the radio; the rain hammered like fists at the windows; the phone beeped in her pocket, sending an electric shock surging through her body. She caught a glimpse of her dad, walking away from her. She banged furiously on the windows; she kicked at the door with her bare feet but was unable to get out and stop him. She watched him disappear into the darkness. Then the squeal of the train brakes came, so piercing that blood started to trickle from her ears.

"Dad!" Gina's scream shattered the silence of the house. She sat bolt upright in bed, her pyjamas clinging to her body with cold sweat.

Half asleep, Mum rushed to her bedside. Gina clung to her.

"Gina, it's okay. You were having a nightmare."

Gina buried her clammy face in her mum's nightdress. "It was horrible. It was me and Dad on that night."

"Shush now, don't think about it."

"Mum, can I stay off school today? It's Dad's birthday. I just want to be at home."

Her mum nodded. "Okay. I'll ask Danny if he wants to stay at home as well. Maybe we could do something nice together; go to the water park or bowling, like we used to do with Dad."

"As long as Tom doesn't come," she said. "He's been calling round every day since he got back. I don't want him here."

"All right, I'll ask him not to come over today but *please* be nice to your Uncle Tom. He's been a real support to us."

"He knows things," Gina whispered.

Her mum looked at her anxiously. "Listen, Gina, Dr. Havers has been phoning. She's really looking forward to seeing you again. She said that she'd fit you in anytime. Isn't that good of her? I'm convinced that you'll start feeling better once you get talking to her. So what do you say? Can I make you another appointment for tomorrow?"

"No! Leave me alone," Gina said, putting the duvet over her head.

She heard her mum sigh and walk out of the room.

Gina turned on the bedside light and looked over at the wall of photographs. "Mum thinks I'm mad, you know, Dad," she whispered. "Your wife, my mum, doesn't believe *me*! What's she planning next? Is she going to have me sectioned and locked up?" Gina looked at her alarm clock. It was three twenty a.m. "By the way, Dad – happy birthday," she said sweetly.

Their plans to go out for the day came to nothing. Gina and Danny decided that they didn't want to go anywhere; instead they spent the morning in bouts of silence as if they were inside a church. Gina wandered into the living room and saw Danny lifting the hood of his fish tank. She cupped her hands around the urn and watched her brother sprinkling the flakes of fish food onto the water.

"The tank's looking great. You've done really well with it, Danny," Gina said, crouching down to see the rush of fish swimming to the surface, their big mouths open, ready to devour the food.

"Yeah, can you believe that they're all still alive?" he said proudly.

"No," she smiled.

"And Gina's doing well," he said mischievously, pointing to the ugly suckerfish scavenging along the bottom of the tank.

"Yeah, Danny's looking great too," she replied, indicating the spiky ball of pufferfish that looked on the verge of popping.

Her skinny brother gave a short-lived laugh before

his face clouded over. "Dad would have loved this, wouldn't he?"

"Oh yeah. He would have loved it." She nodded vigorously, biting her lip.

Danny stared into the tank. "If you look at it long enough, it sends you into a trance. It like…hypnotizes you, and all the stuff going on in your brain just stops and you're somewhere else…but nowhere, if you get what I mean…just kind of peaceful and nice."

Gina wished she could find peace by looking at the tank, but she knew what Danny was talking about. There was something about the combination of elements in it that cast a spell over the observer. The soft light in the hood spread a warm glow over the exotic, watery kingdom; the shimmering fish, their colours a feast for the eyes, gliding elegantly through the swaying plants. The bright, razor-sharp corals sitting on the bed of muted blue stones conjured up images of a tropical reef and the soothing hum of the pump made eyes glaze over.

Danny kept his eyes fixed on the tank as he said quietly, "Sometimes I think it's my fault that Dad killed himself."

"What? Why would you say that, Danny?"

"I'm not stupid or anything; I know Dad didn't do it *because* of this, but I think that I probably made him even sadder when really he needed someone to cheer him up. On the day before he died he asked me to go to the allotment with him, to do some digging, but I was on the

Xbox in the middle of a game, so I said I wouldn't and I let him go on his own. If I'd just gone with him and helped him I might have made him happy and maybe it would have stopped this depression thing."

Gina turned Danny to face her. "Don't you *ever* think that. What happened was nothing to do with you. Dad wasn't depressed. He didn't kill himself!"

Danny looked at her sadly. "Mum says I'm not to listen when you say things like that. She says that you're not thinking straight."

"She's wrong."

"But, Gina, you've spent for ever talking to people and going everywhere. If you were right you would have found something by now."

Gina hesitated, her breathing suddenly heavy with anxiety. "But I haven't been everywhere. There's somewhere I should have gone back to straight away but I haven't been able to face it and the longer I've left it, the more scared I've been." She kissed her brother's soft curly hair. "But I promise I'll go there today. I won't let you and Dad down."

That afternoon Gina came down the stairs in her running gear. She hadn't worn it since the evening her dad had died. She hadn't been able to face running without him, but today, she was going to run *for* him.

She saw the look of surprise and delight on her mum's

face. "Going for a run?" Her mum smiled encouragingly.

"Yeah, thought I might."

"Got your new watch on, I see."

"Yeah."

Her mum was looking at her like she was a baby who'd just taken her first steps. "That's fantastic, love. Have a good time."

Gina limbered up on the pavement, circling her arms, arching her back, stretching her legs against the dwarf wall outside their house. She listened to her bones cracking. She noticed how her athlete's body looked weak and frail after eight months of neglect, and she wondered if running there was such a good idea after all.

She'd discovered her talent for running a few years earlier during a cross-country competition at school. Gina had only entered it because it meant missing double maths. However, she'd glided around the mud-spattered field, adrenalin surging through her. As she'd sailed past the other competitors she knew she was on her way to victory. At last she'd found something she could shine at.

When Gina had come home with the medal and coyly admitted that she "actually quite enjoyed running", her dad hadn't been able to contain his excitement. He'd told her that in the late 1970s, when his family had emigrated from Trinidad, he'd struggled to adjust to life in a grey Britain and running had become his lifeline. He used to love travelling to competitions with the school team in the minibus, having a laugh all the way. During his school days his bedroom shelves had been weighed down with trophies and medals for cross-country events. But then he'd started work at sixteen, married her mum at nineteen and become a father at twenty. There hadn't been much time for sport after that.

Straight away her dad had appointed himself Gina's coach, and borrowed money from their Trinidad holiday fund to buy them each a decent pair of running shoes. He'd revelled in recapturing his youth as he worked out their training programme and mapped out routes for their runs through the local parks and across the city.

Becky and the rest of Gina's friends didn't share her new-found passion. They warned her, half-jokingly, that no girl could look attractive running – it just gave you sweat patches and made everything wobble.

Gina had tried to explain it to them, speaking with the fervour of a Bible-Belt preacher. "But when you run, something brilliant happens," she'd said, her eyes shining. "You feel so alive! It's the challenge of pushing yourself on, especially when your legs feel like lead, your lungs are burning, and you want to collapse – you don't give up! You push through the pain to the other side until everything starts to flow and you're completely in the zone, just concentrating on your breathing until you're almost in a trance! It's fantastic!" she'd proclaimed, looking expectantly at her congregation.

But her friends had just shaken their heads in disbelief. "There's something wrong with you, Gina Wilson," Becky had laughed.

Now Gina looked down the street, took a deep breath and set off. Her neighbour, Bob, called out to her from his doorstep.

"All right, Gina, love? Nice to see you out and about."

She suddenly felt self-conscious and scoured the street to see if anyone else was looking at her; but the only other person in sight was a figure coming out of an alleyway further up the road and he seemed quite oblivious to the world, with his hood up and his head down.

Gina smiled awkwardly at Bob. "Thanks," she said.

She continued down the middle of her street towards the dock road, jumping the speed bumps with relish, luxuriating in the stretch of her legs, which felt like they'd just been unbound after eight long months. However, the feeling was short-lived, as the further she ran the more her body protested. As she panted her way down the dock road she wondered what her dad would say now about her poor posture, her flailing limbs and jarring knees.

By the time she'd reached the main entrance to the docks she found herself staggering to a halt. The biting wind was making her exposed neck prickle and her cheeks burn.

Dave walked out of his security hut and smiled

sympathetically when he saw her bent double, puffing and panting.

"If I was you, Gina, I'd just go home and put me feet up," he advised.

Gina shook her head. "I can't do that," she rasped. "I've got to keep going. There's somewhere I need to be."

She coughed. The thick diesel fumes from the docks were stuck in her throat. She stood up straight, preparing herself to start again, concentrating on taming her breathing. Then Gina set off once more, focusing on every step. Soon her arms were pumping and her spine was rodlike, adjusting her balance as she got into her stride. She felt the change – like a struggling car that had just shifted into the right gear – and her body began to flow. As she quickened her pace and her heartbeat rose, she realized how much she'd missed this feeling.

She ran past the imposing Victorian warehouses that lined the docks, so magnificent in their day, now left to crumble. She turned off the congested road, away from the roaring juggernauts and crossed over to the canal. The miles of pothole-ridden towpaths had provided Gina and her dad with one of their training routes. They would run along them, playing a game of "spot the shopping trolley" in its pea-soup water.

She looked over to the allotments. Gina's breathing faltered as she picked out her dad's patch, neglected and overgrown amongst the well-tended plots. She felt guilty that she hadn't been back to work on it; that her time and energy had been consumed by her enquiries. She knew that her dad understood; she had a job to do. She refocused on the towpath and pounded on purposefully.

13 THE DESTINATION

After a couple of miles Gina left the canal and slowed to a walk. She turned into the deserted cobbled street and shuddered, chilled to the bone. Over the last eight months she'd always known that she would have to return eventually, no matter how distressing, but the thought of coming back here had been too overwhelming – until today.

In the cold light of day, Gina was determined to absorb every last detail. She stood at the spot where her father had parked the car that night, surveying the row of boarded-up terraces and the peeling paint on the useless street lamps, before continuing along the cobbles, towards the bridge. Gina tried to brace herself for the feelings that this visit might stir up, but nothing could have prepared her for being here again, as her thoughts and senses took her straight back to that night.

With each step she took closer to the bridge, Gina felt the rising panic and confusion that she'd experienced as she'd run barefoot from the car, calling out in the darkness for her dad.

She found herself automatically retracing her steps. Gina ran across the old stone bridge, just as she had that night, when she'd hoped beyond hope that she'd find her father standing on the other side, the screeching train nothing to do with him. Now she could see how the cobbled street quickly petered out, she could see the trees and bushes flanking the bridge; she remembered how they'd scratched her flailing arms as she'd frantically thrashed at them, called into them, "Dad! Dad! Are you there?"

That night, peering into the darkness, she'd imagined the trees were denser, not the scrappy collection of neglected bushes and spindly saplings that greeted her now... And the smell of it? Gina closed her eyes and inhaled: the aroma of rotting leaves and blocked sewage pipes sailed up her nostrils. She snorted the air out; it smelled different. That night, despite the driving rain, some other smell had penetrated the air... What was it? Something nice, not putrid. But what? *Think, Gina!* She closed her eyes again, willing her brain to dredge up the smell. A strange mixture...flowers and spices, perhaps? Yes, even in the throes of panic, it had registered as a surprisingly pleasant odour. Could it have come from some scented plant amongst this unimpressive patch of greenery?

She started to walk amongst the bushes and trees; maybe she could find it, sniff it out? But with each step her feet sank into boggy earth that released only rotting fumes into the atmosphere and caked her trainers in mud. She shook her head in frustration and retreated. Why was she wasting her time looking for some flower? That wasn't what she came back for.

Gina walked onto the bridge again, running her hand along its bumpy sides. Stopping in the middle, she looked over the chest-high wall just as she'd done that night. The blood had drained from her face at the sight of the stationary train down on the track. Suddenly she could see herself – it was like having an out-of-body experience – rushing to the end of the bridge and scrambling down the muddy embankment, then sprinting along the sharp gravel on the side of the tracks, not even flinching as the stones punctured the soles of her feet. She watched herself, standing in front of the towering engine, the searing beam of the train's headlights illuminating the dancing rain as she shielded her eyes and looked up at the driver in his carriage, his petrified expression speaking louder than any words. That's when she'd known for sure; that's when she'd started to scream.

Now she was gripped by a sudden compulsion and before she could give herself time to change her mind, she'd heaved herself up onto the side of the bridge. She found herself on her knees, sideways on the narrow ledge.

Her hands gripped the edges of the rough stone. She didn't dare turn her head, so instead stared straight along the wall until she plucked up courage to move into a crouching position, balancing on the balls of her feet. Gina blinked as cold sweat from her forehead trickled into her eyes. She released her hands from the security of the wall, flattening her feet against the stone. Then, painstakingly, she inched her way up into a standing position before sliding her feet to face the train tracks. Once extended to her full height she chanced a look down, but the dizzying distance to the ground upset her balance and she wobbled like a wrong-footed gymnast on the high beam. She rocked back and forth, her arms flapping, but she held her nerve, steadying herself just as the sudden blast of a distant train horn drew her focus down the tracks.

Immediately her brain was telling her to climb down to safety but her eyes were transfixed by the sight and gathering sound of the great metal beast in the distance, veering from side to side as it hurtled along the track.

Standing there, with fear and adrenalin careering through her veins, the questions that she hadn't dared to ask herself were suddenly unleashed.

Is everyone else right? Did Dad stand up here like this? Could he really have left me in that car knowing he was coming here to kill himself? What the hell was going through his head?

The train was approaching at a tremendous speed, but Gina was still in the world of her own thoughts: *Is Tom telling the truth? Was Dad depressed – not thinking straight? But then why was he depressed? Was it an illness – one of those chemical imbalances in the brain – or did something else cause it? Did he have a terrible secret that he couldn't live with any more? A life we didn't know about? Would he have climbed up here, feeling terrified or calm, waiting to jump in front of seventy tons of speeding metal?*

Her glazed eyes came back into focus as one, two, three shrieking blasts of the train's horn confirmed that the alarmed driver had spotted her. It was only a minute or two away.

She panicked as if she'd just been shaken awake in the middle of sleepwalking. Guilt swamped her. How could she think such treacherous thoughts? *NO! Dad would not do this…! But how the hell am I going to prove it?*

The racket of the approaching train shook her insides, turning her legs to jelly.

Get down, you silly cow! she ordered herself. She bent her knees, bracing herself to jump backwards onto the ground when, suddenly, she heard a voice behind her, shouting above the noise of the engine.

"Excuse me. Can I help you?" It sounded like a nervous shop assistant.

Gina turned her head slowly and saw the young man edging towards her. The train was almost at the bridge.

"Where the hell did you come from? Get lost, will you? I'm fine!" Embarrassment made her sound harsh.

"You don't look it. Don't panic. I'm just going to come a bit closer."

"Stay away!"

He craned his neck and saw the train racing towards the bridge. The driver sounded the horn again.

"Come on, don't go ruining my day." He faked a smile, his heart in his mouth. "Look at you, you're gorgeous, imagine what you're going to look like if you jump in front of that train."

"Shut up. I'm not going to jump."

"Great," he said, unconvinced. "So what are you then? One of these weird adrenalin junkies? That's fine by me, really, whatever floats your boat, but just get down, will you, you're making me nervous." He held his hand out to her.

Gina ignored it.

"At least tell me your name so I can tell the police when they come and scrape you off the tracks."

She glowered at him out the corner of her eye, concentrating on keeping her balance. "It's Gina," she snapped.

"Well, lovely to meet you, Gina. I'm Declan."

"I know," she replied curtly. "Declan Doyle – you went to my school."

"What? I thought you looked familiar. You used to have long hair. Gina. Gina Wilson..." Declan paused. "Oh God...your dad...this bridge? THIS BRIDGE! Oh, *please,* Gina, come down."

"I was just about to," she shouted back to him.

"Come on then!"

Gina jumped backwards to the safety of the ground. She heard a final angry blast of the horn as the train rattled past them and off into the distance.

Despite her unsteady legs, Gina brushed away Declan's outstretched hand.

"I wasn't going to jump, I was getting down anyway. I just wanted to…wanted to…" Tears filled her pained eyes.

"I get it. I do," Declan said gently, a trace of an Irish lilt mingled with his local accent. "You just wanted to know how it felt up there. It's crazy, but I get it."

She frowned in surprise… *How could Declan Doyle, of all people, understand?*

She wouldn't have had him down as the sensitive type, although, to be fair, she only knew him by reputation. He'd been the boy in the year above her who'd used a lethal combination of good looks, charm and cheek to talk his way out of detentions and to brighten up the dullest lesson. She knew that he'd had a talent for football and for bunking off school. Predictably, he'd messed up his exams and had to leave. She hadn't heard of him since, though his legacy at school had included a trail of broken-hearted girls who'd fancied him from afar and scrawled graffiti on the walls of the toilets, declaring *Declan Doyle is fit!*

Yes, Gina knew who he was all right and she wanted to get away from him as fast as possible. She cringed inside.

He'd seen her, standing up there on the bridge. It was meant to be private, between her and her dad, but now she had a witness. What if Declan Doyle went around telling everyone; having a laugh with his mates about the pathetic, crazy girl?

She tried to stride off but shaky legs thwarted her exit as she stumbled past him.

Declan bent down and helped her up; her face was burning with embarrassment.

"Thanks," she mumbled, walking on.

"Where are you going?"

"Home," she replied coldly.

"You should stop, get something to drink. You're a bit shaky – mind you, who wouldn't be after standing up there?"

She glared at him. "I'm fine."

"Where do you live? I could get a bus back with you. Make sure you get home all right."

"No. I'd rather run," she said, quickening her pace into a jog.

But Declan was undeterred, setting off after her, following her across the roads and onto the canal towpath.

She looked behind and saw him struggling to keep pace with her, his jeans and thick hoodie too cumbersome for running. Gina picked up speed, widening the gap between them.

He called to her, "Oh, come on now, Gina, have mercy on me."

"Would you *stop* following me!" she shouted.

"I'm not following you. I just fancied a run myself. I love running! Can't get enough of it," he panted.

Despite herself, Gina couldn't help but be amused.

"I won't tell anyone," he called to her.

"About what?" she said, her shoulders rising with anxiety as she carried on moving away from him.

"About you…on the bridge."

She stopped and looked back. He was crouching down on the towpath, desperately trying to catch his breath.

Gina walked slowly back to him.

"You won't tell *anyone*?" she echoed.

"No, I promise," he wheezed.

Her shoulders relaxed and she stretched out a hand to pull him up. "You're best to stand and then bend forward at the waist, your hands on your knees, and take deep, slow breaths." She manoeuvred him into position.

"Thanks." He looked up, his olive cheeks flushed, his brown eyes gazing at her.

She swallowed hard. "How come you were down that street, anyway?"

"I'd just left a mate's on the next road. I spotted you from the end of the street. I nearly had a heart attack! Do you mind if we walk the rest of the way?"

"Okay," she said, mellowing.

They began to stroll.

"I believe this canal is in the top ten of romantic walks

in Britain," he said, looking at the festering waters.

Gina let out a throaty chuckle.

"You've got a dirty laugh." Declan grinned, raising his thick black eyebrows.

"Have I? I haven't heard it for a while."

"Well, yeah." He was suddenly solemn. "I suppose you haven't had much to laugh about. I'm really sorry…about your dad. It must be crap."

"He didn't kill himself, you know," she said matter-of-factly.

Declan squinted in confusion. He was sure he'd heard it was suicide.

"Didn't he? What happened then?"

"I…I don't know yet," she stumbled. "But now that I've stood up on that bridge, I'm even more sure he wouldn't have done it."

She saw pity flood Declan's face.

"Don't look at me like that," she snapped. Her steely eyes made Declan quickly change the subject.

"How's your mum doing?" he asked.

"She's okay. She copes. Mum, me and Danny – he's my little brother – we were all getting on with things in our own way, but this bloke's been hanging around for the last few weeks, upsetting everything," she said with disdain.

"Why? What's he doing?"

"He keeps 'popping in' every day. I wish he'd get lost. We don't need him. Mum certainly doesn't need him."

"Where's he come from?"

"Oh, he's not a stranger. I've known him all my life. His name's Tom. He was my dad's boss; a family friend. He owns a warehouse on the docks, he deals with shipments of cocoa beans."

"So why don't you like him?" he asked.

"I used to think he was okay. Whenever he came round he'd bring me and Danny presents. My dad would tell him to stop, but Tom did it anyway. But then when Dad died, Tom told everyone at the inquest that my dad had been depressed. He said that Dad had hidden it from us because he didn't want to worry us."

"I suppose people do that kind of thing," Declan said gently.

"My dad wasn't depressed."

"But why would his boss lie?" Declan said.

"I don't know, that question keeps going round and round my head." Gina tapped her head with her fist. "But there's other things that Tom has done that make me think he knows something about what happened to my dad."

"Like what?"

Gina suddenly shook her head. What was she doing? This boy had just seen her on top of a bridge and now she was telling him all this! He must think she was a total nutter.

"Nothing, it doesn't matter, it's just he's a liar and now he's round our house all the time, trying to play happy families with us. Well, we're not his family. He should get lost." She couldn't stop herself. Her voice was venomous. She noticed Declan looking at her uneasily. "Sorry...I wasn't always like this," she said, sadly. "Maybe we should talk about something else. What have you been up to since you left school?"

"Well, at the moment I'm lodging with an old lady on Hanover Street, Mrs. Mac. She's great apart from phoning my parents in Ireland to report whether I've been a good boy and checking under my bed in case I've smuggled in alcohol. I tell you, I'm living the dream!"

Gina laughed. "So why are you still here if your parents are in Ireland?"

"I wanted to stay – have a bit of independence – but I haven't been very successful up to now."

"You working?"

"I'm in between jobs at the moment."

"What was your last job, then?"

"A paper round in Year Eight," he grinned.

She rolled her eyes, smiling. "Well, what kind of thing do you fancy doing?"

"What is this, my job-seeker's interview?" he laughed.

"I'm just interested."

"I don't know." He shrugged. "But Mrs. Mac wants to set me up with a job in a funeral parlour."

Gina pulled a face. "That sounds nasty."

"I know! But if I don't find something else soon, she's going to drag me there." Now it was Declan's turn to change the subject. "So, how's the old school surviving without me?"

"Well, the teachers miss you at detention."

"God, I was so immature in those days." He tried to sound sincere.

"You only left a few months ago."

"So I did." Declan grinned. "And what about you? You've got your exams this year, haven't you?"

Gina shrugged. "Yeah, I might scrape by, if I'm lucky."

They walked side by side until they reached her house, their chat punctuated by frequent laughter.

She gestured to the green door. "This is me. I've made it home safely despite your prophecies of doom."

"I was only trying to help."

"I know," she said gratefully. "It was nice of you, thanks."

"Maybe I'll see you around?" he asked, looking hopeful.

"Not if I see you first," she replied, deadpan. She turned her back to him, a secret smile spreading across her face. She couldn't believe it. She'd been dreading returning to the bridge but if she hadn't gone there today, at that time, she wouldn't have met Declan Doyle and she wouldn't be feeling the first spark of happiness since her dad died.

This must be a good sign, Gina thought. *Maybe my luck is about to change.*

14 BEARING GIFTS

As she entered the hallway the smile was quickly wiped from Gina's face by the sight of Tom leaning against the staircase, laden down with parcels. Danny was buzzing around him.

"Hurry up, Gina," Danny ordered. "Tom wouldn't let us open our presents until you got back."

"How was your run?" Tom asked her, teasingly lifting the parcels higher, just out of Danny's reach. "I phoned earlier and your mum told me you'd gone out. That's just great, Gina – your mum's so relieved. She was worried you might never run again."

She saw her mum rush into the hallway from the kitchen and flash Tom a silencing look.

"Hiya, love. How did it go?" Mum asked, planting a warm kiss on Gina's cold cheek.

"Great," Gina said through gritted teeth. "What's *he* doing here?"

"He phoned up and I told him not to come round but he insisted. He's only being nice," her mum whispered apologetically.

Tom approached Gina, handing her a box with a flourish.

"When I heard you'd gone out running I just knew what I had to buy you," he said.

"Wow! Look how much they cost!" Danny pointed to the price on the side of the box.

"Open it up will you, Gina?"

Gina lifted the lid unenthusiastically but found she had to stifle her excitement at the sight of the beautifully crafted running shoes.

"They look brilliant," Danny cooed.

"I know," Tom said proudly. "I went to that specialist running shop in town. I spent ages in there. I never realized there was so much to this running lark. To tell you the truth they made me feel like having a go at it myself. It's about time I got outside instead of going to a sweaty gym getting nowhere on a treadmill."

God, he better not suggest coming out with me. Gina bristled.

"Do you like them, Gina?" Tom waited expectantly.

"If you don't mind, I'll stick with my own," she said, shutting the lid. "You can take them back, can't you? Get your money back."

"Oh, Gina," her mum said, embarrassed. "Don't be so ungrateful. It's such a thoughtful gift from your Uncle Tom."

"My dad bought me these running shoes. I don't want new ones," she said defiantly.

"But your dad would be pleased you've got a great new pair," her mum said, exasperatedly.

"I don't need a new pair. These ones are fine."

They all looked down at her feet and her scruffy, mud-caked trainers, fraying at the seams.

"Well maybe I'll have more luck with your gift." Tom gave a hopeful smile as he handed Danny the square box. "Gently does it," he warned, as Danny threw off the lid.

He reached in and lifted out a water-filled plastic bag. He gazed at the three sleek black-and-white striped fish, their gossamer fins rippling gently.

"Wow, they're so cool!" said Danny, trying hard to hide his disappointment.

"What's up? Don't you like them?" Tom looked crestfallen.

"No, I love them. They're brilliant…but they're tigerfish. I've got photos of them in my aquarium books. Thing is, Uncle Tom…" He hesitated. "I don't think they can go in my tank. It's a community tank."

"What does that mean?" Tom asked.

"Well, it means that all the types of fish you put in it have to get on – you know, not go fighting each other –

and tigerfish are aggressive. They might attack the others."

Tom laughed. "Well, what if these fellas promise to play nicely and not bully the other fish?"

Danny looked unsure.

"Danny, I can't have *two* rejected presents. Come on," Tom cajoled. "They'll look amazing. Put them in the tank, see how they get on, first sign of bad behaviour and you can fish them out, if you'll excuse the pun."

"Okay then." Danny nodded shyly, not wanting to upset Tom. "But you can't just empty them in, you're meant to leave them in the tank in their plastic bag until they get used to the temperature."

"Aren't you the expert," Tom called after Danny as he watched him carrying the plastic bag carefully into the living room.

"And for you…" Tom turned to Clare, who stood sporting a dusting of white flour in her brown hair and a grease stain down her top. "I've bought these." He held out a shoebox together with a flashy-looking carrier bag. "They're the right size. I did a bit of detective work, rifling through the shoe rack when you weren't looking, and as for your dress size…well I just went to that posh frock shop on Hilton Road and mapped out your curves for the salesgirls." He grinned, making an hourglass shape with his hands. "And they knew your size immediately."

"Oh my God! I think I'm going to throw up," Gina muttered.

Her mum blushed as she pulled a sequined dress out of the bag. "It's gorgeous, Tom."

"Wait till you see the shoes," he said, his eyes dancing.

She opened the box to reveal a pair of killer heels.

"How's she meant to walk in them?" Gina protested.

"Oh Tom! The dress. The shoes. The gifts for the kids… They must have cost a packet. You can't go spending your money on us like this."

"But I want to. Who else have I got to spoil? Now go and get that dress on because I've booked us all a table at that new Michelin-star restaurant that was in the paper!"

Gina turned on him angrily. "Don't you know what day it is?"

Tom's effervescence quickly faded. "Of course I do. It would have been your dad's birthday."

"Well, don't you think it's a strange night to go out celebrating?" she hissed.

"Gina's right, Tom. I don't think we should be going out tonight," her mum said.

Tom looked offended. "Clare, do you really think I want to celebrate? That isn't what I'm suggesting. I miss Martin too, you know."

"Of course you do," her mum said remorsefully.

"Listen to me, today of all days we all need cheering up. This is the perfect evening to go out. The three of you have been through so much this year. You deserve to start enjoying yourselves again. To start looking to the future. Isn't that what Martin would want? He wouldn't want you all moping around on his birthday."

Mum looked like she was wavering.

"Danny," Tom called, "you'd like to go out to a fantastic restaurant this evening, wouldn't you? You might even see some footballers in there."

"Really? Okay, but only if it does chips and I don't have to dress up," he replied.

"It may not call them chips but I guarantee they'll be on the menu," Tom laughed.

"All right," he said.

"See, Danny's up for it. Come on, Clare." He looked at her pleadingly.

"Well, maybe you're right about what Martin would have wanted and it would be lovely to get dressed up for once." Her mum was getting excited. "But I'll only go if Gina will come too."

"Well, I won't!" Gina said, crossing her arms.

"Please, Gina, it's so long since we've had a family outing," her mum said.

"But *he's* not part of our family," she retorted.

"Oh, shut up, Gina. You're spoiling everything," Danny pouted. "Just come, will you? I might get some autographs."

"No, you lot go. I'm staying here."

Tom took off his beautifully tailored jacket and hung it over the end of the banister.

"What are you doing?" her mum asked.

"I'll cancel the table." He smiled magnanimously. "I don't want Gina upset over something that was meant to be a treat. So I suggest we stay in and I'll get us a takeaway. What's it to be?"

"Chinese," Danny said immediately. "Barbecue ribs and chips, please."

"Double chips," Tom laughed, ruffling Danny's hair.

Gina was flummoxed.

"This is so kind of you, Tom," her mum gushed. "I'm sorry that we've messed up your lovely plan. Why don't you go and sit down? There's some lager in the fridge. Do you fancy one?"

"Yeah, that sounds great," Tom said, walking into the living room and making himself comfortable in her dad's armchair.

15   THE JOB SEEKER

"**Y**eah?" Danny said, as he opened the door to the tracksuit-clad figure.

"Hi, is Gina in?"

"I think she's still in bed."

"Oh." The young man sounded disappointed. "No worries, I'll come back another time. Just tell her Declan called, would you?"

"Okay."

Clare heard the front door shutting and appeared from the living room in a dressing gown, looking decidedly fragile. She certainly hadn't intended to drink so much the previous night. Gina had insisted on going upstairs straight after the takeaway and Danny had, reluctantly, followed soon after. However, Tom had stayed until well after midnight, chatting to Clare and refilling her wine glass.

"Who was that, Danny?" Clare asked.

"Just some boy for Gina." He shrugged.

"Really?" She scurried to open the door and called after the young man. "Hang on, love. Can I help you?"

Declan turned round sheepishly. "Hi, I'm Declan. I didn't want to disturb Gina. I just called on the off-chance."

"Are you a friend of Gina's?" She eyed up the handsome boy curiously.

"Well…yeah, kind of…we went to the same school."

"Well, come in," Clare said enthusiastically, only too aware that Gina's friends had stopped calling round a long time ago. "I'll tell Gina you're here."

Declan stepped into the hallway.

Clare disappeared up the stairs. There was a shriek from Gina's bedroom and the creaking of floorboards above signalled a flurry of activity. Her mum leaned over the banister.

"She won't be a minute," she called down.

"There's no hurry. I just wondered whether she wanted to come for a run," Declan said.

The next moment a disembodied voice rang out.

"A run?" it repeated.

"Yeah. I told you I love running. Do you fancy it? I've got all the right gear on this time."

Gina flashed her rudely-awakened face over the banister.

"You really *are* serious," she called.

"Yeah. Do you want to come?"

"She'd love to," her mum chirped. "Danny, you look after Declan. Gina won't be a minute."

Danny looked up at the boy and wondered how he was supposed to "look after" him.

"Do you want a drink?" Danny tried.

"No thanks."

"Do you want to sit down?"

"Okay."

Danny led the guest into the living room.

Declan's eyes were immediately drawn to the moving technicolour display in the corner of the room. "Hey, cool tank!"

Danny beamed proudly. "Do you like it? It's mine. I set it up…well, Gina helped, but I got to choose the fish and I look after it."

Declan watched in amusement as a gang of bright minnows bounced around in the stream of bubbles being blown out by the pump.

"Which fish is your favourite?" Declan asked.

"The clownfish. They look brilliant," he said pointing out a little one with orange and white stripes.

"I like the angelfish best," Declan said, as he watched one fan its delicate black and white fins. "And what about this one? He's a funny-looking fella."

"Yeah," Danny replied, "he's a catfish. He spends all day trawling along the bottom of the tank sucking up all the rubbish. I call him Gina," Danny smirked.

144

Declan smiled. *Little brothers – always so kind to their sisters.* "Hey, look at those black ones chasing the guppies. It's like they're hunting them," Declan said, his eyes following the frantic chase around the tank.

"I know." Danny sounded worried. "They're tigerfish. I'm hoping that they'll calm down and stop worrying the other fish. I only got them yesterday. They were a gift. I don't want to offend my uncle by taking them out just yet."

"What you up to today?" Declan asked.

"Playing footy later."

"Oh yeah, do you play for a team?"

"Yeah, the Panthers. We're in the under-elevens Tudor league."

"Really! I used to play in that league. Where are you in the table?"

"Bottom," Danny mumbled. "We're rubbish. We're the reject team, made up of all the players no other team wanted."

"Well, at least the only way is up." Declan smiled encouragingly. "How are you on Fifa?" he asked, spotting the Xbox next to the TV.

"Do you want a game?" Danny ran to get the controls. "I may be useless on the pitch but on this thing – just call me Ronaldo."

"We'll see," Declan grinned, taking a control.

* * *

Gina looked at herself in her dressing-table mirror and groaned. "I look terrible."

"You just look a bit tired. I don't know why, because you went to bed so early last night. You should have stayed up longer with me and Uncle Tom," her mum said.

"No way! What's he playing at, trying to take us all out on Dad's birthday; buying you that dress and those ridiculous shoes?"

"Tom's always been generous. He's just looking out for us, now that Dad isn't here. It's lovely of him. You need to stop this terrible attitude you've got towards him," her mum ordered. "Anyway, you're a sly one, not telling me about this Declan."

"That's because there's nothing *to* tell. I met him when I was out running yesterday."

"And he's on our doorstep this morning? He must be keen," her mum teased.

"Nooo! He just likes running," Gina said, hoping that wasn't true.

"Well, hurry up. Don't keep the poor boy waiting."

Her mum left the room and Gina scrutinized her sleepy face. She opened the bottom drawer of her dressing table and pulled out a bag of make-up. The contents had once been well-used but, for the last eight months, bothering to put make-up on was the last thing on her mind. However, with Declan Doyle sitting downstairs, she suddenly felt the urge to delve into her bag once again.

Danny was three–one up when Gina appeared in the living room in her tracksuit, old trainers and a face that made him cry out, "Why have you got make-up on?"

"Shut up, will you?" Gina said, cringing in front of Declan.

"You're only going running, aren't you? You don't wear make-up for running, do you, Declan?"

"Not personally," Declan said, grinning. "But I think your sister looks good whether she's got it on or not."

Gina could feel her cheeks heating up.

"Uhh, I don't want to know," Danny said, pulling a disapproving face as Declan tried to hold in his laughter.

Gina stuck her tongue out at Danny as she walked over to the display shelf and momentarily cupped her hands around the urn. Declan looked puzzled but Danny ignored her as he concentrated on the game.

"Are you ready to go?" Gina said, heading for the door.

"No!" Danny protested. "Don't make him go yet. The game's only got five minutes and I've just got a corner."

"Fine!" Gina smiled. "I'll wait." She plonked herself down on the sofa. It was obvious that Danny had taken to Declan and for some reason this made her happy.

"Mrs. Mac was on at me again last night about taking that job at the funeral parlour," Declan said, taking a free kick. "I feel *really* cheeky asking you, Gina, especially after what you were saying, but do you know if that Tom has any jobs going at his warehouse?"

Gina couldn't stop her face from falling. *So that's why he's here. He's after a job.*

"God, I hope you don't think that I'm using you, Gina," Declan said, reading her expression. "I really did come round because I wanted to see you, but I just thought there was no harm asking. I'm desperate not to end up working with dead bodies all day. I just need something to get Mrs. Mac off my back."

Gina could tell he meant it. "Okay, I'll ask him. He'll give you a job."

"Really?" Declan said, surprised.

"Yeah," Danny piped up. "Uncle Tom would do anything for Gina because she's being really mean to him and he wants to make her like him."

"Be quiet, Danny!" Gina said.

"It's true! You should start being nice to Uncle Tom, it's not fair on him."

"Look, I don't want to cause a fight between you two," Declan said.

"It's fine. I'll ask him," she said curtly.

"Thanks, Gina, I really appreciate it," Declan said, bathing her in his radiant smile.

"Yeah, whatever." She tried to sound annoyed but couldn't suppress a little smile.

"Now, what about this run?" he said. "There's a burger place about half a mile away. How about we run there?"

16 THE MEETING

Declan approached the table in the dingiest corner of the stale-smelling pub.

"Nice choice of venue," he said, peeling his feet off the sticky carpet.

"Sorry, lad. The Ritz was fully booked," the man scoffed. "Anyway, you're half an hour late. I don't like being kept waiting."

"You try catching two buses out to the back of beyond at this time of night."

The man leaned forward, the yellow light illuminating his weather-beaten face. Declan couldn't tell whether his eyes were open or closed as they were concealed between unruly eyebrows and bags the size of water wings. "This is for your benefit. Do you want people to see us together?"

"Suppose not," Declan mumbled, sweeping his eyes

around the scruffy room in a sudden fit of paranoia. "Do I get a drink?"

"Thanks for offering. Mine's a pint." His battered leather jacket creaked as he held out his empty glass.

Declan huffed and walked to the bar, waiting for the barmaid to finish her game on the fruit machine. He returned to the table with two foaming beers.

"You're still only seventeen. I shouldn't let you drink that," the man mocked.

"You're driving, aren't you? I shouldn't let *you* drink *that*!" Declan retorted.

The man raised his bushy eyebrows, revealing small, bloodshot eyes. He chuckled darkly. "Worried about me, are you, Declan?"

"No, I'm worried about the people you might crash into."

He ignored the boy and took a gulp of beer, the foam forming a white moustache on his stubbly top lip. "So, you've got a job in the warehouse already. How did you wangle that?"

Declan shrugged.

"Was it advertised or did you just go in and show them your incredible CV?" he sneered.

Declan glared at him. "Gina Wilson put in a word for me, I had a quick interview with Mr. Cotter and I started the next day. He didn't even bother asking for references."

"Why not?"

"Because Gina recommended me and he'll do anything to try to keep in with her. She can't stand him. Her dad died a while back. The inquest said it was suicide but Gina won't believe it. She's got it into her head that Cotter knows something about his death."

"Okay," the man nodded slowly, "I'll ask around. You must have made quite an impression on the girl if she's willing to get you a job."

Declan seemed flustered. "Well, not really. She's just nice...*really* nice."

The man let out an exasperated sigh. "Oh, for God's sake, soft lad. This isn't a dating agency. You're not going all Romeo over her, are you?"

Declan stared into his beer. "What d'you think I am, stupid?"

"Do you really want me to answer that?" The man laughed. "Anyway, what do you make of Cotter?"

"I don't know. I've only been working there a week. He seems fine to me. Introduced me to everyone, made sure the other men showed me the ropes, went through all the health and safety stuff. He's training me on the forklift trucks next week," Declan said, trying to hide his enthusiastic smile.

"I'm happy for you," came the deadpan reply.

Declan ignored his sarcasm. "To be honest, I haven't seen much of Mr. Cotter. He doesn't get his hands dirty, which is fair enough – he's the boss. He's in and out. All the lads seem to like him and Kylie in the office seems happy working for him."

"And what about the warehouse: anything there that's struck you as unusual?"

"Everything seems fine. I know you think it's a job you could train a monkey to do, but really there's a lot of skill involved. Watching as those massive containers are hoisted off the ships and transferred to the lorries is pretty awesome. And when they roll up to the warehouse, well, that's when the work really starts. Did you know we have to manhandle every single one of those sacks onto the pallet boards? It's knackering! And then stacking them onto the shelves! If we don't get it *just* right, they'd come crashing down and kill someone. It's actually quite a dangerous job." Declan nodded gravely.

The man rolled his eyes. "Dangerous, my arse. Listen, lad, I've done things that would cripple you with fear. Walk in my shoes for a day, then you'd know what dangerous is."

"No thanks. I bet your shoes stink," Declan retorted.

The man ferreted out an A5 envelope from a plastic bag and handed it to Declan.

Declan looked at him, unsure what to do.

"Well, open it. It's for you to keep hold of. Have a good look."

Declan pulled out a photograph of a tall, bulky, middle-aged black man with a shiny bald head. He was standing on a pavement outside what could have been a hotel or an office block. Declan noted his pinstriped suit and the clashing accessories: a thick gold chain hung across his double-breasted jacket, several chunky rings adorned his sausage fingers and he had a stud in one ear.

"Have you seen this man?"

"No, but he looks like a fella you wouldn't want to mess with. Who is he?" Declan asked.

"You don't need names. He's from the Ivory Coast and he's a person of great interest to me. You just need to keep your eyes open and your ears to the ground and if you come across him, get in touch."

"What's he got to do with Tom Cotter "

"That's one of the things I'm paying you to find out," he said, taking another, thicker brown envelope from the inside pocket of his leather jacket. "This should cover your bus fare home." He slung it at Declan, who opened it and peered inside. The contents made his mouth suddenly dry with guilt and pleasure.

"Put it away," the man ordered. "And don't go flashing it around, or people will start asking questions. You keep your head down and don't draw attention to yourself. And I'm warning you, if you mess me around – try to take the money and just sit back and do nothing – then you haven't quite grasped how easily I could ruin your life."

Declan stuffed the envelope in his back pocket, scowling at his drinking partner.

"Hey, don't look like that." The man stood up to leave and slapped Declan on the back, sending him jerking forward. "You're my number one boy. I'm relying on you. Just remember to keep your mind on the job and don't get distracted by girls. Keep Gina Wilson sweet, keep *all* of them sweet; you need people to trust you, but my advice to you is, trust no one!"

"Especially not you," Declan muttered into his glass.

17 EATEN ALIVE

Danny, Gina and their mum were crouched in front of the fish tank, surveying the carnage. Half-eaten carcasses floated on the surface of the water. Danny was trying to identify the dead.

"They got all the guppies," he said, chewing his lip. "Can't see the pufferfish. And my clownfish, oh no!" His lip started to quiver as he saw the orange-and-white body floating among the debris. "He wouldn't have stood a chance."

Danny scowled at the sleek offenders, who were now imprisoned in a water-filled plastic bag in a corner of the tank. "I should have taken them out earlier. I thought they were going to settle in."

Gina and her mum exchanged anxious looks.

Gina put her arm around Danny's shoulders. "Don't worry about it. We'll sort it out. You've still got plenty of others left. Look, on the stones right in front of you – Gina's survived." She pointed to the catfish with its mouth clamped around one of the blue stones. "And look in the corner, by the air pump – there are three minnows."

"They always hang out in the bubbles. It's like their personal Jacuzzi." Danny gave a feeble smile.

"And the angelfish, look here." She pointed to the fish emerging from the cannon hole of the pirate ship. "She doesn't look too bad."

"They've taken a chunk out of her dorsal fin." Danny winced.

"Yeah, but she's still swimming okay, isn't she?" Gina replied like a spin doctor.

A *rat-a-tat-tat* made them all jump.

They turned to see Tom's cheerful face at the bay window.

"Don't let Tom in here. Don't mention it to him. No need to upset him," her mum said.

"No need to upset him?" Gina echoed. "This is his fault! He needs to see what he's done."

"For God's sake, Gina, it's not a crime scene," her mum replied.

Mum scurried to open the door. Gina could hear her whispering to Tom in the hallway.

She watched him as he walked solemnly into the room, like he was entering a wake. He crouched down next to Danny and ruffled the boy's hair.

"Who'd have known that they'd do this?" Tom said, shaking his head.

Gina flashed him an incredulous look. "Danny tried to tell you, but you made him put those stupid fish in anyway."

"Sorry, Danny," Tom said. "I just thought they'd look good in the tank."

"Don't take any notice of her." Danny cringed. "You didn't force me to put them in, Uncle Tom, it's okay. But what should I do with the tigerfish now?

"No problem. I'll take them back to the shop, donate them. Explain my mistake," Tom said, taking his wallet from his jacket. "Take this and when you get a chance, why don't you go to the shop and restock the tank. I promise not to interfere. I've learned my lesson."

Danny looked at the twenty-pound notes and then over to his mother to see what he should do.

"Well, that's very kind of you, Tom, but that's far too much money," Clare said.

"No. Please take it," Tom replied.

"You can't buy your way out of everything, you know," Gina snapped at him.

"Gina, don't be so rude," her mum scolded.

"Yeah, Gina, leave Uncle Tom alone!" Danny said.

"I'm only trying to help. Like I did when I gave your mate Declan a job," he said pointedly.

Gina fell silent.

"Cup of tea, Tom?" her mum said, trying to diffuse the tension.

Tom followed Clare into the kitchen. The radio was playing softly in the background and the smell of freshly-washed clothes on the radiator mingled with the scent of the shepherd's pie cooking in the oven.

"You'll have to excuse Gina. It's not been a good day; she's upset for Danny and then we've had this come from the council."

She handed Tom a letter.

"It's upset us all, but especially Gina. You know how she is about her dad."

Tom read the correspondence.

Dear Mrs. Wilson,
We are writing to bring to your attention the fact that Plot 64 on the Canalside Allotments has not been tended for many months and has fallen into an unacceptable state. We are aware of the sad passing of your husband and so have delayed taking any action regarding the plot until now. However, as you will appreciate, the council has a lengthy waiting list for these allotments and we are therefore at a stage where we require a renewed commitment from you to retain this plot. We look forward to your reply within two weeks. If we do not hear from you within this time period we will automatically assume that you are

terminating your tenancy and will reallocate the plot.

Yours sincerely,

Mr. Michael Blake (Parks and Gardens)

"They shouldn't be allowed to do this," Tom said angrily.

"Of course they should. I can see the council's point. But it doesn't make it any easier. I haven't been able to face going to the allotment since Martin died and Gina's only been back once. It must look a right mess. It needs someone to work on it and I haven't got the time. But then, of course, Gina's up in arms. Says there's no way we should give it up. I know she sees it as losing another part of her dad."

"Well, why don't you let her look after it?"

"She's saying she will, but I can't let her. She's meant to be studying and it's far too much work for her."

"Well then, it sounds like you've got no choice. You'll have to give it up. Don't worry about Gina; she'll get over it," he said harshly.

Clare's face fell. "I know you're right, but Martin loved that plot. He was convinced we could be self-sufficient, never have to buy fruit and veg again." Clare gave a hollow laugh. "He was fighting a losing battle of course, the soil is terrible. We never got anything out of it."

"Why did he keep at it then?"

"You know Martin, he wasn't a quitter, and to be honest he liked to have his own space sometimes; a place to think about things." She handed Tom a mug of tea. "You know he went there the day he died, don't you?"

Tom's eyes widened. "No! Are you sure?"

"Yes, Gina found out. Martin was there that afternoon, digging. Sometimes I picture him standing in his allotment, looking out over the docks with all his terrible thoughts; contemplating killing himself."

Tom listened, intently.

"And what I do is" – Clare's voice started to crack – "I rewrite that day in my mind. I'm not sitting at the stupid checkout, making small talk with the customers. No, I imagine that I know instinctively that he's in trouble and I march out of work, still in my uniform, and I go straight to the allotment and find him there and I go up to him and hug him so tightly and whisper in his ear that whatever it is that's wrong, however bad he's feeling, I can make it better. And then he kisses me and says to me, 'Thank God you found me, Clare.' And I take him home and keep him safe until all those terrible thoughts have passed."

Clare's shoulders started to shake, the sobs building up in her chest. Tom pulled her to him and wrapped his arms around her. He kissed the top of her head, stroked her dark hair, holding her tight as she buried her head in his chest. Tom tilted her chin up. The anguish on Clare's tear-stained face mirrored his own.

"Don't worry, Clare," he whispered. "I'm going to look after you. All of you." He bent his head down, cupped Clare's soft, round face between his hands and kissed her on the mouth; a kiss full of such intensity that it shocked and thrilled her in equal measure.

The sound of footsteps approaching sent Clare into a panic. She tussled out of Tom's embrace.

"Don't say anything," she said to Tom, opening the oven door and practically sticking her head in it.

"Are you okay?" Gina eyed her mother, noting how flustered and flushed she seemed.

"Yes," Clare said blithely. "Just getting the pie out of the oven."

"Won't you need the oven gloves for that?" Gina said suspiciously.

"Oops, silly me," Clare said.

Gina turned her gaze to Tom. His blue eyes were shining. He looked slightly ruffled – not his usual immaculate self.

"What's going on?" Gina asked.

"I'll tell you what's going on," Tom announced. Clare looked at him in alarm. "Your mother's told me about the council and the allotment and I'd like to help. I know how much that allotment meant to Marty so, if you'll let me, Gina, I'm going to maintain it so that the council can't take it off you."

"Really!" said Gina and her mum in unison.

"I didn't know that you were into that kind of thing. Don't you have a gardener to do your *own* garden?" Gina asked.

"Yeah, but this would be different. I'd like to do it… in memory of your dad."

"But me and Danny would want to help," Gina said.

"Of course! You don't think I'm going to do it all on my own, do you? Just give me a bit of time to do all the back-breaking stuff and then you and Danny can do the planting and get all the glory." He broke into a dazzling smile and Gina, for once, found herself returning it.

"Danny," she called out. Her brother ran into the kitchen.

"Danny, Tom's going to help us with Dad's allotment so the council won't be able to take it off us."

Danny's face lit up. "Brilliant. Hey, Uncle Tom can we play cards in the shed, like I used to do with Dad?"

"Sure." Tom shrugged.

"And can we raise the stake? Cos Dad only let us play for pennies."

"Pennies? It'll have to be twenty pence a game, or I'm not playing," Tom teased.

Tom's ears pricked up as a familiar song filtered through from the radio.

"Hey, Danny, turn up the radio, will you?"

Danny kept his finger on the volume button until the song blasted out.

"It's old people's music," Danny protested.

"It is not!" his mum said defensively. "It's Abba! Everyone loves Abba."

"Come on, Clare." Tom circled an arm around her waist. "Let's show these boring youngsters how it's done."

He barrelled her out of the kitchen and into the hallway and started to serenade her.

"I'm diggin' *my* dancing queen!" He winked.

Danny put his hands over his ears. "Embarrassing! Embarrassing!" he chanted, secretly revelling in the fun.

Gina and Danny followed them into the living room as Tom swirled their mother around, the floorboards creaking beneath them. Clare shrieked as he bent her backwards so her hair swept the floor and then pulled her up sharply, nose to nose, his eyebrows raised in mock seduction.

Clare's eyes shut as the room spun around her, her mouth plastered with a smile, breathless and giddy. Gina watched her mother's glowing face and, despite herself, she couldn't help feeling happy for her, even if it was Uncle Tom she was dancing with. But none of them noticed the marble urn, jumping closer to the edge of the shelf with each footstep that thumped in front of it. The next circuit of the room sent the urn leaping off the shelf and crashing to the floor. The lid flew off it and the grey, gritty contents spewed out. Some landed on the cracks between the floorboards and instantly seeped down them, disappearing for ever.

Gina scrabbled on the floor, trying to brush the ashes away from the cracks. "No, no, don't, please don't," she jabbered to them. Gathering up what remained, she returned the ashes to the cracked urn as if they were gold dust.

Her mum, Danny and Tom stood still, their mouths open in horror like they were playing some terrifying version of musical statues.

Gina turned her distraught face to Tom. "That was all I had left of my dad," she whimpered.

Tom shook himself out of his paralysis, replying nervously, "It'll be okay. I'll make everything all right again, you'll see."

18 THE PASSENGERS

Tom found a tube of glue in Martin's old toolbox and, with trembling hands, set about meticulously mending the cracked urn.

Danny watched, saying sympathetically, "It's okay, Uncle Tom. It wasn't your fault. It was an accident."

"There," Tom said, replacing the restored vessel on the shelf. "I've done my best."

"Are you staying for tea?"

"No, I don't really feel like eating. Anyway, I'd better go, Danny. I've caused enough upset for one day."

"Well, don't go without the fish." Danny pulled the clear plastic bag out of the tank and handed the three tigerfish to Tom. "Make sure the water is kept warm enough."

"Yeah, sure." Tom wagged a finger at the fish. "I promise that I'll take these naughty boys back to the shop in the morning. Night, Danny." He patted the boy's shoulder in a manly way. "I suppose you're too old for kisses now."

Danny suddenly jumped up at Tom and gave him a peck on the cheek. "Are you coming round tomorrow?"

"Yeah, if you want me to."

"I want you to," came the reply, as Danny ran upstairs.

"Night, Gina," Tom shouted hopefully in the direction of Gina's bedroom, but there was no response.

He walked to the front door with Clare. "I'm so sorry about the urn, Clare."

She searched his troubled face. "Don't be silly. I was dancing too. Anyway, there's no harm done."

He couldn't look at her. "And I'm sorry about kissing you. I shouldn't have. I got carried away. I was out of order."

"No, not out of order just...well...things are so confusing, everything still feels so raw and I've got to think of the kids, of Gina! But please don't feel bad." She smiled and squeezed his hand. "Everything is better with you around, Tom."

Tom got into his car, giving Clare a last wave as she lingered at the door. He shuddered as he started the engine and he sank into the heated leather seat. He couldn't get the ridiculous thought out of his head.

Martin's urn falling like that, just when I was dancing with Clare...just after I'd kissed his wife! He put the car into gear and pulled out. *Don't be so bloody stupid,* he chastised himself. *Get a grip, man!*

* * *

Forty-five minutes later Tom's car had left the heaving city behind and was gliding along the dual carriageway, where smart suburbs eventually gave way to countryside. He reached the scenic surroundings of his own home. Here the air smelled of pine from the woods and tasted of salt from the sea that lapped up on the beach nearby. He turned down the bumpy unadopted road. In Tom's neighbourhood potholes in the road symbolized how exclusive it was, not how rundown.

Tom pressed a zapper and sent the electric gates sweeping open and a bank of security lights blazing. He cruised up the driveway, coming to a halt outside the imposing house, whose facade had been cleverly designed to look like a country house hotel even though it was less than ten years old. He picked up his cashmere overcoat, briefcase and the plastic bag from the passenger seat where the fish had enjoyed a smooth ride.

He stared at the fish and groaned. His hands full, Tom used an elbow to nudge the car door shut but then, instead of walking towards the glow of the lantern above his porch, he strode to the left of the house until he reached a grey wheelie bin placed discreetly amongst the conifer trees. Tom put his briefcase down, draping his coat neatly over it, before lifting the lid of the bin and dropping the plastic bag inside. With a flick of his wrist, the lid slammed shut, leaving the fish to their fate.

19 THE ATTENTIVE FRIEND

Every evening Gina had butterflies in her stomach as she waited to see if Declan Doyle would turn up. Every evening she convinced herself that he wouldn't, that he'd found something better to do than go running with her. After all, why would he want to spend time with *her* when he could probably pick any girl he wanted? But then, every evening, the bell would ring and she'd rocket down the stairs, pausing to compose herself before opening the door and greeting the smiling boy with a casual "Hi".

She'd steal glances at him while they paced around the park and along the canals. He always looked like he was enjoying himself and, as they ran, he kept her entertained with stories that made her laugh, especially the ones about his landlady, Mrs. Mac, and her flirty friend Bridie.

"I'm not joking," he told Gina in pretend shock. "Bridie

asked me to pick up her stick and when I bent down, she patted my bum!"

Gina couldn't believe how thoughtful Declan was. He always wanted to know how things were at home and what was going on with Tom. He listened to her complaints about Tom's daily visits and he didn't tell her that she was being paranoid when she said that every time she turned round it felt like Tom was there.

He was so easy to talk to that when she found herself explaining how it had felt to see her dad's ashes disappear through the floorboards, Declan seemed to completely understand. Then, when she told him about the tigerfish eating half of Danny's tank, he volunteered to take Danny to the aquarium. Gina wondered whether he really meant it but, just as he had promised, he turned up the following Saturday and went with them to Neptune's. She stood back and watched the delight on Danny's face as he led Declan from one tank to the next, debating which fish to buy and which coral looked the coolest. Danny begged Declan to come back to the house to help him settle the new fish and by the time they were finished, evening was drawing in.

"You've wasted your day helping us," Gina said, apologetically.

"It's not wasted. I spent it with you," Declan said, causing her cheeks to burn.

* * *

One evening Gina and Declan were just finishing a run along the canal when the rain started to pour down. They dived into a greasy-spoon cafe on the dock road and sat, side by side, in the steamy window, eating bacon cobs and sipping strong tea. Gina looked at him nervously before reaching into her little rucksack and pulling out the tatty notebook.

She'd spent days plucking up the courage to show it to him. She was scared that he'd think she was crazy but, despite this, she wanted to share it with him. She felt that he, of all people, might understand.

"What's that, then?" he asked.

Gina explained about the evidence she'd been gathering about her father's last day, tentatively asking, "Do you want to see it?"

"Of course I do." He nodded supportively. "Why don't you talk me through it?"

He leaned towards her, his shoulder touching hers. She tried to stay focused as she went through the pages. She could see him trying to mask his surprise at the amount of detail she'd scribbled down, but he listened patiently as she deciphered the words for him and explained the timelines. He didn't interrupt as her jumbled thoughts tumbled out. He didn't once look at her like she was crazy, but she noticed his eyes widen when she described the man she'd seen outside her house on the day of the funeral.

"What's the matter?" she asked him.

"Nothing," he answered emphatically.

When she'd read out all her notes, she looked at him expectantly. "So, what do you think?"

"I don't know. I *really* don't know. There's definitely parts of the story that seem strange but they may or may not be suspicious."

"So you think I'm wrong?" she asked, holding her breath.

He hesitated, looking into her desperate eyes. "I think that you knew your dad and that you completely believe that he wouldn't have killed himself but, whether he did or not, there are still questions that haven't been answered about his death."

She breathed out a sigh of relief. "That's good enough. So will you help me?"

"Yes, of course. I'll do anything."

"Then would you keep an eye on Tom in the warehouse?"

Declan shifted uncomfortably in his seat. "I'm not sure I should do that. He's my boss."

"But it's not like you'll be spying on him, you work there anyway. Just let me know if he does anything that seems dodgy, if he says anything odd about my dad. Please, Declan, I need you on my side."

"Okay," he said. "But don't be disappointed if I have nothing to report."

"Thank you, thank you."

"Don't thank me. I haven't done anything."

"Yes you have; you've listened to me. You haven't said that I'm wrong about everything. You're helping me, Declan. You're brilliant!" She broke into an enormous smile.

But her words seemed to upset him. Declan suddenly seemed tense and awkward around her.

"I've got to get home," he said abruptly. He didn't even look at her as he said goodbye and walked out of the cafe. She was left sitting on her own, feeling embarrassed, wondering what she'd done wrong.

20 THE BUSINESS ASSOCIATE

"**O**oh! Look at those muscles," Kylie cooed as she trotted past Declan, who was carrying a bulging sack across his shoulders.

Declan smiled through gritted teeth, straining to maintain his grip on the coarse jute that, even in the three short weeks he'd been working there, was already causing calluses on his hands.

"Where are you off to?" he asked. "It's not even dinnertime."

"Tom's sent me for an early lunch," she said gleefully. "There's a couple of fellas just arrived. I think he wants a private meeting."

"Who are they?"

"I don't know." She shrugged. "Some business associates, I guess. There's a skinny, old guy with a funny accent – he was very polite, not like the big guy! He swaggered into the office like he owned the place and then tried to chat me up," she said, feigning outrage. "Said I was far too glamorous to be working in a warehouse. Said I was as beautiful as the women back home in the Ivory Coast. Wanted to take me out for a drink."

"You said no, then?"

"I didn't say anything. He wasn't all bad. He's got some impressive jewellery on him and he's a sharp dresser."

Declan's ears pricked up. "Really?"

"Ooh, Declan, you're not jealous, are you?" she trilled. "I thought your heart belonged to someone else."

"Who?"

"Well, Tom tells me that you can't keep away from Gina. Knocking around with her all the time. I'm happy for you, babe. You make a cute couple and Gina's a great girl, but she's been through a terrible time, so make sure you treat her right – you'll have me to answer to." Kylie didn't look like she was joking.

Declan looked flustered. "But we're not going out."

"Well why not? Don't you fancy her?"

"Yeah I do, I *really* do," Declan blurted out. "But things are complicated."

Kylie rolled her eyes. "How complicated can things be at your age? Stop making excuses and just ask Gina out. I'll see you later, handsome."

Declan watched Kylie walk away, swinging her handbag. He groaned. *If only she knew.*

Declan couldn't let his thoughts dwell on Gina. He had to focus. He grunted as he threw the cocoa sack off his shoulders and back onto the shelf. He rubbed his hands to get rid of the welts the sacks had left on them, brushed down his overalls and headed towards the office.

As he approached he could see the three men through the grubby windows. Tom had his elbows on his desk, his hands in a steeple, fingers touching his lips. In the corner of the office sat a skinny, sallow-looking man, with a wispy grey comb-over and half-moon glasses perched on his bony nose. Tom's other visitor strode up and down, his substantial frame dominating the room and the thick gold chain across his jacket bouncing on his chest. The man gesticulated and smiled like he was delivering some sort of entertaining lecture, and every so often he pulled a spotted silk handkerchief from the pocket of his pinstriped suit and patted his bald head.

Bingo! Declan thought, his pulse quickening. *That's the man in the photo. And it could be the same guy who was outside Gina's house.*

Declan stepped closer to the windows, straining his ears, whilst trying to think of a legitimate reason to be there. As he looked into the office, he saw Tom staring back at him. Tom came out of the room.

"Hey, Declan," he said. "I hope you're not slacking. There's a whole batch in Aisle Four needs shifting. Get Pete to give you a hand. Use the forklift – you've been trained."

"The windows, Tom," Declan said hesitantly. "I just thought I'd give the office windows a clean, they're filthy." He began to rub the glass with the sleeve of his overall.

Tom looked at him, baffled. "Maybe later, hey," he said. "You may have noticed that I'm *trying* to have a meeting here." Tom shooed him away and went back into the office, shutting the door behind him.

"Idiot," Declan mumbled to himself, as he walked away. But he was determined not to mess this up. He backtracked, finding a good position at the side of a towering shelf. He still had a clear view of the office, even if he couldn't hear the conversation.

Declan felt like he was watching a silent movie as he observed the visitor getting back into his stride. Whatever the man was saying was clearly upsetting Tom. Tom threw his hands up in protest. The swaggering man smiled and seemed to be pointing at the stumpy fingers on Tom's left hand. Declan caught a look of sheer terror on Tom's face before he shot out of his chair, squaring up to the big man.

A full-scale argument seemed to be raging now. Declan suddenly noticed the sickly-looking man in the corner. He appeared to be fighting for his breath, like a fish out of water. The man ferreted around inside his coat and pulled out an inhaler. Shaking it vigorously, he put it to his mouth and took two sharp puffs. This caught the attention of the other two, who pulled away from each other. The sickly man looked over his half-moon glasses and spoke. Whatever he said seemed to finally calm them down.

The big man handed Tom a slip of paper. He hesitated before taking it. He glanced at it and put it in the inside of his jacket. Declan thought that the big man seemed triumphant, smiling broadly and extending his hand to Tom, who reluctantly shook it. The big man laughed and headed towards the door. His colleague eased himself out of the chair and bowed sharply to Tom.

Declan watched the two men leave the office. He followed them at a distance out of the warehouse and saw them get into their cars, the big man into a silver Mercedes, the other into a Fiat Punto. Declan grabbed his phone from the pocket of his overalls and, as the engines fired up, he took surreptitious photos of the cars' number plates.

Declan walked back towards the office feeling pleased with his quick thinking. Maybe he was going to be quite good at this, after all.

He positioned himself back in his secluded spot and observed Tom, who was seated back at his desk. Tom ran his hands down his grim face before opening the side cupboard of his desk and pulling out a whisky bottle and a glass. He poured himself a large measure and, steadying his hand, raised it to his lips, slugging it down in one go. Declan leaned forward, peering closer as Tom stood up. The man's face was twisted, his knuckles white around the glass. He let out a growl as he flung the glass to the concrete floor; the shards ricocheted up at him.

Declan flattened his back against the shelf in alarm.

What the hell is going on? he thought.

21 THE JACKET

Gina sat despondently at her dressing table. A pile of school books loomed next to her like the leaning tower of Pisa and her physics past-paper lay neglected in front of her. She'd been trying to work through the same page for the last half-hour but her mind wouldn't stop wandering. For months now her thoughts had been consumed with trying to prove that her dad hadn't killed himself. However, over the last few weeks, she found that they'd been infiltrated by someone else.

She shook her head and screwed up her eyes. *Come on, Gina, concentrate.*

She looked at the physics sheet again. The law of velocity came into focus but, within minutes, her eyes glazed over as her thoughts turned to Declan.

Gina knew that she was no expert on boys. Her limited experience had involved a disastrous encounter at an ice rink when she was fourteen. Becky had set it up, concerned that Gina seemed more interested in running than going out with boys.

Becky's choice was a boy of few words who'd spent the "date" dragging Gina around the ice rink at thirty miles per hour. She was on the verge of throwing up when he'd then tried to stick his tongue down her throat.

Since her dad's death, boys, like everything else, had held no interest for her; but then Declan Doyle had walked into her life.

When they were together she loved hearing him talk about his family and his Uncle Shaun's farm in Ireland. Despite all his funny anecdotes, she could see in his eyes how much he missed them all. She loved the fact that some evenings, even after they'd been for a run, Declan would ring her just to say goodnight and they'd end up chatting for ages about everything and anything. She loved it when he sent her funny YouTube clips and music links that he thought she might like. She knew it meant that he was thinking about her, but could he picture every detail of *her* face the way she could his? Did he imagine kissing her the way she did him and, when they stood close to each other, did he feel that same aching need to touch?

She was still confused by his abrupt departure from the cafe the other day. But since then things had carried on as normal.

Gina blinked as the doorbell rang. She strained her ears,

then her face became a picture of embarrassment as the lilting voice floated up the stairs.

"Hello, Mrs. Wilson."

"Come in, Declan, Gina's working in her room. She could probably do with a break. Gina, love, Declan's here to see you," her mum called up the stairs.

Declan was a little flustered. As much as he loved to see Gina, the real reason for his visit was to bump into Tom.

Upstairs, meanwhile, Gina grimaced, frantically fanning her hot face with her hands.

"Gina? I'm sending Declan up, okay," her mum shouted.

"No, I'll come down," she called back, but as she stood up he was already knocking at the door.

"Hiya, Gina. Can I come in?"

"Yeah, of course." She headed for the sash window, struggling to get it open.

"Here, I'll give you a hand." He was so close to her that she could see where the chocolate dust from the warehouse had settled on his long eyelashes. The sweet smell reminded her of her dad coming home from work.

He pushed up the window and cold air rushed in.

"You feeling okay?" He looked at her with concern. He put his hand on her cheek; her eyes widened.

"I'm fine. It's just so hot in here, isn't it?" she mumbled.

"It's probably your brain getting overheated with all that revision," he teased.

"Yeah, must be."

"Is Tom here?"

"Of course he's here," she said disapprovingly. "He came straight from work. He's practically moved in."

"I might just go downstairs and see him."

"Oh." Gina was disappointed. "Why do you want to see him?"

"I just need a quick word. Then I'll be all yours."

Gina quickly looked away, pretending to rearrange her school books as her cheeks threatened to burst with heat. "Fine, go ahead. I'll be down in a minute," she said nonchalantly.

Declan headed down the stairs. He knew he wouldn't have much time. He just needed to get his hands on the piece of paper he'd seen Tom slip into his jacket pocket earlier. He hoped Tom might be in one room and his jacket in another. But as he dithered over which room to try first, Gina's mum called to him from the kitchen and beckoned him in. As he entered, Declan's eyes fell on Tom's jacket, draped over a chair at the kitchen table.

"Declan," Gina's mum began, "I wanted a quick word with you, while Gina isn't around."

"Okay, Mrs. Wilson."

"Oh, you're so polite." She smiled. "But you don't need to call me Mrs. Wilson, just call me Clare."

"Okay, Clare."

"Listen, Declan." She leaned towards him, her eyes

bright. "I just wanted you to know that I'm *so* pleased you're around. You becoming friends with Gina has been great for her. You've really taken her out of herself. You know she took her dad's death extremely hard, don't you…? Especially the circumstances." Clare coughed, trying to hide her own emotion.

"Yeah." He nodded, looking uncomfortable.

"Things have been difficult this last year. I've been sick with worry about her. She'd become obsessed with certain ideas about her dad's death, so to see her taking an interest in things again, to see how much she enjoys being with you, well…it makes me hopeful she's coming out the other side." Tears sprang into Clare's eyes. "Oh sorry, how embarrassing." She tried to dry them with the washing-up gloves that encased her hands.

"Don't apologize, Mrs…I mean, Clare," Declan stumbled. "I'm glad you think I'm helping. I really like being with Gina. She's a great girl."

"And you're a great boy!" she replied, throwing her arms around him and giving him a heartfelt hug.

Declan looked mortified. "I don't deserve that," he mumbled.

"I know," Clare laughed. "What young man wants to be hugged by a middle-aged woman? I tell you what, let me make you a cup of tea instead."

"No…" Declan saw his chance. If he could just get Gina's mum out of the room, he could search through

Tom's jacket. "You go in the living room and put your feet up and I'll make everyone a cuppa." He tried to guide her out but Clare was having none of it.

"Declan, this is my house and you'll do as you're told," she said playfully. "Danny and Tom are in the living room. Go in and see them."

Declan walked past the jacket, eyeing it up longingly.

He stood in the open doorway of the living room watching Danny and Tom standing at the fish tank. Danny was in full flow about his restocked tank, oblivious to the fact that Tom was sipping his whisky with his eyes cast down to the floor.

"Uncle Tom, you haven't really looked at my tank since I got all the new stuff. Can you see the three clownfish? They love swimming in and out of the pirate ship. And what do you think of the new coral?" Danny was saying excitedly. "I think the colours look amazing, especially against all the blue stones." He pointed to the floor of the tank. "It looks cool, doesn't it?"

"Yeah, yeah, great," Tom muttered, without looking.

"Uncle Tom…" Danny turned to face him. "Could I come and help at the allotment at the weekend?"

"Not yet, Danny. I'm still doing all the heavy work."

"That doesn't matter. I don't mind the digging and stuff. I'm good at it. I'm stronger than I look," he said, flexing his puny arms, hoping to raise a smile from Tom. But the solemn-faced Tom didn't speak. He seemed to be looking right through Danny.

"Go on!" Danny tugged at Tom's shirtsleeve. "I could bring a pack of cards. I'll even make us some sandwiches."

"Haven't I already told you? I'll let you know when you can help," Tom snapped.

Danny's face dropped. He turned quickly back to the fish tank, trying to hide his embarrassment and hurt.

Declan felt the boy's upset and swiftly announced his presence with an overly cheery "Hello!"

Danny and Tom looked round, surprised to see him standing there.

"How you doing, Danny?" Declan asked warmly, patting the boy on the back. "How's that footy team of yours getting on?"

Danny looked worried. "I'm in goal tomorrow. First time! Only because Max Reece is having his tonsils out. I don't even want to be in goal. I'm best on the wing but Big Paddy, our coach, he says I won't be missed and I'm better off in goal because I've got big hands."

Declan tried his best not to laugh.

"I'm going to be rubbish and we're playing the Thunderbolts and they're *well* dirty. One of their players got banned last season for punching the ref. They'll probably kick my teeth in when I go down for the ball."

"Well we can't have that. Your teeth are your only good feature," Declan said.

"Get lost!" Danny shoved him, chuckling.

"What time is kick-off?"

"Six-thirty at Ryland Park."

"Okay, well how about I call round for you after work, about five-thirty. We could go to the park and I'll shoot a few penalties at you, give you a few tips?"

"Yeah, all right," Danny chirped. "That'll be good, thanks. Hey, Uncle Tom, do you fancy a training session in the park tomorrow?"

"What? No. I'm too busy," Tom answered gruffly.

The three of them stood in an awkward silence, which was only broken when Gina breezed in. She said "Hi" as she walked over to the display shelf and cupped her hands around the mended grey urn.

Tom glared at her. "For God's sake, Gina, do you have to do that?"

"What? What have I done?"

"What have you done?" Tom said incredulously. "It's that weird thing you do with the urn every bloody time you come into this room."

Gina's stomach turned over.

"I…I…it's my dad," she spluttered.

"It's not your dad! It's just a load of ashes and most of *them* will be from the burned-up coffin." His voice was rising. "Isn't it about time that urn was moved somewhere so we all don't have to keep looking at it? We know Martin's dead. We don't need it there to constantly remind us."

Gina stood in stunned silence.

"That's a bit out of order, isn't it?" Declan said, coming to her defence.

"Shut up. This doesn't concern you," Tom barked.

Gina's mum rushed in from the kitchen.

"Tom, what's going on?" Clare asked sharply.

Gina found her voice. "Don't you dare tell me what to do with my dad's ashes." She squared up to him, anger in her eyes. "What the hell are you doing here anyway? This isn't your house. We aren't your family. Why don't you just get lost!"

"Look, let's all calm down," her mum said gently. "I've made tea. We'll go in the kitchen and sit down."

Tom shot a withering look at Clare. "Is that your solution; a cup of tea? You've got to tackle this, Clare. You've indulged this behaviour and it's not helping her. She needs to snap out of it. Can't you see that? If I'd been here, I would have sorted Gina out long ago."

"But you weren't, were you?" Clare snapped back. "You went off travelling after you said you'd be here for us."

"I'm sorry, Clare. But I'm here now and I'm going to help."

Gina felt Tom's hands come down firmly on her shoulders. "We all miss your dad but he's dead and nothing is going to bring him back. He killed himself, Gina. I know it's painful but your refusal to accept that hasn't just been damaging you; it's been torturing your mother and distressing Danny. It's selfish, Gina. You've been making it so much harder for everyone. It's time to move on."

Gina met Tom's steely gaze.

"You know that my dad *didn't* kill himself," she said accusingly.

"What are you on about?" Tom retorted.

Gina pushed his hands off her. "You know things. You did things. The phone call, saying he was depressed, that text you got after our house was broken into."

Tom bubbled with fury. "I've had enough of your insane talk. This has got to stop. You're ridiculous!" he roared.

Danny gasped in shock at Tom's outburst. Declan reached out to Gina but she turned and ran out of the room. Her mother went to follow her.

"Leave her, Clare," Tom shouted. "Let her mull over things. It's for the best."

"But she was getting better…making progress. There was no need for that," Clare fumed.

"There was every need. Just wait, you'll see I've done the right thing," Tom said.

"Mum, should I go and see her?" Danny asked, eyeing Tom nervously.

"No thanks, Danny. Why don't you go to your room for a minute? Tom's just going, aren't you, Tom?" she ordered.

Declan panicked and stepped out in front of him. He had to find out what was on that piece of paper. "Did you bring a coat, Tom? I'll get it for you."

"I'm capable of getting my own jacket, thanks," Tom growled.

Clare walked into the hallway with Tom following her, protesting, "I'm not being chased away, Clare. We need to discuss this now."

"Can I just use your loo?" Declan said to no one in particular as he rushed past them.

Declan ran up the stairs and into Gina's bedroom without stopping to knock.

"Gina!" he hissed. She was banging a fist on the wall in an effort to stop herself crying.

Gina raised her head, mortified as she realized he was standing there. "What are you doing in here?" She turned her face away from him. "Get out, Declan! I don't want to see anyone. I just want to be left alone."

"Listen, Gina," Declan said urgently, sitting down on her bed. "I need your help. I need it right now. I need you to come downstairs and talk to Tom."

"Talk to him! Are you joking? I can't even bear to look at him." She was still talking to the wall.

"Gina, I need you to stall him. He's about to go home and I need to do something before he goes."

Curiosity overwhelmed her. She looked at him.

"What do you need to do?"

"Nothing much." His foot tapped nervously on the side of her bed. "But it's important, Gina, *really* important and if I don't do it now I'll miss my chance."

"You tell me what it is and I might do it for you."

"No! I just need you to stall him. Keep him in the living room for two minutes, that's all."

"No deal." Gina crossed her arms. "*You* keep him talking. *I'll* do the business."

Declan's eyes danced manically as he considered his options. "Okay, okay. It's his jacket. It's on a chair in the kitchen. There's a piece of paper; it should be in the inside pocket. I need to know what's written on it. Don't take it, just look at what it says, okay?"

Gina frowned. "What's this about?"

Declan put his hands in praying position. "Please, Gina, I haven't got time to explain."

"Is Tom up to something?"

"He could be. That piece of paper might tell us if he is."

"Then why didn't you just say so? You said you'd let me know if anything happened. Did someone give it to him?"

"Yes, some big guy from the Ivory Coast. He could be a business associate. He came to the warehouse. I don't know who he is."

"So why do you think it's something dodgy?"

"Call it gut instinct. I just have a bad feeling about it all and I want to see what's on that paper."

Gina's face split into a grateful smile. "Thanks for doing this for me, Declan."

"S'okay," he mumbled to the ground. "Just hurry up!"

As Declan raced down the stairs he was relieved to see

that Tom hadn't moved from the hallway, where he was still arguing with Gina's mum.

"Clare, she needed to be told," Tom was saying.

"I'm not going to talk about this any more," Gina's mum huffed, walking away from him and passing Declan on the stairs. "Go home, Tom."

Tom's face was like thunder as Declan approached him, thinking fast. "Tom, I know it's not a good time but I need to discuss something important with you."

Tom scowled at him. "Can't it wait, for God's sake?"

"No, it's about the warehouse, the stock. I meant to tell you earlier."

"What is it?" Tom said impatiently.

"Well…" Declan began, walking into the living room, desperately hoping Tom would follow. "It's about the air-conditioning system. I don't think it's working properly. The left side of the warehouse felt really humid today."

"What? Are you sure?" Tom said, following him in.

"Yep."

"But the beans have got to be kept cool or else they could be ruined," Tom said.

"I know. That's why I knew you'd want to be told," Declan said, shutting the door behind them with relief.

Gina watched, unseen, as her frazzled-looking mum disappeared into the bathroom. She seized her moment and crept down the stairs and past the living room, where Tom's exasperated tones cut through the closed door.

"This is all I need; that air-con system cost me a bloody fortune. It'd better not be playing up. There's thousands of pounds' worth of stock in that warehouse."

As she entered the kitchen, Gina spotted the jacket straight away. Shutting the door as quietly as possible, she picked it off the chair, unzipped the inside pocket and felt around. Nothing. She delved her hand into the left-side pocket and pulled out Tom's car and house keys and a packet of chewing gum. In the right-side pocket she found a leather wallet. Her eyes flashed to the door as she pulled out the wallet and opened it. She flicked through the rows of credit cards and an impressive array of membership cards for clubs where he entertained important clients. Gina bristled; sure, Tom was generous and, over the years, he always seemed to enjoy visiting them, but she couldn't remember him ever taking her dad to any of his clubs. It suddenly struck her that maybe Tom had thought that a warehouse foreman wasn't good enough to mix with his wealthy friends.

Focus, Gina, don't get sidetracked. She opened the wallet's main compartment and pulled out the wad of crisp, clean notes. Placing the pile of money on the kitchen table she fanned it out and, as she swept her hand over the fifties and twenties, she spotted a white piece of paper folded amongst them.

She picked it out and opened it, revealing a set of numbers: *874351/54/208/23/10/13*

What – is that it? She turned it over to make sure she hadn't missed anything. She rifled through all the pockets of the jacket again – there was nothing else. A creak from the living room door sent her heart jumping into her mouth.

No way will I remember those numbers, she thought. *Pen? I need a pen.* She looked around the kitchen in a panic, as if the place was unknown to her.

Messy drawer! She scrambled to open the drawer next to the cooker and fought through a tangle of elastic bands, batteries, and sellotape until she unearthed a pen. *Paper?*

She heard Tom's voice in the hallway. "I'll check it out on my way home."

"No, wait." Declan's voice boomed a warning. "Do you want me in extra early tomorrow, in case there's loads of sacks to sort out?"

"Are you after a pay rise, Declan?" Tom said half impressed and half mocking. "Just let me go to the warehouse and see for myself."

"So you're going then!" Declan said loudly.

Hurry up! Hurry up! Gina panicked.

She copied the numbers from the paper onto the back of her hand before frantically gathering up the money, placing the folded paper in between the notes again and stuffing them all back into the wallet.

"For God's sake, Declan, I'm not deaf…" Tom stopped dead as he opened the kitchen door to find Gina, one hand deep inside a pocket of his jacket.

"Gina! What are you doing with my jacket?"

"Did it fall on the floor, Gina? Were you just picking it up?" Declan prompted her from behind Tom.

Tom turned his head to Declan; the look on his face silenced the boy. "I wasn't asking you. I think it's best you go home."

"But—" Declan began to protest.

"Home!" Tom jabbed a finger at him, before shutting the kitchen door.

Gina felt the blood drain from her face. "I…I…was just looking to see what make it was. I reckoned it was probably Armani. I wanted to check."

Tom eyed her suspiciously. "Come off it. Since when have you taken an interest in my clothes – in *any* clothes, for that matter?"

She cast her eyes to the floor, licking her suddenly dry lips.

He took the jacket from her and picked his wallet out of the pocket. Opening it, he ran his fingers over the top of the crumpled notes.

"How much have you taken?" His voice darkened.

Gina's heart was beating out of her chest. "Nothing," she whispered.

"But you've been through my money, Gina, you must have taken something."

Gina swallowed hard, keeping her eyes on the floor.

"Listen, I know that you're angry with me, but you can't go stealing from me."

"I wasn't stealing, honest," she muttered. "It was for Mum."

"What was for your mum?"

"I was looking for money because I wanted to buy something for Mum. I've only got a tenner and I wanted to get her something decent."

"It's not her birthday for months," he said accusingly.

"It's not for her birthday. I wanted to get her something to show her that I'm sorry for being such a pain since Dad died. I know I've been a pain, Tom – what you said has made me think."

"Really?" Tom softened on hearing her admission. "Well, that's good to know, Gina."

"And I would have paid you back anyway."

"Either way, you don't have to steal from me. If you need money then you only have to ask. You know I'd give you anything you wanted." A smile played on his lips as he pulled a note out of the wallet.

"Here, have this, buy something nice for your mum."

"No! I can't take it," she protested, seeing it was a fifty.

"Take it," he insisted. "You don't have to pay me back." He grabbed her hand. She froze – the numbers she'd copied down were clearly visible. He dragged the hand towards him; she tried to maintain his gaze, willing him not to look down. She twisted against his grip, relieved to see the numbers roll out of sight as her palm appeared.

"You didn't take much persuading," he laughed, pressing the note into her palm and closing her moist fingers around it.

"Thanks," she whispered, hoping he hadn't noticed how her hand trembled.

Tom stood staring at her in baffled amusement. "You're full of surprises, aren't you, Gina?"

Her mum came bustling into the kitchen. "There you are! I thought you were up in your room." She scrutinized her guilty-looking daughter and sighed. "Have you two been having a go at each other again?"

"Not at all. Gina and I have just made up. Haven't we, kiddo?" He put his arm around her stiff shoulders.

"Yeah." She faked a smile.

"We've had a good talk. Cleared the air." He squeezed her closer to him.

Her mum beamed with relief. "Well, that's just great. It would make me so happy if you two could get along." She threw her arms around them, rocking them. "You sillies. No more falling out, hey?"

"Don't worry. Gina and me are the best of friends. We understand each other now, don't we?" he said, with a wink that sent a shudder down Gina's spine.

22 SOMETHING GOING DOWN

"**D**ive to the left, Danny!" Declan shouted as he booted the ball from the penalty spot yet again. The ball flew past Danny and into the back of the net.

"I can't do it. I haven't saved *any* yet. I'm so rubbish," Danny grumbled, retrieving the ball.

"Don't be a baby. You can. You've got to react faster, concentrate more."

"Let me take a shot," Gina said, placing the ball on the penalty spot.

"Okay, now come on, Danny, focus," Declan coached. "Watch her as she runs up and see if you can work out where she's going to place it. Stretch your arms out, bend your knees; get ready to dive."

Gina took a short run-up and blasted the ball. It rocketed towards the right-hand corner of the goal. Danny dived and stretched his arms like they were made of plasticine. His fingertips just made contact with the ball, and deflected it away from the goal.

Declan sprang up into the air and did a somersault. He ran up to Gina and they threw their arms around each other, mucking around; cheering like Danny had just saved a penalty in a World Cup Final.

Danny picked himself off the AstroTurf, grinning. "Calm down, you two. It was only Gina's shot and she's a girl, so it doesn't count."

Gina released Declan but he kept his arms around her; he seemed reluctant to let her go. She smiled to herself.

"Get off the pitch," Danny suddenly shouted. "Big Paddy and the team are here and there's the Thunderbolts' minibus!"

They watched apprehensively as a team of bruisers piled out of the minibus.

"Are you sure they're under-11s?" Declan asked.

"Yep," Danny groaned.

Gina and Declan exchanged worried looks.

"You'll be fine," Declan said breezily. "Just remember everything we've gone through."

"Yeah, okay," Danny said, walking to the goalmouth like a condemned man.

Gina and Declan stood on the touchline, watching the game under the glaring floodlights.

"God, I can't watch any more," Gina said, looking through her fingers as another ball sailed past Danny and into the net. "This is a massacre!"

Declan nudged her. "Don't let him see you looking like that. Come on, Panthers!" he shouted at the sorry-looking team.

"I've been thinking about those numbers on Tom's piece of paper," she said in a low voice, although no one was in earshot. "Maybe they're details of a bank account, or the code to a safety deposit box or a safe?"

"Yeah, they could be." Declan shrugged. "We just don't know."

"But then, I was thinking that maybe the last three sets of numbers could be a date." Gina got her notebook out of her bag and showed the sequence of numbers to Declan.

"Look – 874351/54/208/23/10/13. Couldn't the 23/10/13 be a date?"

Declan nodded, impressed. "Possibly, in which case, it's very soon."

"So, as we haven't got anything else to go on, I reckon we shouldn't take our eyes off Tom on that day, and see if anything happens."

"Okay, I can do that at the warehouse and you can take over in the evening, if he comes to your house."

"We've got to be careful though. We don't want him getting suspicious. I nearly died when he walked in on me in the kitchen. At least he didn't realize what I was up to, but the way he was acting…he really gave me the creeps."

"Yeah, he had a go at me this morning about the air-conditioning – said I'd wasted his time. We should definitely keep this to ourselves."

"But what about my mum? She needs to know if he's up to something."

"No!" Declan seemed alarmed. "Don't say anything. We need to suss out what's going on first. It may be nothing and then you'll just look like you're making up stuff and your mum will be upset with you."

"Yeah, you're right. We'll keep it to ourselves for now." Gina turned her attention back to the game. "Ooh…come on, ref! That was a foul! Number eight just elbowed that little number six in the face!"

The final whistle blew and there was relief all round that the slaughter was over.

"I think Danny's going to need a little more coaching," Gina said.

"Leave it to me. I'll make him into a Ninja goalie before the end of the season," Declan laughed.

Gina fought back an urge to hug him. It felt so great to have him around, to know that she wasn't alone in this any more. Declan was helping her. He believed in her.

Declan looked at his watch. "Do you fancy seeing a movie tonight? If you get Danny home and I get changed and call back for you in half an hour?"

"Yeah, that sounds good. What were you thinking of?"

"Any – your choice." Declan shrugged.

"My choice? But what if I want to see a chick flick full of women buying shoes and complaining about men?" she teased.

"I'll watch whatever makes you happy." He smiled.

Gina tried to mask her excitement. *Oh my God! He's actually willing to see a chick flick with me. What boy does that unless they fancy you?*

"See you in half an hour then," she trilled.

Gina made Danny rush home. Once they were in the house she ran upstairs, calling to her mum that she was getting ready to go out with Declan. Twenty minutes later, most of the contents of her wardrobe were piled on her bed. She'd changed half a dozen times, looking in the mirror and shaking her head.

The doorbell rang. She put on another coat of lipstick, slipped on her new shoes and clung onto the banister like she was walking downstairs on stilts.

She smiled when she saw the look on Declan's face as she opened the door.

"Wow! You look nice." He couldn't take his eyes off her.

"Oh thanks," she said casually, "I just threw on the first thing I saw."

"Well come on, your chariot awaits."

"Where?" She looked around.

"On the High Street. It's the number six bus. We'd better run, it's due in a minute."

"No way, I can't run in these heels!" she protested.

"Then I'll give you a piggyback." He turned round and offered his back.

"You must be joking."

"No. We'll miss the movie and you don't want to sit through it with sore feet, do you? Come on, hop on."

"Oh my God, I can't believe I'm doing this!" She jumped up onto his back. "Giddy up then."

He started to run up the street with Gina clinging to him, her arms around his neck, laughing so hard she thought she was going to fall off.

"Thanks for not making me watch a chick flick," Declan whispered to her in the darkened cinema.

"It's okay. I like thrillers better, anyway." She lowered her hand into the cavernous tub that Declan was holding.

"Wow, you really like popcorn," he whispered, rattling the near-empty tub.

She squirmed. "Have I eaten it all? The weird thing is that I could hardly eat after my dad died and now I can't seem to stop. It's since I've met you, you're a bad influence on me."

"I hope so." He grinned. "Open up then."

He held a piece of popcorn up to her mouth but, as she lunged for it, her lips accidentally sealed around his fingertips. Declan froze. He swallowed hard. She immediately released his fingers and nearly choked on the popcorn.

"Sorry," she spluttered.

"No worries," he whispered, flustered.

For the remainder of the film Declan didn't seem to move a muscle. Every time Gina sneaked a look at him out of the corner of her eye, he was sitting with his hands on his knees, staring intently at the screen.

After the movie they jumped in a taxi home and by the time they were at her front door she was willing him so hard to kiss her that she felt sure he'd be able to read her mind. She stood up on the doorstep so that she was level with him.

"Thanks for a lovely night," she said, looking into his languid brown eyes.

"No, thank *you*," he said, grinning. But then his phone vibrated in his pocket, and the grin fell from his face as he answered it.

"Hi…okay…I'll ring you back." Declan's voice was cold.

"Who was that?" Gina asked.

"Just a mate. I need to get back to him. I'll see you soon," he said, with that same tense look that she'd seen in his eyes before, and he left her standing alone on the doorstep.

* * *

203

Declan sat in his flowery bedroom and rang back his least favourite person. "Have you worked out what those numbers I gave you mean?" Declan asked the man.

"No, but something's going down, lad. Cotter wouldn't get a personal visit like that unless there were things in the pipeline."

"Well, Gina reckons the last few digits could be a date."

"What do you mean 'Gina reckons'? Why the hell have you told her?"

"Because I wouldn't have even got the information without her," Declan replied indignantly.

"What does she know?"

"Only that I think Tom might be involved in something dodgy. She was more than willing to help. She doesn't want him around her family, especially her mum. She thinks he knows things about her dad's death, doesn't she? What about the stuff in her notebook that I told you about? What about her description of the guy outside the house? It sounded like it was the same man who came to visit Tom, the man in the photo. You said you were going to look into it?"

"Yeah, yeah, don't worry about that," he said dismissively. "The bottom line is, I've asked people who know and they say that Gina Wilson is unstable. All this stuff about her dad not killing himself – it's rubbish. She hasn't been able to handle his suicide and she's been taking it out on Cotter."

"Are you sure?" Declan asked.

"Yes, I'm sure." He sounded irritated.

Declan didn't want to believe it. Gina was so convinced about her dad and she'd trusted Declan to help her. He felt so guilty about what he was doing. He despised the person on the phone but, on the other hand, there was no reason for the man to lie about this. If it was true, it meant that Gina wasn't well; that all her thoughts and theories were just delusions that she'd built up to protect herself from reality.

"Poor Gina," Declan whispered to himself.

"Just don't get sucked into her problems. You've got a job to do; so keep a clear head and for God's sake don't tell her anything else!" he said, infuriated.

Declan gave a hollow laugh. "What could I tell her? I don't know anything. If something's about to go down, then maybe it's time you told me what you've got me involved with."

"I've told you as much as you need to know and that's the way it's going to stay. Your immediate problem is making sure the girl keeps her mouth shut about this. We can't have Cotter knowing he's being watched."

"I'll do my best," Declan said quietly.

"I need better than that. There's too much at stake here for you to cock this up."

"I hate all this lying. It's not something I'm good at," Declan protested.

"Oh, don't be so modest, Declan. I'd say you had a real talent for it," he replied, sneeringly.

23 THE DATE

The forklift truck whirred as Declan pulled the lever and the sacks rose up into the air. The machine juddered as he brought the load safely down onto the shelves, sending a cloud of chocolate dust into the atmosphere.

"Well done, Dec. You've really got the hang of this," Pete, his workmate, shouted up to him.

Declan smiled beneath his hard hat. Yeah, he was okay at this and actually enjoying the job had been a surprise bonus for him.

He climbed down from the truck and went to see if he could spot Tom. He'd been trying to keep an eye on him all morning. If Gina's theory was right, if the last set of digits on that piece of paper did represent a date, then today was the day, and he didn't want to let Tom out of his sight.

As Declan strode down the aisle he spotted Tom heading out of the warehouse and towards his car. Declan rushed into the office and found Kylie dunking a biscuit into a steaming cup of tea.

"Hiya, Declan, fancy a cuppa?" she asked.

"No thanks. I was just wondered where Tom had gone?"

"He said he had to pop over to Clare's house. Said he'd be back in a couple of hours."

"Thanks," Declan said, his mind racing. He jogged out of the warehouse and onto the quayside into the bracing sea air.

He got his phone out and started to text. *Please have your phone on, Gina,* he willed.

Mr. Hannigan, the history teacher, was fighting a losing battle, trying to enthuse class 11H about the War of the Roses, when Gina's phone vibrated from inside her schoolbag.

She ducked down to answer it before Mr. Hannigan noticed.

She opened the text from Declan: *Phone me now, urgent.*

Gina's hand shot up. "Sir!"

"Good to see that someone was listening." The ageing teacher smiled. "So, what *was* the turning point in the conflict, Gina?"

"Er...I don't know, sir, but can I be excused? I've got

really bad stomach cramps. I think I need something from the nurse."

The teacher looked uneasy – he knew the code for female problems and wasn't about to question her.

"Off you go, then," he said wearily.

Gina headed for the toilets and phoned Declan.

"What is it?" Gina whispered.

"Tom's just left the warehouse to go to your house. Is anyone home?"

"No, Danny's at school. Mum's working till six."

"You know what the date is?"

"Of course I do."

"Then can you get back to your house and see what he's up to?"

"What? Now? But I'm in school!"

"So? Haven't you ever bunked off before?"

"No," she replied, sounding disappointed in herself.

"Well there's a first time for everything, Gina. Just walk out confidently like you've been given permission. It's easy," the expert advised. "It's got to be you, Gina. It's your house. It will look too weird if I turn up."

Gina felt her pulse quickening as she started to rehearse her lines to get past the school receptionist.

She could see Tom's car parked outside her house. As soon as Gina entered the hallway she heard noises coming from upstairs. She reached the landing and listened. He was in her mum's bedroom. She opened the door quickly, hoping to catch him, but for a second her world froze.

She gawped at the figure with his back to her. He was crouched over a drawer that had been pulled out from the wardrobe. His head was bent forward. All Gina could see was the green tweed jacket he was wearing: her dad's favourite jacket. The one he wore for best. The one he'd worn for so many happy celebrations in their lives.

She didn't know why she said it. It made no sense but, for a split second, despite all logic, every fibre in her being willed it to be him.

"Dad?" she called out, her voice tremulous.

But the face that turned to her was Tom's.

"Oh, Gina. What must you think?" He looked dismayed and guilty. He stood up and approached her.

She stepped back, shaken. "What are you doing? Why have you got my dad's jacket on? Why are you going through all my dad's things?"

"I'm clearing out, for your mum," he answered gently.

Gina looked around at the plump black bags sitting around the room, her father's clothes poking out of them. She saw that all the bedroom furniture had been pulled away from the walls. Box files of her dad's paperwork lay open on the bed.

"I'm so sorry if I've upset you with the jacket. I didn't expect you'd be home. I saw it in the wardrobe and...

I know this is going to sound strange, but I suddenly needed to put it on. I can't explain it, but wearing it, I feel close to Marty, connected with him somehow."

Gina watched Tom's face crumple with emotion.

"How did you get in?" she asked coldly.

"Your mum gave me a set of keys."

"Well give them back!" she ordered, putting out her hand.

"No, Gina. Someone should have a spare set, in case of emergencies. Listen, I'm only trying to help. Your mum hasn't been able to face clearing everything out. I suggested that I could make a start; bagging his clothes up to give to charity."

Gina couldn't be placated. "How convenient. You, getting rid of any trace of my dad. Do you think it will make it easier for you to take over his family?"

Tom looked wounded. "I'd never try to replace your dad. I'm not half the man he was."

"Well at least you've got that right."

"Why are you determined to battle against me? Your mum and Danny don't have a problem with me. They like having me around."

She put her hands on her hips, eyeing him suspiciously. "Why *are* you always here? Do you fancy my mum?"

Tom shook his head disapprovingly. "What kind of question is that?"

"She's hardly your type, is she?"

"I didn't think that I had a type," he replied.

Gina laughed derisively. "Come off it. You've been out with so many boob-job blondes half your age that I bet you couldn't tell them apart."

"Okay." Tom nodded. "I'll put my hands up for being attracted to a certain type of woman, once upon a time. But I've changed, Gina. I've grown up. I don't expect you to understand. I'm middle-aged and my friend is dead – it's made me realize what's important in life...*who* is important in life. Your mum is a wonderful woman and I think the world of her, but all I'm trying to do is to look after you all. It's what your dad would have wanted."

Gina scrutinized his face.

He seems so sincere. So bloody sincere!

"But..." she began. Tom held his hand up to silence her.

"But nothing, Gina. You need to show a little more respect. I thought we'd come to an understanding after the other day. Have you bought something nice for your mum yet, with the money I gave you?" His tone was accusatory.

Gina bit her lip, seething. "Give me my dad's jacket... please!"

He took it off and held it out. She grabbed hold of it, but Tom didn't let go; instead he pulled it towards him. His bowed face was only inches from hers. The intensity of his gaze made Gina's skin prickle.

"You look so like him, Gina," he said in a hushed tone.

"It's not just the eyes and the lips. It's the little things, like the way you stick your chin out when you're annoyed. You know that, because of you, Marty will never be completely gone."

Gina ripped the jacket out of his hands and held it tightly to her like a comfort blanket.

"You need to go now," she said, fighting the tremor in her voice.

"Okay," he said, heading for the door. "I understand how upsetting this is, but remember, no matter how much you try to push me away, I'll always be here for you."

24 UNCLE STEVIE

Gina sat on her bed, tightening the laces on her trainers. She needed to get out and clear her head. She just kept thinking about the numbers on that piece of paper. She was so frustrated that nothing had happened on the day and was desperate to find out what Tom was up to.

She looked over at her bedroom wall. Her eyes fell on the photo of her dad at one of the Running Club presentations. In it, she was holding up a medal. He had his arm around her proudly. He looked so smart in his best jacket. The one she'd found Tom wearing. She shuddered at the thought of how weird Tom had been with her.

She'd told her mum about it, asked angrily, "Why was he clearing out my dad's things? Don't you think you should have mentioned it to us?"

Her mum had been upset, apologetic. "I'm so sorry, Gina. Of course I would have discussed it with you but I didn't know. Tom had mentioned it and I'd vaguely agreed that it had to be done at some point, but then he just went and got on with it."

"Well, I hope you're going to tell him that he's out of order."

"I can't do that. He was only trying to help. We just got our wires crossed."

"And why has he got our house keys? You've got to get them back off him."

Her mum had been flustered. "I can't ask for them back, Tom wouldn't be happy. He thought he should have a set, in case of emergencies. It seemed like a good idea."

"But that means he can let himself into our house whenever he wants!"

She'd sounded exasperated. "Of course he won't. This is your Uncle Tom. Stop talking about him like he's a stranger."

Now Gina blew a kiss at her wall of photos and ran to Hanover Street. She knocked on the door, trying not to breathe in the pungent aroma from Mrs. Mac's bizarre floral display in the window boxes.

The crinkled old lady opened the door. "Hello." She smiled. "What can I do for you?"

"Hi, Mrs. McManus? Is Declan home? I'm his friend, Gina."

It was as if the Pope had just appeared on the doorstep.

"Bridie!" Mrs. Mac called. "Come on to the door. Gina's here."

"Gina?" a puzzled voice said. A diminutive figure shuffled to the door. "Holy mother of God – isn't she the girl that Declan is courting?" Bridie ferreted around in her cavernous handbag and found her glasses. Putting the milk-bottle lenses on, she inspected Gina with her enormous eyes.

"Well, your hair is too short but you're an angel nonetheless," Bridie trilled. "No wonder Declan's dropped all his friends to spend time with you."

"Has he?" Gina said in surprise. "I wondered why he'd never introduced me to any of them."

"Well, I've warned him," Mrs. Mac said. "He shouldn't go dropping his friends just because some girl has caught his eye. You never know how long these romances are going to last."

"But I'm not his girlfriend," Gina said coyly. "We're just good friends."

"What?" Bridie said, outraged. "Well what's wrong with you, girl? Isn't our Declan good enough for you? I tell you, if I was forty years younger I'd court that young man myself."

"Oh Bridie, that would still make you a child snatcher," Mrs. Mac tutted. "Now leave the poor girl alone. To be honest, Gina, darling, it's a relief to hear that you and Declan aren't courting. I was starting to get a bit worried. You know where these things can lead and, in the absence of his parents, I'm in charge of his mortal soul. It's a great responsibility," she said solemnly.

Bridie cackled. Mrs. Mac scowled at her friend. "I'm glad you find it so amusing, Bridie. Thank God the poor boy hasn't got you as his moral guardian. Now, Gina, I'm sorry to tell you that Declan isn't in. He left about half an hour ago. I just assumed he'd be with you."

"Oh," Gina said, disappointed. "Well, I'll get going then. It's been lovely to meet you both."

"And you," Mrs. Mac said.

"Yes, angel, and if ever you need advice about matters of the heart, I'll be glad to help," Bridie piped up. "There's nothing I haven't seen."

"Or done!" Mrs. Mac said, her eyes fluttering in disapproval.

Gina headed for the park, determined to do a few laps even if it wasn't going to be as much fun without Declan.

She'd just finished her fourth lap around the perimeter when she spotted a hooded boy on a bench. She peered at the figure. He certainly sat like Declan: one hand on each of his knees, back straight, broad shoulders pulled back.

I notice far too much about that boy, Gina thought to herself.

But he had company – a rather unkempt man, who looked like he'd seen life, was sitting on the same bench and Declan seemed to be talking to him.

Maybe a homeless guy? She smiled. *Typical Declan, he chats to everyone.*

She jogged across to him, trying not to appear like a bounding puppy.

"Hi, Declan, I knew it was you!" she called out as she approached him.

Declan raised his head and the look of panic on his face was unmistakable.

"Wow," Gina said playfully. "What are you up to? You look guilty as sin."

"Nothing. No. I'm just surprised to see you." He pulled at his hood nervously.

"Sorry if I've interrupted your chat," she said politely to the unkempt man.

"Don't worry about it, love. I was just catching up with my nephew."

"Oh!" Gina couldn't mask her surprise. "You're Declan's uncle?"

"Yeah. I'm his Uncle Stevie, and you are?"

"Gina."

The man extended a hairy hand. "I've heard all about you! He can't stop talking about you – isn't that right, Declan?"

Gina tried to suppress a rush of joy. Declan shot Uncle Stevie a murderous look and the "uncle" put an arm around his "nephew".

"Come on now, lad. Don't be coy. Best to get things out in the open." One of his bushy eyebrows seemed to wink at Gina. She didn't know how to respond. "He's a knock-out kid, isn't he?" He tapped Dec's cheek with his fist.

"Suppose so," Gina answered, sensing the hostility oozing out of Declan.

"We're as thick as thieves. Very close. Declan feels more like a son to me." The man was clearly enjoying himself, while Declan seemed to be squirming.

"Really? Why have you never mentioned your uncle, Declan?" she asked.

Declan shrugged, his eyes cast to the ground. The man answered for him. "Maybe he's ashamed of me." He gave a rattling laugh.

Gina got the impression she was intruding on a private joke, which Declan didn't find very funny. The palpable tension between the two was now making her feel uncomfortable.

"Well," she said, after an awkward silence. "I'd better be off. I'll see you soon then, Declan?"

Declan nodded, stony-faced.

Uncle Stevie gave a crocodile smile that exposed nicotine-stained teeth. "Try keeping him away."

25 QUALITY CONTROL

The warehouse was a buzz of activity. A ship from West Africa had docked that morning, bringing with it six-metre-long containers full of cocoa beans for Tom's clients. Declan and his workmates hadn't stopped all day; supervising the discharge from the quayside and then stacking the sacks onto the warehouse shelves. Here the sacks would remain until lorries arrived to take the beans on the last leg of their mammoth journey: to the chocolate makers around the UK.

Declan had been enjoying the job so much that sometimes he forgot that the only reason he was there was to keep an eye on Tom Cotter and his activities. In fact, Declan couldn't believe how great his life was at the moment – if it wasn't for the inconvenient fact that it was based on lies.

He wanted the reality to be that he'd just been incredibly

lucky – getting a job he enjoyed and meeting a girl he loved being with and, despite his best efforts, couldn't stop thinking about. Sometimes he thought he saw signs that Gina felt the same way and it was getting harder and harder to hold himself back. He vowed never to go to the cinema with Gina again. It had been torturous sitting next to her in the dark, having to force himself to keep his mind and hands off her.

Guilt gnawed away at him every time Gina thanked him for being such a good friend, every time her mum invited him to stay for tea with a look of gratitude on her face. Declan knew he was a liar, so he was determined to do the only decent thing he could in the circumstances; he was determined not to show Gina how he really felt about her.

It had been three weeks since "the date" and Declan was still no wiser about the numbers on that piece of paper. In fact, since the meeting he'd witnessed between the three men, nothing at all out of the ordinary had happened at the warehouse.

Declan had just stopped for a well-earned tea break when he heard Tom's voice call down from the heavens.

"Declan, come over here, will you? Bring a pen and paper."

He looked along the aisle and then craned his neck to see Tom, high up on the rolling ladder that could be swished along the full length of the shelves to reach any point. Declan watched as Tom dragged out one of the sacks from a shelf and slit across it with a gleaming knife. A sweet aroma sailed out of the sack. Tom pulled a shiny silver scoop out of his pocket and sank it deep into the mass of brown beans. He lifted out the scoop and started to inspect the contents, turning the beans with his fingers, before rolling them between the palms of his hands and bringing them up to his nose to inhale their scent.

Tom nodded to himself, satisfied.

He called down, "Write this down, will you, Declan, and ask Kylie to log it on the computer."

Declan had his pen and paper poised. "Go on!"

"874351/12/102/23/10/13 – condition good," Tom shouted.

Declan froze, the pen still floating above the paper, his mouth slightly agape. "What did you say?" he asked in astonishment.

"Pay attention, will you? I said, '874351/12/102/23/10/13 – condition good'. Have you got that?"

"That's what I thought you said," Declan replied, eyes wide. "Sorry, could you just repeat it one more time?"

Tom rolled his eyes and repeated the numbers. Declan copied them down, nodding vigorously, and started to sprint towards the office.

Tom shook his head in frustration. "I'm sure that lad's not all there," he muttered to himself.

Declan burst in on Kylie.

"Oh, hello, gorgeous," Kylie said, startled. "You seem keen to see me."

"Tom wants some info putting on the system."

"Is it quality control?"

"Yeah."

"Let me just get the right spreadsheet up." Her long fingernails tapped on the keyboard. "Fire away."

Declan moved behind her and bent over her shoulder so he could see the screen.

Kylie swivelled in her chair; their faces were almost touching. "Are you trying to look down my top, you naughty boy?" she grinned.

"I'm interested in how the system works." Declan's olive skin blushed.

She let out a laugh that sounded like a horse neighing. "Oh, Declan, you are funny." She fluttered her eyes slowly, so that her fake lashes brushed his cheek. "I'm only teasing you. Now, have you asked Gina out yet?"

Declan coughed nervously. "No, I think it's best if we just stay mates."

She cupped his face between her hands, pouting. "Is it still 'complicated'?"

Declan nodded.

"Well you know what they say, don't you? 'Tis better to have loved and lost than never to have loved at all'." Kylie laughed at herself. "Get me...quoting poetry. But what

I'm saying is, Declan, you should just go for it."

Declan swallowed hard as she released his face.

"Now what was the data you had for me?" she asked breezily.

He repeated the numbers Tom had given him and watched as they appeared on the spreadsheet under the different column headings:

SHIPMENT	LOT	SACK	D.O. DEP	D.O. DELIVERY	CONDITION
874351	12	102	23/10/13	13/11/13	GOOD

His heart started to beat faster.

"Kylie, can you just run through what all the numbers stand for?"

"Are you after my job?"

"No, I just want to know how all the different bits work together. I find it fascinating," he said.

"Really? Well, Tom devised the system, it's quite straightforward, look." Kylie pointed to the screen. "It's always the serial number of the ship, the lot number, the sack number, the date the cargo left the port in the Ivory Coast, then we record what date the shipment docked here, and finally what condition the cocoa beans arrived in."

"Of course, all the sacks have numbers on," Declan said excitedly.

"Yeah, they each have a lot number and an individual

number. Every sack has to be accounted for. This is big business, Declan. If a sack goes astray or gets nicked, we need to know about it."

"And who decides which sacks to check?" Declan asked, trying to stay calm.

Kylie shrugged. "As far as I know it's just random. Tom chooses sacks from different lots, just to get a sample."

"And is it only Tom who checks them?"

"Well it is now. But Martin used to do it before… before…"

"Before he died." Declan finished her sentence.

"Yeah," she said, suddenly choked up. "Martin was the only one Tom trusted to do it properly. You have to know what you're doing. They spend a long time in those containers on the ships. Things can happen: temperature changes, condensation. The beans can start going mouldy. Tom can tell if they're okay by the feel, smell and colour. He has to separate out any bad beans. Our clients don't want damaged goods." Kylie was getting into her stride now. "It really is lovely to see you taking an interest, Declan. I'm sure the rest of the lads think all I do is sit here and text my mates all day. I play a vital role in this business, you know. Without me and my spreadsheets this place would be in chaos."

"I know, Kylie. You're wonderful." He beamed.

"Do you want to see my spreadsheets for when the stock leaves the warehouse? They really are impressive: lists of buyers, dates, quantities, how they were transported." She smiled proudly.

"Maybe some other time. I'd better get back to work before Tom accuses me of skiving."

"Don't you worry about Tom. I'll tell him what an interest you're taking in the business. He'll be impressed."

"No," Declan said hurriedly. "Don't do that. I don't want him to think I'm a creep."

Kylie looked at her watch. "Hey! Don't bother getting back to work. It's clocking-off time already. Come on!" She turned off the computer and ushered him out of the office, locking the door behind her.

"Right…okay, well I'd better get home quick then. Mrs. Mac is cooking one of her special stews," he announced, heading towards the entrance.

Minutes later the warehouse staff were gathered at the small doorway cut into the closed sliding doors.

"Good work today, guys," Tom said to them. "Are you off for a well-earned pint?"

"We sure are," they chorused.

"Are you coming?" Kylie asked.

"No, I'm going to Clare's for my tea."

The men exchanged knowing looks.

"You spend more time at Clare's house than your own," Kylie said.

"I like being with her and the family. Anyway, she's a wonderful woman," Tom replied enthusiastically.

"Mmm, wonderful," Kylie repeated, knowingly.

Tom rolled his eyes and changed the subject. "Where's Declan?"

"He got off sharpish. His landlady is making him stew."

Tom pulled a face. "Do you think the boy might be a bit slow?"

"No!" Kylie protested. "I think he's sweet and he's keen to learn the business. Really keen, Tom."

"If you say so, Kylie," Tom said, turning the main lights off and switching on the alarm. "Everyone out!"

There came the sound of keys turning in the outside locks and footsteps walking away.

Only then did Declan come out of his hiding place. He was convinced now that he knew what the numbers on the paper meant. He looked around the vast, silent warehouse and steeled himself. He had a lot of searching to do.

26 THE LOCK-IN

D eclan tried Stevie but the voicemail kicked in yet again. "Why haven't you got your phone on?" Declan said in frustration. "I need you, now! This is urgent. I think I've sussed out the code on that paper. I think it's one of the sacks of cocoa beans that came in on today's shipment. I'm in the warehouse right now, looking for it."

Declan knew that they'd stored all of today's shipment on Aisle One, so at least that narrowed down his search, but his heart sank as he looked at the thousands of sacks piled on the mile-long shelving. He couldn't chance using the forklift truck to move any sacks, in case the noise aroused suspicion from outside. He tried to be methodical. First he had to locate lot number fifty-four and then check every sack in that section. He started on the first bottom shelf and checked the numbers on the mounds of sacks. He struggled to read the red print on the sacking in the glow of the warehouse nightlights. The shelves were so deep that he had to crawl to the back of them to reach all the stock. Despite the air conditioning, as he pulled and pushed sack after sack, beads of sweat started to run down his face.

This could take all night, he thought, as he climbed up the rolling ladder and began searching the next shelf.

Outside, the port that never slept was still working at full throttle and every creak, shout and clatter was making Declan so twitchy that when his phone vibrated in his pocket, he nearly jumped out of his skin.

"Oh, Mrs. Mac, it's you."

"Yes, Declan, it's me," she said sternly. "But where are you? Your dinner's on the table. You're not in the pub, are you? You may work with men but you're only a boy, just you remember that. You'd have been far better off with Mr. O'Rourke at the funeral parlour. He's teetotal."

"No, don't worry. I was just about to phone you. I'm working tonight, so I won't be home until really late."

"What? But you usually finish work at five," she said, puzzled.

"Yeah, I do normally but this is just a one-off. One of the docker crews at the quayside has offered me a night shift. I can't pass it up. It's good money."

"Oh, I'm proud of you, Declan," she trilled. "Working so hard. Wait till I tell your mammy."

"Thanks, Mrs. Mac. Don't wait up, okay?"

As he ended the call Declan suddenly panicked. *What if Tom comes back to find the sack? Say he catches me by surprise and finds me in here? What do I do? What do I say? Tom said he was going to Clare's for tea. I need to know his movements. I need to phone Gina.*

"Hi, Gina, is Tom there?" Declan said.

"Yeah, very close, actually." Gina flashed a look at Tom, who was sitting opposite her at the kitchen table.

"Could you keep an eye on him for me? Let me know if he leaves," Declan asked.

"Gina, no mobiles at the table," her mum chastised. "Who is it anyway?"

"Don't tell her," the paranoid Declan whispered.

"It's Becky," Gina answered.

"Oh," her mum said, pleasantly surprised. "Well, that's lovely. I suppose if it's Becky you can take the call."

Gina put her hand over the receiver, whispering to her Mum, "I'll take it outside. She's traumatized. I think she's been dumped."

"I wouldn't use my mobile at the table if you let me have one," Danny chipped in.

"Danny, how many times do I have to tell you? You don't need one until you go to Rylands," his mum said impatiently.

Gina scurried out of the back door and into the yard. "Declan," she whispered, "what's going on?"

"Nothing," he said unconvincingly.

"Either you tell me, or I'll tell my mum that Tom is up to something," she threatened.

"You can't do that! We can't prove anything yet."

"I'm willing to take my chances. This is obviously about Tom, so I want to know exactly what you're up to."

"That's blackmail," he hissed.

"It's for your own good. I want to help."

Declan groaned. "I'm in the warehouse. I think I've sussed out what those numbers mean."

"What! And you weren't going to tell me?"

"I've only just worked it out and I could be wrong," Declan protested.

"So, what do they mean?" she asked excitedly.

"I think the numbers identify a particular sack of cocoa beans from a particular shipment. You were right; the end numbers are a date, but they're the date the ship left Africa, not the date it arrived here. That shipment came in today so I think that sack is in the warehouse right now and I need to see what's inside it."

"Oh my God! I'm coming to meet you."

"No, you're not! It could be dangerous."

"Then you don't want to be there on your own, do you?"

"I didn't know you were some kind of bodyguard in your spare time," he retorted. "Anyway, I could be here all night and still not find this thing."

"All the more reason for me to come. Two pairs of eyes will be quicker than one."

"But I'm locked in. So even if you got past the port gates, you won't be able to get into the warehouse."

"Don't underestimate me," she said confidently. "See you as soon as I can get away."

"No! Don't, Gina! Gina?" Declan was talking to himself.

Gina played the dutiful daughter. She couldn't do enough for her mum. She volunteered to tidy up the kitchen before joining them in the living room. She sat next to Danny on the floor without making a detour to touch the urn. This caused her mum and Tom to exchange pleased looks.

As the chat show on the TV blurred out, Gina watched Tom out of the corner of her eye. He was sitting in her dad's armchair as if he was the man of the house. Her mum was on the sofa close by. Gina bristled as she saw Tom reach across to her mum and squeeze her hand. Her mum's cheeks flushed. Gina held her tongue and bided her time.

It wasn't long before Tom rose from the armchair and announced, "I should be getting home."

"Already?" her mum said.

"I need an early night," he answered.

This was Gina's chance to put her plan into action.

"Phone!" she said suddenly, waving her mobile at them.

"I didn't hear it go off," Danny said.

"It's on vibrate, dunce. It's Becky." Gina walked out of the room, chatting. "Hi, Becky. How's it going?"

She stood just outside the door having her pretend conversation for all to hear, and, by the time she came back into the room, Tom had his jacket on and was ready to leave.

"Mum, Becky's invited me for a sleepover," she said hurriedly.

"Oh, that's nice, love. I'm so glad you two are friends again. When is it?"

"Tonight."

"Tonight? It's a bit short notice, isn't it? And it's a school night. Sorry, Gina, I'm going to have to say no."

"Oh, come on, Mum! She needs me. She's in the middle of some boy crisis and it's *really* nice of her to ask me, because you know how crap I've been with all my friends since Dad died."

"Don't say crap," her mum said.

"But, Mum, I'm just beginning to get back in with them. It'll really help me. You went on and on at me about going out with my friends more, and now I get the chance you won't let me! Becky's going to think I don't like her and everything will be terrible again, just when things were getting better," Gina pleaded breathlessly.

"But what about school?"

"Becky's mum's dead sensible. She won't let us stay up too late and she said she'd drive us to school in the morning. I'll just take my uniform."

She could see that her mum was wavering.

Tom intervened, whispering, "Go on, Clare, let her go. It'll be good for her. You know I'm right. Wasn't I right about the urn business?" He looked pleased with himself.

"Well, I suppose you need a break, a bit of fun. One late night won't be the end of the world, will it? I'm just happy that you're getting on with your old friends again."

Her mum smiled and hugged her. Gina swallowed her guilt.

"This is so unfair," Danny wailed. "I want to go on a sleepover on a school night."

"You can…when you're sixteen," Gina smirked.

"This is age discrimination. There's probably a law against it."

"Get over it, Danny." Gina kissed her squirming brother.

"Why don't I drop you off?" Tom said. "It's dark out there."

"Thanks! I'll just grab my stuff." Gina ran upstairs, throwing her uniform into her schoolbag.

They'd only been travelling a couple of minutes when Gina piped up, "It's just here." She pointed to the end terrace on the street opposite the entrance to the docks.

He stopped the car. "Have a good time, Gina. And just remember – I'm the one who persuaded your mum to let you come here tonight. I'm on your side." He patted her knee. She flinched, opening the car door urgently and jumping out.

"What's wrong?" he asked, perplexed.

"I've got to go," she said, unnerved. "I'll go down the alley. They never use the front door."

Gina disappeared down the stranger's alleyway. She waited and watched as Tom drove off and then rushed to the end of the street, just in time to see his car turning into the entrance of the docks.

She phoned Declan in a panic. "Declan, he's just driven into the docks!"

She heard a clatter as Declan nearly fell off the ladder. "Shit!" he said. "I've got to hide."

Gina didn't have to wait long before she saw a juggernaut, signalling to turn into the docks to pick up cargo. She ran across the road and hid by the side of it, out of sight of the security hut and the nightwatchman. As the barrier went up, she entered the port using the monstrous lorry for cover.

Meanwhile, Tom was turning the keys in the warehouse locks.

The alarm sounded a warning as he opened the door. He hurried over to the panel and punched in the code to silence it. Declan watched as Tom started up one of the forklift trucks and headed towards Aisle One.

Gina had never been allowed in the docks at night and creeping around it now, she was spooked. Floodlights blazed everywhere and she scuttled from one pocket of darkness to the next, trying to avoid the gaze of an army of CCTV cameras.

As she approached the quayside, she stood transfixed by the sight of ghostly ships emerging from the rolling fog, their horns bellowing as they came in to dock; their immense bows looked ready to crash through the quayside, destroying everything in their path.

A crew of dockers in their luminous uniforms came towards her, like fireflies. She ducked between piles of crates. As they walked past, she felt something brush against her legs in the darkness. She put her hand over her mouth to stop herself from screaming. Looking down, she saw a black rat, nearly the size of a cat, scurrying away.

As soon as she dared, Gina made a run for it, heading past the freight trains. She gazed anxiously up at the cranes, which were lowering vast containers onto the waiting carriages. She made it to the complex of warehouses. Fleets of lorries, their headlights on full beam, were standing outside many of them, but all seemed peaceful at the cocoa warehouse, with just one lone car at its entrance.

Gina started walking briskly towards it when, from round the corner, a sudden torch beam threatened to expose her. She dropped to the ground, her knees and hands splashing into a pool of diesel oil. The security guard's radio crackled and she heard him reply.

"No, it's as quiet as the grave tonight. I'll just finish my route and come back. Put the kettle on, will you? I'm freezing."

Gina didn't move a muscle as the torch beam passed

over her head and the security guard went on his way.

She ran behind Tom's car and phoned Declan.

"What do you want, Gina?" he whispered. "Tom's in here."

"I know. Let me in. I'm outside."

"What? No! Go home!"

"Security will catch me. You've got to let me in. It can't be hard. The warehouse is big enough for him not to see you."

Declan knew that she wouldn't go away until he did. He snuck out of his hiding place and painstakingly edged his way between the aisles towards the door. When he reached it, he eased it open, flinching at every creak.

He pulled Gina inside and out of sight.

"For God's sake, Gina. What are you doing here?"

"I've come to help," Gina whispered, her eyes shining with adrenalin.

"Help!" he hissed. "You're going to get us both caught. This isn't a game."

"Don't you think I know that?" she said earnestly. "I need to be here. What if whatever's in that sack has something to do with my dad's death?"

27 THE NIGHT WATCH

"I'm going to see what Tom's doing. You stay here," Declan whispered to Gina.

He crept to the end of Aisle One and poked his head round the corner. He could see Tom in the truck about halfway down the aisle. His boss was using the forklift to lower a stack of sacks from one of the upper shelves, but Declan was too far away to really see what Tom was up to; he had to get closer. He started to crawl along the piles of sacks on the bottom shelves and got as close as he dared before taking out his phone ready to take photographic evidence.

The warehouse fell into silence as Tom cut the engine and jumped down from the truck. With his back to Declan he began sifting his way through the sacks before separating out one in particular. Declan leaned out from the shelf, his phone poised to take the photo, but Tom turned round! Declan froze. *He's going to see me!*

There was a sharp tug on his jeans and Declan felt himself sliding backwards and out of sight. He turned and gave Gina a wide-eyed smile of gratitude. Neither of them dared speak. Tom stepped over to the truck and picked a gleaming knife from the seat. He kneeled down in front of the sack and slit it open like a butcher. Declan and Gina strained to see, but Tom's back blocked their view. Tom started to rummage around inside it, cocoa beans spilling out all around him. After a moment, he pulled something out, inspected it and put it in his jacket. He then climbed back into the forklift and proceeded to carefully lift all the other sacks back onto the shelf. When he'd finished, he turned the forklift off and gathered up the open sack and all the spilled cocoa beans. Gina and Declan pressed themselves against the back of the deep shelf as he passed by on his way to the exit, carrying the open sack. He reset the alarm, turned off the main lights and left, locking Declan and Gina inside.

"What do you think it was?" Gina asked, scrambling out from the shelf.

"Don't know. Couldn't see," Declan groaned.

"Are we locked in?"

"Yep. He's put the mortise lock on."

"Well, should I call the police?"

"And tell them what? That he's come into his own warehouse and taken something out of one of his own sacks? They're not going to be interested. We're the ones who aren't meant to be in here. If you phone the police, we're the ones who'll end up in trouble."

"So we're here for the night?"

"Yeah, unless…"

"Unless what?" she asked.

"Nothing," he answered, distractedly. "I'd better phone Mrs. Mac, make up some excuse for not getting home. What about you? How are you going to explain this?"

"I'm all sorted," Gina said with a mixture of pride and guilt. "My mum thinks I'm at a sleepover."

Declan walked out of her earshot and made his call.

"Yeah," said the gruff voice.

"Why the hell haven't you been answering your phone?" Declan said. "I've left loads of messages. Why didn't you get back to me?"

"My phone's been off. I was on a job," Stevie replied.

"Well, it's your loss, because Cotter has just been in the warehouse, taken something from one of the sacks of cocoa beans and left."

"What the hell was it?"

"I don't know. I couldn't see."

"You're useless!"

"Get lost! You should be thanking me. I've just found out that Cotter's probably involved in some sort of smuggling racket."

"Where is he now?"

"How should I know? He left the warehouse and now I'm locked in here." Declan omitted to say that Gina was there too. He knew it wouldn't go down very well with Stevie.

"Well," Stevie scoffed, "it won't do you any harm. You can just sit tight until someone opens up in the morning."

"But how am I going to explain being locked in the warehouse all night?"

"Use your bloody initiative, soft lad! You don't want Cotter finding out you were there. Listen, you've done okay," he said begrudgingly. "I'll speak to you in the morning."

Tom looked in his rear-view mirror and saw the blue lights flashing in the darkness. His instinct was to put his foot down, try to outrun them but, as if they could read his mind, the siren began to wail its warning. He pulled over onto the hard shoulder and took a deep breath, smoothing his hair back with his hands.

The two policemen kept him waiting as they sat in their car, checking his registration number on their computer database. They then walked along either side of his vehicle, shining their torches into it.

Tom put his window down and asked politely, "Can I help you, officers?"

"Driver's licence, please," a thickset officer said.

Tom got it out of the glove compartment and handed it over for inspection.

"Would you mind getting out of the car, sir, and going over to my colleague on the grass verge?"

Tom did as he was told.

"Look, could you please tell me why you've pulled me over?" Tom asked tensely.

He didn't get an answer. He watched anxiously, as the light from the officer's torch probed every corner of the car's interior.

"Would you open the boot for us please, sir?" the second officer asked.

Tom obliged and the door of the boot glided open to reveal the gaping sack inside.

"What's this?" the officer said, feeling around the contents.

"They're cocoa beans, officer. It's my business. I import them. These particular ones were damaged so I was going to dispose of them. Now, are you going to tell me why you've stopped me?"

"We clocked you travelling at a speed of ninety-six miles per hour. Do you know what the motorway speed limit is?"

Tom's tense face cracked into a smile.

"Do you find breaking the law amusing, sir?" the burly officer asked.

"Of course not," Tom replied.

"Blow into this." The second officer produced a breathalyzer and held it to Tom's mouth.

The breathalyzer pinged and the policeman shook his head. "He's clear."

The burly policeman seemed disappointed. He handed Tom his licence back. "You'll receive a letter in the post regarding a fine and points on your licence. I hope that I won't have to pull you over in the future, sir."

"Oh, so do I, officer," Tom said with genuine sincerity.

Gina climbed up the rolling ladder and checked the lot numbers on the mound of sacks that Tom had just replaced there.

She pulled out her notebook and found where she'd copied down the numbers. "Yeah," she called down to Declan. "They're all lot number fifty-four, the same number as on the piece of paper. You were right about the code. Do you think it could be drugs?"

"Could be." He didn't sound convinced. "But if it is, we're only talking tiny amounts. It fitted in his jacket!"

"Yeah, but it could be a sample of some new super-drug or…what about some kind of detonator for a bomb?" Gina suggested, her mind whirring.

"We could guess all night, but we'll never get to know, stuck in here." Declan gave a frustrated sigh.

"I can think of worse places to be stuck," Gina said,

pressing her nose into the mound of coarse sacks. "God, I love that smell! I love this place! It just reminds me so much of my dad; even the ladders." She tapped the rung with her hand. "Sometimes, when I came to visit the warehouse, Dad would let me climb a little way up, and then he'd push it and I'd go whizzing along the shelves. It was great."

"I could push you on it now, if you want?" Declan said, brightening up.

"Go on then." She grinned, gripping onto the rungs.

"Hold tight," Declan warned, as he gave the side of the ladder an almighty shove. He watched in alarm as Gina rocketed down the length of the aisle, the ladder rattling along the runners. It hit the rubber stoppers at the end and rebounded, almost throwing her off. He ran to her.

"Are you okay? I had no idea it would be *that* fast or that loud."

She laughed giddily, unable to let go of the ladder. "That was brilliant!"

Declan helped her down.

"Do you want a go?" she asked.

"No, we need to keep the noise down." He plonked down on the nearest pile of sacks. "You haven't got any food, have you? I'm starving."

Gina pulled out her lunchbox from her schoolbag and sat down beside him. "A soggy sandwich and a half-eaten packet of crisps – my leftovers. It's the best I can do."

He took them gratefully.

Gina wasn't even aware that she was staring at him as he ate. She let out a tiny sigh. Declan looked at her looking at him and started to pat his mouth.

"Have I got something on my face?" he asked.

"No," she replied.

"Oh, only you were looking at it like I had." He shrugged.

Gina felt her face heat up. "Yeah…well, maybe there was a little something but it's gone now," she lied.

She was grateful when his phone vibrated and took his attention off her.

"It's my mum," Declan said in surprise. "Mammy, it's a bit late for you to be phoning, isn't it?"

"Hi, sweetheart. Well I'm just lying here awake so I thought I might as well give you a ring. I know I shouldn't disturb you when you're busy, but Mrs. Mac rang to say that you were doing extra work, a night shift! I just wanted to tell you how pleased me and your daddy are."

"Oh, it's nothing…just a one-off."

"You know we miss you, love." Her voice quivered. "Please think about coming over. The life here will be good for you, Declan."

"Mammy, you're talking like you're in Australia or something. You're only a boat ride away. When I get some more money together I'll hop over and visit. I promise."

"Okay, see that you do. Now, Mrs. McManus tells me you've got a new *friend*. A girl, Gina, isn't it?"

"Mrs. McManus is very good at keeping you informed,"

he said, rolling his eyes at Gina.

"Well, someone has to; you never volunteer any information. Anyway, what's she like? Would *I* approve of her?"

Declan looked across at Gina and smiled. Gina shrugged, mouthing to him, "What?"

"Yes, Mammy, you'd approve," he said, holding Gina's baffled stare.

"Umm, okay then, but don't be getting too serious. You've got your whole life ahead of you."

"You can talk. You and Daddy met when you were still both in nappies."

"That is entirely different," she said self-righteously.

"How?"

"Well…I don't know, it just is. Now don't be questioning me, I'm your mother."

Declan chuckled. "Okay, Mammy, whatever you say. Look, I've got to get on. I'll speak to you soon. Give my love to everyone."

"I will, sweetheart, and Declan…"

"Yes, Mammy?"

"Remember to stay out of trouble."

"What was that about?" Gina asked, when Declan had rung off.

"Just my mam fussing. She seems to be under the impression that we're going out together." She picked up a forced laugh in his voice.

"Us! Going out? Ha!" She rolled her eyes in mock outrage, while inside her head she shouted at him, *Please say you want to. Go on, Declan, say you want to!*

"I know, ridiculous, isn't it?" His frivolous tone was gone. His voice sounded rich and serious. Every other noise seemed to have been silenced. All Gina could hear was her own breathing; all she could see was Declan's face. Was she imagining it, or did he just lean in, ever so slightly, towards her? Did his head just tilt a fraction? Did his lips just part, the tiniest bit?

This is it! He's going to do it, she thought. *Why's he being so slow, so shy? I'm just going to have to go for it. It's now or never!*

Gina shuffled towards him and tilted her head in the opposite direction to avoid clashing noses. She closed her eyes and leaned in until she was a hair's breadth away from his lips. There she hovered in exquisite anticipation. But seconds passed and nothing happed. Gina opened one eye to investigate.

Declan found himself eyeball to eyeball with her. He was convinced that she could see into his very soul and he shot away, like she'd given him an electric shock.

"What is it? What's wrong?" she asked, dismayed.

"Nothing. I just can't, I'm sorry," he mumbled.

"But...but you looked like you wanted to," Gina said, mortified.

"Well I can't. I don't."

Gina saw how flustered he was and a thought suddenly dawned on her. "Oh my God! I know what you're up to!"

"What? Do you?" Declan panicked, his voice squeaked.

"You've got a girlfriend, haven't you? You're feeling guilty. That's why you haven't introduced me to any of your mates. You're afraid that they'll tell me or tell *her*."

Declan tried to hide his relief. "No, I haven't got a girlfriend, honest!"

"Then what's the matter?" she said, feeling literally repulsive.

"It's me, not you," Declan said hurriedly.

She winced. *Is he really using that line on me?*

"I'm sorry. It's complicated. It's not a good time for us." He looked pained.

"What does that even mean?" she said, confused and humiliated. "Oh, forget it. It's my mistake." She picked up her bag, sucking in her cheeks to try to stop herself from blubbing. "I'm going to sleep down there."

"Okay," he said quietly. "I'll stay awake. We don't want them to open up in the morning and find us snoring."

"Fine, thanks," she muttered as she lay down on the itchy sacks, wishing the earth would swallow her up. It was going to be a long night.

Tom pulled up in the car park of the motorway motel. He looked around at the smattering of other vehicles and, seeing that they were all empty, he bent down and felt inside the leather lining of the driver's seat. He pulled out the pouch and put it in his pocket.

He walked through the slightly tatty reception area and gave a friendly nod to the young woman behind the desk. He took the lift up to the second floor and gave two sharp knocks on room 203.

"Mr. Egon, it's me," he said.

A sickly-looking face peered round the door, inspecting Tom through his half-moon glasses. "Come on in, Mr. Cotter," Mr. Egon wheezed. "I hope you're not going to disappoint me this time."

28 THE SURPRISE

Gina yawned as she walked slowly home from school. She'd hardly been able to keep her eyes open all day, after a sleepless, awkward night in the warehouse.

Her phone rang and she cringed. It was Declan.

"Hi," she answered flatly.

"Howdy partner, did you make it to school okay?" He sounded far too breezy.

"Yeah."

"You were a real pro at sneaking out of the warehouse this morning. I had to creep out, hide round the corner for a bit, and then come back in, pretending I'd just arrived. Kylie was convinced I'd been out on the beers all night; she said I looked shocking." He laughed but Gina didn't join in.

"You feeling okay? You don't sound very happy," he asked tentatively.

"I'm fine," she said brusquely. "What do you want, Declan?"

"Just wanted to see you were all right. You know…after last night."

"What do you mean? Why shouldn't I be all right?"

"No reason. It's just you didn't really say much after… after…" he stumbled.

"After I made an idiot of myself, you mean?"

Declan gave a heavy sigh. "Oh God, Gina, you didn't. I think you're brilliant, you know that, don't you? I love hanging out with you but…"

"But you don't fancy me. It's okay. I've got the message." She bit her quivering lip. "My mistake."

"I just can't get involved with anyone right now."

"Why? Have you taken a vow of celibacy?" Sarcasm didn't make her feel any better.

"Please say we can still be mates," he pleaded.

"Declan, the truth is I need you. I want to find out what Tom is up to. I want to know what was in that sack; if it's got anything to do with my dad. So yes, we're still mates."

"I want to help you."

"Thanks. Then let's just pretend that the most cringeworthy moment of my life never happened last night, okay?"

"Okay," he said quietly.

"Anyway, what's Tom been up to today?" she asked in a businesslike manner.

"I've hardly seen him. He's been in and out of the warehouse all day. He seems very pleased with himself. Him and Kylie have been deep in conversation in the office. She's been on the phone loads, but she won't tell me what's going on. She says that I might tell you and spoil the surprise."

"Well, I've just walked onto my street and his car's outside our house so let's see what he's got to say for himself."

"Don't ask him about the sack! Don't say anything to anyone," Declan panicked.

"Of course I won't. Do you think I'm stupid? I'll speak to you later."

Gina braced herself as she opened the front door, still thinking about how she could question Tom without raising his suspicions. However, her plans were abandoned as she walked into a whirlwind of activity and excitement. Her mother was flapping around, with Danny standing in the hallway, grinning like a Cheshire cat.

"Gina!" Danny ran to her. "Uncle Tom's taking us all to Disneyland for the weekend!"

"What? Disneyland, Paris?"

"Yep! Isn't that brilliant?" Danny said, dancing around as if he'd just scored a match-winning goal.

"But why?"

"Don't ask me." He shrugged. "He just thought it would be a nice surprise. Even Mum's dead excited and she gets sick on the teacup ride."

Gina grabbed her mother mid-flap.

"Mum, what's going on?"

"Oh, Gina, love. My head's spinning. Tom arrived saying he's just closed a really good business deal and he's taking us all away to celebrate. He just sprang it on me. Sorry I didn't have time to tell you, but don't worry, I've packed for you already. Go upstairs and check that I've put in the right things."

"But when? How?"

"Flight leaves in three hours, taxi should be here in thirty minutes. Tom arranged everything secretly – can you believe it! And we're spending a night in Paris itself. Paris, Gina! I've always wanted to go there." Her mother's face lit up. "Oh, sorry, love, how was Becky's? Did you get any sleep?"

"Forget Becky's," Gina said in frustration. "We shouldn't go anywhere with Tom."

Her mum looked stunned. All the joy drained out of her.

"What are you talking about? Of course we're all going."

"I'm sorry, Mum. We really shouldn't. We don't know what he's playing at."

Her mum looked close to tears. "He's not playing at anything. Your Uncle Tom is doing something lovely for us. Please, Gina, don't be like this."

Danny had been watching in confusion. "What's up, Gina? What's your problem?"

"Sorry, Danny, but I don't think we should be going away with Tom."

"Why?"

"Because...because. Don't you think it's odd, him just whisking us off like this?"

"No! I think *you're* odd, Gina. Why do you try to spoil everything that Uncle Tom wants to do for us? It's not fair!" he shouted at her.

Tom emerged from the living room. "What *do* you think I'm playing at, Gina? I'm dying to know."

His presence cast a shadow over her.

"Nothing," she mumbled. "It's just all too quick. We need more time."

"But spontaneity makes things much more exciting." He smiled broadly. "Now, enough of this silliness. Everything's paid for. Do as your mum says. Go and get ready." He gestured towards the stairs.

She swallowed hard. "No."

"This is the last time I'm going to ask you, Gina. Go and get ready," he said threateningly.

She stuck out her chin defiantly.

"All right then, me, your mum and Danny will go without you," he said matter-of-factly.

Gina looked to her flustered mother.

"Oh, no, Tom. I can't go without Gina."

"Yes you can. Danny, will you go without Gina?" Tom asked gently.

Danny scratched his head nervously. He couldn't look at his sister. "Yeah. I'm sorry, Gina, but I really want to go and you're just being weird about it. It's only a couple of days. You'll be all right without us, won't you?" he asked, talking rapidly.

"Of course she will," Tom insisted.

Clare ushered Tom into the kitchen. They were whispering intently for what seemed like an age. Then it sounded as though Tom was making a phone call. When they finally stepped back into the hall it was her mum who spoke, as if she was reading from a script.

"Gina, I'm going to ask you again. Will you come and have a lovely time in France with us?"

"No, I'm not going with him." She saw Tom cross his arms.

"*Please* come, Gina," Danny begged. "It won't be the same without you."

Gina shook her head sadly at Danny. "I'm sorry, Danny."

Her mum continued. "Well, in that case I'm going to let you stay here, but not on your own. We've phoned Kylie and she's kindly agreed to stay with you for the weekend."

"I'm sixteen! I don't need a babysitter," Gina protested.

"They're my conditions. You either agree to be looked after by Kylie or we'll make you come with us," her mum said firmly.

"Fine, but you shouldn't be going either."

Tom broke his silence. He smiled coldly. "No matter how hard you try, you can't offend me, Gina. I understand your behaviour. Your road to recovery is bound to suffer setbacks, but we can't let your illness damage this family. Your mum won't let you dictate what happens any more. It's not helping you get better. We all just want to see you well again."

"Oh, Gina!" Her tearful mum flung arms around her.

"Don't worry about me, Mum. I'll be fine. You go and have a nice time. I'll go up to my room and let you get sorted." Gina started up the stairs. "By the way, Tom, thanks for dropping me off at Becky's last night."

Her mum noted Gina's sudden mood swing with dismay.

"Oh," Tom said in surprise. "That's fine. I was glad to help."

"Did you get home okay?"

Tom looked puzzled. "Yeah."

"Did you go straight home?" she asked casually.

"Yeah," he replied.

"You didn't stop off anywhere?"

Tom's eyes flickered up to her, his brow suddenly furrowed. "Why the interrogation? No, I didn't stop off anywhere."

"Okay, well have a nice time in France."

As she climbed the stairs she sensed their baffled eyes on her.

Gina closed her bedroom door and chose a photo to talk to amongst the collage.

"Don't worry," she told her dad; he was carrying a toddler-sized Danny on his shoulders. "I'm going to find out what that liar is up to, even if it kills me."

29 THE DAY TRIP

Gina and Kylie sat on the sofa in their dressing gowns, eating bowls of cereal and watching music videos on the TV.

"What do you want to do today, babe?" Kylie asked. "I was thinking we should hit the shops. We could even get a free makeover in a department store. All we'd have to do is go to the make-up counters and pretend I'm getting married and you're my bridesmaid."

"Whatever you want," Gina laughed.

"Of course we could always phone Declan? Invite him to hang out with us; that's if you don't mind me tagging along, playing gooseberry." Kylie winked.

"You wouldn't be a gooseberry. There's nothing going on between me and him," Gina mumbled.

"Oh God, you two!" Kylie said, exasperated. "You need

your heads knocking together. I don't know what you're waiting for."

"Declan doesn't fancy me."

"Yes he does, he told me."

"Then he lied to you because I know he doesn't for a *fact*, so please let's not talk about it."

"Okay." Kylie grimaced, seeing how upset Gina looked.

"Kylie." Gina lowered the volume on the TV. "Where do the sacks of cocoa beans come from in the warehouse?"

"Hey? Why on earth do you want to talk about that? Declan was asking all about the business as well. You two aren't thinking of going into competition with Tom, are you?" She gave a neighing laugh.

"I'm just interested. I know they come from the Ivory Coast, but who supplies them?"

Kylie switched into work mode. "Well, we deal with a few different suppliers. The Ivory Coast is the world's largest producer of cocoa, you know. We go with the most competitive price, but we like to keep continuity. It's good for Tom to build up a working relationship with suppliers."

"So does he ever get to meet them? Do they ever come to see him?"

"He's certainly been on a few business trips there over the years, but most communication is done by phone and email nowadays."

"Declan told me that Tom had a couple of visitors a few weeks back and you got sent out for an early lunch."

"Oh, yeah." Kylie smiled knowingly. "Henri Sissouma. He took a shine to me. He's some kind of business associate of Tom's from the Ivory Coast. First time I'd met him. The poor fella with him looked like he was at death's door, jaundiced and thin as a twig."

"Have you seen them since?" Gina asked.

"No, but Henri's phoned the office to ask me out. He didn't even remember my name but he must be keen. He left me his number and said if I ever fancy dinner, to give him a call."

Gina sprang up from the sofa. She knew this must be the man who gave Tom the code for the sack.

"You've got his number?"

"Yeah, what can I say? I can't help it if I'm irresistible to men." Kylie batted her eyelashes. "Anyway, why are you so excited?"

Gina's mind was racing. Her eyes darted around as Kylie looked on in bemusement.

"Kylie," Gina said gravely. "I need you to do me a massive favour."

"Anything for you, babe," Kylie answered dubiously.

"Would you call up Henri Sissouma and see if he'll go out with you, just the one date, that's all?"

"Why?"

"I just need you to find out more about him. What exactly he does, what's his connection with Tom; normal stuff you'd talk about on a date."

"But why do you want to know?"

Gina chewed her lip, debating how much to tell Kylie.

"I think there might be something dodgy going on between this man and Tom."

"Like what?"

"I'm not sure. That's why it would be great if you could get him to talk to you."

Kylie shook her head. She got up and walked over to the fish tank. She stared at the fish silently gliding around in the water and sighed.

"Gina, I know you've got some issues with Tom but this is taking things a bit too far, babe. I've worked with him for six years – I'd know if something dodgy was going on."

"Yeah, I know I'm probably wrong, but all I'm asking is one date, one chat."

Kylie lifted up the hood of the fish tank. She opened the tub of flakes that sat next to it. "Say there is something going on, it's not as if this fella is going to confess to me over dinner, is it?"

"No, of course not, but he might tell you something useful."

Kylie started to shake the fish food into the tank as she stared into space. "He was quite an impressive-looking fella, I suppose, and I bet he'd take me somewhere nice. Hmm… Oh, go on then, one date, and if I don't find out anything, you've got to promise you'll get off Tom's case."

Kylie suddenly noticed the hundreds of fish-food flakes sinking slowly into the water. "Oh God, look what I've done. I've emptied the whole tub in!"

"Don't worry. I'll sort it out later. You're a star!" Gina trilled. "Can you phone him right now? If he takes you to a restaurant I could be there; on another table, in case you need me."

Kylie let out another neighing laugh. "That's sweet, but I won't need a wingman. I can handle myself."

"But—"

"But nothing. I do this my way, or not at all."

Fifteen minutes later Gina phoned Declan's mobile. She could hear heavy rock music in the background; definitely not Declan's choice.

"Declan," she said. "Where are you? Can you come round?"

"Sorry, I can't. I'm spending the day with Uncle Stevie."

"Oh, are you doing anything nice?"

"I don't know yet. He's taking me on a bit of a mystery tour." Declan scowled at the driver.

"Listen, Declan, Tom's taken Mum and Danny to Disneyland. I refused to go. But the good news is that I've persuaded Kylie to go on a date with the man who gave Tom the code."

"What! The guy who came into the warehouse? How did you do that?"

"Don't panic. I kept it vague. Kylie doesn't think Tom's ever done anything dodgy but she's willing to find out more about this guy for us."

Declan looked nervously at Stevie, hoping he couldn't hear Gina, but Stevie seemed engrossed in his music, humming tunelessly as he drove.

Declan lowered his voice. "That would be great but it could be dangerous. We don't know who we're dealing with."

"I do," Gina said, pleased with herself. "Didn't Kylie tell you that he rang her to ask her out? His name's Henri Sissouma and I'm *not* putting Kylie in any danger. They've arranged to meet in a restaurant in town on Monday night, where there'll be plenty of people around. He's travelling up from London."

"Still, I'd be happier if I was there, keeping an eye on things."

"I've already suggested that. She won't let us."

He saw Stevie give him a sideways glance. "Look, we'll talk about it later. I've got to go," Declan said hurriedly.

"Okay. Have a nice day with your uncle."

"Was that the Wilson girl? You've been spending far too much time with her. Remember that Cotter is who we're interested in. The girl was only ever a means to an end."

His words made Declan feel sick with shame. "Actually it was Kylie, Tom Cotter's secretary," he lied. "We're friendly. She likes to tell me all the gossip. She phoned to say that she's going on a date with Henri Sissouma."

Declan watched for Stevie's reaction. The man's wild eyebrows shot up.

"So you know who I'm talking about?" Declan said. "What else do you know about him?"

Stevie didn't answer his question. "Did I hear you say that you're going to be there, keeping an eye on things?"

"My, what big ears you have," Declan sneered. "No, she won't let me."

"Well, I want a report of every word Sissouma says to her, do you understand?"

"Sure. Are we nearly there? We've been driving for ages."

"God, it's like taking a toddler out!" Stevie griped. "Yes, it's down here."

He turned down into a road where fine-looking, detached houses flanked the tree-lined pavements. The car crawled along, until they neared the one house that stood out from the rest. It was dilapidated and set back from the road. Ivy was beginning to creep over the rotting windows and the front garden was neglected and overgrown.

"That's the place." Stevie pointed. "Now we just sit and wait."

"What for?"

"For the owner to leave."

"Who lives here?"

"You'll see. Now, how about more music? We might be waiting some time." Stevie leaned across and rifled through his CD collection in the glove compartment. "What about a bit of Pink Floyd? We could play some air guitar together. Would you like that?" The man gave a throaty chuckle as Declan dropped his head into his hands.

It was an hour before the spindly man appeared at the end of the driveway. The wind lifted his wispy comb-over so that it flapped in the breeze. He patted it down, smoothing it across his head before pushing his half-moon glasses up the bridge of his nose, wrapping his coat up to his chin and setting off down the road.

"That's him!" Declan said excitedly. "That's the man who was in the warehouse with Mr. Cotter and Henri Sissouma."

"Of course it is." Stevie shook his head, despondently. "This isn't a coincidence, soft lad. I tracked him down from the car reg you got me."

"Well, now what? Are we going to follow him?"

"No, *you're* going to get into the house."

"What do you mean 'get into the house'?"

"*You*" – he poked Declan in the chest – "get inside *that* house."

"What? *Break in?*" he said in disbelief.

"You may not have to. Look at the state of it. Looks like it's about to fall down anyway. There's probably some window hanging off its hinges at the back," Stevie said helpfully.

"No way!" Declan protested. "You do it."

"Don't be so stupid. I can't do stuff like this."

"And neither can I! What if he catches me? He'll call the police."

"He won't and if he did, I'd sort it out. Anyway he's not going to catch you, is he, because he isn't there. Now, off you go and take pictures with your mobile of whatever you find, but don't touch anything." He handed Declan a pair of gloves. "You'd better wear these."

"This is breaking and entering. There must be another way to do it."

"Sorry, lad, sadly for me, at this point in time, you're all I've got. But the better the job you do, the sooner you'll be off the hook. Now, don't worry, remember, I've got your back." He winked.

Declan's heart was pounding as he climbed over the high rusty gate at the side of the house and jumped down into the back garden. The back of the house looked even more neglected than the front. The garden was so overgrown that there could have been a tiger lurking in the tall grass. The untamed plants, trees and hedges shielded the whole area from nosy neighbours and every curtain on every back window was shut.

He tried the peeling back door but it was rock solid. He tried to prise open the windows on the ground floor but they were stuck down with paint. He looked up to the top windows. They too appeared to be closed and he wasn't going to attempt to shimmy up the rotting drainpipe to see if he could open them.

He ran his hands down his face in despair, knowing that Stevie would never leave him alone if he came back empty-handed. He took a step back and surveyed the house again. His eyes started at the top and worked their way down, slowly. That's when he noticed the glimmer of light peeping out from behind a row of overflowing bins. The bins were lined up against the back wall. He pushed them out of the way to reveal a row of long, narrow, filthy windows.

"A cellar!" He grinned.

He lay down on the damp ground and wiped the grubby panes, but soon discovered that the filth was on the inside as well. He used his fingernails to try to prise each of the windows open. The last one came away easily and he held it triumphantly aloft with one hand and put his head and shoulders through the narrow opening.

Everywhere was covered in a film of gritty dust. The room reminded him of the metal workshop at his old school. There were partitioned workstations along one wall, each with a piece of equipment in it and an angled lamp shining over it. He recognized a circular saw, a rotating stand, clamps, planes, files, even a microscope. There was a sink nearby with long, thin hoses attached to the taps. A battered chair on wheels sat by the workbenches. Declan pictured the sickly-looking man using it to whizz from one workstation to another. *Maybe he's a mad scientist building a bloody space rocket!* he thought with amusement.

In the centre of the cellar was a large wooden table strewn with tools, many of which he couldn't identify. But he did recognize the silver electronic weighing scales. He knew that they could be used to weigh bags of money. He knew that they could be used to weigh drugs.

I need to get a better look. He leaned further through the narrow window, stretching his neck like a tortoise venturing out of his shell. He stopped.

There's something moving inside the house! It's coming from upstairs. It's getting closer! What the hell is it? He strained his ears. *Clattering? Scratching? Panting… Oh my God, it's a DOG!*

Before he could move, the canine flew down the cellar steps and leaped up at him, its jaws a whisker away from biting a chunk out of Declan's face. Declan pulled away in shock, whacking his head on the window frame. He cowered on the ground, one hand on his throbbing head, the other on his thumping chest, as the enormous dog bounced up and down at the window, barking and snarling.

His phone went off. He grappled around for it in the pocket of his hoodie.

"What?"

"Get out of there now," Stevie barked. "He's come back

and he's heading for the back garden. I can hear that dog from here!"

Declan looked around in panic, ready to run, but the man was already approaching him.

"Can I help you?"

Declan noted the man's distinct accent. *What is he? German? Austrian?*

"You nearly gave me a heart attack," Declan gasped. "I'm just looking for my cat. I think he may have crawled in here. He's just a kitten – he keeps getting lost." Declan's performance screamed "liar" to anyone watching.

"I suppose you think it must be easy to break into my property? Who's going to stop you? After all, I hardly look able to. Be warned though, you don't want to mess with me."

"No, honest. I wasn't going to rob you or anything. It's just my cat."

The man gave a wheezy laugh that shook his bony frame. "If you really do have a cat down there," he said pointing to the cellar, "then I'm afraid my dog will have torn it apart by now. Why don't you give me your address and maybe I can send you the pieces in the post?"

Declan laughed nervously. "You're joking, right?"

"I'm not known for my sense of humour."

"It's okay. I don't reckon he went in there after all. He's probably found his way home by now." Declan stood up to leave. "I'll let you get on. I'm sorry for coming on to your property." He started to walk away, hardly daring to believe that the man would let him go.

The man held up his hand to stop Declan. "I won't bother the police about this because I have friends who could easily find out who you are and where you live. They would pay you a visit that would leave a lasting impression on you. Now run home to your *moeder* and don't ever think of coming back here. And remember, don't be afraid of me, be afraid of who I know."

30 TOUGH LOVE

"It looks worse than it did yesterday," Kylie groaned, as she swished the little net through the murky waters of the fish tank. "All those flakes have gone gooey."

"Don't worry," Gina said. "Danny will be okay about it. I'm sure there'll be something he can put in it to clear the water."

The noise of a taxi engine sent them both to the front window.

"They're back!" Kylie tottered to open the front door.

Gina's mum and Danny bustled into the hallway. Tom was behind, laden down with bags.

Gina's kisses and hugs stopped abruptly when she got to Tom.

He smiled at her, saying, "Gina, you missed a great weekend!"

"Yeah, Gina, it was the best. You should have come,"

Danny said, bounding into the living room.

Kylie tried to intercept him. "Danny, don't panic, but I had a little accident. Put a bit too much food into your tank. It looks worse than it is, doesn't it, Gina?"

"Yeah, it'll be easy to sort out," Gina said optimistically.

Danny's face fell when he saw the green hue of the water. "Are the fish all right?"

"They're all fine. I've counted them," Gina said.

"Don't worry about it, Danny boy," Tom said. "I'll sort it out."

"Well, I'll be off then." Kylie sidled towards the door.

"Thanks so much. Have you girls had a good time?" Clare asked.

"Yeah. Kylie's been great." Gina smiled.

Tom rooted through the numerous bags. "This is for you, Kylie. Just a small thank you."

Kylie clapped her hands, taking the Tiffany's bag and pulling out the small rectangular box.

"Oh, Tom!" she gasped, as she pulled out a delicate white-gold necklace. "It's beautiful and it's from Tiffany's!"

"Well, Clare and I wanted to show you how much we appreciated your help with Gina."

Gina bristled. *Clare and I…! Your help with Gina!*

"Don't look so fed up, Gina." Tom was looking directly at her. "We've got a present or two in here for you."

Tom plonked himself down in her dad's armchair.

"I'll be off," Kylie said, blowing a communal kiss.

"Gina, you would have loved Paris." Her mum's eyes sparkled. "It's such a beautiful city."

"No, Disneyland was loads better," Danny interrupted. "I wasn't into all the Mickey Mouse stuff, but the park had brilliant rides."

Tom looked pleased with himself. "Well, seeing as this trip was such a success, we ought to think bigger next time."

Next time? He's trying to take over our bloody lives, Gina thought.

"I've been thinking about summer. I think this family deserves to go somewhere really, really special."

Gina was becoming more agitated. There was something in Tom's pompous tone that unnerved her.

"Where?" Danny asked, wide-eyed.

"Somewhere you've always wanted to go, all of you," he said teasingly. "Somewhere I know your dad was desperate to take you."

"Trinidad?" her mum said in disbelief.

"Trinidad!" Danny punched the air.

"*Trinidad!*" Gina said in outrage.

"Yes, what could be better than fulfilling Marty's ambition to take his family home?" Tom proclaimed proudly. "We can visit relatives, go to his childhood haunts, we could even scatter his ashes there…he'd have liked that, wouldn't he?"

Gina was flabbergasted. "You've got no right! There's no way *you're* taking us. Why are you doing this? Are you

272

trying to buy yourself a family…? Because we're not for sale!"

Tom looked rattled. He smoothed his hair back with his hands. "I'm doing this for your dad."

"You weren't even a good friend to my dad," Gina said.

"You don't know what you're talking about," her mum snapped. "Tom *was* a good friend."

"Well, it seems to me that you were happy to come here and play at being 'Uncle Tom', but you never let my dad into your *real* world, did you? The world of your posh clubs and rich associates. Didn't you think he was good enough to mix with them?"

"You couldn't be more wrong," Tom said. "Years ago, before you'll even remember, I took your dad to all my clubs; tried to introduce him to good contacts in the business world. Isn't that right, Clare?"

Her mum nodded.

"But it was your dad who wasn't interested," Tom said.

"Well maybe that was because of the kind of people you deal with," Gina said accusingly.

"No, it was because your father lacked ambition," Tom barked back.

Gina glared at him. Tom immediately looked remorseful.

"I'm sorry, Gina. I shouldn't have said that." Tom turned to her mum. "I didn't mean it, Clare. I thought I could handle all this abuse, but I'm beginning to wonder if I can."

"Gina, apologize to Tom," her mum said angrily.

"So you're siding with him?" Gina said.

"There are no sides," her mum said wearily. "This isn't a battle."

"It is, and I'm not going to let him win," Gina said, storming from the room and grabbing a set of keys from the kitchen drawer.

Gina ran all the way to the allotment. She unlocked the creaking wooden gate and surveyed her dad's plot in confusion. It looked like a digger had turned over the earth. Great mounds of soil had been piled up at the sides.

Gina's attention was caught by the flapping doors on the shed. She looked in and found that floorboards had been ripped up, exposing the grass below. Their table, chairs and gardening equipment had been thrown into one corner like it was a scrapheap.

"What the hell has he done to Dad's allotment?"

"Gina!" Mum had followed her, puffing and panting. "What's happened here?"

"It's Tom! He told us he was going to look after Dad's allotment but he's wrecked it."

Her mum stumbled around for an explanation. "Tom must have some reason for this."

"Then you phone him now and ask him."

"I'll phone if you promise that afterwards we can talk about you and Tom."

Her mum phoned and Gina listened in.

"Tom, I'm with Gina at the allotment. We just wanted to know what's going on with it. We're a bit surprised by how it looks."

There was a momentary silence before he made a laughing sound. "God, I'm sorry. It must look terrible to you. Don't worry, I had to get rid of all the bad soil. I'm going to cover it with some good quality stuff."

"And the shed?" her mum asked.

"Well…the floorboards were rotting. I'm getting a new one, bigger, better. I wasn't going to tell you until it was all done. I thought it would be a nice surprise."

Gina shook her head and her mum said, "It would have been good to be consulted, Tom."

"Yeah, sorry, Clare. I suppose that I've been overenthusiastic."

"It's okay. You meant well. I'll see you later," she replied.

"Mum, he's lying. Our shed wasn't rotting."

Her mum put a hand up to silence her. "Tom's explained things and I'm happy with that. Now forget the allotment. We need to talk about you and him. This appalling behaviour towards him has got to stop. I understand about Trinidad, but Tom's heart is in the right place."

Gina looked gravely at her mother. "We've got to get him out of our lives, Mum. You don't really know him."

"For God's sake, I've known Tom for years."

"He's up to something," Gina blurted out. "At the warehouse…there's something going on."

"What are you talking about?" Her mum sighed.

"We saw him…me and Declan. In the middle of the night. Tom came back to the warehouse, slashed open a sack and got something out."

She saw her mum's face cloud over. "What the hell were you doing in the warehouse in the middle of the night!?"

"We were trying to find the sack. Tom had this code, you see, written on a piece of paper, and Declan sussed out that it identified a particular sack of cocoa beans. So we went looking for it, but then Tom came in and took something out of one of the sacks…we couldn't see what it was, but it must have been something dodgy, otherwise why would he have waited to get it until night-time? Anyway, once he'd got whatever it was, Tom left and we were locked in the warehouse all night," she said breathlessly, waiting for the revelation to hit her mother.

"Was this the other night; when you told me you were at Becky's sleepover?" Her mum's hackles were rising.

"Yes," Gina replied meekly.

"So, let me get this straight." Her mum crossed her arms, her voice irate. "You lied to me and then sneaked off and spent the night with Declan in Tom's warehouse, where you spied on him, because you thought you'd found a secret code that meant he was coming back to his warehouse to get something out of a sack, is that right?"

"You make it sound bad when you say it like that, but yeah."

"And do tell me again, what exactly was in the sack?"

"Well…we couldn't see, could we, but he definitely took *something* out of it," Gina said with conviction.

"So, in fact, it could have been a handful of cocoa beans, for all you know?"

Gina hesitated. "Well yeah…but…no! Why would he come back at night to get some beans?" she said triumphantly.

"Why the hell shouldn't he? Maybe he had to check them urgently. Maybe he was worried that they were damaged cargo he had to do something about."

"But the next day, when I asked him what he'd done that night, he said that he'd just gone home." Surely this was the winning blow?

"So what? Maybe he didn't think it was even worth mentioning that he'd gone to his *own* warehouse *before* going home. He's not answerable to you, young lady. You and Declan have either got two of the most fertile imaginations or you're just being unbelievably malicious, coming up with this ridiculous story to try and turn me against Tom."

"No, it's true, Mum, honest!"

She watched tears prick her mother's eyes. "For God's

sake, Gina, your mind's so twisted against Tom that I bet you jumped at the chance to believe some rubbish that Declan told you. I've a good mind to tell Tom that you broke into his warehouse."

"No! Please, you mustn't tell him!" she panicked. "I didn't break in anyway, Declan just stayed in there after work. We didn't do any damage."

Her mum's lips pursed. "So, what *did* you and Declan do all night, locked up in there?"

Gina couldn't meet her mother's stare. "Nothing, Mum, honest. Nothing happened."

"I thought Declan was good for you but it sounds like he's just winding you up even more than before."

"He's not."

"Maybe I should stop you seeing him."

"You can't! It's not his fault. I made him spy on Tom. He didn't want to," she said protectively. "He's done it for me. Please don't stop me hanging around with him. I like being with him."

"Yeah and I like having Tom around and so does Danny. Tom cares about us. He's been a great support to me."

"Is there something going on between you and him?" Gina asked in trepidation.

"No, it's too soon for me, but who knows what will happen in the future."

"But what about Dad?" Gina's lips trembled.

"Can't you understand? I will never forget your father.

I will always love him, but he's dead, Gina and I'm still alive." She struck her chest. "So let *me* have a life!"

"But please, Mum, not with Tom. He's involved in something illegal. He knows what happened to Dad. Dad didn't kill himself!" she said fervently.

Clare threw her arms up in the air, and looked to the sky. "Enough, Gina! I can't go on like this. Your dad sent you a text, for God's sake. He was saying sorry to you for what he was about to do. What else do you need? Wouldn't it be simpler for all of us if we could believe that it was just a terrible accident? That your dad didn't kill himself and leave me with the guilt of thinking that I failed him? Do you have any idea how that makes me feel, Gina? And, all this time having to cope with you and your relentless denial and your paranoia about Tom."

"But—"

"But nothing! You've got to stop it, Gina," her mum shouted in despair. "Wake up now and accept what happened. It's time to move on, look to the future, and if I want Tom around, then he will be, and you'll just have to get used to it!"

Clare had just laid her exhausted head on the pillow when her mobile rang.

"Hi, Clare," Tom said. "Sorry to ring you so late but I just wanted to know if Gina had settled down. I stayed with Danny as long as I could, but I thought it'd be better if I was out of the way when you got back. She really upset him."

"I know and after he'd had such a great weekend too. He's fast asleep now. I had it out with Gina and when we got home she went straight to her room. I let her cry herself to sleep. Listening to her nearly killed me but I've decided that I've got to try a bit of 'tough love'. If she won't go back to see Dr. Havers then I have to think of my own strategies to bring her out of this."

"You're doing the right thing, Clare. I'm sorry that my Trinidad idea upset her. I really wanted to make her happy."

"It's a lovely suggestion, Tom, but you know how Gina's been about you since the inquest. She's focusing all her anger on you. It's out of hand. She's even been making Declan spy on you."

"What? Why?" Tom sounded alarmed.

"She's just determined for Declan to dig up something dodgy about you, about the business, any excuse to get rid of you."

"And what's the little toerag come up with?" His voice had stiffened.

Clare immediately regretted mentioning it. She didn't want to get Declan into trouble. He was a good lad really, even if he did have an overactive imagination. She suddenly felt the need to protect him.

"Oh, forget it, Tom. Declan hasn't said anything," she lied. "I think the poor lad's been caught in the middle. I know he loves working for you, but he'd also do anything to make Gina happy."

"So, he's been digging for dirt and come up with nothing?"

Clare heard the anger in Tom's voice.

"Yes, nothing," she said emphatically.

"I've got a good mind to sack him! Is this how he repays me for giving him a job?"

"Please, Tom, don't do that. He's just a teenager trying to impress a girl. Despite this, Declan's good for her. She's been so much better since she met him, and healthier – she's eating properly again and she's stopped touching the urn every time she comes into the room."

"Yeah, but that's thanks to me," Tom boasted.

"Maybe, but one thing's for sure, Declan makes her happy, so *promise me* you won't sack him."

There was a long pause.

"Promise, Tom!" Clare said earnestly.

"Okay, anything for you."

"And you won't hold a grudge against the boy, will you?" she asked nervously.

"No, of course not. I've forgotten about it already," he answered with an icy breeziness.

31 KYLIE'S DATE

Henri Sissouma had hardly paused for breath and they were already onto dessert. He'd spent the last hour and a half quaffing numerous glasses of champagne and regaling Kylie with details of his many assets.

His London apartment overlooked the Thames; his Italian leather sofas were the best money could buy; his home cinema system was the same one all top Hollywood stars insisted on having; and he invited Kylie to feel his biceps as testament to the quality of the gym in his spare room.

Kylie shovelled in another spoonful of tiramisu in order to stifle a yawn. The string quartet struck up again in the corner of the candlelit room.

Kylie tried to interrupt his flow. "This is a lovely restaurant, very classy. My last date took me to Pizza Hut."

Henri Sissouma tutted. His chunky rings clinked

against the champagne bottle as he refilled her glass. "How dare he? A woman of your refinement deserves the finer things in life, Karen."

"Oh, you've done it again." She wagged a manicured nail at him. "It's Kylie, not Karen."

"Of course, forgive me. Such a beautiful name, how could I forget it?"

"So, Henri," she said, deciding it was time to make her move, "I've heard all about your fast car and your swish apartment but what you haven't told me is what you do. You must have a great job. What are you? One of those entrepreneurs?"

He nodded approvingly. "As people say here, I have my fingers in lots of pies. I manage the business concerns in this country for a very wealthy and important man back home in the Côte d'Ivoire."

"And you do business with Tom?"

"Yes, we've been doing business together for a number of years."

"So, you deal in cocoa beans? Of course you do, our shipments are from the Ivory Coast."

The big man threw his head back, letting out a booming laugh that strained the buttons on his waistcoat. "My dear Karen, my boss doesn't supply beans."

"Oh," she said, stifling her annoyance. "What does he supply, then?"

"I don't wish to talk about business when I have such

283

beautiful company." He reached across the table and took her hand.

"Henri," Kylie said, giving him her sweetest smile, "I bet a man as impressive as you supplies something very special." She placed her other hand on top of his.

There was a twinkle in his champagne-blurred eyes as he replied, "Let me just say this; the chocolate made from the cocoa bean is said to induce a feeling of great happiness. Well, what my boss supplies also induces great happiness but it costs much, much more."

Kylie slapped his hand, playfully. "Henri, stop talking in riddles and tell me what it is."

"I've said too much already, *ma petite cherie*."

"Oh, go on," Kylie pouted. "I'm intrigued."

He smiled broadly and beckoned her to him. Kylie leaned across the table and Henri Sissouma whispered in her ear, his voice deadly serious. "If I told you, I'd have to kill you."

Kylie shot away from him, but her shocked expression only made Henri Sissouma roar with laughter.

"Oh forgive me," he spluttered, patting tears of laughter from his cheeks. "I am joking, of course, but the business between myself and Mr. Cotter is a private matter, you do understand, don't you?"

"Yes, of course," she said through gritted teeth.

Henri Sissouma pulled the chain of his gold fob watch, lifting it out of his waistcoat pocket. He flicked open the cover and tried to focus on telling the time.

"It's getting late, Karen, and I'm staying in a lovely hotel. I have a suite with a balcony. Would you like to come and see the view?"

Kylie rose from her chair, scraping it across the marble floor. "Sorry, Henri, but I make a rule of only going back to hotel rooms with men who can remember my name. Thanks for dinner though." With that, Kylie flounced out of the restaurant, leaving Henri Sissouma open-mouthed.

32 ALL AT SEA

Danny bounced up and down, the wind whipping him into a frenzy.

"After three," Danny shouted, his eyes wild. "One, two, three – GO!"

Danny, Gina and Declan took a running jump off the top of the towering sand dune. Declan flew through the air, landing on the beach, Gina collapsed in a heap at the foot of the dune and Danny remained near the top, entangled in the tall spiky grass that bound together the shifting sands with its roots.

"That's not fair. You two have got longer legs than me," Danny called out indignantly.

Declan scrambled back up the sliding sand and released him.

"Let's get you to the bottom," Declan said, rolling the boy down the hill.

Danny reached the beach, spitting sand out of his mouth. "Brilliant!" he said giddily. "Do it again!"

"Leave Declan alone and go and chase some sticks or something," Gina said.

"Just because you want to be alone so you can snog him," Danny sang.

Gina lunged at her brother. Danny sprang up and ran off along the massive expanse of beach. He held the ends of his coat out behind him, hoping that the fierce wind would lift him up like a human kite.

Gina shook her head in protest. "Ignore him. Danny's off his head. You do know that I'm *so* over that, don't you?"

"Yeah, I know," Declan muttered.

They walked along the beach, the wind blowing away the grime of the city.

"Why do you think Tom invited me today?" Declan asked.

Gina shrugged. "I suppose he's just trying to get in with me. He probably thinks I'd want you here. He's desperate to play happy families with us and Mum is letting him; she won't listen to me."

"What do you mean? You haven't told her anything, have you?" Declan sounded worried.

Gina clammed up. She couldn't bring herself to tell him about her confession to Mum. She knew he'd never trust her again if she did.

"No!" Gina said, as if she was insulted by his question.

"Anyway, do you still think it's drugs?"

"Well, what was it Sissouma told Kylie? 'It induces great happiness but costs much, much more.' Doesn't that sound like drugs to you? He's talking about getting high."

"Kylie reckons Sissouma's full of bull and she doesn't think Tom would be involved in drug trafficking."

"Well then he must be making a fortune from cocoa beans. Just look where he lives. Must feel like he's on holiday all the time here," Declan mused.

Gina knew what Declan meant. When stepping out of Tom's luxurious home they were greeted by alpine-scented woods, not the grey narrow streets outside their own houses. And a short walk through the trees brought them to these undulating sand dunes with views from the top that laid the whole horizon bare. The massive expanse of sand, the foaming waves crashing onto the shore, the huge skies, with the dazzling sun playing hide and seek behind the racing clouds. This place had always seemed to Gina like a different world from her neighbourhood, with its harsh docks, diesel-filled air and constant cacophony.

"If he takes us back to his house again we might get a chance to look around," Gina said.

"I wouldn't count on it. I felt his eyes on me all the time. Even when I went to the loo I found him loitering outside."

"You're being paranoid," Gina said uneasily.

"Hey, you two!" Tom's voiced boomed behind them.

"Keep walking straight on. We're heading to the marina. I want to show Declan something."

Declan pulled a face. "What's that about?" he asked Gina.

"Don't know," she replied, turning round and scowling as she saw her mum and Tom strolling shoulder to shoulder along the beach.

"It's wonderful here, Tom," Clare said, inhaling the sea air. "Look at Danny – he's in his element." She pointed to him, flapping his arms and running around in the distance.

"You need to come here more often; a lot more often," Tom said. "I'm rattling around in that big house. It gets lonely. You and the kids should stay over at weekends. Danny could learn how to surf, Gina could run for miles along the beach instead of that stinking canal, and you… well, there's a lovely spa down the road, I could book you treatments. You deserve to be pampered for once."

Clare gave a bittersweet smile. "You make everything sound so tempting. I wish things were as straightforward as that."

"Don't worry, Gina won't be like this for ever. We'll get her better," Tom said, rubbing her arm comfortingly.

They all reached the marina and stood on the jetty, where Tom's Mirror dinghy was tethered. The steely grey water was jumping up at them and slapping against the jetty's wooden slats.

"I thought you might fancy a quick sail," Tom said to Declan, holding the mooring rope in an effort to steady the rocking boat. "In you go."

"You're joking, aren't you? It's a bit rough out there," Declan said.

"Perfect sailing conditions," Tom chirped.

"Thanks for the offer, Mr. Cotter, but I'm not much of a sailor. The ferry over to Ireland is the extent of my seafaring experience."

"Well, then, that settles it. You definitely need a lesson." Tom gripped Declan's arm and pushed him down into the bobbing boat.

Gina saw the look of trepidation on Declan's face. "Can I come too?" she asked hurriedly.

"Yes," Declan said relieved, reaching up and taking her hand, but Tom pulled them apart.

"Sorry, but there's only room in the boat for two. Let Declan learn the ropes, we don't want him distracted by you, Gina."

"Go on, Declan, don't be a baby." Danny grinned.

Tom stepped down into the boat and told Danny to untie the rope.

"Where are the life jackets?" Gina asked.

"Under the seat," Tom answered.

"Then put them on," she demanded.

"And don't stay out too long. It looks wild out there," her mum added.

"Stop fussing. Anyone would think we were off on a round-the-world voyage," Tom laughed.

Gina, Clare and Danny watched from the jetty as the fragile-looking boat grew smaller and smaller. Even in the distance they could still see that the turbulent waters were tossing the little boat around.

Inside the dinghy, Declan's face had turned a sickly shade of green. He reached underneath for the yellow life jacket.

"Don't bother with those," Tom said with a sly smile. "They're useless; punctured. I've been meaning to replace them for weeks."

Declan looked petrified, gripping onto the side of the boat with white knuckles.

Tom laughed, slapping the boy hard on the shoulder. "Come on, shipmate, this is meant to be a sailing lesson. Get the jib up."

"What the hell is the jib?" Declan whimpered, feeling his stomach heave.

"Here." Tom handed him ropes. "Get the sail up. I'll stay at the helm and sort the mainsail."

Declan regretted pulling the ropes. As soon as the wind caught the red sails the boat was propelled forward as if someone had lit the fuse on a rocket.

"Lovely work." Tom grinned, delighting in the boy's discomfort. "Now we tack."

Without warning, Tom slackened the ropes and the

boom swung across the boat, skimming Declan's hair. "Move to the other side of the boat, quickly!" Tom ordered as Declan floundered in the middle in confusion. The boat rocked and rolled. Tom grabbed him by his hoodie and plonked him down on the bench next to him.

"That thing could have knocked me out," Declan protested, pointing to the boom.

"You have to be quick on your feet. When I say 'move' you shift to the opposite side asap, do you understand?"

"Listen, Mr. Cotter, this is really nice of you but I'm better on dry land. Can we go back now?"

"No, you'll soon get the hang of it. Look how we're powered up. Isn't it exhilarating?"

Declan didn't answer. His head was hanging over the side of the boat, the contents of his stomach emptying into the waters.

"Ready for another one?" Tom said, releasing the boom again. "Hike out!" he shouted to the dribbling young man as he nimbly ducked and stepped to the opposite side, leaning, straight-backed, over the side of the boat. The sails billowed, the boat changed direction sharply and Declan clung onto the seat opposite for dear life. Tom slid his feet into the toe straps screwed to the deck and chose his moment carefully. He waited until Declan had struggled onto the bench, then he leaned in and eased the ropes, taking the wind out of the sail. This caused the dinghy to list so violently on Declan's side that it catapulted him out of the boat, heels over head, into the wild waters. Tom worked quickly to rectify the vessel. His eyes scanned the churning waters, but there was no sign of the young man.

Declan was lost under the dark, paralyzing water. The shock of the cold felt like a vice around his chest. He was so disorientated that his brain couldn't work out whether he was thrashing up to the surface or down to the depths. He tried to open his eyes, but the stinging saltwater forced them shut. The longer it took to see daylight the more he was panicking. He found himself praying, something he hadn't done for years, despite his mum's best efforts.

Please, God, get me out of here. Please let me be heading in the right direction. I'll try and be good. I'll start going to Mass again, I promise.

The tension fell from Tom's face as he saw the hand appear above the water, quickly followed by Declan's head, his mouth open and gasping. Declan was frantically treading water as the sea tossed him about.

He spluttered, waiting for Tom to sail towards him, but instead he watched in disbelief as Tom started to circle the boat around him like a shark eyeing up a shipwrecked sailor.

Declan strained to wave with one arm, battling against the water with the other to keep him afloat.

Gina narrowed her eyes. What was going on out there? They were too far to be sure but, from the jetty, it looked like the boat was circling. She thought she could only see one figure on the dinghy. What had happened? Was one of them lying on the deck? Had one of them fallen overboard?

"Get me out of here," Declan spluttered through chattering teeth.

"Don't be so impatient. A few more minutes will clear the cobwebs away."

"I'm freezing…please!"

"Have you been spying on me, Declan?" Tom shouted to him.

Declan felt like his heart had stopped pumping.

Oh my God, what does he know? What do I say?

The boat continued to circle the flailing boy.

"NO!" Declan called.

"What have you seen at the warehouse? Come on, Declan. I'm dying to know."

"Nothing, I don't know what you're on about," he said breathlessly.

"Clare says you've been spying for Gina. Trying to dig up some dirt on me," Tom shouted.

Declan's frozen mind crunched into action. He'd been given a lifeline. How could he use it?

"No…well yes…but not really," he spluttered, the saltwater slapping his face. "I…I…I told Gina I'd keep an eye out but I haven't been and I haven't seen anything, honest."

"But you *have* been spying, Declan. You're always taking an unhealthy interest in my business."

"Yeah…but not because I'm s-s-spying," he chattered through blue lips. "I…I want to learn the business. I like it, I think I could be good at it."

"So you want to import cocoa beans for a living?" Tom sneered, unconvinced.

"I…I…want to be rich, like you. That's all, Mr. Cotter. I just want to be like you." He gulped in the biting air, unable to catch his breath.

Tom's eyebrows arched in amusement. "Well, it seems I have a fan. I like the idea of that. What do you want to be, Declan? A mini-me? I hope you're not going to turn into a stalker, are you?" he laughed.

Another wave engulfed Declan, crashing over his head. He bobbed up again. "P-p-please, Mr. Cotter, get me out of here. I can't feel my legs, I'm sinking," he pleaded.

Tom steered the dinghy towards the floundering boy. Declan grabbed the side, clinging on like a limpet. Tom looked down at him.

"I'm a very private person, Declan. I don't like anyone knowing my business. And I don't like you trying to dig up dirt on me in the hope of getting into Gina's knickers. Do you understand?"

Declan nodded, his face quivering.

Tom reached over, took hold of the waterlogged hoodie and pulled Declan into the boat like a fisherman hauling in a catch. Declan lay, coughing and shaking, on the wooden floor. Tom calmly took the helm, heading for shore.

"Let's get you back and out of those wet things before you catch your death." He smiled benevolently.

"But…but you could have drowned me." Declan stared up at Tom in shocked anger.

"What are you on about?" Tom said darkly. "It was your own fault that you fell out of the boat. You didn't listen to my instructions. You're not used to sailing." He glared at the boy, daring him to disagree.

Declan sat up and wrapped his arms around his trembling body. "You did it on purpose," he whispered into his knees.

Tom pointed. "Can you see them waiting anxiously on the jetty? You've given them a real scare."

Declan looked over at the figures; Gina was jumping up and down, waving frantically at the boat, her shouts lost on the wind.

"I look forward to hearing you telling them how it happened, okay?"

Declan's blue lips quivered with cold and impotent rage. He nodded meekly.

Tom leaned over and gave him a hearty slap on the back. "Good boy. Now let me just make myself clear; I like young men with ambition, they remind me of myself, but if I ever even suspect that you're spying on me, we'll go for another boat trip and next time I'll dump you a mile out at sea and I won't be so quick to fish you out. You understand, don't you, Declan?"

Declan looked into his boss's cold blue eyes. Yes, now he understood what kind of man Tom Cotter really was and he felt sick with fear.

Gina held out her hand to Declan as the dinghy came in to land, bumping against the side of the jetty. "God, Declan, you gave us a fright."

Declan didn't respond as he stepped unsteadily out of the boat.

"He's had a shock; he's freezing. Come here, love, let's get you back to Tom's house," her mum said, drawing her coat around the silent boy.

"How did you fall out?" Danny asked.

Tom answered for him. "He stood up. He didn't listen to me."

"You're a right divvy," Danny laughed.

Declan's face remained grim.

Danny suddenly realized it wasn't a laughing matter. "I'm glad you're okay," he added.

"He's fine. He just needs to find his sea legs," Tom said encouragingly.

* * *

Back at the house Tom was an attentive host. Fussing over Declan, insisting that he kept the change of clothes he gave him and trying to coax him to stay for dinner, but all Declan wanted to do was to get as far away from his boss as possible.

"I really need to get home." He smiled at Tom through gritted teeth.

"We'll all go," Gina's mum said.

"No, please don't. I'll get the train, it's no bother." His voice was blank.

"Well, I really enjoyed our little sailing lesson, Declan. Anytime you want another one, just let me know," Tom offered, generously.

Declan shot him a cutting look.

Gina followed Declan out of the front door and onto the sweeping driveway.

"Are you sure you feel well enough to go home alone?"

"Stop fussing, Gina, it was only a dip in the sea." He gave a weak smile and began to walk away but suddenly rushed back to her, throwing his arms around her and squeezing.

She tapped three times like a submitting judo opponent. "Declan," her muffled voice called out from his chest. "I can't breathe."

He released her.

She saw his crumpled face, his eyes watery. "What's wrong?"

"Nothing. It's just all that sea water, still stinging my eyes." He backed away and strode down the path. "Please, take care, Gina," he shouted without turning round.

By the time Declan stood on the railway platform his fear and shock had turned to anger. He waited impatiently for his call to be answered.

"Hello, Declan," the thick voice said.

"He's on to me!"

"What are you on about?" Stevie asked.

"Cotter, he's just nearly drowned me in the sea. He knows I've been spying on him. He threatened me. He'll let me drown next time."

"You didn't tell him anything, did you?" the man asked anxiously.

"Of course I didn't! I'm not stupid."

"Good lad. You've done well. We've got him on the run."

"It doesn't feel like it. It's not safe. I can't do this any more." Declan's voice wavered.

"We can't stop now. You'll be fine. Cotter was testing you out and you held your nerve. People make mistakes when they're rattled and Tom Cotter is obviously a nervous man. You've got nothing to worry about; I've got your back!"

"Why doesn't that make me feel any better?"

33 SOMETHING IN THE AIR

Danny opened the door to their bathroom and found Tom in a haze of steam and scents, a towel wrapped around his waist, his toned torso stretched as he vigorously rubbed another towel over his wet hair.

"Sorry," Danny said in sleepy surprise. "I didn't know you were here. I'll wait outside."

"No, come on in, I've finished. I stayed over last night, downstairs." He beckoned Danny in and then spun him round, tutting playfully. "Let me have a look at that bedhead. You need some serious attention."

"You can talk. You look like you've got a hangover," Danny retorted, looking at Tom's bloodshot eyes.

It was true that Tom wasn't looking his best. Yesterday evening he'd come round to see the family after work, determined to stay the night. Before Clare knew it, it was late and he'd drunk too much whisky to drive home. He'd quietly suggested to Clare that he might sleep over, on the sofa bed in the living room. At first she'd seemed unsure. "But what about Gina?"

"Be strong, Clare," Tom had replied. "Remember, 'tough love', you're the one in charge, not Gina. And I'm only sleeping on the sofa, for God's sake."

Clare had taken his advice and refused to listen to Gina's protests.

When Tom brought in his washbag from the car, Clare was surprised. "You've come prepared," she said.

He laughed it off, replying, "I was a boy scout, you know."

Gina had gone to bed that night, seething and unsettled knowing that Tom was sleeping in their house.

However, despite his little victory, Tom was regretting staying over. His nerves were in tatters after a torturous night lying in the sofa bed with Martin's urn looming over him from the shelf opposite. Tom never used to be a superstitious man, but all night he'd been convinced there was a presence with him in the freezing room. He lay awake, unable to tear his eyes from the urn; haunted by his thoughts.

"Don't be cheeky," Tom said to Danny. "It's not a hangover, I just haven't slept very well. All my beds have those memory foam mattresses, it's like sleeping on a cloud. You should all spend more time at mine. I've got those five bedrooms and they're all en suite."

"Yeah." Danny nodded enthusiastically. "I've always thought your house was amazing. I love your snooker room."

"Well, if I knew you were going to be staying more, I'd think about having a swimming pool built. Would you like that?"

Danny looked like he might burst with excitement. "Oh my God! A swimming pool! That would be brilliant. You've got to get one."

"We'll see." Tom grinned. "Now come here and get some gel on that hair." He skimmed some from a pot on the basin and worked it through Danny's soft curls.

"Good man, that's more like it. But if you *really* want the ladies to go wild for you—"

Danny screwed up his face. "Get lost, I don't want any girls after me."

"That's what you say now, Danny boy, but next year, when you hit secondary school, you'll be falling in and out of love on a weekly basis. So best to start working on your image now, preparing the ground...and I have just the thing."

He picked out a small cellophane-wrapped box from his washbag. He unwrapped it and pulled out an ornate bottle. With a flourish he eased out the bottle's glass stopper and poured a couple of drops of the clear liquid onto his hand, clapping his palms together and then patting them on Danny's cheeks.

"Urgh, you've made me smell like a girl," Danny protested.

Tom roared with laughter. "You should be thanking me. This little of bottle here cost a hundred and eighty pounds!"

"A hundred and eighty quid, for that!" Danny pointed at the bottle in disgust.

"And worth every penny!" Tom declared.

"Is that the bottle you got in France?" Danny asked.

"Yep, I found it in an exclusive perfumery on our Paris trip."

"Yuk, so it *is* for girls!"

"No, it's aftershave, Danny. Only real men can get away with wearing this." He gazed at the frosted bottle admiringly. "I thought I'd never be able to get hold of this stuff again. I'd been looking for it for ages; couldn't even get hold of it on the internet. Everyone said they'd stopped making it."

"Yeah, that's probably because the fumes were killing people." Danny grimaced.

"You've got a lot to learn. This stuff is like a magic potion. It casts a spell – just a couple of drops make you irresistible to women – and I'm talking women who look like models."

"I've got more important things to think of than stupid girls, Uncle Tom; my fish tank is still a mess," he said, trying to wipe the aftershave off with a towel.

Tom snatched the towel from him. "I know, I noticed that the water was getting greener."

"Yeah, you can hardly see the fish. They might be suffocating or maybe they'll all get some horrible disease and die!"

"Well, what can you do about it?"

"I put in a tablet but it hasn't worked. I need to go to the aquarium, get something stronger."

"Tell you what, little man. Why don't you leave that to me?" Tom said.

"Really?" Danny said gratefully.

"Sure, as long as you promise to keep that aftershave on all day. Trust me, Danny, report back after school and tell me if I wasn't wrong." He put the bottle back in his washbag, which was perched on the side of the bath. He winked at his protégé and exited the bathroom. Danny locked the door and stood on his tiptoes, admiring himself in the mirror, half convinced that perhaps now he really *was* a babe magnet.

Seconds later the handle turned, followed by a knock.

"Danny, is it you in there? Hurry up! I'm running late."

Danny scowled. "Don't I get any privacy?"

"Just open the door, will you?"

Gina entered and sniffed the air.

"What's that smell?" Her voice was a whisper.

"Oh God, does it stink? He told me women love it."

"Love what?"

"His stupid aftershave. He put it on me."

"Come here." She pulled her brother's face towards hers and inhaled deeply.

"What are you doing?" he said indignantly.

She stood staring into space, her hands still clasped on his cheeks. Danny stamped on her toe and she released him with an "Oww!"

"Bloody hell!" Danny exclaimed. "Uncle Tom said it cast a spell but not on your sister, that's just sick."

"Is it Tom's?"

"Of course it's Tom's. It cost a hundred and eighty quid a bottle!"

"Is it new?"

"Yeah, he got it in some stupid shop in Paris. He was going on about how it was his favourite."

"Have you got the bottle?"

"He put it in his washbag over there. What's wrong with you? You're acting weird again."

"Nothing. Just go, Danny. I need to use the bathroom," she ordered.

She shut the door behind him and grabbed the washbag from the side of the bath. She took out the ornate bottle and hesitated. "Maybe I *am* insane!" Gina said, looking at her shaken reflection in the mirror.

She held the bottle to her nose and pulled out the stopper with a *POP!* The aroma escaped like a genie. A wave of nausea washed over her, causing bile to rise in her throat. She eased herself down onto the bathroom floor, waiting for the feeling to pass. A rap on the door startled her, but it was her mum's voice that called out: "Come on, Gina! You're going to be late for school."

Gina got off the floor and opened the bathroom door.

Her mum's brow furrowed on seeing Gina's sickly-looking face. "Are you okay, love?"

"Yes, fine." She forced a smile. "Listen, Mum, do you know about this new aftershave Tom got from Paris?" She showed her the frosted bottle.

"Oh yes, lovely, isn't it? But you shouldn't be touching Tom's things, Gina."

"Has he ever used it before?"

"Yeah. It used to be his favourite. He's looked everywhere for it. You should have seen him when he found it in this perfumery; he was like a big kid." Her mum smiled to herself at the recollection.

"When did he used to wear it?"

"How am I meant to remember that?" She straightened her supermarket uniform. "You should ask him yourself."

"No, I was just being nosy. I was thinking I might get Declan a bottle."

"Gina, you won't be able to afford a bottle of that stuff. I bet Declan would be happy with something much less expensive. I could pick you up something from my place, if you want?"

"No, don't worry. I'll leave it for now," Gina said,

making a show of replacing the bottle in Tom's washbag.

"Okay, love. Just hurry up."

Gina waited for her mum to walk into the bedroom before retrieving the aftershave from the washbag and putting it into her pocket.

She loitered on the landing, trying to think of a way of avoiding Tom, but she knew that if she waited for him to go to work she'd be late for school. She began walking down the stairs using the banister for support. Tom came into view. He was standing in the living room doorway, staring across at the murky green water in the fish tank.

"Look at the state of it," he huffed, glancing up at her on the stairs. "Bloody Kylie and her fish-keeping skills. Don't worry, Gina, I'm going to get this sorted for Danny. There must be a simple way to get rid of all that algae, mustn't there?"

Her silence prompted him to look up at her properly this time. He noticed how tightly she was holding onto the banister. She seemed as twitchy as a mouse cornered by a cat.

"Are you okay, Gina? Aren't you feeling well?" he asked, concerned.

Gina couldn't look at him. She ran down the stairs and out of the front door, shouting, "I've got to get to school."

34 THE CURIOUS HAPPENING

Only Gina's body had spent the day at school. Her mind was somewhere entirely different. She'd wandered from lesson to lesson on autopilot. In the classrooms, she was unable to absorb a word the teachers were saying, despite being reminded on numerous occasions that this was her exam year and she couldn't afford to be staring into space.

At lunchtime, Becky and Tanya called her over.

"Come and sit with us, Gina," Becky said, encouragingly.

Over the last couple of months, Becky had started chatting to her, asking what had happened to make her seem happier, hoping that she was getting over her grief. Gina hadn't told her anything and she couldn't talk now. Today, she couldn't think about anything else, not even Declan; all she could focus on was the scent in that bottle.

"Sorry," she shouted to Becky. "Can't right now."

Gina went to the girls' toilets and locked herself in a

cubicle. She took the aftershave bottle out of her rucksack, opened it and inhaled. The aroma made her feel sick again; it seeped into the very core of her brain, making her head pound, making her doubt her sanity.

That evening, her stomach clenched as she walked into the living room to find Tom with his arm around Danny's shoulders discussing the fish tank. She took a deep breath. *Get a grip, Gina. You're being ridiculous.*

"How have you done it?" Danny asked Tom in wonder. "All that green water's starting to clear."

"It's the ultraviolet bulb, see? I attached it to the hood," Tom said proudly. "I asked a mate of mine and he said that the quickest way to get rid of algae in a fish tank was to use a UV light. Mind you, he did say not to leave it on too long."

"Why?"

"Oh, it was something about the exposure being bad for the fish. But he was being ultra cautious. We'll just use it to blast the algae, get the water all lovely and clear again, and then take the bulb out."

"Great," beamed Danny. "How much was it, Uncle Tom, because I'll pay for it? It *is* for my tank."

"Don't worry. I'll put it on my expenses," he laughed. Danny faked a laugh to be polite, even though he didn't know what Tom meant. But Gina did and an idea suddenly struck her that sent her hurrying to her bedroom to make a phone call.

"Declan, do you know if Tom keeps a record of his business expenses?" she asked urgently.

"Well, I suppose he has to, doesn't he, for tax and things," Declan replied.

"So they might be on the computer. Kylie might know about them."

"Kylie probably does them. She's probably got them on one of her amazing spreadsheets."

"Brilliant! Well, tomorrow, when Tom's not around, can you get Kylie to look something up for me?"

"What is it?"

"I need you to look up all his expenses for a date – it's from quite a while ago, though."

"What date?"

Her voice faltered. "It's the date my dad died."

"Why?"

"Just do it for me, please, Declan." He could hear the anxiety in her voice.

"But, Gina, even if Kylie does have records of his expenses, they'll be confidential. She won't let me look at them."

"She will! Tell her it's for me. Tell her I won't ask her any more favours after this. This is important, Declan. I feel like I'm going mad; this might tell me whether I am or not."

"Gina!" Tom's voice boomed up the stairs. "How do you fancy a movie and dinner?"

"Declan, I've got to go. I'll speak to you tomorrow," she said, rushing to end the call.

"No thanks," she shouted hurriedly to Tom. "I've got loads of homework to do."

But he wasn't about to take no for an answer. She heard him bound up the stairs and before she had a chance to get to the door he was in her room.

"Come on," he cajoled, his sky-blue eyes smiling. "All work and no play makes Gina a dull girl."

"No really, I've got a ton of work to do." She pointed to the pile of books on her dressing table.

She watched him nervously as he loosened his tie, undid the top button of his crisp white shirt and rubbed the back of his neck, his eyes momentarily closed, groaning. "*I've* been working hard all day and *you* need a break from all this studying. An evening out will do us the world of good and anyway, your mum will be home in a minute and I don't want her to have to start cooking."

"Then I'll make tea," Gina said, heading for the door, but he stepped in front of her, barring her exit.

"Gina, come and sit down." He gestured to the bed.

"I don't want to sit down. I've got things to do."

"I think we need a chat." He corralled Gina towards the bed, where she sat stiffly. She fixed her eyes on the wall of photos.

The bed creaked as he sat down beside her. The smell of his aftershave wafted towards her, making her feel nauseous. He followed her gaze to the photos.

"I know how much you miss Marty. I miss him too, Gina, but you're letting your dad down," he said solemnly.

"I am not!" she snapped.

"But you are. Your dad would be grateful that I'm helping and supporting his family. He'd be upset to see how you behave towards me. How you're determined to stop your mum and Danny being happy again. I love being part of this family. I can't even imagine my life without you all in it. I understand that you're ill, Gina, that's why I've been patient, but now it's time you got better. Am I making myself clear?" He stood up and loomed over her. "You're not going to get rid of me, so the sooner we start getting along, the easier it will be for you."

Gina kept her eyes on the photos; her breathing was ragged.

"As soon as your mum gets home we're all going out. Okay?" It didn't sound like a question.

Gina gave the tiniest nod, desperate for him to leave.

"Good girl!" Tom said triumphantly.

He strode out of the room, leaving Gina's insides churning.

Gina had been grateful for the cover of darkness that the cinema had provided. She'd sat as far away from Tom as possible. In brooding silence she'd watched the antics on the massive screen, listening to Tom and Danny guffawing at the gross-out comedy. In the restaurant there was nowhere to hide. She stabbed her fork into her dinner, watching as the food and wine kept coming, noting how Tom's voice and gesticulations were getting progressively louder and bigger as more alcohol slipped down his throat. He'd left his car outside their house, insisting that he wanted to "make a proper night of it". Her mum's cheeks were rosy, her eyes bright, as she and Danny hung on Tom's every word. He started to draw up plans on a napkin, the outline of a swimming pool.

Danny was agog. "Is it going to be indoors?"

Tom grinned. "Of course, with a sauna and Jacuzzi at the side."

"Oh my God, my mates will be so jealous. Can they come round with me and use it?"

"Of course they can." He ruffled Danny's hair. "And what about you, Gina? What can I do for you? There's a stable right by the beach. How about I get you some riding lessons at the weekends?"

"No, I don't want anything," Gina mumbled, shrinking back into the velvety chair.

Her mum looked at her watch. "Would you look at the time!" she exclaimed. "Tom, I've got to get the kids home. It's a school night and I'm on an early shift in the morning."

"You only live once, Clare. A few nights out will keep us young and the kids happy."

"Yes, but you've had years of practice at being a party animal. I haven't. Me and Martin never went out like you do. We couldn't afford it for a start, but a good film and a curry in front of the TV was always enough for us." Her mum suddenly sounded wistful.

Gina noted how Tom's eyes narrowed in annoyance. "Right then, let's get a couple of taxis," he said sharply. "By the way, have any of you seen my new aftershave? The one I bought in Paris? I thought I put it in my washbag this morning but when I got home it wasn't in there."

Mum flashed Gina a curious look, but Gina shook her head emphatically.

"Danny boy, have you taken it because the girls mobbed you today?" Tom half teased.

"No way! The girls liked it but my mates were saying that I had perfume on," Danny said indignantly.

"I'll look for it. It's bound to be in the house somewhere," her mum said. "You're welcome to the sofa bed again, if you don't want to get a taxi all the way to yours."

Gina looked alarmed.

"No thanks, Clare," Tom replied firmly, thinking of his sleepless night in the living room. "I'll call round in the morning to pick up my car."

Gina let out a sigh of relief.

* * *

It was nearly midnight by the time the taxi pulled up outside their house. Danny bounded into the hallway, intoxicated by thoughts of swimming pools. Her tipsy mum was laughing, trying to restrain him as if he was an overexcited puppy, but joining in the fun was the last thing Gina felt like doing.

"You two, bed!" Her mum giggled. "Don't forget to clean your teeth and, Danny...*don't* sleep in your clothes!"

Her mum followed them upstairs and within ten minutes the house was silent. Danny fell asleep as soon as his head touched the pillow but, as the night ticked by, he became restless, his eyeballs flitting behind his eyelids, until, suddenly, he was sitting bolt upright, gasping.

It was a dream, Danny thought with relief. *The fish are fine; they're not dead, floating on the surface of the water, frazzled by the ultraviolet bulb...but they could be!*

Panic rose in him again and he scrambled out of bed. The only light in his room was a gloomy orange glow from the street lamp outside.

I shouldn't have forgotten. I meant to check them. Uncle Tom's mate said they shouldn't be exposed to it for too long. How many hours has it been on? He pressed the button to illuminate his Homer Simpson clock: *4:18. Oh, God, I haven't looked at them since we went out.*

He stepped out onto the silent landing and felt his way down the stairs. He pushed open the living room door and approached the tank. A broad smile spread across his

315

sleepy face as he saw his fish, darting through the now clear water like shimmering rainbows under the stark light of the ultraviolet bulb. Danny crouched down to the socket on the skirting board and switched off the light. As he began to rise, something in the darkened waters made him do a double take.

"What?" He was on his knees, his nose pressed against the glass.

He tried leaning back to see if gaining perspective would alter what he saw, but no, there on the floor of the tank, dotted amongst the blue stones, plants and pirate ship, were five incredible glowing beacons. They shone out of the darkness like red-hot embers.

He turned his head away, blinking several times before looking back at the tank again. The blood-red stones seemed to pulsate. He wasn't dreaming.

"Wow! What the hell…?"

Just a moment ago, all those stones looked the same as usual, didn't they? There were no red ones – nothing was glowing – I would have noticed! Maybe it's something to do with the light? It's never happened when I've turned the normal light off.

Danny scampered up the stairs and into Gina's room. If his mum had been like all the other mums and let him have a mobile phone he could have taken a photo of it himself but, as it was, he needed a witness. Say they'd stopped glowing in the morning? No one would believe him. They'd say he'd been sleepwalking or just making it up. He needed Gina to see them, now!

He shook the duvet-covered mound. "Gina, wake up. You've got to come and look at this," he said in a loud whisper.

"What?" she groaned.

"Come downstairs. I want to show you something; it's amazing."

A disembodied hand emerged from the duvet, swatting him away like a fly. "Get lost, will you? I'm asleep."

"Please, Gina. You'll love this."

"I'll see it in the morning," she murmured.

"No, it might not be the same in the morning. You need to look now. Come on, Gina. It's so cool!" he proclaimed, whisking the duvet off the bed and revealing her in foetal position.

"Danny, I hate you!" she said, swaying groggily as she sat up. "This had better not be just a boy kind of cool, as in *rubbish*!"

Taking her hand, Danny led the zombie-like Gina downstairs and into the living room.

He felt pleased with himself as he watched her expression. "Wow! They look amazing? When did you put *them* in?"

"I haven't put anything in. They're the normal blue stones that have always been there. I came down to turn the light off and everything looked normal but when I turned the bulb off, those stones started to glow."

"Weird, but you're right, that is cool. Why would they suddenly start doing that?"

"I reckon it must be the UV bulb Uncle Tom put in. It's the only thing that's changed. Can we look it up on the computer?" he asked eagerly.

"Not now, Danny." Gina yawned. "We'll do it in the morning, hey?"

"But say they stop glowing. Say they never glow again! No one will believe us."

"Don't be such a drama queen, of course they'll believe us and if it *is* something to do with that light then it'll happen again. Now, get up to bed, please," she begged.

Danny tutted and shuffled up to bed but Gina remained standing there, in the unlit room, mesmerized by the shining blood-red stones at the bottom of the dark, humming tank.

Curiosity got the better of her; she walked over to the family computer and sat down.

I might as well look it up now. I'm awake anyway. It'll be quicker without Danny jumping around me.

The screen flickered into life and she brought up a search engine. She paused, pondering how to describe what she'd seen.

She tried a few keyword combinations until some relevant results came up. Gina's brow crinkled as she scrolled down the screen. Links to articles about the same topic kept coming up, again and again. She opened the first one and her eyes scanned the text.

"No way," she laughed to herself. She clicked on the next link and the next and despite her cynicism she became more and more engrossed – all the articles seemed to agree.

She shook her head. *There must be some other explanation.* She focused on the other suggestions and read carefully, but none of them really matched what she was seeing.

She looked back to the fish tank. The glow from the stones was fading fast! Gina rushed across to it. Her instinct told her to get the stones out while she could still identify them. She lifted the hood and slowly sank her arm to the bottom of the tank, delicately plucking out the five stones, trying not to distress the fish, who were darting around frantically like they were looking for a fire exit.

"Sorry," she whispered as she put the hood back down and waited for the disturbed water to settle again. She turned on the main light in the living room and examined her catch. Five chunky, cloudy blue stones, their surfaces rough and uneven. She ran her fingertips over their bumpy exteriors then, one by one, she held them up to the light. There was no trace of any red, of any glow. Now there was little to distinguish them from the hundreds of other stones that lined the floor of the tank. Some may have been slightly bigger, some were smaller and, between them, they covered the whole spectrum of the colour blue, but all looked nothing out of the ordinary.

35 THE DESECRATION

Danny put his head under the pillow, trying to block out his alarm clock.

"Doh! Get up, buddy! You're late," Homer Simpson declared. Danny groaned, hitting Homer's shiny head to silence him. Opening one eye, he looked at the clock display. He *was* late, really late! Why hadn't he heard the first alarm go off? Why hadn't he heard his mum coming into his room, telling him to wake up?

He shot out of bed, tussling with his uniform until he was fully clothed. Excitement suddenly bubbled up in him as he remembered the strange discovery of last night. He went to get Gina, but her room was empty. Danny headed down to the living room and found a yellow Post-it note stuck on the fish tank.

Danny, I've taken the glowing stones out of the tank. (Don't panic, I was careful.) Just want to find out more about

them. I'll get them back to you soon. Hope you don't mind.
Gina x

"What!" He threw his hands up in protest. "That's not fair." He stomped into the kitchen, frustrated that he had no one to complain to.

The doorbell rang and Danny opened it to a blurry-eyed Tom, dressed in a crisp work suit. Tom didn't wait to be invited in. He headed for the kitchen, groaning, "I'm just picking up my car but, God, I need a strong coffee! Has your mum gone to work?"

"Yeah. There's only me in, but I'm late for school."

Tom stood over the kettle, spooning coffee into a mug. "Give me a minute and I'll give you a lift. Did anyone find my aftershave?"

"Don't know. Not sure." Danny shrugged. "You look terrible."

"Thanks. This time it *is* a hangover. Let my face be a warning to you about the evils of drink." He gave a weak smile. "Anyway, what were you shouting about? I could hear you from the pavement."

"It's Gina! She's gone and taken the stones," Danny began to rant. "She didn't even ask me! It's not fair, because she made me go back to bed and she said we'd *both* look it up in the morning but now she's gone and taken them and they're mine! I wanted to bring my friends back and show them. They're so cool!"

Tom winced at the noise level.

"What are you raving on about, Danny?" he said wearily.

"The blue stones in the fish tank. You know…chunky, kind of…cloudy-looking."

"I've got to be honest with you, I hadn't really noticed, but I'll take your word for it," Tom said, pouring the boiling water into the mug.

"The thing is, Uncle Tom, I came down last night to check the fish were okay. I was worried about them after what you said about that bulb you put in. Anyway, I hadn't turned it off. I thought the fish might be hurt or something. But they were fine."

"I'm glad to hear it. Has it done the trick?" Tom yawned, picking up the mug.

"Yeah, the water's all clear. It's brilliant! But the mad thing is, when I turned that light off, five of the stones at the bottom of the tank just started to glow, and I mean *really* glow, blood-red – it was incredible – like magic."

Tom froze. The mug hovered by his lips.

"Cloudy *blue* stones that glowed *red*." His voice was a whisper, his bloodshot eyes narrowed.

"Yeah. You should have seen them, it was amazing!"

"And the UV bulb had been on?"

"Yes, but they only started glowing when I switched if off."

"Your dad bought you that fish tank, didn't he?" Tom asked urgently.

"Yeah, for my birthday. It was last thing he ever bought me. That's why Gina had no right to take those stones. I want them back."

"When did he give it to you?"

"He didn't get a chance to give it to me. He'd gone and got it the day he died. It was in the back of his car when he went to that bridge with Gina." Danny's voice began to quiver; he didn't want to associate the present with this memory.

Tom stepped towards Danny, fixing him with a manic stare. "Did you choose the stones?"

"No, they came with the tank."

"So your dad chose them?" He sounded like a cross-examining barrister.

Danny shrugged. "I don't know. Maybe, but it could have come as a package, you know, with the tank and filter and stuff," he said, increasingly baffled by Tom's questions.

Tom threw the mug down on the kitchen table and charged towards the living room. "Are any still glowing?"

"No! Haven't you been listening, Uncle Tom?" Danny said, exasperated.

Danny followed and watched as Tom stared into the tank, before switching on the UV bulb and swishing the front curtains closed.

"Shut the door, Danny, and close the curtains down there," he ordered, pointing to the far end of the room.

"I don't know why you're bothering. They're not in there," Danny said as he shrouded the room in darkness.

"Ssh!" Tom hissed, crouching in front of the tank to scrutinize the bed of stones.

Danny could only hold his silence for a minute before blurting out in frustration, "Gina's taken them. We'll just have to wait till she gets home and I'll show you then."

"What about her bedroom?" Tom said, thinking out loud.

He sprinted up the stairs and into Gina's room. He scanned it and, not seeing the stones on display, he began to rifle through her cupboards. He felt along the top of the wardrobe, got on his hands and knees to look under her bed, tossed her pillow and duvet off the bed before upturning the mattress, pushing her pile of revision books onto the floor and feverishly prising open trinket boxes from the drawers of the dressing table. Danny stood in the doorway, watching open-mouthed as the room was turned upside down. "Why are you doing this? What's wrong?" he squeaked.

Tom didn't answer; he turned to the wall collage that bombarded him with images of Martin Wilson. Sour sweat glistened on Tom's forehead. His breathing heavy, he stood like a pumped-up boxer, waiting for the bell. "You crafty bastard, Marty," he muttered to the photographs.

Tom lurched down the stairs two steps at a time, with Danny at his heels.

Back at the fish tank, he turned off the light and held his breath. The tank remained in darkness.

Danny opened the curtains, letting the sunlight flood the room. "They're not in there."

"But are you absolutely sure she took them all?"

"Well…I think so, probably," he wavered.

"I need to be sure," Tom said, flinging up the hood of the tank and, without even pausing to roll up his sleeves, plunging his arm into the watery world.

"What are you doing? Stop it! You're going to hurt the fish!" Danny howled.

"There could still be some buried underneath that haven't been exposed to the light," Tom growled, grabbing a handful of stones from the bottom, and unearthing a maelstrom of debris that instantly polluted the waters. Plants that had been embedded in the stones began to float up to the surface and the fish swayed violently in the turbulence.

"Don't just stand there! Go and get me some plastic bags, anything I can put these stones into."

"No! Stop it! Stop it!" Danny's face was hot with rage and distress.

"Do as you're told!" Tom barked, this time dragging his hand along the bottom of the tank like a dredger.

Fish began to wash over the sides of the tank in a tidal wave of water. Danny watched in horror as the ground became awash with bright, shimmering bodies, flapping frantically against the floorboards.

Danny scrambled around the floor, delicately lifting the dying fish into the palm of his hand. "Move out of the way!" he shouted at Tom. "I've got to get them back in the water."

But Tom shoved him away, causing the fish to catapult out of his hand.

Danny felt rage overwhelming him. He ran at Tom, springing up onto his back, wrapping his arms around Tom's neck and his legs around his waist, trying to pull the big man away from the tank.

The shock of the attack caught Tom off guard; he stumbled back for a moment, but regained his balance and fought to prise Danny's limpet limbs from him.

"Danny, get off me!" His voice was strangulated.

"You leave my tank alone!" Danny bawled into Tom's ear, tightening his grip as the man tried to shake him off. Danny clung on like a cowboy at a rodeo, but he could feel his hands beginning to slide apart, his ankles unlocking. Tom grunted as he separated Danny's hands and sent him flying backwards through the air. He landed on the ground with a thud.

Tom's febrile face loomed over him. "Don't you dare get up!"

Danny immediately sat up, defiantly.

"I'm warning you," Tom hissed, jabbing a threatening finger at Danny's face. "Stay down!"

Tom took off his jacket and laid it out on the floor. He continued scooping out handfuls of the blue stones and deposited them onto the jacket. He groaned in frustration; it was taking too long. He walked over to the display shelf, grabbing a weighty metal running trophy with Martin's name engraved on the plaque.

"Cover your face," he ordered.

"No!" screamed Danny, as he saw Tom swing the trophy from behind his head and smash it into the fish tank. The impact created a pinhole crack in the centre of the glass and, for a split second, the sheet seemed to have survived. But then as Danny watched in horror, fracture lines started to crackle outwards, until the whole sheet of glass suddenly shattered, and water flooded out, carrying with it the remaining fish.

There was the sound of squelching and crunching as Tom stepped on flailing fish and broken glass to lean into the desecrated tank. He picked out the flaccid plants and coral. He discarded the pirate ship, before shovelling the rest of the stones into the jacket on the ground. He then bundled it up and tied it like a bulging knapsack and went to leave.

He stepped past Danny, who was sitting, hugging his knees, head bowed. Tom swallowed hard, his voice thick. "I'm sorry, Danny. This is important. I promise I'll get you a new tank. Don't cry, eh? Forgive your Uncle Tom."

But Danny didn't answer. He bit his lip, desperate to stop his tears, afraid of this man who was suddenly a stranger to him.

36 CUSTOMER SERVICES

Gina was nearing the school gates when her phone rang. *Home* flashed up on the screen.

"Hello?"

"Gina…Uncle Tom has gone mental," Danny sobbed. "He's looking for those glowing stones. He smashed up my fish tank. He wrecked your room. He was *really* scary. He'll be looking for you. He knows you've got the stones. I've tried to get hold of Mum but she's not answering. I don't know what's going on."

"Calm down, Danny. What did he say about the stones?"

"Nothing! He just went crazy."

"Listen, you're best off in school. Have you got money for the bus?"

"Yeah."

"Then go to school. I'll keep trying Mum."

"But what if he's there when I get home? I don't want to be on my own with him."

"Don't worry. Mum will sort it out. I'll see you later. Love you!" Gina said anxiously.

As the call ended, her phone beeped. Someone had been trying to get through. She listened to the message.

The voice made her stomach lurch. "Hi, Gina, it's Uncle Tom. Give me a call, will you, as soon as you can?"

She opened her school bag and unzipped her fluffy purple pencil case. The five cloudy blue stones sat atop an assortment of pens, compasses and protractors. She zipped it up again and turned away from the school gates, swimming against the tide of students who were flooding towards the entrance. As soon as she was out of sight of the school buildings she started to run.

As Gina entered Neptune's Aquarium she was relieved to see that Jamie was there.

"Hi, Jamie," she said as she approached him.

"Hi, nice to see you again. How's your brother's tank doing?" he asked.

"Actually, I've come about some of the stones that were in it." She emptied the stones from her pencil case into Jamie's hand. "They glow red – do you sell ones like these?"

Jamie inspected them. "No. We do sell glowing stones for decoration in the tanks, but they're made of shiny, hard plastic material. Your ones are real stone. They look more like some of the bedding stones we stock." He handed them back to Gina. "Sorry if I haven't been much help."

"No, don't worry. You've been really helpful, thanks."

Gina's phone went to voicemail yet again. Tom cursed. He tried to think things through. *She usually has her phone on her but she'll be in school so she's probably turned it off. Maybe she'll check it later. Okay, I'm wasting valuable time here. I've got to get things moving.*

Tom dialled another number.

"Mr. Egon, it's Tom Cotter here."

"Hello, Mr. Cotter. I wasn't expecting to hear from you."

"No, well…I'd like you to come and see me. I have items that may be of great interest to you."

"Really? I haven't heard about this from Mr. Sissouma," he said, puzzled.

"That's because they're nothing to do with him. I would like you to come and verify these objects."

"But what about Mr. Sissouma?" Egon said gravely.

"Don't worry about him. If these objects are what I suspect they are, your visit will be very worthwhile."

Gina arrived at P.J. Harpers and loitered outside, deciding what to do.

It's too crazy, isn't it?

Her phone rang. She ignored it – it was Tom yet again.

How many times is that? Five? Six? Look at how he's behaving. What he did this morning. Yeah, I need to go in there.

The bell on the door rang out as Gina entered the jeweller's. She stood nervously in the carpeted square surrounded on three sides by cabinets displaying seductively lit jewellery.

She approached the flash sales assistant in the sharp suit, who eyed her suspiciously.

"Hello," she said, trying to sound as mature as possible.

"Can I help you?" he asked curtly.

"I'm hoping so." She smiled stiffly. "I have some stones that I'd like you to look at, please."

The sales assistant watched as Gina got out her fluffy purple pencil case and handed him the five objects.

He looked disapprovingly from the dull stones to the teenage girl. "Are you sure you need a jeweller's? These look like something you'd buy from a seaside rock shop."

"Please just look at them."

"Sorry, I can't help you. We're busy. But thanks for calling," he said sarcastically.

Gina surveyed the empty shop and narrowed her eyes. "Look, you obviously don't know much. Could I talk to someone who does?"

The man seemed most put out.

"I'm not leaving until I see someone who actually

knows their job," she said, folding her arms and standing firm in the middle of the shop floor.

The man huffed and called out, "Mr. Fenton, there's a girl here who's refusing to leave the shop unless someone looks at some grubby old stones she's got."

An older man appeared from the back of the shop. "Is there a problem, Mr. Drake?"

"This girl wants us to check out these stones." He rolled his eyes, whispering loudly, "She's a total time-waster – look at the state of them."

"Shouldn't you be at school, young lady?" Mr. Fenton asked archly.

"It's a teacher training day," Gina replied.

"Then why are you in your uniform?"

"I forgot, didn't I – turned up, wondered why the place was so quiet." She pulled a gormless face. "Anyway, would you look at these stones for me?"

"Will you leave without any fuss if I do?"

"Yeah, of course."

"Come on, let's see what we've got then." Mr. Fenton spread the stones out on a black cloth and pulled a loupe out of his pocket, putting it to his eye. He picked up one of the stones with tweezers and examined it with the magnifying lens. He turned the stone slowly around before picking up the next one, then the next. He scrutinized each one without comment, but Gina noticed an almost imperceptible twitch of his mouth.

He lowered the loupe from his eye and proceeded to put one of the stones to his lips.

"Lovely and cold," he whispered excitedly. "Gary, get the tester out."

"Which one?" Gary Drake asked.

"The one that checks for thermal conductivity."

"No!" he said incredulously.

"Yes! Now!"

"What are they? Please tell me." Gina was practically dancing on the spot.

"Patience," Mr. Fenton replied, placing the stones gently inside the little open box. He touched wires to each of the stones in turn, his eyes and grin getting wider with each reading.

Gina felt like she was about to burst. "Please tell me what they are."

"What you have here, young lady," Mr. Fenton announced, "are gem quality, blue rough diamonds. Quite extraordinary! In all my years of working in this shop I've never even seen a genuine blue diamond. They estimate that for every ten thousand diamonds mined only one will be of colour. These stones are extremely valuable."

"But they just look like grubby cloudy stones," Gary Drake protested.

"They're uncut, Gary. This is what diamonds look like when they come out of the earth. You've only seen them all cut and polished and ready to sell to our customers. An expert diamond cutter could transform these stones into breathtaking gems."

"They glow red, you know, when they've been under a UV light," Gina said, giddy with excitement. "I looked it up on the internet but it just sounded too crazy that they could be diamonds."

"Where did you get them from?" Mr. Fenton's voice was suddenly stern.

Gina hesitated. "They…they were my dad's."

"And where did *he* get them from?"

"I don't know." She shrugged.

Mr Fenton frowned. "This is all very unusual. I'm afraid I can't let you walk out of here with these gems. I need to keep hold of them and you need to stay here while I make a phone call. I think you and your dad will have some questions to answer so we can get to the bottom of this."

"You don't understand! I've got to go. Please give me my stones back."

"Didn't you hear what Mr. Fenton said? You've got to stay, until we sort this out," Gary Drake said, surreptitiously pushing a button under the counter.

The button set off a clanking sound. Gina looked to the front of the shop and saw metal grates starting to roll down over the windows and doorway of the jeweller's.

She leaned right over the counter, her feet off the ground, and grabbed the stones out of the box.

"No you don't!" Gary Drake said, seizing her by her

school jumper. Gina wriggled like a fish on a hook until she'd managed to slip out from his grip, leaving the jumper in Drake's clenched hands. She grabbed her bag and ran to the door, the grates now nearing the ground. Drake jumped over the counter after her. She swung the door open and dropped down onto her stomach, sliding under the clanking metal that was only centimetres above her. She pulled her feet clear just as the grates clanged to the ground, trapping the furious assistant behind them.

"Raise the grates, Mr. Fenton," she heard Drake cry as she sprinted away.

37 THE GUESSING GAME

Gina sat on the park bench, catching her breath, deep in thought. She looked at her phone, waiting for it to ring. She didn't have to wait long.

Seeing Tom's name appear, she muttered, "I'm ready for you."

"Hi, Gina, you've answered at last." Tom sounded so relieved. "How you doing?"

"Fine," she said coolly. "How are you?"

"Oh, I'm great."

"I've only just noticed you've left me a load of messages – anything wrong?" She feigned innocence.

"No, not really. It's just that Danny was telling me about that weird thing in the fish tank. You know, those stones glowing red."

"Aah…" She sounded bored.

"Have you got them? How many were there?"

"How many should there be?"

"What? How should I know?" He sounded rattled. "I'd love to see them."

"Why?"

"Because it sounds 'so cool', as Danny would say. I've always had a bit of an interest in geology, ever since I was a lad."

"Really? I never knew that." Her words dripped with an unveiled sarcasm.

"Oh," he said cheerfully, "there's a lot you don't know about me, Gina."

"Actually, I know more than you think."

"What do you mean by that?" he said with a nervous laugh.

She ignored his question. "Why do you think those blue stones would glow blood-red?"

"I really don't know."

"Well, should I tell you then?"

"Yeah, sure. If you've got a theory."

"It's called phosphorescence. It's a physical property of the stones which means they've reacted to the UV light that you put in to get rid of the algae. If those stones are exposed to ultraviolet light they will start to glow, but only after the light has been turned off. Isn't that cool?"

"Yeah, wow! You seem very well informed, Gina."

"It's amazing what you can find out from the internet. But listen, it gets even more interesting, because any old stones can't do this. Only *very* special stones."

"Well, I wouldn't get carried away. I doubt there's much special about stones in a fish tank, but I'd like to see them all the same. I have a mate who could look at them for us and tell us exactly what they are. He's probably more reliable than the internet."

"Thanks, Uncle Tom, but we don't need your mate. You see, I've been to a jeweller's, got them checked out myself, and can you guess what they told me?"

"No," Tom said tensely.

"Oh, come on now, Uncle Tom, I want you to guess," she said in a sing-song voice. "What do you think those stones are?"

"Really, Gina, just tell me. I don't know."

"Hard luck, if you won't even guess then I'm not telling you. Bye."

"Gina!" he jumped in. "Don't hang up. Okay, I'll guess. It's a stupid, random guess but I suppose, if you're saying that they're very special…well, I suppose you could be talking about something like diamonds?"

"Wow! Well done! What a great *guess*. You're so clever, Uncle Tom," she said with bite. "Yes, the jeweller said that those cloudy, dirty blue stones from the bottom of Danny's fish tank are rough diamonds. He got very excited actually, said that those unimpressive-looking stones are worth a fortune. How about that then?"

"They're mine!" Tom blurted out.

"I don't think so," Gina retorted. "They belong to my dad."

"No! He stole them from me and I want them back."

"Have you been looking for them, all this time? Is that what this has all been about? Going through my dad's things, digging up his allotment, taking his shed apart? And what about the day of Dad's funeral, when our house was broken into and everything turned upside down – you organized that, didn't you, Uncle Tom?"

He didn't deny it; instead he said, "I only want what's mine, Gina. You just need to hand over the stones to me."

"No! I'm not going to do that." She ended the call defiantly.

38 CALL THE POLICE

Declan put the shopping bags down on the pavement to answer his phone.

"Hi, Gina, what are you doing using your mobile at school. You bad girl."

"I'm not in school. Is Tom in work?"

"No, he hasn't been in all day. Even Kylie doesn't know where he is."

"Where are you? It doesn't sound like the warehouse."

"No, Kylie said it would be okay to take a late lunch so I could help Mrs. Mac and Bridie do their weekly shop. We're just outside Mrs. Mac's. I'm unloading the car and then I'll head back to work." His voice dropped to a whisper. "Bridie drove; she nearly killed us."

"Listen, Declan, I've found five blue diamonds – rough, uncut diamonds."

"What? Where?"

"You're not going to believe this, but they were in Danny's fish tank, just lying there, all this time, with all the other stones on the bottom of the tank."

"Come off it! That's crazy. Are you sure they're diamonds?"

"Yeah, a hundred per cent. I've had them checked out. But it's Tom. Tom's involved. He knows about them; he wants them. He's just phoned me – he says they belong to him and that my dad stole them from him. But that's crap, isn't it? My dad wouldn't do that."

"But…but what the hell were they doing in the fish tank?"

"My dad bought the tank for Danny. He had it in the car on the day he died; he must have hidden them in there. He mustn't have told anyone. But Tom's been looking for them all this time. I know he has."

"But where are they from?"

"I don't know. My head's spinning."

There was silence. Declan's brain was racing so fast he couldn't speak.

"Declan, are you still there?" Gina asked.

"Yeah, sorry." He sounded distracted.

"Did you find out anything about his expenses, from Kylie?" Gina asked anxiously.

"Yeah, she had spreadsheets for all his business expenses going back the six years that she's worked there. She wasn't happy, but she let me look at them. There wasn't much on that day, just a payment for petrol. Nothing for any hotel and I checked through the whole of that week for hotel payments but there's nothing recorded."

Gina's voice jumped on him. "Nothing! Are you sure?"

"Well, that's what Kylie's spreadsheets say."

"Declan…" Her voice trembled. "He lied. Tom knows the truth about my dad and I'm going to make him tell me."

"How?"

"I've got something now that he's desperate to get his hands on, haven't I?"

"Oh, please, Gina, don't do anything stupid! Where are you now?"

"I'm in the park but I'm going to head home. I can't get through to my mum. I want to get to the house before Danny. I need to keep Tom away from him. He terrified Danny this morning."

"Listen, Gina," Declan said gravely. "I need to make a phone call. I'll get back to you in a minute."

"Who are you calling?" she asked.

"Someone who'll know what to do."

Bridie bustled up to Declan, observing his troubled eyes and furrowed brow.

"What's wrong, Declan, darlin'? You look like you have the worries of the world on your shoulders. Deidre! Put the kettle on, will you, Declan's not himself."

Mrs. Mac came for a closer inspection. "Oh yes. Definitely not himself."

Declan looked down at the two concerned pensioners. "Thank you, ladies, but I haven't got time for tea," he said, bounding into the house.

Declan chewed his nails, waiting for Stevie to pick up.

"Hello, Declan," came the gravelly voice. "Any news for your Uncle Stevie?"

"Yes! You need to phone the police, now!"

The man guffawed down the phone. "Have you forgotten, lad? I *am* the police."

"**Y**eah, I know...but I mean proper police," Declan said. "We need police cars with their sirens blazing. We need to find Cotter and arrest him, right now, before Gina gets to him or he gets to her."

"I feel a bit insulted, Declan. I've been a 'proper' policeman for twenty-five years. I've got more experience than most of the uniforms put together. Us plain-clothes are the real deal. You should show more respect."

"Whatever!" Declan snapped. "Just arrest Cotter, will you?"

"There's nothing I'd like to do more, but why?"

"How about if I told you what Cotter and Sissouma are smuggling in those sacks of cocoa beans."

"Go on, I'm all ears."

"It's diamonds! Rough diamonds."

"Diamonds, hey!" His usually sarcastic tone sparked

with excitement. "Can you be sure of that?"

"Oh yeah, just wait until you hear what Gina's found in the bottom of her brother's fish tank," Declan said triumphantly before launching into the tale of the glowing stones.

"Oh my God, lad, this is beautiful, just beautiful! I could kiss you!"

"This is what Sissouma was talking about when he said what his boss supplied induced great happiness but cost much more. I thought it must be drugs, but it's diamonds."

"It sure is," Stevie said excitedly.

"Did you know about this already?" Declan asked, puzzled.

"I had my suspicions."

"Well, what are you waiting for? Find Cotter and arrest him before he gets to Gina. She's got the diamonds. She's talking about using them to get the truth out of Cotter."

"The truth about what?"

"About her dad."

"Well, she may not like what she hears. If Martin Wilson hid those stones, he must have been in it up to his neck. Where is she now?"

"Heading home."

"We'll use unmarked cars and keep an eye on her but I can't arrest Cotter yet. I need to hold back and see how this plays out. I still haven't got any solid evidence. I don't want to blow my chance of nailing him."

"But you can't hold back. Cotter is dangerous. Look what he did to me."

"He won't touch her."

"You don't know that."

"Listen carefully, lad, because I need to explain to you what we're dealing with here. Then maybe you'll understand how important it is to get these bastards," Stevie said ominously. "I've known something was going on since the day of Martin Wilson's funeral. We had a tip-off from the Met that Sissouma was in the area. My colleagues down in London had him under low-level surveillance; they knew he was working for a dangerous man back in the Ivory Coast. They suspected he coordinated some kind of money-laundering operation but they hadn't managed to get anything on him.

"I was assigned to tail him that day. I saw him outside the Wilsons' house. I saw him get out of his car and nod to Cotter when he looked out of the upstairs window. A second later Gina Wilson looked out but Sissouma didn't even notice her. It got me wondering what the connection was between the two men. So I started to take an interest in Cotter. I figured that with his warehouse business, shipments from the Ivory Coast and some kind of connection with Sissouma – Cotter was in a great position to get involved in smuggling something."

"Then why didn't you raid his warehouse?" Declan asked.

"I did what I could. I tipped off the docks security and

they did a spot check – got the sniffer dogs in, but there was nothing. I even got my boss to persuade the tax office to have a good look at Cotter's finances, but he must have a top-notch accountant – the guy came out squeaky clean.

"After that I got my knuckles rapped by my Super. I was told to lay off Cotter, that there wasn't enough to go on, but I was convinced it was worth keeping an eye on him. The next minute Cotter goes and disappears – off on his travels. I think the sudden interest in him must have rattled his cage. But I didn't forget about him and when he turned up again six months later I went back to my Super and asked for some manpower, resources for surveillance. He refused, said that he couldn't justify the budget unless I had something more solid to go on. But then, Declan, you walked into my life. A little gift from above; my very own 'covert human intelligence source'…cheap at half the price." Stevie gave a raucous laugh.

"I'm glad you find it funny. You turned me into a bloody informant. Lying to people – to good people!"

"It was your own choice."

"Come off it, Detective Sergeant," Declan spat. "You made sure I didn't have a choice."

"Don't be bitter, you've done a great job. You got hold of the code, worked out what it meant, and if you hadn't seen Egon in the warehouse and got his car reg I'd still be none the wiser."

"Why, how does Egon fit into this?"

"Well, I started doing some digging around about our friend and things became *very* interesting. He came over here from Belgium about ten years ago, to retire. He wasn't on anyone's radar; just a normal, law-abiding citizen. An old bloke in ill health, bothering no one. But guess what his job was back in his home country?"

"Just tell me, will you?" Declan said, getting increasingly stressed about Gina.

"He was a diamond cutter in Antwerp; one of the biggest diamond centres in the world."

"What! Why the hell are you only telling me this now?"

"Because the less you knew before the better. I'd stake my life that all the equipment you saw in his cellar was for diamond cutting. He must have come out of retirement to set up his very own underground business. No one would have suspected him. They may have illegal cutting operations going on in Antwerp, but it's not something we'd be on the lookout for in this country."

"So they're smuggling rough diamonds out of the Ivory Coast in the sacks of cocoa beans, which get unloaded directly to Cotter's warehouse, where he retrieves them from the sacks and then what…he passes them on to Egon?"

"It certainly looks like it. Diamonds are perfect to smuggle, easy to conceal, hard to detect – not like drugs that the dogs can sniff out – and just a few of those stones can be worth a small fortune."

"So what does Egon do with them?"

"Well, once he's cut them he or Sissouma will have buyers lined up; the kind of buyers who aren't going to ask questions about where the diamonds came from."

"But where *do* they come from? I mean…how do they get hold of them in the first place?"

Stevie let out a heavy sigh down the phone. "I've read the Met's file on Sissouma and the man he works for. It makes for chilling reading. His boss is a warlord in the Ivory Coast. He runs his own army; he even recruits kids to fight for him. He has control of one of the diamond mines in the north of the country. He has men, women and children working in appalling conditions: bent double in the rivers all day, panning for the stones. And then he uses the rough diamonds to buy weapons, landmines, ammunition, fuel. He'll use them for bribes, for blackmail, everything and anything he needs to hold onto his wealth and power. They're blood diamonds, lad, used to finance war and terror; ironic, isn't it, that they end up being given by romantic idiots as tokens of undying love."

"And Tom Cotter is part of all this?" Declan said in disbelief.

"Yep. We've uncovered something very important here, lad. God knows how long they've been running the operation. They could have smuggled millions of pounds worth of blood diamonds through his warehouse. *Now* can you see why I have to make sure I get my evidence."

"But you can get a search warrant for Egon's cellar. You've got Cotter telling Gina that those diamonds belong to him. What more do you want?"

"You don't understand. It's not enough. Egon could just say that he was keeping the equipment for old times' sake – it's not illegal to own it – and I'm not arresting Cotter before I know what I've got will stand up in court. I want these men sent down! I'm not going to trial to have one of their flashy barristers tear our case apart, convince the jury it's all circumstantial and hearsay and get them off on some technicality. I've seen it happen too many times. The bigger the criminal the better the defence he can afford – that's our justice system for you!"

"But you can't use Gina as bait to get your evidence!"

"She's using herself as bait! She wants to get the truth out of him, doesn't she?"

"But you can't *let* her."

Stevie grunted in frustration. "I know what I'm doing. You've no need to worry. I've got her back."

"What! Just like you had *my* back when Egon caught me trying to break into his house?" Declan scoffed. "No way, I don't trust you. You don't care about Gina, you just want your evidence. You'll let it go too far. It would be better for your case if Cotter hurt her, wouldn't it?"

"Now you listen to me," Stevie rumbled. "I've put my reputation on the line over this investigation. I've had no support. My boss thinks I've been wasting my time. Are you seriously suggesting that I blow my one chance to prove him wrong? Don't you want to see scum like Cotter behind bars? Haven't you understood what's behind the smuggling – war, weapons, murder?"

"But we can't stop all that," Declan said, exasperated.

"No, but we can smash this smuggling operation. It will starve Sissouma's boss of serious funds."

"I understand what you're saying, but I'm sorry, I can't chance Gina getting hurt. I've got to keep Cotter away from her."

"Come on now." Stevie suddenly sounded unnervingly nice. "We've been a good team. We're so close to nailing these bastards. We've just got to hold our nerve."

"It's too risky."

"Listen," Stevie growled. "If you jeopardize my investigation by going anywhere near Gina Wilson, then our deal is off. I'll pull every string possible to make sure that you go down. If you stop this from playing out, I'll make sure that you end up in the worst young offenders' institute in the country. They'll send you to one out in the wilds, where no one can afford to come and visit you. So you keep away from her. You let me do this my way."

"No! The deal's off, Stevie. I'll take what's coming to me but I'm not standing back and letting Cotter hurt her."

"What? You think you can do this to me?" Stevie

roared. "I'm going to have you arrested for obstructing a police officer. You aren't going anywhere, you little piece of sh—"

Declan cut him off.

40 THE UNEXPECTED GUEST

Tom opened the green door to the spindly man.

"Mr. Egon, please come in," he said, showing him into the living room. "I really appreciate you rushing over here like this. As I said on the phone, I need you to verify some stones, but there have been exciting developments; it appears we *are* dealing with the real thing and exquisite specimens too. I think once you see them for yourself you'll realize that your journey has been worthwhile."

The frail man eased himself down onto the sofa, surveying the smashed fish tank and the glass-strewn floor without comment.

He looked over his half-moon glasses at Tom. "You were rather vague about where you procured these stones and why Mr. Sissouma isn't involved."

"They're nothing to do with Sissouma. He doesn't need to know. This is just between you and me."

Egon gave a wheezy intake of breath. "It would be very foolish to try to bypass him. He's not a very understanding man and this *is* his business, after all."

"Listen, Mr. Egon. If you keep it between ourselves then I guarantee you'll get a great deal. I'm keen to offload as soon as possible."

"Sissouma has contacts everywhere. He'll trace them back to me, then to you. We've been doing business with him for years. I don't want to jeopardize our working relationship, to say nothing of my life."

"I'll make it worth your while. Wait till you see them. Not only are they blue diamonds, they also glow blood-red after exposure to UV light. You know how rare that makes them."

Mr. Egon's eyes widened. "Well, if that's true then they are indeed extremely precious. Maybe they'll match the quality of the Hope Diamond in Washington." He licked his dry lips hungrily.

"Exactly! So how valuable could they be?" Tom asked, salivating.

"The quicker you show them to me, the sooner we'll both know."

There was a split-second hesitation before Tom replied confidently, "I'm just waiting for their delivery. They'll be here very soon. In the meantime you may wish to sift through this." He presented Egon with his bound jacket and untied the knot to reveal the blue stones that had lined the fish tank. "It may be that one or two of the diamonds are still amongst these."

"I hope you're not wasting my time," Egon said sharply.

"No, Mr. Egon. Please check them. We need to be sure."

The phone in the hallway rang out. Tom went and hovered over it, waiting for the answering machine to kick in. He noticed Clare's switched-off mobile also sitting on the hallway table. She must have walked out without it this morning.

Gina's voice came over the speaker. "Hello, Danny? Are you home? Pick up if you're there, it's me. I'm on my way. Tom's got a key to the house so, if you get back before me, put the bolt on the door; don't let him in, okay? That's important – *don't* let him in! I'll see you soon."

Tom smiled at the phone, relieved. "Yes, I look forward to seeing you soon, Gina."

Declan paced his bedroom, retrying her number.

Gina answered, slightly breathless as she marched towards her house. "Declan. Have you made your call? Who did you ring? What did they say?"

He avoided her questions and asked one instead. "Where are you?"

"I'm nearly home. There's no one in the house – I've just phoned. I'll get back before Danny."

"Listen, Gina. Keep away from Tom. I don't want him anywhere near you."

"Don't you understand? I *want* to meet him. He's going to tell me the truth."

"Let the police deal with him."

"No, not yet. You know what a great liar he is. He'll just deny everything, they'll never get the truth out of him, but I can. If he wants these diamonds he'll have to play ball."

"You don't know what you're dealing with, Gina. It's dangerous."

"I can handle him," she said defiantly.

"But it's not just him you've got to worry about. It's Sissouma, he works for a warlord in the Ivory Coast. Tom's involved with them too – it's not just the diamonds in the fish tank. That's what they've been smuggling in the sacks of cocoa beans. That's what he must have got out of the sack that night we saw him in the warehouse. They're blood diamonds."

"Blood diamonds? What are blood diamonds?"

"It's complicated; it'll take too long to explain."

"Then talk fast!" she ordered.

Mr. Egon gave a sigh of annoyance. He pushed his glasses up onto his comb-over and rubbed his eyes. "There's nothing here of any value." He started to pack away his equipment.

"Please, Mr. Egon, forgive me. I just wanted to make sure I hadn't missed anything. But I can guarantee you that the delivery is the real thing. Be patient, she's on her way."

Tom started at the sound of the doorbell.

"Is this her?" Egon asked.

"No, she's got a key," Tom said, heading to the front window, recoiling on seeing the caller. The colour drained from Tom's face. "Why the hell is *he* here?"

"I invited him. I phoned him as soon as I heard from you. I value my life, Mr. Cotter, even if you don't," Egon said, his bones cracking as he got up to open the front door.

Henri Sissouma swaggered into the room, flashing a crocodile smile at Tom.

"Mr. Sissouma, I don't know what Egon has told you but I can explain," Tom garbled.

Sissouma held his hands up to silence him. "No, there's really no need. It's perfectly obvious what is going on. You were going to cheat me out of my diamonds. Mr. Egon, very wisely, phoned me and told me all about it. We have years of dealings with each other. Mr. Egon understands the consequences of not being honest with me. You, on the other hand, seem not to have learned your lesson." He stared at the finger stumps on Tom's left hand.

"No! You know that I'd never cheat you!" Tom protested.

"Are you calling Mr. Egon a liar?"

Egon pursed his thin lips.

"Of course not." Tom's body tensed, poised to take flight, but he knew he had to hold his nerve. "There's just been a misunderstanding. I wanted him to come and check out the stones and then, if they turned out to be the real deal, I was going to inform you straight away. I know what a busy man you are. I didn't want to waste your time, dragging you here for nothing."

Sissouma laughed mockingly. "Oh, I see. How very considerate of you." He held out his hand. "Let me see the stones."

"I'll have them in a minute."

"I thought you had them now! Where are they?"

"Gina Wilson, Mrs. Wilson's daughter, has got them. She's on her way here. As soon as she comes through that door, they'll be yours."

"Why has the girl got them?" Sissouma asked.

"I believe that they're the missing diamonds: the package that was swapped last year."

"The package of useless stones you passed on to poor Mr. Egon?"

"Yes. We thought they had been swapped in transit but it now appears that Martin Wilson, Gina's father, must have stolen the diamonds from the sack. He was my foreman at the warehouse – he had access to all the stock. He hid the diamonds before he killed himself. He jumped in front of a train."

"Why would he kill himself?"

Tom shrugged. "I don't know. Maybe he developed a guilty conscience."

"Well, it's fortunate for him that he took his own life because, if I had caught him, his death would have been long and painful. That is what happens to people who try and steal from me. As you know, Mr. Cotter, my employer was extremely upset about the loss of that particular consignment. He was anticipating a large return from them."

"I know, I'm sorry, but it really wasn't my fault."

Mr. Sissouma tutted. "*Au contraire*, Mr. Cotter, this *was* your fault. I hold you personally responsible for employing thieves, and now you add insult to injury by trying to cheat us out of our property once again. But here's what I'll do. If you return my diamonds to me you will be punished but you will survive. However, if I don't get them back, or if you try to disappear with them, then I will find you and I *will* kill you. You do believe me, don't you?"

Tom strained to answer. Sissouma's words were like a hand squeezing his neck.

"Answer me!" Sissouma bawled, speckles of spit showering Tom's face.

"Yes, I believe you," Tom croaked.

Sissouma stepped back from him, his lips curled in a smile. "Now, let's all calm down and wait for the girl. Perhaps we should all have a cup of tea, Mr. Cotter. Anger always makes me thirsty."

41 MISCARRIAGE OF JUSTICE

Declan walked out of his bedroom. He was going to Gina's house. He figured that at least if he was with her, he could stop her doing anything stupid.

The doorbell rang. He heard Mrs. Mac answer it. Her voice suddenly went twittery.

"Declan," she shouted nervously up the stairs. "You'd better come down here. There's two policemen wanting to talk to you."

He stopped dead on the landing.

"Are you not going to invite them in, Deirdre?" he heard Bridie say. "I hope young Declan isn't in trouble, officers. He's such a lovely boy. Whatever it is, it's bound to be a mistake; a miscarriage of justice. You hear about that kind of thing all the time."

"I'm afraid this is a serious matter and we must insist Mr. Doyle comes down." The officer sounded irritated.

Shit! Stevie wasn't bluffing, he's having me arrested. Declan turned on his tiptoes and started creeping towards the bathroom, the landing floorboards creaking with every step.

The officers rushed up the stairs, shouting, "Stay where you are!"

Declan ran into the bathroom, locking the door behind him.

The men thumped on the door. "Open the door, son. We don't want to have to knock it down."

"I haven't done anything," Declan said, clearing all Mrs. Mac's lavender soaps and bubble baths from the window ledge and hoicking up the sash window.

"Declan Doyle, we're arresting you for obstructing a police officer," a voice boomed through the door.

Declan stuck his head out of the window and looked down onto the roof of the outhouse.

"This is your last warning," the officer said, as Declan swung his legs out of the window.

"We're coming in!"

The flimsy lock was no match for their hard shoulders and within seconds the door flew open to reveal the empty room.

The policeman hurried to the window just in time to see Declan jumping from the outhouse roof into the yard and running out of the back gate.

42 A TANGLED WEB

Gina glanced through the window into the empty living room before turning the key in the lock. She pushed the door open, pausing on the doorstep, watching and listening. The house was silent. She stepped inside and immediately noticed her mum's mobile on the hall table.

No wonder she hasn't been answering!

The red light from the landline answer machine blinked at her from the table. One message – her message. No one was home.

Gina felt her shoulders relax as she started to lift her bag off her shoulder and over her head. She froze, the bag suspended in mid-air: she could hear a faint wheezing sound coming from behind the kitchen door. It came again and again at regular intervals.

An image flashed into her head – someone collapsed on the kitchen floor, struggling for breath. *Danny? Mum?*

"Danny!" Gina ran down the hallway, flinging open the kitchen door. She jolted to a halt at the sight of the wheezing figure sitting in her kitchen, flanked by Tom Cotter and a burly man in a shiny suit. She recognized him. He was the man who'd been standing in the street the day their house had been broken into.

"Gina, don't panic. We're here to talk to you," Tom said, approaching her.

She bolted back down the hallway, grappling with the doorknob, which suddenly felt like it had been smothered in butter. Tom was behind her like a shadow, his outstretched hand holding the door shut. She was trapped! He'd just take the diamonds from her; this wasn't how it was meant to be.

Her survival instinct kicked in – she snapped at him, sinking her teeth into the sinews of his hand, biting down until she drew blood. Tom yelped, tearing his hand from her mouth, looking at her in disbelief. She didn't hesitate. As soon as he removed his hand from the door Gina took her chance. She opened it and rushed out onto the pavement, nearly knocking over a woman walking her dog. The woman seemed about to shout at her, but saw the wild look on Gina's face and the two men who charged out of the house after her. Her dog barked, warningly.

Tom grabbed hold of Gina's arm.

"Let's go back inside," he growled, blood springing from the teeth marks on his hand.

The woman put her hand on Gina's shoulder. "Are you all right, love?" she asked, eyeing up the two intimidating men.

"She's fine," Tom answered. "I'm a family friend. It's family business. Come back in the house, Gina, and we'll sort this out."

"Is that right? Are you okay?" the woman asked again.

"Yes," Gina said, taking Tom by surprise. "But I'm not going back in the house. They can go back in, I'm staying here."

The woman waited until the men retreated. Tom had to stand behind Sissouma, as the man's frame filled the whole doorway.

Gina turned to the concerned woman. "Thank you, I'll be fine."

"Okay, if you say so." The woman nodded, coaxing her barking dog away.

Sissouma tried to take control of the situation. "Come in, please, young lady. It's no good doing business on the doorstep. These are private matters."

"I'd rather stay here."

"Very well. I'm sure by the end of our conversation you'll be persuaded to enter. Now, where to begin. Firstly, Gina…that is your name, isn't it? I believe that you have something in your possession that belongs to me."

"How do you know that they're yours? Tom Cotter says that they're his and *I* think that they belong to my dad."

"'Oh, what a tangled web we weave when first we practise to deceive'," Sissouma quoted with a flourish. "It appears that Mr. Cotter was hoping to cheat me out of my diamonds today, although he's trying to persuade me that it was all a silly misunderstanding. What do you think, Gina, should I give him the benefit of the doubt?"

She looked beyond Sissouma to Tom; the muscles in his face were twitching.

"I wouldn't trust him," she said coldly.

"Then you're a wise young woman. But let's speak frankly. Those stones didn't belong to your father either. He was a thief. He stole them from me. He caused a great deal of trouble, but you now have a chance to make amends."

"My dad wasn't a thief!"

"I'm afraid the facts prove that he was. Now please, return my property."

"What if I don't give them to you?"

Sissouma shook his head, his eyes downcast. "Then there will be terrible consequences for you and your family. And it will be when you least expect it. Maybe you will be lying in your beds one night and you'll awake to find the house engulfed in flames... It will be such a terrible accident."

Tears of fear welled up in Gina's eyes.

"Don't look so worried, Gina. Once you've given me my stones the matter will be closed – order will be restored. You'll never see me again, I promise. Now, in you come." He beckoned her inside.

But Gina didn't move. Her eyes flittered from one end of the street to the other, her heart pounding; her decision made.

"Tell Tom Cotter," she shouted into the hallway, "if he wants the diamonds, he'll have to come and get them." She turned on her heels and fled up the street.

An incensed Sissouma stood aside and addressed Tom.

"Bring back my property," he hissed "or *you* are a dead man."

Tom bolted out of the doorway like a greyhound out of its trap, his sights set on Gina, who was blazing up the road in her school uniform, her shoulder bag banging against her side.

Tom saw her turn left at the top of the road but, by the time he reached the intersection, she was nowhere to be seen. He knew that she could have disappeared down any of the alleyways which led off from the main road and behind the houses on the side streets. He started to run along the road, looking down each alley, hoping to catch a glimpse of her.

Gina made her way down, across and up the labyrinth of cobbled alleyways, traversing street after street until she reached the backyard that she was looking for. She smiled with relief on seeing the gate was open. She scanned the lane, checked that no one was looking and entered the yard, rapping on the back door, praying he was in.

43 THE PURSUED

Declan couldn't shake them off. From the bathroom window the two officers had been able to see the direction he was heading in. They'd radioed for support and he'd found his path blocked as he reached the top of Gina's street. He'd panicked and begun running around the alleys like a headless chicken, the policemen closing in on him. He had to get out of there! He made it to the end of the alleyway opposite the entrance to the docks and recklessly sprinted across the heaving road.

He waved frantically at the security guard on the gate.

"Dave! Raise the barrier, quick!"

Dave seemed amused. "You're a bit keen to get back to work, aren't you, Declan?"

The breathless Declan put his thumb up in thanks and scarpered into the docks.

Dave was still smiling after him when, a minute later,

two panting officers and a police car with its siren whirring appeared in front of him.

Gina left the yard and headed for the dock road. She'd done the best that she could under the circumstances but things weren't going to plan and she was plagued by doubt.

Oh my God! Have I just made a massive mistake? They may not even remember what I told them. But what other choice did I have? Where the hell is Declan?

She paced up and down the pavement of the busy road, making herself as visible as possible. As the minutes ticked by, she became more stressed – what if he didn't find her?

She gave a sigh of relief when Tom Cotter appeared from one of the side streets and spotted her. She waited until he got closer and then she started to run.

Daylight was fading as she sprinted along the canal with Tom in pursuit. Tom's leather shoes pinched his feet, his tie flapped up into his face, his arms pumped, his legs pounded. Gina had stamina but Tom had speed. He was gaining on her. As Gina looked behind at him, her foot dipped into a pothole in the towpath and sent her flying forward. She scraped along the cobbles. Her tights ripped, her knees burned and her shoe got stuck in the pothole.

She saw Tom come skidding past her as he tried to stop. He halted and started to walk back towards her, hands on hips, panting heavily. He couldn't see what Gina saw: a teenager on a bike, racing along the towpath at the speed of light. Gina saw the look of bemusement on Tom's face as she suddenly rolled to the side of the path. An aggressive shout came from behind Tom: "Get out of the way!" But he didn't have time to react before the cyclist rocketed past him, clipping his shoulder, sending him stumbling over the edge and into the green waters of the canal.

Gina picked herself up. She glanced at her smarting knees, checked in her shoulder bag to see that she still had everything and headed back to retrieve her shoe. But Tom was already clawing his way out of the canal, looking like a swamp creature, covered in a layer of green scum.

She had to abandon her shoe and keep going, blocking out the pain in her knees, and the jarring of her foot against the cobbles. She skirted around a young couple having a stroll along the stagnant canal. Seconds later she heard their cries of protest as Tom ploughed through them. He put a spurt on, closing the gap, getting so close that he lunged at her, but his fingers slid down her back, unable to get a hold. She pulled away. She heard his breathing turn ragged, losing any rhythm. That's when she knew that she could outrun him, that's when she kept her pace steady and led the exhausted man to where she wanted them to be.

Gina made it. She got out her phone and left a breathless message.

"Declan, where are you? I'm at the bridge, the place we first met. Tom's going to be here any second… He's here! I can see him! I'm going to make him tell me the truth. I've got to go."

44 MAD LAD

Danny opened the front door and stepped inside the house.

Everything's okay, he reassured himself. *Uncle Tom will still be at work. Mum and Gina will be home soon. I'll just play Xbox until they get back.*

As he swung the door shut, a man lunged from behind it, slapping his hand across the boy's mouth. Danny's eyes were huge with shock.

"Shush now," Mr. Sissouma told him. "The last thing I want to do is to hurt you."

The port police were quickly informed about the suspect: a seventeen-year-old called Declan Doyle, who worked in Cotter's cocoa warehouse. He'd been seen running into the port area only minutes before.

They checked on their database for his security ID and a photo of his cheeky, smiling face appeared on the screen. It wasn't long before they spotted him on their bank of CCTV screens. They put a call out – the suspect was heading for the warehouse.

Declan thought he'd slipped into the warehouse unseen. The sliding doors were fully open and his workmates were too busy loading up a truck to notice him. He disappeared down an aisle and secreted himself amongst the sacks, but less than a minute later he heard a kerfuffle, as a mixture of security guards and police arrived at the entrance, demanding to search the building.

Kylie tottered out of the office.

"What's this about, fellas?" she asked.

"An employee here, Declan Doyle. He's resisted arrest. He's been seen running into the warehouse. We need to look for him," one of the officers said.

"What's he meant to have done?" Kyle asked, shocked.

"He obstructed a police officer."

"Oh, is that all," Kylie said, raising an eyebrow. "He's hardly on the Most Wanted List, then."

"This is serious. We don't need your permission to search the premises," the police officer said, walking past Kylie and her workmates.

Kylie hurried back into the office to call Tom.

He needs to know what's happening, she thought. However, Tom was far too busy to answer his phone.

Declan quickly shifted the sacks around him to make a hiding space. He held his breath as footsteps echoed down the aisle. They stopped in front of him. He cringed as he noticed his trainer was sticking out between the sacks. He inched it out of sight, but he was too late.

The cry went up, "Over here! Aisle Six."

Declan kicked the sacks at the policeman and scrambled into the aisle. He started to run but was met by a blockade of uniformed men. He turned to try the other way but now both ends were covered. They stampeded towards him. He spotted the rolling ladder attached to the shelves and realized that the only way was up! He climbed to the top like a demented monkey and stepped off, onto the highest shelf. Looking down, he saw that two of the officers were already on their way up.

Declan ran along the top of the long, towering shelf. Puffs of cocoa dust burst into the air with every step, but his path of sacks was uneven and kept sliding dangerously beneath his feet. His pursuers were too nervous to look down. They followed him with slow, shuffling steps. There was no need to hurry, anyway. The boy had reached the very end of the shelving. Where could he possibly go from here?

"It's the end of the line, son," one of the officers called as he shuffled towards Declan. "So why don't we all just get down from here before we break our bloody necks?"

Declan moved to one side of the shelf and started rocking on his feet like he was powering himself up.

"No way!" said the man in alarm. "Don't be crazy. You could kill yourself!"

Declan ignored him, keeping his focus on the shelf on the next aisle and trying not to think of the two-metre gap between them and the twelve-metre drop below. He gritted his teeth and ran across the width of the shelf before leaping into the air. His outstretched arms slammed down on the shelf opposite. He dug his fingers into the stored sacks and tried to lever up his dangling body, but terror gripped him as he felt the sacks starting to slide. There were gasps from the ground below as he started to slip. Declan grabbed for the next sack along, like he was on the monkey bars in a playground. He prayed that it could take his weight as he started to haul himself up.

He felt like kissing those sacks of beans as he lay safely on top of them for a brief moment, but he had no time to waste; he was quickly up and running, locating the aisle's rolling ladder. His pursuers suddenly lost sight of him as he slid down the ladder. They ran around to where he should have landed, but he was gone.

Kylie had been craning her neck, watching Declan's escape attempt with her heart in her mouth. She too had lost sight of him and went back to the office to try Tom again but, as she crossed her legs under her desk, they hit something.

"Aww," Declan whimpered, as her stiletto dug into his ribs.

She looked under the desk, her mouth open.

"Declan," she hissed.

"Ssshh." He put his finger to his lips, breathing heavily.

"Hello, officer!" Kylie suddenly announced. "Have you lost him?" Declan curled up in a ball. Kylie's long legs pressed against him.

"Don't worry. He can't stay hidden for ever," the officer said confidently. "He's a mad lad though, isn't he – did you see that jump?"

"Yeah, and he's probably legged it out of the warehouse by now. You won't mind if I don't see you out? We're trying to get the deliveries sorted."

"We'll go when we're good and ready," the policeman said gruffly.

Clare sighed with relief as she walked into her hallway. She was looking forward to a relaxing night in. She half hoped that Tom wouldn't visit tonight. She wanted to spend some time on her own with the kids. She put her bag on the table and spotted her mobile.

"There it is." She tutted to herself. "I'd lose my head if it wasn't screwed on."

But a sense of unease descended on her. The house seemed far too quiet, no TV, no music, no footsteps from upstairs.

They can't be doing their homework! Clare thought incredulously.

She called out, "Gina! Danny! How was school? I've brought home a steak pie. I hope you two haven't been eating loads of biscuits, you'll spoil your tea."

The sight of Mr. Sissouma and Mr. Egon emerging from her living room made Clare jump.

"Who are you?"

"Please don't be alarmed," Mr. Sissouma said. "We are business associates of Tom Cotter's." Mr. Egon gave a sharp bow and a sickly smile.

"Mr. Cotter had to leave on an urgent matter and asked us to wait here. He shouldn't be long. He's told us that you wouldn't mind. He said that you were a most hospitable lady."

"Where are my children?" she asked anxiously.

"Gina is out, I believe, and your delightful son is in here."

The men ushered her into the living room where she found a drained-looking Danny on the sofa.

"What's happened, Danny?" Clare asked in alarm as she saw the destroyed tank.

Danny remained silent.

"A little accident," Sissouma reassured her.

Clare turned and headed for the hall.

"Where are you going, Mrs. Wilson?"

"I'm going to phone Tom. Find out what this is about," she said firmly.

"It's not a good time to phone him. He's busy."

"Please don't tell me what to do. In fact I think it's best that you and your colleague wait somewhere else for Tom. Why don't you go to his warehouse?" She gestured to the door.

"I'm sorry, Mrs. Wilson. I'm afraid I must insist we stay here until Tom returns."

"And I must insist you leave. I'm busy. This isn't a good time."

Mr. Sissouma snatched her mobile from the table and put it into his jacket pocket. "There will be no phone calls. Please sit down quietly with your son. He needs his mother to set a good example. Once Mr. Cotter returns everything will be all right."

45 TAKEN FOR A RIDE

She watched as Tom, bent double and panting, wiped the green scum from his face and hair.

"For God's sake, Gina, why have you brought me here?"

"You know what happened here, don't you?" she said, keeping her distance from him.

"Of course I do. This is where your dad killed himself."

"Have you been here before?"

"No."

"Didn't you want to see where your friend died?"

Tom shook his head, still trying to catch his breath. "No, I made the decision not to. It would have been too painful and I was right. Listen, Gina, just give me the diamonds and we can go home."

"No, not yet." She looked up at the blackening sky. "It's getting dark, isn't it?"

"Yeah and this isn't a good place to be in the dark."

"We'll be okay. The street lamps will come on in a minute," she said, nodding towards the rows of lights down the cobbled street.

"No they won't, none of them work," he said. "We'll be standing here in the pitch-black soon, if we don't sort this out."

Gina struggled to remain calm but she could feel herself beginning to tremble. "How do you know that if you've never been here before?"

"What? Well...I don't know... It was just an educated guess. Look at the state of the street; full of boarded-up houses, it's unlikely the street lights would still be working."

"You don't have to guess, do you, Uncle Tom," she spat, "because you were here that night, weren't you?"

Tom threw his arms up. "What the hell are you talking about? I spent that night in a hotel in Glasgow. I was on business up there. You were so traumatized I don't expect you to remember. I didn't come home until your mum phoned me in the early hours of the next morning – I drove back at a hundred miles an hour all the way, to be with you all."

"Liar!" Gina bawled. "You weren't in Glasgow. Your own business expenses don't show any payment for a hotel that night."

For a second he was speechless; then he went on the attack. "Have you been looking at my business expenses? You're obsessed, Gina. Did it ever cross your mind that

I may just have forgotten to claim for it?"

"Really! Well, now that these diamonds have turned up, I'm sure that the police will be interested in checking the hotel's records – then we'll know whether you stayed there that night."

Tom's demeanour changed; he puffed his chest out and sneered at her. "Are you *really* saying that I was on this bridge that night? Did you see me then, Gina? Strange how you haven't mentioned this before."

Gina started to back away from him and towards the cluster of bushes and trees at the side of the bridge. She opened her school bag, pulling out the bottle of aftershave.

Tom watched open-mouthed as she started to sprinkle drops of the perfume into the greenery.

"What the hell are you doing with my aftershave?" he demanded.

"I'm just trying to jog your memory. It sounds like you've forgotten that you were hiding in those bushes. When I ran to the bridge that night, looking for Dad, I came over here and there was a smell, an expensive, exotic smell that, even in my panic, I realized was odd – out of place. The smell lodged itself somewhere in my memory until you brought this bottle back from Paris. As soon as I smelled that scent again I could see myself standing right here, in this spot, on that night."

"This is ridiculous!" he bellowed. "You're mad! Clare should have dragged you back to that psychiatrist, instead of letting you get worse and worse. I'd advise you to keep your mouth shut. The police have got better things to do than to follow up the crazed rantings of a teenager who can't accept her father's suicide. Be careful, Gina. The doctors will put you on so much medication that you won't even know what day of the week it is. I was in Glasgow that night, everyone knows that!"

"Everyone knows what *you* told them," she shouted. "No one had any reason to doubt you. But you didn't stay the night in a hotel, you came back here, to this bridge, to meet my dad! It was about the diamonds, wasn't it?"

"Enough!" He powered towards her, pinning her against the wall of the bridge. He ripped the bag from her shoulder and over her head. Throwing it open, he emptied the contents onto the ground, then rifled through the textbooks and exercise books, her PE kit and lunchbox. He searched the bag again and found her phone in a side pocket, but no stones.

"Where are they?" he snarled in her face, his perfect white teeth bared like a dog poised to attack.

She shrugged defiantly. He started to frisk her, his hands sliding over her body.

"Get off me," she screamed, swiping her nails across his face.

He recoiled. His bitten hand flew to his stinging cheek. His frame trembled with rage but he was desperate to appear in control.

He held out his hand. "Give them to me. I need them, Gina...*we* need them. Have you any idea what kind of man Sissouma is? And the person he works for? Don't mess with these people. They're dangerous."

"I know all about you and your warlord and your blood diamonds," she said in disgust. "You help smuggle a murderer's diamonds in the sacks of cocoa beans, you get them out and pass them on to an illegal cutter."

"Where did you get that story from? Not Declan Doyle by any chance?"

Her eyes dived to the ground, betraying the answer.

"How does he know all this? Who's he working for?" Tom asked.

Confusion spread across Gina's face. *How* does *Declan know so much? Why didn't he tell me who he phoned?*

Tom leaped on her doubt. "It seems that your friend Declan has been keeping you in the dark. Maybe he's not really your friend at all. Maybe he's been using you to find out about me. Weren't you the one who recommended that I take him on in the warehouse? Did he ask you to get him a job with me?"

Her body felt suddenly hot and clammy as the truth dawned on her.

"Oh, poor Gina," Tom said mockingly. "You've been taken for a ride."

She bit her lip, holding back the urge to burst into tears.

46 THE DEAL

"**K**ylie, I've done nothing wrong," Declan whispered from under the desk. "I've got to find Gina. She's not safe, but how am I going to get out of here with all of the port police looking for me?"

"Don't worry, I'm on it," Kylie answered. "There's only a couple of the coppers left here now. The rest have gone to look around the dock."

Much to Declan's relief, Kylie stood up. He uncurled his aching limbs. She passed a yellow hard hat under the desk.

"Right, put the hat on and, when I say so, you get out from there and follow me to the entrance of the warehouse, but keep your head down," she warned.

Declan did as he was told and Kylie led him to the Chunky Chocs lorry that had just been loaded up with cocoa sacks for the chocolate factory.

Kylie opened the passenger door of the cabin and ushered Declan in.

"Hey, Kylie, what are you up to?" the surprised lorry driver asked, lowering the bacon cob that had been heading for his mouth.

"Hiya, Charlie. You know Declan, don't you?" She smiled sweetly. "I just need a little favour. Could you be a wonderful man and give Declan a lift out of here?"

"Well, yeah, no problem."

"Only thing is, he needs to lie on the floor until you get through the gates," she said, pushing Declan onto the litter-filled floor of the cabin.

"Why? What have you been up to?" he asked Declan.

"Nothing bad," Kylie interjected. "Just a little game of hide and seek with the port police. You'll do this for me, won't you, Charlie?" She pouted at the pot-bellied driver.

"Anything for you, Kylie," Charlie replied, revving up his engine.

Declan waited until they were clear of the dock road before he got up.

"Thanks a million, Charlie," he said, checking his phone.

The driver glanced over and saw the look of panic on the young man's face as he listened to Gina's breathless message.

"What is it?" Charlie asked.

"I need one more favour," Declan said. "Can you make a little detour to drop me off somewhere?"

Gina tried desperately to compose herself. "I don't care about some stupid boy," she blustered to Tom. "So what if he's used me? At least he's told me what I needed to know. At least I know what you've been up to; the kind of man you really are, working for this warlord when you know how…how *evil* he is."

"It's just business," Tom retorted. "I'm not responsible for what some man is doing thousands of miles away, in a country I don't even know or care about."

"But those diamonds help pay for his weapons."

"If it wasn't me then someone else would be profiting."

"How long have you been doing this?"

"Long enough. It's been easy money. It's a simple system that had never caused a problem before…"

"Before what?" she demanded.

Tom clammed up for a moment. "Just tell me where the diamonds are, Gina. Time's running out!"

She laughed viciously. "But the thing is, 'Uncle Tom', time's not running out for me, only for you."

"What does that mean?"

"I haven't got the stones. I've given them to someone – someone you don't know – and I've told them that if they don't see me within an hour then they're to take the diamonds to my house and give them to Sissouma. And I gave this person a very important message to pass on to

Sissouma; they're going to inform him that the stones are from me, *Gina Wilson*, because you, *Tom Cotter*, were planning to take them and disappear. So you see, if anything happens to me, those diamonds will be delivered to Sissouma and then *he'll* come after *you*."

"I'll just phone him and tell him it's a lie," Tom said brashly.

"And you really think he's going to believe you?" Gina scoffed. "Didn't he tell me that you'd already tried to cheat him once today? The only thing that will save your skin is if *you* hand him those diamonds. That's the only way that he can be sure that you weren't going to run off with them; you know I'm right, don't you?"

Tom didn't answer. She saw his fists clench.

"I'm prepared to do a deal with you," she said, repeating the words she'd been rehearsing in her head. "If you tell me the truth about my dad, how he got those stones, what happened on this bridge that night, then I'll tell this person not to take the diamonds to Sissouma. *But* if you won't tell me, or if I think you're lying, then I'll make sure that you never get a chance to take the stones back to him."

"How can I tell you what happened, when I wasn't there?" Tom hissed.

"We both know that's a lie."

"Do you understand that you're playing with my life here?" his voice rumbled.

"Of course, I do," she answered coldly.

He moved closer, looking down on her. She could smell the stagnant canal on him; his clothes were filthy, his tanned face haggard, his immaculate veneer gone.

"Gina, you don't make deals with me. You'll do as you're told. You're going to phone whoever you gave the stones to and tell them that you're fine and that we'll come and collect them. Under no circumstances are they to take them to Sissouma."

Gina shook her head at the ground. "I'm not going to do that."

His face darkened. "Don't make me hurt you."

She looked up and held his gaze, forcing her voice to be strong. "Wow! Aren't you the big man? You can do what you like. I won't tell you anything, or phone anyone."

He lunged at her, seizing her by her school shirt, pinching her skin. He raised his other arm high above her head.

"Make the call."

"No!"

His arm swished through the air, his hand slapping her across the face with such force that it rocked her off her feet. He let go of her, and she stumbled against the side of the bridge, grappling around for support. Her ear rang from the impact of the blow. Tears of pain and fury rolled down her blazing cheek.

"Please don't make me do this, Gina." He looked genuinely pained. "Phone the person you gave the stones to."

She straightened herself, brushing her clothes down before declaring, "You really are a special kind of 'uncle'."

"You're forcing me to do this," he mumbled.

"Do you want the name of the person I gave them to?"

"You know I do."

She paused, as if it was on the tip of her tongue, but then said, with a supercilious smile, "Sorry, it's slipped my mind."

He snapped, grabbing her again and delivering a blow to the same side of her face that was twice as brutal. It felt like he'd hit her with a brick. She crumpled to the ground; a sliver of blood trickled from her red-hot ear. He stood over her as she struggled to get up only to fall back again.

He looked on the verge of tears – for himself? For her? She couldn't tell.

"For God's sake, Gina, tell me who's got them."

She slurred like a punch-drunk boxer. "No. And if you hit me again I'll pass out and then you'll never know." She started to chuckle manically, red-stained saliva dribbling from her swollen mouth.

Tom crouched down to her slumped body and held her face in between his hands, his wild eyes searching her dilated pupils.

"Do you want him to kill me, Gina? Could you live with yourself knowing you could have stopped it?"

Gina's eyelids drooped, her head fell forward. He shook her skull. "Come on, Gina, *please* phone them!"

She rallied, easing herself into a sitting position against the bridge wall. "I'll phone them," she mumbled through ballooning lips, "but only after you tell me the truth about what happened that night with my dad." Her blurred eyes strained to focus on her watch. "Tick-tock, Tom, your time is running out. Only thirty minutes before they give the diamonds to Sissouma."

She waited for his next move, desperately trying to hold her nerve, terrified at the thought of another blow. But Tom didn't touch her. Instead he bowed his head and hid his face in his hands. He remained crouched like this, as if he'd retreated into his own world. Her instincts told her not to break the unbearable silence, so she sat and watched, fear keeping her throbbing brain alert.

The silence was only broken by the sound of a train, which sped beneath the bridge, making Tom's whole body shudder. He uncovered his face; the weight of his stare pressed down on her.

"You've got to promise me that you'll stop this person taking the stones to Sissouma, because I'm going to tell you the truth."

At that moment Gina knew that he meant it and a terrible sense of dread flooded her.

"I always make sure I'm at the warehouse if I know I'm getting one of my special deliveries," Tom began, "but this shipment arrived two days early from the Ivory Coast. I was up in Glasgow so Marty just took control; he got the cargo stored and carried out the quality control checks on random sacks of beans. And that's when he found them – a fluke. I suppose, after all these years of getting away with it, my luck just ran out that day. Of course, your dad wasn't stupid. He guessed what they were; why else would a pouch of stones be hidden in a sack of cocoa beans?

"He phoned me straight away, told me what he'd found, said he was about to contact the port police to hand them over. I told him not to. Pretended I didn't know what the hell was going on. I said that I wanted to see them for myself before we brought the authorities in. Alarm bells started ringing for him. He asked me outright, 'You're not involved in this, are you, Tom?'

"I said, 'Of course not. How many years have you known me? It's just I'm the boss, it's my business and it's not your place to go making decisions before I've even had a chance to assess the situation.'

"He agreed but I could tell he had his doubts.

"I told him that I'd drive straight back from Glasgow. I'd been having meetings, I hadn't even checked into my hotel. I told him that we'd meet up so he could show me the stones and that he wasn't to tell anyone yet, in case one of the lads in the warehouse was involved. I said to send everyone home, shut up the warehouse and that I'd phone him to let him know where to meet when I was close to home.

"I spent the whole drive with my stomach in knots, working out what I was going to say to your dad. How I was going to convince someone as straight as Marty to give me the stones. I knew what was at stake. If Marty blew the whistle, I was more scared of what Sissouma would do to me than the police. By the time I got to the city it was dark, the weather was foul and I was so wound up that I stank of sweat and stress. I doused myself with aftershave to try to mask it. But I tipped the whole bottle on myself, I was so nervous.

"I needed to meet Marty somewhere secluded, away from prying eyes. I came straight here. I know this place well. I never tell anyone, but this is the street where I grew up. That was my house in the middle. Even back then it was barely fit to live in.

"I phoned your dad, told him where to meet me. He said that he couldn't, that he was outside the sports centre picking you up. He said that he'd see me tomorrow, but I couldn't let that happen. I knew that the more time Marty had to think about it the more likely he was to go to the police. I insisted he came to meet me. I told him it wouldn't take long, that he should leave you in the car, well out of sight. I told him that you'd both be home in no time and that you'd be none the wiser. He wasn't happy but in the end he agreed.

"I was already on the bridge getting soaked to the skin by the time I heard Marty's car. The moon was the only light but my eyes had adjusted to the dark, so I was able to watch him as he felt his way towards me. I waited until he was close and I whispered, 'Where's Gina?'

"'In the car, down the street. She can't see anything, she knows nothing.'

"I said, 'I really appreciate this, Marty. Let's sort this thing out, hey? Have you got the stones?'

"Marty patted the pocket of his overalls.

"'Let's see them, then.'

"He handed me a leather pouch. I tipped the contents into my hand and inspected them as best as I could in the bad light – there were five of them, rough, dull and bluish stones. They looked like what I'd expected to see. Sissouma had already informed me that this delivery was particularly special – not the usual white diamonds.

"Marty said, 'Okay, now you've seen them. Are you going to phone the police?' He was calling my bluff.

"'Listen, Marty. It's not that simple.'

"Your dad shook his head at me, full of self-righteous disapproval. 'What the hell are you involved with, Tom?'

"He bombarded me with questions about where the diamonds were from and how I got involved in this racket. He wanted to know how it all worked. I was careful what I told him. I thought I knew how to play him. I kept it simple, didn't tell him that they were blood diamonds; said it was a smuggling operation for a mine owner; someone who wanted to avoid paying taxes, had their own cutter and buyer all organized, so all I had to do was retrieve the stones and get them to the cutter. I tell you, my heart sank as I watched his stony face.

"I said, 'Don't look at me like that, Marty. It's not like I'm helping to smuggle drugs or something. With this racket, no one's getting hurt. The only one losing out is the tax office. It was a good business opportunity and I reckoned I might as well get involved. There's never been any problems,' I said, 'and that's why I'd like you to benefit as well, Marty – share in my good fortune. I can cut you in on this. All you have to do is keep your mouth shut. You'll get paid for doing nothing. Just think of what that extra money could buy for Clare and the kids. You could take that holiday to Trinidad, buy a decent car. Whatever you want! Your family deserve this. Do it for them.'

"But your dad shook his head and said, 'Look, I've heard enough. Gina will be getting worried, wondering where I am, so I want this sorted now. We go back a long way, Tom. I always knew that you were a tough businessman but I liked you, saw the best in you, but right now, I feel like I hardly know you. I'm going to give you a chance. Give me the diamonds and tomorrow I tell the port police that I found them in the cargo. They can take it from there. I won't mention you. You can do what you want, deny all knowledge…or you can tell them the truth.' He raised his eyebrows at me, knowing that this wouldn't happen in a million years. 'But one thing is for sure,' he said, 'this has to stop! I need you to promise me that.'

"I shouted at him, 'Are you out of your mind?' I could feel panic taking hold of me; I wasn't going to be able to persuade him. I knew Marty. Your dad was a man who wouldn't even look twice at an attractive woman in a pub without feeling guilty. I had to make him understand. I said, 'For God's sake, Marty, you don't want to mess with these people. I need to get these stones to the cutter. If you get the authorities involved we'll both suffer the consequences. The people I deal with won't take kindly to their business being ruined and I guarantee that they'll come looking for you.' He thought I was threatening him.

I said, 'It's not a threat. It's what will happen.'

"He hesitated and, for a second, I thought I'd got through to him, but then he took out his phone. He said, 'Sorry, Tom. This is your last chance; agree that I hand those stones over to the authorities tomorrow and that you'll stop all this *for good* or I phone the police, right now.'

"I said, 'No, I can't let you do that!'

"I saw the screen of his phone light up and that's when I lost it!

"I remember grabbing for the phone and then Marty taking a swing at me and suddenly we were on the ground…grappling with each other on the wet cobbles. I must have knocked the phone out of his hand, it spun off along the ground and the next second I'd dragged Marty up and had him pinned against the side of the bridge. I was so pumped up, it was like I was possessed or something. When I held him there I didn't see my friend, I could only see this man who was going to ruin my life; everything I'd ever worked for. All those years of fighting to make something of myself, clawing my way up from the bottom of the pile. But I didn't mean it to happen; you've got to believe me, Gina. I don't even know *how* it happened! I lifted him off his feet. I just kept lifting him, higher and higher…the look of horror on his face – as if *he'd* realized what I was going to do even before *I* did. He grabbed for me but I hit his hand away and the next moment I'd somehow bundled him over the side of the bridge.

"There was a sickening thud. I looked over and saw your dad's body sprawled across the tracks... He was facing upwards, his eyes shut; one of his legs was twisted behind him like he was made of rubber. The rain was pelting down on him, but he didn't move, not even a twitch. I stood there staring at him, frozen to the spot, not knowing if he was dead or alive. It was only the blast of the car horn that brought me round. It made me jump out of my skin. I realized that it must be you, waiting in the car, wondering why your dad was taking so long. And then I saw the headlights of the train in the distance, cutting through the darkness, rocketing towards us, and I knew that I had to get Marty off the tracks...

"I could have done it; I could have run down the embankment and dragged him off, called an ambulance, saved my friend, taken the consequences...but I didn't," Tom whispered, as if he still couldn't believe it. "Instead, I found myself scrambling on the ground, looking for Marty's phone. I was shaking so badly that I could hardly press the keypad to write the text."

"*Forgive me. Dad,*" Gina whispered. "You wrote that?"

"Yes, and then I got your number up, pressed send and threw the phone onto the track like it was a red-hot coal. I didn't dare look down again, I just ran to the other end of the bridge and I crouched in those bushes, my heart thumping out of my chest, the sound of the train getting closer and closer until I heard the screeching of the brakes."

Tom's voice tailed off. He shook his head; his hand covered his mouth.

"You haven't finished," Gina said. "Go on."

"No, Gina, please. I've told you everything," he pleaded.

"I said, go on!" she bawled, the veins in her neck straining. "I want you to tell me every last detail. All your lies, all your deceit. What did you do when you heard the brakes screeching?"

Tom bowed his head. "I put my hands over my ears, screwed up my eyes, rocked on my heels to make the image go away."

"And then what?" she demanded.

"The train came to a stop and for a second all I could hear was the hissing noise from the engine, but then your voice rang out from the dark, calling for your dad. The sound of it made me retch. I swallowed back the bile, watching you through the undergrowth as you ran frantically about the bridge. You suddenly came in my direction, scanning the trees; you lingered there, leaning into the bushes. You came so close that I could see your bare feet, hear your panicked breathing and I just curled up tighter, into a ball, willing you not to see me.

"Then I saw you cross the bridge and head down the embankment and I took my chance. I shot out of the bushes and sprinted across the bridge and down the street. I'd parked my car on the next road and as soon as I reached it, I locked myself in, as if someone was chasing me, ready to drag me from it. I wrapped my arms around myself, trying to control the shaking. My teeth were chattering so hard I thought they'd shatter. I squeezed myself tighter and tighter but a furnace couldn't have taken away the feeling that my blood had frozen.

"I knew there'd be sirens and people lifting their curtains and coming out of their houses to see what they were missing. I had to get moving. I steadied my hand to get the key in the ignition and I drove out of the city, knowing that I couldn't go home. I booked into some crappy hotel, paying cash, using another name.

"I sat in the room in my wet clothes, sobbing and shaking, drinking my way through the contents of the minibar. I was woken at four in the morning by my mobile. I had to peel myself off the bathroom floor to answer it. It was your mum, hardly able to speak, she was so shell-shocked. She just kept repeating 'Why would Martin do this? Why would Martin do this?' I told her that I'd drive home straight away. I had to end the call to throw up in the sink.

"I splashed cold water on my face. I forced myself to look at my reflection in the mirror – it disgusted me. I didn't know how I could live with what I'd done but I knew that I had to. I gave myself a good talking to: what was the point in the truth coming out? Marty was dead, there was nothing I could do to change that. I knew that it looked like suicide. I could help that theory along by telling people that Marty had been depressed, but I swore that I'd try and make amends by being there for you, Danny and your mum. I could provide for you, look after you, offer you a comfortable life.

"Once I'd made that decision I blocked out everything else. I pulled myself together, cleaned myself up and went to drop the stones off at the cutters. It only took him one look to raise his suspicions. When he examined them and announced that they were fakes I felt sick.

"Sissouma was soon on the scene and I knew I was in trouble unless I could convince him that I didn't know where the real diamonds were. He had to believe that when I retrieved the stones from the sack, they'd already been swapped. He had my house turned upside down, he threatened to torch the warehouse and, of course, I couldn't exactly go to the police about it. I tried to tough it out but then, for some reason, I started getting unwanted attention from port security and then the Inland Revenue wanted to check my books – it seemed as if someone had tipped them off. I got too twitchy. I thought it was best to disappear for a while until things had died down. I felt so bad; I'd promised your mum that I'd be there for you all and then I'd bolted.

"Sissouma's boss was furious about the missing diamonds and Sissouma questioned anyone who'd been part of the smuggling operation but, even with his interrogation methods, he was getting nowhere. So he sent people after me and when they tracked me down I ended up losing two fingers before he was satisfied that I didn't have anything to do with it.

"But despite the violence, I never told him about Marty. I didn't want him thinking that the family may know where the stones were. He would have come after you. I did everything I could to protect you."

"Don't pretend you were protecting us," Gina raged. "You didn't tell him because you thought Dad might have hidden the real stones and you wanted to find them, make money out of them. That's why you came back."

"No! I was never sure if your dad had swapped the diamonds or if he'd found the fakes in the sack. But now I *do* know. Your dad just didn't trust me enough to hand them over, so he swapped them with stones for a fish tank." Tom let out a genuine laugh of approval.

"Yeah and that's because my dad must have known what a greedy, deceitful bastard you really are!"

"Maybe," he replied, his laughter gone. "But I came back for you, your mum and Danny. Don't you think it would have been easier for me to disappear? I didn't want to be involved any more, but I came back to look after you even though it's meant Sissouma following me, threatening me and dragging me back into this business; even though it's meant having to face what I did every day; being in your house, surrounded by memories of Marty, having to look at his ashes on that bloody shelf every day! It's been torture, but I've done it because I wanted to be there for you, to be part of your family. I wanted to give you all a great life."

Gina shook her head in disbelief. "You murder my father and then try and take over his family, make moves on his wife, play at being our new *dad*! What kind of sick bastard are you?"

"I was trying to make things better and I will, I can, even now. Just make that phone call. I'll go and collect the diamonds, give them to Sissouma and disappear out of your lives for ever. I promise that you'll never have to see me again. I'll sell the business, leave the country. I'll transfer enough money into your mum's account to make sure that you'll be comfortable for years to come."

"You think that you can buy me off!" she spat.

"That's not what I'm trying to do. It's just what you deserve. Please, Gina, I've told you everything. Every word is true. Now make the phone call like you promised." He snatched a quick glance at his watch. "We only have twelve minutes before they go to Sissouma."

"No!" she said. "I'm not going to."

"What? But you've got to! You promised!"

Gina looked him unflinchingly in the eye. "I don't have to keep a promise to the man who murdered my dad."

She turned to walk away from him but was stopped by the sight of a lorry pulling up across the end of the street, *Chunky Chocs* emblazoned on its side.

The driver honked his horn and drove away, leaving Declan standing in the road.

Declan ran to Gina, distressed on seeing her battered face.

"Did you do this to her?" Declan roared at Cotter.

"Don't worry," Gina said through her swollen lips. "This is nothing compared to what Sissouma will do to him."

"Tell her to make the call!" Tom implored Declan. "She's going to get me killed!"

"Gina, what's he talking about?"

Gina remained tight-lipped, gripping her phone.

"She's left the diamonds with someone – they're going to take them to Sissouma, tell him I was going to cheat him. He'll kill me. We've only got a few minutes. She's got to stop them."

Declan looked at Gina's tear-filled eyes. "Come on,

Gina. You can't let this happen," he said gently.

"He killed my dad," she whispered. "Why shouldn't I let Sissouma kill him?"

Declan turned to Tom, open-mouthed. Cotter's silence, an admission of guilt.

Declan was in turmoil, thinking what to say.

"Because…because…you're not like *him*, Gina. You wouldn't let someone die. Trust me, I know you. You won't let this happen."

If looks could kill, Declan Doyle would have died on the spot. He didn't know why Gina stared at him like that, he only knew that he wasn't getting through to her.

"Let the police deal with him," Declan said.

"No! He killed my dad and made everyone believe that it was suicide. I hate him. I want him to suffer."

"And he will. He'll be banged up for years. He'll have nothing, he'll be nobody."

"It's not enough!" she cried, tears starting to roll down her face.

"Listen, Gina. I never knew your dad but I know how much you loved him, what a fantastic guy he must have been. Do you think *he'd* want Cotter dead? Do you think *he'd* want that kind of justice?"

There was a flicker of change across her face that Tom seized upon.

"Gina, your dad would do the right thing and I know that you will," Cotter pleaded.

She hesitated, staring at the man for whom she felt such a terrifying hatred and then she reluctantly loosened her grip on the phone and tapped in the numbers.

"Thank you, thank you," Tom jabbered with relief.

"I'm not doing this for you," she said. "This is for my dad."

"Hello…" an Irish voice sang in Gina's ear.

"Hello, Mrs. Mac—" Gina said urgently.

"…Sorry, I can't make it to the phone right now. Please leave your message and number after the beep and I'll be getting back to you. Bye bye."

Beep!

"Mrs. Mac, this is Gina. Are you there? Pick up the phone if you're home. It's urgent! Mrs. Mac, don't take that parcel I gave you round to my house. It's very important that you DON'T take it! Please phone me back as soon as you get this message."

"Where is she?" Tom barked. "Phone her mobile, for God's sake!"

Declan answered gravely. "Mrs. Mac doesn't have a mobile. She doesn't approve of them. They go off in church. She gets very upset."

49 THE PERSISTENT CALLERS

Clare put her arm around Danny but he shuffled out of her reach.

"It's okay, Mum. I'm not afraid of him," he said, glaring at Sissouma. "And as for that one; I could beat him up with my little finger." Egon groaned at Danny and took another sip of his tea.

Sissouma let out a belly laugh. "Young man, you would make a brave soldier. I imagine you like all those computer games where you shoot the figures on the screen. I've noted that in this country all the boys love the war games. But if you were in my country, working for my boss, you could be doing that for real. He is a great commander and he does not discriminate against the young. He knows that many of the finest, fiercest soldiers are children and he looks after them like they are part of his own family. Would you like that, Danny? Would you like to be a real soldier, carrying a real gun?"

"Shut up! Leave him alone!" Clare snapped.

A knock on the front door silenced the tense room.

Clare got up defiantly from the sofa. Sissouma grabbed her arm and pulled her back down.

"No, Mrs. Wilson," he whispered. "We don't want any unnecessary visitors. Let's just sit quietly until they go away."

They sat and listened, each knock and ring of the bell making Clare flinch.

Bridie and Mrs. McManus stood on the doorstep of the Wilson household.

"I don't think anyone's in, Deirdre. The living room curtains are closed and you've done enough knocking to wake the dead," Bridie said.

"But they must be in. Gina was very clear. She said to bring it round now."

Bridie put on her glasses and looked at her wristwatch. "Actually, she said to leave it an hour, and that means we're ten minutes early."

"Well, you know I can't abide being late for anything," Mrs. Mac said.

"Yes, but maybe this fella isn't here yet."

"Give it one more try then. Let him know why we're here. He might think that we're Jehovah Witnesses or something."

Bridie bent down to the letter box, held the flap open and bellowed into the hallway.

"Cooee! Is there anyone home? We've got an important parcel and message for a Mr. Sissouma. Well, I suppose it's more of a pencil case than a parcel and the message is a bit odd, but Gina asked us to come over and tell you. We're nothing if not reliable, isn't that right, Deirdre?"

Mrs. McManus nodded solemnly.

"So, Mr. Sissouma, if you're there, love, would you come to the door? I can't be bending down like this all day, I'll seize up."

Sissouma came rushing out of the living room and opened the front door.

"I'm Mr. Sissouma," he said, helping the elderly lady straighten up.

Bridie's magnified eyes twinkled. "Well, aren't you a strapping fella?"

"You said that you have a parcel and message from Gina Wilson?"

"We do indeed," Mrs. Mac said, waving the fluffy purple pencil case.

"Then *please*, come in."

Mr. Egon gathered his equipment from the kitchen table and beckoned Sissouma out of the living room.

"So sorry to interrupt you, Bridie, but my colleague

needs me for a moment," Sissouma said, as he stopped the old lady mid-sentence and walked into the hallway.

Egon wore a broad smile across his gaunt face.

"How nice to see you looking so happy, Mr. Egon. Have you got some good news for me?"

"Oh yes, Mr. Sissouma. I can verify that we have in our possession quite exquisite specimens. The finest that I've ever seen."

Sissouma clapped his hands together in delight and stepped back into the living room to address the gathering.

"Well, ladies and Master Wilson. I would love to stay and hear another of Bridie's stories of her triumphs in the bingo hall but, unfortunately, Mr. Egon and I must bid you *au revoir.*"

"Oh, what a pity. I could talk to you all day. What charming friends you have, Mrs. Wilson," Bridie trilled to the nervous woman and her rather rude son, who sat glaring at Sissouma.

"Thank you very much for your hospitality, Mrs. Wilson," Sissouma continued. "We will leave you good people in peace, now that order has been restored."

Clare looked at him in confusion and relief. "That's it? It's over? Gina will be left alone?"

Sissouma bent down and whispered in her ear. "Yes, I promise that we won't bother you again as long as you don't report anything to the police. So you see, 'All's well that ends well', except, of course, for Mr. Cotter."

The phone in Tom's pocket beeped. He got it out, his breathing ragged with nerves, like the accused standing in the dock, awaiting the verdict.

He opened the message from Sissouma. Gina and Declan watched as Tom's face paled, his eyes closed. He'd been found guilty as charged and handed down a death sentence. He knew there would be no form of appeal.

"Is it from Sissouma?" Declan asked.

Tom's eyes darted around like a hunted animal. "I've got to get as far away from here as possible. The man is going to kill me."

"Then hand yourself in to the police. It's the least you can do for Gina; it's your safest option. Sissouma can't get you if you're banged up."

"I wouldn't be safe in prison. I'd be a sitting duck. He has contacts everywhere. All it takes is for him to call in a favour, grease a few palms and I'd have my neck broken in the shower, or my back stabbed in the exercise yard." Tom began to stride away.

"Where do you think you're going?" Gina shouted after him. "You don't get to walk away from this. That's not justice!"

"No, but it's survival, Gina. I'm sorry."

"You'd better stop, right now," Declan shouted.

Cotter turned round; a sneer played on his face. "Or what? Are *you* going to stop me, Declan? Are you trying to play the knight in shining armour? It's not going to work. Gina knows that you've been making a fool of her, lying to her, using her to get at me."

Declan glanced, shamefaced, at Gina.

"Gina, don't listen to him," Declan begged.

"Why? Is he lying?" she asked, already knowing the answer.

"Well…no, not exactly, but now's not the time to talk about this. He's just trying to distract us; divide us. He's the enemy, Gina, not me. I'm not going to let him get away."

"You stay where you are," Tom barked. "Just remember your little dip in the sea."

Declan charged at him, ramming his shoulder into Cotter's stomach, wrapping his arms around the man's legs and pulling his feet from under him. Cotter hit the ground like a felled tree. Groaning, Tom struggled to release his legs from Declan's grip. He delivered sharp little kicks into Declan's stomach until the young man could hold on no longer. Cotter scrambled away from him, but Declan pounced on him again, straddling his waist, raising his fist, ready to hit Tom in the face. But he wavered – he'd never hit anyone before, not even in a playground scrap.

Declan's hesitation cost him dearly, as Tom powered a right hook into Declan's side. Declan's breath was trapped in his throat and a searing pain from his kidney travelled through his body. He fell backwards in agony and Tom wasted no time in exchanging positions. Now Tom sat on top of him, grinding his knees into the crooks of Declan's arms, pinning them down. Declan let out a yelp.

"Never hesitate," Tom hissed, delivering a vicious punch to Declan's face. The skin above his left eye split. Warm blood began to trickle from it, getting caught in his eyelashes.

"Stop it!" Gina screamed, trying to drag Tom off him, but Tom flung her away, effortlessly.

"By the time I'm finished with him, he won't be able to get up, let alone come after me," Tom promised, landing another punch to the side of Declan's head.

Gina looked around frantically and saw the bottle of aftershave on the ground. She picked it up and pulled out the stopper. She heard the dull, sickening thud of another punch. She approached the kneeling man from behind; reaching her hand under his chin, she jolted his head back.

Tom's startled eyes looked up at her as she poured the aftershave into them.

He let out a howl, rolling off Declan and staggering around blindly, his hands over his burning eyes.

Declan mumbled to Gina, "Run down to the main road. Get help. I'll phone the police."

Police cars and an ambulance arrived at the bridge within minutes. Gina had grabbed a passer-by to help, but Tom was in too much pain to put up any resistance. The paramedics tended to his eyes. They were hidden under an angry mass of swollen skin.

Gina did a double take as "Uncle" Stevie emerged from one of the cars.

"Your uncle is a copper?" she said to Declan, in surprise.

"He's not my uncle," Declan admitted.

"But I am a copper," Stevie added, shifting the paramedics aside to get at their patient.

"Thomas Cotter, I'm arresting you on suspicion of the murder of Martin Wilson, assault and the smuggling of illegal diamonds."

Tom tried to open his eyes to find Gina. "Hey, Gina," he shouted out. "Now we know what your little friend is. Declan Doyle is a grass! The lowest of the low."

"I think *you* deserve that title, Mr. Cotter," Stevie said drily, slapping the handcuffs on him.

"I'm going to accompany Cotter to the hospital but I need you two to come down to the station. I'll get the duty doctor to have a look at you. You both look like you've been in the wars."

"Am I under arrest?" Declan asked nervously.

"No! I'm a happy bunny, Declan. I've got my result. We've got Sissouma and Egon. We had unmarked cars on Gina's street. We waited until they left the house and then we picked them up, diamonds and all, and now we've got Cotter – that's what you call a full house!" He grinned smugly.

"Then just give me a few minutes with Gina," Declan said. "I've got some explaining to do."

The detective looked at Gina's stormy face and took a sharp intake of breath. "Well, good luck with that. I'll see you both later; that's if you survive, lad."

51 OVER A BARREL

Gina and Declan slumped against the wall in stony silence, watching the cars and ambulance pull away.

"Go on, I'm waiting," she said ominously.

Declan cleared his throat nervously. "Okay, but before I begin I just need to remind you that I have been beaten up already today, so go easy on me."

"Shut up! Just tell me what you've been playing at."

"Right, here it is." He swallowed hard. "The other month I was caught nicking lead off a church roof."

"Charming," Gina said curtly.

"The place was derelict. It was about to be stripped and bulldozed anyway," he protested. "It was me and a couple of mates, thought we could make some easy money. I was sick of having no job, no cash. Anyway, my mates were down below and they legged it when they saw the security guard but I was left stuck up on the roof, with no way to escape. I ended up down the cop shop. I was booked in, fingerprinted, locked in a cell for hours – it stank; I was freezing and hungry."

"My heart bleeds for you."

"Okay…I don't deserve any sympathy. But after a couple of hours I was taken to one of the interview rooms and this scruffy, wild-looking fella comes in, no uniform. I've never seen anyone who looked less like a cop. Anyway, he sits down at the table, doesn't turn the tape on. I asked for the duty solicitor and he just said, 'All in good time, lad. We haven't started official business yet. This is just an informal little chat.'

"So, then he says that he doesn't usually deal with this kind of case but that he's taking a special interest in me because he's been informed that I used to go to Rylands High. I told him that I left last summer. Then he mentions your name. Says you're a pupil there, wants to know if I know you, especially as we live in the same neighbourhood. Well, I told him that I only knew *of* you, used to see you around the school, heard about your dad killing himself.

"Then he asks if I knew a bloke called Tom Cotter. I'd never heard of him. So he sits, staring at me, stroking his stubbly chin; he was freaking me out. 'You know,' he said eventually, 'I think you're going to get a custodial for this. Caught red-handed.'

"I panicked. It was my first offence. I'd never been in trouble before. Anyway, he tells me that magistrates are

415

coming down hard on lead strippers, wanting to make an example of them. 'This lead theft business has become an epidemic,' he says. 'The magistrates are upset about it, especially when it's nicked from a place of worship.'

"'The church was going to be demolished!' I said.

"'It was still God's house.' He gave a phlegmy chuckle, amused with himself.

"Then he starts asking me all about my family. When he finds out that they're in Ireland and I'm here on my own, he seems pleased. He was really getting to me, putting on a pathetic Irish accent, saying 'What would your mammy and daddy think about their lovely Catholic boy nicking from a church?'

"I told him to get lost. I told him that I wanted to be interviewed by someone else, but he just carried on, saying, 'Listen, Declan. I'd hate to see you locked up in a young offenders' institute. You'd be mixing with some nasty pieces of work – violent, disturbed, drug-addled. They'd stab you with the cutlery if it wasn't made of plastic. You'd come out a different lad…ruined. You know what I mean, don't you?' He was being sadistic.

"I was trying to look like I didn't care but I felt like I was going to burst out crying. He stood up and leaned over the table, his cigarette breath in my face, saying, 'Don't worry, Declan. I think that we might be able to help each other out of this mess. Let's put you back in the cells for a while and I'll make a few phone calls.'

"He left me in the cells for hours with nothing to think about but how I'd survive being locked up with a bunch of psychos and the shame on my family of having a son in the nick; all my job prospects gone before I'd even earned my first wages. By the time I was taken back to the interview room I was a wreck. So when he breezes in, telling me it's my lucky day, he's got an offer for me that I shouldn't refuse, I was so grateful I would have agreed to anything. He told me the terms – he wanted me to keep an eye on Cotter. He said that Cotter was friendly with your family, had been your dad's boss. The plan was for me to get in with you, get as much info out of you as possible about Cotter and use you to try and get a job at the warehouse."

The blood leached from Gina's face. "So that day when you saw me on the bridge – was that a coincidence?" she asked in trepidation. "You said that you'd been at a mate's house on the next road?"

Declan cringed. "I followed you from your house. I'd been keeping an eye on you, working out your daily routines; you've got time to do that kind of thing when you're unemployed. I was waiting for a good chance to accidentally bump into you. So when I saw you limbering up for a run that day I thought that I could just run after you and pretend I was jogging too, but once you got into your stride you were so fast that I almost lost you when you turned off the canal. I stood at the end of the street catching my breath and watching you. I nearly died when

I saw you climb up on that bridge. I thought you were going to jump. I really did come over to help you."

Tears of anger and humiliation welled up in Gina's eyes. "So, all the time we've spent together! All the attention you've given me! Oh my God...that night in the warehouse!" Her hands flew up to hide her face. "No wonder you didn't want to kiss me. That was beyond the call of duty, wasn't it? I'm sure it was bad enough for you, having to pretend you liked me, without having to actually have physical contact with me."

"It *has* been terrible, Gina, because I like you, and I mean I *really*, *really* like you. I was dying to kiss you that night, but I couldn't. It wouldn't have been right. I felt a complete shit."

"That's because you *are* a complete shit," she hissed at him. "Have you been having a good laugh about me with your 'Uncle Stevie'? And have you told him how you got into my family's good books. Coaching Danny, being Mr. Nice guy with my mum?"

"No, it wasn't like that. Danny's a great kid. I want to help him with his footy. And your mum, she's so nice. Please, Gina, I love being with you and even if I wasn't being forced to do this, even if I wasn't being paid, I'd still want to be with you."

Gina's eyes widened, her nostrils flared. "You were getting paid?"

Declan grimaced. "That sounds bad, doesn't it? But

really, I would have been daft not to take the money. It's completely legit. 'Covert Human Surveillance Operatives', that's what the police call them; they pay you! It's like a proper job, isn't it?" he said in desperation. "Stevie said that they wouldn't press charges if I helped him. I'd be let off, but even then I didn't say yes straight away. I stalled, said I needed time to think. I hated the idea of spying on people…being his informant. He gave me until midnight that night. If I refused to help him or he didn't hear from me, he'd make sure I was charged and that it went to court." Declan put his hands together as if in prayer. "Please believe me, Gina. I didn't want to do it, but what else could I do?"

She didn't speak. He couldn't read her face. An unnerving calm seemed to have descended on her. He flinched as she turned towards him, but she put her arms out, as if to embrace him.

He gave a nervous smile as she held his shoulders. She pulled him towards her, whispering in his ear, making the hairs on the back of his neck tingle. "Thanks for your help today."

His aching face cracked into a relieved smile.

She understands! She forgives me! God, that wasn't so bad.

"I never want to see you again," she continued in the same low tone. "You don't call me, text me, you don't even get to walk down my street. Do you understand?"

The smile dropped from his face. "Gina, don't say that. Give me a chance, *please*."

"No," she said with conviction. She hauled herself up and walked away from him, her head held high.

52 FATHER'S DAY

Gina, Kylie, Danny and her mum stood, arms linked, surveying the allotment. The sun shone on the transformed plot of land. Months of back-breaking work, tilling tons of topsoil, had turned the barren earth into fertile ground.

Now, fragrant sweet peas climbed up garden canes. Blooms of bright dahlias swayed in the warm breeze. Patches of wild strawberries ripened under green netting and the first shoots of carrots had broken through the soil. In the far corner stood a large pitch-roofed shed, its flower-filled window boxes lending it the air of a countryside retreat.

"This is all down to Declan," her mum said. "He's worked so hard. He even insisted on paying for the shed."

"Well, I'm sure he could afford it with all the money he got for *spying* on us," scowled Gina.

"Gina, you should have come to help. Me and Declan have had a right laugh working on the allotment," Danny said.

"No thanks, I'm not going anywhere near that boy."

"Oh, come on, Gina," Kylie pouted. "Declan has been like a lost puppy. He's pining for you, babe. And you're just making yourself miserable without him."

"Yeah, give him a break!" Danny lectured.

"You all seem to have forgotten that he was spying on us, conning us," Gina said indignantly.

Her mum shook her head. "He was spying on *Tom*, not us, and if anything we should be grateful to him."

"Grateful?" Gina protested.

"Yes. Listen, Gina, you know how sorry I am for not believing you. You were always right about your dad, and you didn't give up until you got to the truth, but Declan helped you. Without each other you wouldn't have found out what Tom Cotter was really like, what he did." Her mum's face went ashen. "I was so taken in by him."

Kylie put her arm around her. "Come on now, Clare. He fooled everyone. Don't think about him. He's where he belongs. Banged up for years, frightened of his own shadow. I even heard that he's asked to be put in isolation for his own protection."

Gina squeezed her mum too. "Kylie's right. This is Dad's day. He would have loved to see the allotment like this. I can't think of a better place to say a proper goodbye to him."

The allotment gate creaked open and Gina's jaw dropped as Declan entered, looking decidedly sheepish.

"What are *you* doing here?" Gina hissed.

"I invited him," her mother said. "This silliness between you two has gone on long enough. I know Declan is sorry for how he did things but, as I said, we should be grateful to him and that's why I want him here today."

Gina's eyes threw daggers at him as he stood a safe distance from her.

Her mum opened the lid of the grey marble urn and walked slowly along the row of people, shaking a handful of ashes into cupped hands.

Each of them strolled to different areas of the allotment and stood for a moment, wrapped up in their thoughts of Martin Wilson, before they scattered the ashes onto the earth. Gina looked out over the sun-bathed docks with a melancholic smile. "I really hope that heaven looks like Trinidad, Dad." She let the ashes run through her fingers.

Gina saw her mum wipe away tears and put a smile on her face before saying, "Danny, Kylie. Come on, let's go back to the house."

Gina started to follow, but her mum turned to her.

"No, Gina. You're not leaving this allotment until you've spoken to Declan."

"But, Mum!"

Her mum ignored her protests and walked away.

Declan was standing like a lamb who'd been left in a field with a wolf.

"How have you been?" he asked nervously.

She stared past him but he continued regardless.

"Hey, are your exams nearly over now? Your mum told me that they were going well. Are you going to stay on for sixth form? You should, you're clever enough – not like me."

"You're clever enough, you're just too lazy." She scowled.

His big brown eyes widened, delighted that she'd spoken to him.

"You've never replied to any of my texts," he said.

"Of course I haven't. I should have got an injunction out on you. Calling me, texting me, writing me letters. I told you not to – it's harassment."

"Did you read the letter?" he asked hopefully.

"No, I threw it in the bin," she replied coldly.

Declan looked crestfallen. "Oh, well if you'd read it, Gina, you'd know how sorry I am. You'd know how I feel about you."

"Yeah well, sending Mrs. Mac and Bridie round was a bit desperate, wasn't it?"

"I didn't send them round!" he protested.

"Come off it. It was like the Spanish Inquisition. Mrs. Mac in our kitchen, saying, 'I don't know what tiff you two have had but he's in a terrible state. He's off his food – he hasn't touched any of my stews.' And then Bridie going on,

424

'Do you want to talk about it, Gina? You know that I'm a woman of the world.'"

Declan couldn't help laughing. "I'm sorry about that, but you know I can't control those ladies. Anyway, my mum wants me over in Ireland."

"Are you going?" A flicker of panic crossed her face.

"No, I've told her I've got a job here."

"Oh really, who are you spying on this time?" she said, arms crossed.

"No one. Mr. O'Rourke still had an opening at the funeral parlour. I've been carrying coffins for the last few months."

"Wow, you must *really* not want to go to Ireland."

"No, I just *really* want to stay here…with you," he answered.

Her mouth opened and shut but no words came out.

"Listen, Gina," he continued earnestly, "what if you pretend that we'd never met before. We could start all over again – properly this time." He extended his hand to her and she eyed it suspiciously.

"Go on, take it," he coaxed.

She tried hard to maintain her most withering expression. "This is stupid," she said, putting a limp hand in his.

He squeezed her hand gently, saying, "Hi, I'm Declan Doyle. I shower every day, I'm kind to my mammy and I've a job for life at the funeral parlour because, as Mrs. Mac so rightly says, 'There's always going to be a good supply of customers.'" He mimicked his landlady perfectly. "So, Gina Wilson, would you do me the honour of coming out with me tomorrow for a pizza?"

"Sorry, I'm washing my hair tomorrow."

"Well, how about the day after?"

"Can't, I'm cutting my toenails."

"Well, have you got any night free over the next year, because I'll wait. I'm a very patient person."

Her eyes danced mischievously. "Actually, I might have a free night."

Declan's face lit up. "Great! When?"

"When hell freezes over," she proclaimed with relish.

"You're just cruel, Gina Wilson," he said, employing his best puppy-dog eyes.

She stuck her tongue out at him. "You deserve it."

"Declan!" Danny bounded through the allotment gate. "Mum says have you two made up yet? She wants you both to come back to the house and have some food."

Declan hesitated, looking at Gina. "I'm sorry, Danny, I don't think I should. Gina doesn't want me around."

Danny grabbed his arm and started to drag him out of the allotment, shouting, "Of course she does. She's read that stupid letter you sent her about a hundred times. She keeps it under her pillow – I've seen it – it nearly made me throw up!" He screwed up his face in disgust.

Gina started flapping. "Danny! That's private. Don't you dare go through my stuff!"

Declan stopped in his tracks, an elated grin spreading across his face. He trudged back to Gina, dragging Danny behind him.

She rolled her eyes, her lips twitching with a suppressed smile.

"Don't look so smug, Declan Doyle."

"This face isn't smug," he said innocently. "But does this mean you've forgiven me?"

"Of course I haven't." She grinned.

He leaned towards her so that they were nose to nose. "Would it be okay if I kiss you?" he said with trepidation.

"No! It would be horrible," she answered, putting her arms around his neck and sealing her lips on his.

"Gross! Do you two have to?" Danny protested, attempting to pull the couple apart. But his efforts were futile.

ACKNOWLEDGEMENTS

A big hug and huge thanks to my wonderful agent, Jo Unwin – I'll miss you! To all at Usborne who do such a magnificent job in every department and who make me feel so valued. Special thanks to my fabulous editor, Rebecca Hill, for being patient, insightful and exacting. Thanks also to Becky Walker for all her hard work on the copyedit.

To enable the writing of *Blood Tracks* I undertook research in several areas and I'm indebted to the following people for allowing me to interrogate them and for providing such vital expertise: Mairin Casey, David Egbokhan, Cathy Scheib, Eloise Gaillou, Steve Copplestone and last, but not least, Old Sea Dog himself, Karl Bird. Thanks to you all.

I'm so grateful to my mother-in-law, Diana, and my brother-in-law, Chas, for their kindness in opening their houses to me when I needed to hide away and write.

Love and thanks to Stan, Archie and Sadie for filling our home with noise and normality and reminding me that all work and no play makes writers duller people. Finally, thanks to my husband, David, for his love and unfailing support – I'm a lucky devil!

ABOUT THE AUTHOR

Paula Rawsthorne was an award-winning writer before she had even published her first book. One of her very first stories won the BBC's 2004 Get Writing competition and was read by Bill Nighy on Radio 4. Paula then became one of the winners of the Undiscovered Voices 2010 competition with her first novel, *The Truth About Celia Frost*, which also went on to win both the Leeds Book Award, the Sefton Super Reads Award and the Nottingham Brilliant Book Award. *Blood Tracks* is her second novel.

Paula lives in Nottingham with her husband and three children, where her writing is fuelled by a diet of coffee and cakes.

THE TRUTH ABOUT CELIA FROST

PAULA RAWSTHORNE

CELIA FROST IS A FREAK.

At least that's what everyone thinks. Her life is ruled by a rare disorder that means she could bleed to death from the slightest cut, confining her to a gloomy bubble of "safety". No friends. No fun. No life.

But when a knife attack on Celia has unexpected consequences, her mum reacts strangely – and suddenly they're on the run. Why is her mum so scared? Someone out there knows. And when they find Celia, she's going to wish the truth was a lie.

A buried secret, a gripping manhunt, a dangerous deceit... What is the truth about Celia Frost?

"Riveting." *The Independent on Sunday*

"Electrifying." *The Independent*

"Fast and fun." *The Guardian*

"Nail-biting and thought-provoking." *The Bookseller*

"A page-turning thriller that's impossible to put down."
Lovereading4kids.co.uk

POWERFUL...
CAPTIVATING...
BRAVE...

Discover more incredible novels at
www.fiction.usborne.com